CASIDDIE WILLIAMS

Never Run Again

Contents

Preface

Content Warning:

This book contains sensitive matters including but not limited to sexual, mental, and physical abuse. Rape (off page). Violent loss of a pregnancy. Domestic abuse.

This book is a why choose MMMMF contemporary romance where no one in the relationship chooses, and everyone loves each other.

Characters in this book are fictional, and although there is neurodivergent representation, it is not meant to downplay or be insensitive to anyone with this diagnosis. Autism and ADHD are a spectrum, and everyone's experiences are different, including the characters in this story.

Although this book does end on a cliffhanger (don't hate me) I won't keep you hanging for long.

Your mental health matters. You are Enough!

Acknowledgement

It feels like it took forever to get to Spencer's story. So many other characters screamed louder in my ear than she did… until one day, it was her turn.

The amount of "what do you think of this" moments that happened between me and my Alpha far exceeds any of my other words. KK Moore is a freaking saint and sometimes the devil on my shoulder. No matter the struggles, the best story always comes out.

Thank you to my wonderful team of Betas and ARC readers for always supporting my wild ideas and getting to read them first!

As I come up on my first year of publishing (July 10th) I can't thank you, my readers, enough! I wouldn't be where I am today if it wasn't for you. I far exceeded any conceivable goals I had for myself when I saw a TikTok and said, "I could write a book about this." Hazel's book turned into Annie's book, then Dellah's, and by the time my anniversary rolls around, I will have published nine of my own works (maybe ten if I can sneak one more in) and have been published in two anthologies.

THANK YOU FROM THE BOTTOM OF MY HEART AND THE TOP OF THE TALLEST MOUNTAIN!!!

~Casiddie

1

Spencer

"I'm going as fast as I can, Justin. Nicole is already at the hospital, Blake and Cole are with her, and Hannah is with Annie and the twins. Relax." I hear his heavy sigh from the passenger seat of the ambulance as his leg bounces with nerves.

We were across town having lunch when my best friend got the call that his wife, Nicole, was in labor with their second child. I'm breaking all the rules for him by driving lights and sirens toward the hospital to get him there as quickly as possible.

A moment before we approach an intersection, I take a deep breath as I hit the button to change the tone of the siren. I've become accustomed to the different pitches of each siren warble and know what to expect.

"Spencer," Justin whines and I try to empathize with his anxiousness.

"Two minutes."

"Are you sure you don't want to stay?" Yes. I'm sure I don't want to watch your wife give birth.

"One of us has to work. I'm dropping you off and heading to the station to pick up Miller. Call me when he's here, and I'll come by and bring your bags."

As I pull up to the Emergency Department entrance, Justin is out the door yelling goodbye before I stop the rig.

I'm excited for my best friend. He's come so far in the eight years I've known him. I've watched him go from a broken man to a husband and father. We've been paramedic partners for the past six years, and he's my rock and I'm his.

Pulling up to the fire department, Miller is already waiting for me with a smile on his stupidly handsome face. I wish Justin had never pointed out I have two men in my life vying for my attention, Miller being one of them. I never noticed how his dark, shaggy hair would fall over his eyes. Or how blue said eyes are, surrounded by skin that always looks sun-kissed.

"Hey, Smithy. Heard you were looking for someone to ride...with." He punctuates his dirty joke with a panty-dropping smile and a wink.

"Just get in. And why do I have to continuously remind you not to call me that?"

"When you tell me why you keep a small arsenal in your house, I'll stop reminding you of the sexy little red *Smith and Wesson* you showed me that day at the range."

"I never should have taken you with me." Miller laughs as he buckles his seatbelt and settles into a comfortable position.

"So what's for lunch?"

"I've already eaten. We are stopping by Justin and Nicole's to get their go-bags and deliver them to the hospital. Nicole was out shopping when her water broke."

"Woo-hoo, field trip." The corner of my lip twitches at his

enthusiasm. He's adorable when he acts like this. *Shut up, Spencer. You can't allow yourself to fall for his boyish charm.* "I asked Chief if I could fill in for Justin while he's out on paternity leave. I keep wondering when he's going to decide to retire. We all know he doesn't need to work."

"He works because he wants to, and he likes the satisfaction he gets when he helps the community. Why are you a firefighter?"

"Chicks dig the uniform." I can hear the smile in his voice without looking at him. Miller's easygoing nature allows me to understand what he's saying without any pretense. His tones and inflections perfectly match what he means, and I never have to play a guessing game with him. "Are you telling me you could resist me in full uniform, smelling like a fresh fire and danger?" I stop the shiver wanting to run down my spine, and once again, I want to curse Justin for pointing out Miller's attraction to me. So no, Miller. I can't resist you, and please don't ask me again.

"I've seen it before. It was resistible." But only because I wasn't attracted to you then.

"I'd call you on your bullshit, but you don't usually BS me, so maybe you don't find me attractive. I'm wounded, Spencer. You might need to pull over and use the defibrillator to restart my heart."

As I open my mouth to attempt a snarky comeback, the radio crackles, and my heart skips a beat. The baritone voice that stirs the butterflies in my belly bellows over the speaker.

"Unit 25, please respond to 723…" My stomach drops for a completely different reason, hearing my favorite voice recite my father's address and use the code for a mental health crisis.

3

"Spencer, Spencer, what's wrong? All the color just drained from your face." I feel Miller's hand on my forearm, but I'm numb to the sensation as I flip on the sirens and make the safest U-turn I can while putting my mask in place.

I quickly glance at Miller, whose pinched brows and wide eyes show his concern for me. I don't know what could be happening with my father, and I need to give him a heads-up about where we're going before we arrive.

"Wait. Why do I know that address? Don't you live on that street?" I shift my eyes to look at him, and he stares at me intently.

"That's my father's address."

"Oh shit. What's going on?"

"I honestly don't have any idea, Miller, but we're about to find out."

As we turn onto my street, two patrol cars are parked in front of my father's house.

"Unit 25 on scene."

"10-4. Subject is calm at this time." Why was he not calm? What's going on, Dad?

Miller shoots me uneasy glances as we pull the gear out of the rig and roll the cot to the front door. I can hear men talking inside and steal my emotions before stepping in.

"Gentleman, I need to speak to my daughter. Can you please—"

"Dad."

"Oh, thank god. Spencer, you need to go. I saw him. There's been a vehicle parked at the end of the block for the past week. I walked past it today, and it was him." I walk over and grab his shoulders, leading him to sit on the couch.

"Okay, Dad. It's okay."

4

"But it's not, honey. I'm getting too old. I can't protect you. What if he—"

"Dad." I cut him off with my curt tone. All eyes in the room are on us, but this is not a conversation that needs to be shared.

-Crackle- "Unit 25. Status check." The portable radio on Miller's hip grates on my nerves as he looks at me expectantly.

"Status, Smithy?" I want to berate him for using his nickname for me around all these people, but the momentary reminder of guns and his soothing tone help ease my rising anxiety.

"I'm good. I'm going to take him in the other room and talk to him. You can call us clear." He shoots me a concerned look before leaving in the direction of the front door with the two officers.

Turning back to my father, I give him a weary sigh. "Okay, Detective. Tell me what you saw?"

2

Miller

Spencer spent ten minutes inside with her father after we left them alone. I've never heard her mention him before and assumed he had passed or they were estranged, but seeing as he lives in the house at the front of her driveway, I have even more questions now.

Spencer's home is at the back of a long driveway, past a larger house that sits near the road. I always assumed she rented her little pool house, but it appears she has a reason to live back there.

She may have perfected the art of reading people's microexpressions, but as she walks down the path toward the ambulance, her mask is down, and her face shows pure pain.

The freckles across her nose and cheeks, which turn adorably darker in the summer, are crinkled, and her blue eyes are dull. My fingers twitch in my lap with the need to hold her and fix whatever has caused the look on her face.

When she opens the driver's door and looks up at me, I see her mask click into place.

"Smithy, don't do that."

"Do what?" She knows exactly what I'm referring to, and I hate that she feels uncomfortable with me right now.

"You don't need to mask around me, Spencer. If you don't want to talk about what just happened, we don't have to, but please be yourself." Her brows twitch as she considers what I just offered before I see her shoulders relax.

"Thank you." She offers me a small smile, and I nod in response. "Were you still hungry? We can stop somewhere and grab you food."

I give her my goofiest grin and clutch my heart. "Why, Spencer? You sure do know the way to my heart."

"Through your stomach?"

"Yes, ma'am." I see her lip twitch and know, even if just for the moment, I've distracted her from whatever happened with her father. "Smithy, if you want to talk, I'm a good listener." I see her give me a quick side glance and a nod. I got my point across, and that's good enough for me. She knows I'm here if she needs me.

I hear a buzzing in the cupholder and see Spencer has a new text.

"Will you check on that for me, please?"

"Um...I don't have a good track record with answering your texts. I think I still have PTSD from the last time." I cringe at the texts I saw the day that Justin's wife, Nicole, his girlfriend at the time, found guns hidden all around Spencer's house and a letter that Justin had written to her explaining his mental health journey.

How long ago was that? Wow. About two years. I can't believe it's been two years since Justin committed himself to an inpatient facility to get his mental health in order. Nicole lived with Spencer for a few weeks while he was away, and the compassion she showed Nicole is what really started my heart's downward spiral for this woman.

Fuck. I can't believe it's been over two years of fawning over this gorgeous redhead sitting beside me. I know I'm not the only one, either. She has her choice of guys, and she's choosing none of us. She's the most stubborn, infuriating, intelligent woman I know.

"Miller?" *Shit.* I spaced out. "You were staring."

"Stop being so incredible looking and it'll make it easier not to stare." She sighs, and it's adorable.

"Just check my messages, please. It's probably Justin giving us an update on the baby."

"Oh, baby!" Without any more hesitation, I grab the phone and open the text.

"Holy fuck!" I play hot potato with Spencer's phone in my hand, trying to unsee the image that was just on the screen.

"What? What's wrong?"

"That was…Oh god, Spencer. There was a…" I'm acting like a child. I'm a grown-ass man. "Spencer, someone sent you a dick pic."

"Could you repeat yourself, Miller?" I grab the end of the phone with two fingers and gently place it back in the cup holder like a grenade without a pin.

"No. No, I will not repeat myself, Spencer. You heard me. Just think about what I said."

"Who is it from?"

Is she serious? "I'm sorry, but I don't keep a catalog of everyone's dicks for reference."

"Miller, don't be ridiculous. Can you pick it up and see who it's from?"

"No. You can either pull over now or wait the two minutes

until we get to Justin's house and check it yourself." I jump in my seat when the phone rings, and the tune *"I'm Too Sexy"* plays through the cab. "Um, Spencer?"

"Stupid Axel."

"What?"

"That's Axel's ringtone. He changed it in my phone, and I keep forgetting to fix it." When was Axel in close enough proximity to Spencer's phone that he was able to mess with her ringtone? "Will you answer for me, please?"

Ugh. I cautiously pick up the phone and swipe the screen, turning the call to speaker.

"Tails. Oh my god. I'm so sorry. Jesus." What is Axel going on about?

Spencer pulls into Justin's driveway and puts the rig into park. She runs her hands over her double French braids—the reason Axel calls her Tails.

"Axel, what are you rambling about?" Spencer looks as confused as I am.

"Did you...but I...Fuck. That text wasn't meant for you."

A growl rumbles through my chest. "The dick pic was from you, asshole?"

"Miller? What the? Did you see my...?"

"Dude, aren't you too old to be sending women pictures of your junk?" There's a heavy sigh on the other end of the phone.

"Axel, I will delete your miss-sent picture, but you'll have to figure out a way to make it up to Miller on your own." That's easy for Spencer to say; she didn't see the picture. Although if she's going to delete it, I suppose she'll have to look at it then.

"Fuck. I'm really sorry, guys. I meant to hit Stacy, and

9

I guess I was one name off." There's evident remorse in his tone, and I want to be mad at him, but I know he's embarrassed.

Spencer quietly mouths that she'll be right back, and I watch her disappear into Justin's house.

"What the fuck, man? Spencer isn't in the rig at the moment, so tell me what's going on. Quickly."

"I...Man, fuck. I don't know. It was an honest mistake. When I realized who I sent it to, I froze and waited for Spencer to call me. She didn't call, and I panicked thinking that was worse than her calling. I saw the text was open, but not in my wildest dreams would I have thought *you* would be the one opening it." I burst out in laughter, remembering a conversation I had with Spencer two years ago.

"You losing it over there, man?"

I attempt to regain my composure by taking several deep breaths. "I was just remembering the time I teased Spencer and told her I didn't want to answer her phone for fear of seeing a dick pic. She joked that if anyone would be sending her one, it would be you. I saw your fucking dick, bro."

"Listen, it's a nice dick, and anyone should be honored to be graced with its eye candy." Despite my initial shock, it did seem like a nice-looking dick from the quick peek I got. Glancing at Justin's front door, I minimize the call screen and open Spencer's text threads.

Axel: <Attachment: 1 image>

I shouldn't look at it. I. Shouldn't. Look. At. It. *Fuck it.* My thumb presses his name on the screen. The image shows Axel's hand squeezing firmly at the base of his extremely hard cock, his curly brown hair represented in his trimmed pubes. The purple vein on the bottom of his long shaft bulges from the force of his strong hand. My eyes travel the vein to the tip of his...pierced. Fucking. Head.

"Axel." His name is breathy on my lips.

"Yeah, man?"

"Oh fuck!" I forgot he was still on the phone, and it slips through my fingers from my shock. It slides across the mechanical panel between the two front seats down to the footwell of the driver's side. "Shit, shit."

"You okay, Miller?"

"Um, yeah. I just dropped you. Hold on." Justin's front door opens, and my pigtailed goddess steps out with two bags slung over her shoulder. Why didn't I go inside to help her with those? *Shit. Focus.* I'm scrambling to unbuckle my seatbelt and crawl over the console when Spencer reaches the door and opens it.

Fuck. I'm out of time. Spencer's eyes dart between my awkward position in the cab and where my outstretched hands seem to be pointing. She sees her phone and reaches down to grab it. My head drops between my shoulders in defeat. I know what she sees on the screen. I can feel the effects of the picture squished between my stomach and the armrest of the seat.

"Pierced. Impressive."

"Spencer?"

"Axel? You're still on the line? Well, it appears that Miller was admiring your picture, but I'd like to commend you on your virility. It's quite impressive. And those piercings look like they would cause great pleasure to whomever you used them with."

I have no words. No fucking words.

3

Axel

"...those piercings look like they would cause great pleasure to whomever you used them with."

Did she just say those words to me? And, wait. Miller was looking at my cock? Oh my god. He totally looked at my cock.

"Um. Thank you. I think. You can go ahead and delete the picture now. Unless you'd like to keep it, and I'd be okay with that too, Tails." I hear a masculine groan in the background and realize I must still be on speaker, and Miller heard my offer.

I was lying here in bed, unable to fall back asleep after my night shift, when my mind began to wander like it often does. More like squirrel, but at this point it's all the same. I saw her this morning as I was leaving. Spencer was pushing a patient into the Emergency Department as I was leaving my night shift. Being a nurse on nights allows me to see her often, even if it's only from afar.

"Have a good night, Axel. Sleep well."

"Oh, I'll be sleeping well, Tails. You'll be starring in my dreams."

I shot her wink, and I walked out to my car. Little did I know I'd be having a very awkward conversation with her a few hours later.

"Axel?" Fuck. I'm still on the phone.

"Sorry, Tails. You rendered me speechless." She honestly did. She complimented my cock. Spencer. Complemented. My. Cock.

"Well, that's a fucking first, asshole."

"Shut up, Miller. Go back to staring at my dick pic and stop talking."

Miller and I have been friends since before either of us knew Spencer, but the red-headed vixen drew us both in, and we've made it a little friendly competition to try and catch her.

"If you boys are done comparing dick sizes, I have better things to do to occupy my day." What I wouldn't give to help occupy her day.

"Are we all good, Tails? No hard feelings about my fat finger slip?"

"Axel, seeing a picture of the male anatomy isn't something that will even be a notable moment of my day. Would it bother you to see someone's breasts in the ED?"

If they were yours, it would.

"Point proven. Have a good day, you two." I hang up the phone because now I either need a cold shower or to finish what I started when I took that picture.

I know I have a reputation around the hospital for being a player, but I like giving women pleasure. My body count would shock people because they assume I sleep with every

14

woman I hook up with. In reality, my hands are the ones that get around. Women come to me for the orgasms I give them. A skill that I've perfected over time and I'm proud of. Does it make me a terrible person that I like to please women? Maybe the amount of women, but I've never had any complaints. Also, I really like getting head. I'm a man in my prime—sue me.

I flop back onto my pillows and stare at the ceiling. I can't sleep, and honestly, masturbating sounds like too much work at the moment. I should check in on Justin to see how the baby progress is going.

Axel: How's my favorite Mama doing? Do we have a baby yet?

Justin: She's doing fantastic. I still have a whole hand, so we aren't that far into it yet. I'll make a group chat and let everyone know when he arrives.

Axel: I'm so proud of you, man. Can't wait to meet him.

Justin: I'm getting the stink eye. I have to focus back on my Pumpkin.

I decide not to respond because I know firsthand how Nicole can be when she wants something, and right now, she wants all of Justin's attention. She deserves it.

I'm off tonight and might as well start my day since sleep seems to be evading me. I'll take my pill and a cold shower. I will not think about Spencer *or* Miller getting up close and personal with my favorite body part.

After my shower and my rigorous hair care routine, which takes at least thirty minutes longer than most guys, I'm in desperate need of coffee. Since meeting Nicole, I've perfected the maintenance of my curly hair. As a hairdresser, she gave me her knowledge of how to manage and maintain my curls, and I appreciate it every time I look in a mirror.

What to do with my day? Justin is having a baby. Miller is with Spencer. *Lucky bastard.* Lincoln.

Axel: I need coffee.

Lincoln: Thanks for the info.

Axel: Wanna go on a coffee date with me? ;)

Lincoln: Only if you're paying. And I'm not a cheap date. S'morgasm or bust.

Axel: Damn, man. Who knew I was paying for a high-end companion?

Lincoln: You did. 30 mins? I'll meet you there.

Axel: Fine. But it better come with a happy ending.

Lincoln and I met under not the greatest circumstances. He was shot in the leg and rolled into my ED by more uniformed brass than I knew we had on the police force. He's the best of the best when it comes to being a police officer. Unfortunately, the injury left him unable to go back into the field. He dispatched while recovering, and although the department tried to convince him to retire with a good portion of his pension, he refused. Now, he happily roams the halls at one of the local high schools as a resource officer and fills in at dispatch when needed.

As I walk in the front doors of S'morgasm, I'm overwhelmed by the smell of sweet chocolate and bitter coffee. My stomach growls in protest reminding me I haven't eaten since around three a.m. and it's now well after noon.

"You ready to share a s'mores setup, Pookie?" A firm hand

grasps my shoulder, and I hear kissing sounds in my ear. A smile spreads on my face as I roll my eyes and turn my head, pursing my lips to kiss attack his cheek.

"Hey. I don't know where those lips have been. Get back." He releases my shoulder and steps away in mock horror. His deep, throaty chuckle booms in the room, making a few heads turn.

Lincoln is a good-looking man, and I'm not ashamed to admit it. His baritone voice even gets *me* hot and bothered sometimes. His green eyes pierce into your soul, making him swoon-worthy to all the ladies. He personifies tall, dark, and handsome.

In answer to his teasing statement, I'd usually say something like "Your mom's bed" because I have that kind of juvenile humor, but his mom passed away over a decade ago, so I'll contain that comeback. I know his father remarried but he never talks about her and I never bring it up.

"I'm always happy to show you where they *could* be." My eyebrows wiggle, and I make more kissy motions with my lips. Lincoln's large hand covers my mouth to stop my advances, and I lick it.

"Seriously, man. Did you just lick me?" He wipes his hand on his jeans and scowls at me.

"Don't pretend you didn't like it. I'll do it again if you order your funky s'mores concoctions and make me eat it with you." The V between his eyes deepens as he scowls harder.

"Fine. You drive a hard bargain, but I'd rather not swap anymore spit with you." He realizes what he's said as soon as it comes out of his mouth. I know his preference leans toward men, and he once confessed his attraction to me when we were drunk. It's become a fun source of good-humored teasing for me. "Don't do it, Axel."

"Don't worry. I'll spare you the embarrassment if you add rainbow sprinkles to our s'mores." He huffs, and I wink. I know I've won this round.

"So what's up, Axel? Shouldn't you be sleeping?" The ground looks really appealing as I shake my head and rub the back of my neck.

"Yeah, well. I um…" I lean close to his ear so no one in line with us can hear. "I sent an accidental dick pic to Spencer." His brows scrunch as he considers who I'm talking about. I understand his confusion. Spencer is typically a masculine name, and considering the conversation we just had, he's trying to put the pieces together. "Justin Webb's partner."

"Oh, Spencer. *Ohhh.*"

"Yeah. Oh. *That Spencer.*" I've never been shy about my attraction to her. She's a wonderfully complicated woman.

"I have so many questions, but I don't think I want to know. Maybe after some caffeine and sugar." We reach the front of the line, and I let Lincoln order for us. He orders a s'mores set up with my rainbow sprinkles, white and milk chocolate, nuts, and chocolate chip cookie crumbles. He listens to my threat and doesn't order the raspberry jam he usually gets because it's weird, even though he shoots me a look when the barista asks if he'd like any more toppings.

I pat him on the back, whisper good boy into his ear, and watch the blush creep on his cheeks.

Once we have our coffees in hand, we find a seat on a buttery soft brown leather loveseat. S'morgasm has a rustic industrial feel with exposed beams and pipes. The coffee is always excellent, and the s'mores setups, which are little tabletop sternos with the toppings of your choosing, are unique, and frankly just fun.

"Linc, remind me why a stud like you is still single?" His shoulders stiffen, and he inhales a sharp breath. I turn in my seat to face him better and glare. "Are you keeping secrets?"

I try to contain my need to bounce with excitement as he takes a sip of his coffee and clears his throat. He's hoping to buy himself some time but I won't give up that easily.

"Don't be coy, mister police officer. Spill the beans."

"Okay, listen. I'm not sure how he feels about being out, so I don't want to say anything, but yeah, there's a guy."

"Do I get any more details?" He gives me a side-eyed glance, and my instincts tingle. "Wait. Do I know him? Is that why you're being cryptic?" I couldn't be happier for this guy. He's broody on a good day, especially to someone he doesn't know, but once you're in his inner circle, he has total golden retriever vibes. If he has a man in his life, I know it must be someone special.

"If I say yes, you're going to try and pry the details out of me, aren't you?"

"Well, that's basically an admission, but I'll respect you. Begrudgingly." He smiles at me appreciatively. A waitress brings over our food, and we dig in. "By the way, this isn't the happy ending I expected."

He rolls his eyes at me and stuffs his face with marshmallows.

4

Spencer

"He's beautiful, Nicole. He looks just like you, curly hair and all." The tiny sleeping baby in my arms has a sweet face and rosy cheeks. "How are you feeling?" Nicole came home from the hospital yesterday, and Justin has been flitting around like a butterfly on steroids.

In the past, I might have seen this behavior as worrisome, but this is who he has become as a father. He's overly attentive in an annoyingly loving way, and he's taken his role as a father and husband better than I could have ever expected. The man I met eight years ago, who was barely alive and overdosing in an attempt to take his own life, is a person of the past.

"She's doing great for having a baby three days ago." Justin comes into the room smiling with Hannah, their two year old daughter, hanging on his hip.

"Brudder!" Hannah's arms jet out toward the baby in mine.

"Baby Miles." Justin looks lovingly at his son.

"Baby My-ees." Hannah's eyes light up as she attempts to say his name.

"Hey, Spence, why don't we take these two little ones to the other room and let Nicole rest?"

"Justin, I'm fine."

He steps up to Nicole, who's lying in bed and kisses her forehead.

"And so are they. Get some much-deserved rest, Pumpkin. We love you." She smiles at him with love and admiration and nods.

"Love you, too. A nap does sound nice."

Justin and I leave the bedroom with the little ones, and I take a seat on the living room couch while he steps into the kitchen to get Hannah a snack.

"So, I don't think I ever asked if there was a reason you named him Miles. Does it have a special meaning to either of you like Hannah does?"

Justin chuckles nervously. "We haven't told anyone." He looks at me for a long moment, considering whether to tell me.

"I'd never judge your choice of names, and you don't need to feel obligated to tell me. You know that, Justin." Miles stirs in my arms, and I readjust my hold and pat his butt.

"I'm not worried about you judging; I'm just laughing." I put on my mask, and my face goes blank.

"I'm ready."

"Don't do that. You can laugh. I can take it from you." He finishes slicing the apple for Hannah and adds it to the plate with cheese and crackers. "So, you know my childhood was crappy. And you know it was my job to tend to the cows." I nod because this is all knowledge I already possess. "I had...a favorite cow. After Ivy passed, the cow was all I had. Even though she was one of our milking cows, I had named her when I was too young to know the difference between a heifer and a bull calf. I was joking one night with Nicole when we were thinking of names, and she loved the significance of it and the humor behind it."

I can't imagine how much that meant to him that she liked the name. Ivy was Justin's little sister. She died in an ATV accident when he was seven, and she was five. He was driving them, and it took a lifelong toll on him.

I feel the bubble of laughter that wants to rise in my chest, but I contain myself for his sake. "It's a strong name."

"Yeah, yeah. You can laugh. I named my son after a misgendered cow."

"Don't do that, Justin. Don't deflect. It has meaning. Own it and appreciate the significance."

He watches Hannah eat with reverence, and I know he's thinking about her name. Hannah is named after his little sister Ivy's favorite doll.

The silence sits comfortably between us in the room. The sound of Hannah humming, broken up by sleeping baby coos as we each care for them.

Justin's phone buzzes on the counter, and his brows furrow when he looks at the caller ID.

"It's Katy. Isn't it the middle of a school day?"

"As far as I know."

"Hey, Katy. What's u—" He pauses, listening, and concerned lines burrow deeper on his face. He moves across the room out of Hannah's earshot before speaking again. "Sweetheart. Calm down. I can't understand you. Where are you?" Katy and Justin have a special relationship. The same day I met him was the day she saved his life. "Are you safe right now?"

"Justin?" I don't like his last question.

"Are you hurt other than…fuck. Don't move." He looks at me with panicked eyes as they ping-pong between Hannah and Miles.

"I'm bringing him to Nicole." He nods and rubs a hand over his shaved head.

"I'm going to stay on the phone with you, but I need to talk to Spencer, so I'm putting you on mute. But I'm here. Okay?"

I walk into their bedroom and Nicole is asleep, so I gently place Miles in the bassinet next to the bed. When I come back into the living room, Hannah is no longer at the kitchen table, but Justin looks even more frantic.

"Katy, Spencer is back. I'm still here, but give me a minute to talk to her." He's using his victim work voice, and the hairs on the back of my neck stand on end. Why is he using that tone with her?

"What's going on?"

"Katy is in the alleyway between the gas station and the fast food place across from her high school."

"Why isn't she in school?"

"She walked across the street to get lunch, and…she was attacked."

"Justin. Attacked as in…" His answer is a single nod. "Tell her I'm on the way, and don't get off the phone with her until I get there." I grab my keys from the bowl by the door and leave.

As soon as I pull out of Justin's driveway, I turn on the Bluetooth in my car and listen to the ringing.

"Tails, are you making a booty c—"

"I don't have time for your comedy right now. Are you busy? I need your help." There's a pregnant pause before he

23

answers. All joking has left him.

"What and where? Anything you need." I give him the location and the only other information Justin gave me, "A man attacked her."

"Fuck, Spencer. Call the police."

"Axel, she called Justin. She didn't call 9-1-1. Let's assess the situation first, please."

He sighs heavily, but I can hear motion in the background and a car door shut. Despite his protest, he's showing up for me.

"And this is Katy? Justin's Katy?"

"Yes. We owe it to him to help her. He has enough on his plate right now."

"I'm on my way, Spencer. You don't ever have to ask twice. I'm there."

Pulling up to the gas station, I have no idea what condition I'm going to find Katy in. I knew I was coming no matter what information Justin gave me, so I didn't bother to ask. Axel pulls up next to me and grabs a bag from his trunk. I get out and do the same. I know we both keep medical supplies on hand at all times.

"Where is she? What do we know?"

"I don't know any more than what I've already told you, and she should be right down there. Justin was staying on the phone until I arrive." Axel's attention drifts over my shoulder, and he nods. I turn to see who he's acknowledging and quickly turn back.

"Did you call him?"

"Lincoln? Yeah. He's a friend. I assumed, based on the location, that Katy goes to school across the street. Linc is the school resource officer there."

"I said, no police." My annoyance slips through, and knowing who's about to walk up behind me, I put my mask in place. It will be easier for Katy if I'm in full work mode anyway.

"He knows Katy. It's okay." He attempts to reach for my shoulder, and I sidestep his arm.

"We're wasting time." I walk away with purposeful intention, not wanting to give him an opportunity to say anything.

The alleyway is dark, but there's a sliver of light bouncing off the fast food restaurant's wall from the afternoon sun.

"Katy?" I call her name quietly, not wanting to scare her more than I'm sure she already is.

"Spencer? Justin, she's here." I follow the sound of her voice on the phone and find her curled in a ball behind a dumpster. I crouch down next to her and hold out my hand.

"Can I talk to him?" Katy's hand shakes as she extends the phone to me. "I've got her, Justin. I'll keep you updated. Take care of your family. I've got her." He hangs up after thanking me.

Movement scuffs at the front of the alley, and Katy jumps. I turn and hold up a hand for them to wait.

"It's alright, Katy. I have friends with me. They are both men. One is a nurse from the emergency room. His name is Axel. The other, I believe you know, is Officer Reed, your resource officer. We are all here to help you. Is it okay if they come closer? If not, I'll send them away."

Katy's eyes dart around, unsure of how to answer me.

In a weak, scared voice, I hear, "Okay." I turn back to Axel and Lincoln and nod.

5

Lincoln

I don't know if I'm more shocked to see Spencer, the ruby-haired beauty who flashed through my life a month ago, or Katy, the fierce, level-headed junior cowering in the corner.

When Axel called me fifteen minutes ago, I didn't answer because I was working. But when he sent a 9-1-1 text, I immediately called him back.

"What's wrong?"

"Junior at your school. Katy. I don't know her last name. Brown hair and eyes. Funny. Didn't come back to school after lunch. Do you know who I'm talking about?"

"I think so. Let me check the attendance." I scroll through the attendance on my tablet and see that Katy North was marked absent for sixth period. I know Katy, but that's not her usual behavior. "Okay, yeah. What's up?"

"We have a situation." He sighs, and it's filled with disgust. "Meet me across the street at the gas station parking lot. She was attacked, Linc."

"The fuck? I'll call the station—"

"No."

"No? Why not? If she was...taken advantage of, we need to report it."

"Lincoln, this is Webb's Katy, the little girl that saved him. She called Justin directly. We need to handle this situation with the utmost of care."

"Fuck." I rub my hand across my forehead.

"Yeah."

This is wrong. As a trained police officer, I know what I need to do. Report the incident. But I also know his story, and I know how important Katy is to Justin being alive today.

"Okay. I'll meet you there and assess the situation. But Axel, I make no promises. I'll help you because I know Katy and Justin, but if she was raped, we're taking her to the hospital for a workup."

"I understand."

From the front of the high school, I watch the parking lot like a hawk. I don't want to spook Katy. She called Justin, and Axel is somehow involved. I drive over as soon as I see his truck pull into the gas station.

I recognize Spencer's braided hair as I approach and see the interaction she has with Axel. She's tense, but a situation like this would make anyone feel that way. As happy as I am to see her, I'm more grateful a female is here to help.

The first and only time I'd laid eyes on Spencer, she was giving her statement to a fellow police officer after we were held at gunpoint one morning getting coffee. While her striking natural beauty is hard not to reminisce about, seeing her and my stepbrother playing tonsil hockey in the heat of the moment was completely unforgettable. To my knowledge, he hasn't heard from her since that day, despite giving her his card and an open invitation to his club, Midnight Moonshine.

As Axel and I enter the alleyway, Spencer lifts her hand for us to stop. She's explaining who we are to Katy and asking if she's comfortable with us coming closer. I already respected Spencer after realizing who she was. I was her dispatcher for a year while I was in recovery, but hearing her in action, I'm in awe.

She waves us over after getting Katy's approval, and when I approach, I immediately sit on the ground. I don't want to stand over her and overwhelm or intimidate her. Axel stands back, waiting to help however he can.

"Hey, Katy. Thank you for letting us help you." My visual assessment shows scrapes on her hands. She's wearing a dress and it looks to be ripped down the front. Her chocolate-colored hair looks muted and disheveled, and her face is tear stained, makeup lines running down her cheeks. "Hey Axel, do you have a jacket or hoodie in your truck? Katy could use a little cover-up." A small smile tilts Katy's lips as she tightens the fist she's using to hold her top closed.

"Yeah. Be right back." His footsteps retreat as I turn my attention back to Katy.

"Are you injured anywhere? Is there anywhere you're significantly hurt?" Her eyes bob back and forth between Spencer's and mine before casting down. "Would you feel more comfortable if I left and you could talk to Spencer?"

"No. No, I'm..." She inhales a hiccuping sigh. "Stay. Please."

Behind me, Axel whispers my name and reaches out with a zip-up jacket.

"Thanks." I open it in front of Katy, and she leans forward

to let me drape it over her shoulders. "I'll turn my head so Spencer can help you get this the rest of the way on." I look toward Axel and use my hand as an extra shield while I hear Katy and Spencer shuffling around. The sound of the zipper closing lets me know they are situated.

"Thank you. Um. My hands hurt." She reveals them to us palm up and we can better see the scrapes and small pieces of gravel and dirt embedded into them.

"Can Spencer clean those for you?" I'm not sure why Spencer is letting me take the lead on this since she's the experienced paramedic, but unfortunately, Katy isn't my first sexual assault victim, and maybe Spencer can sense that.

Katy nods at Spencer and shifts her arms closer in her direction. Spencer opens her bag and brings out the necessary supplies.

"Anywhere else?"

She closes her eyes and nods again. "My knees...I was on them when he..." Her words trail off as sobs wrack her body. Every fiber of me wants to console her, but I know I can't. If she needs comfort, I hope she can find it in Spencer. "I'm a...was...a virgin." Katy pulls her hands from Spencer and curls into an even smaller ball.

"Katy, you're safe now." I hesitantly place my hand on her arm, hoping not to scare her but letting her know I'm here. She throws herself into our arms. With one arm slung over both Spencer and me, Katy sobs and hiccups, and I know if we don't calm her down, she's going to hyperventilate.

With a gentle hand, I smooth down her hair, whispering words of encouragement and strength. From my knowledge of Spencer, I know this can't be comfortable for her.

"Katy, I'd like to take you to the hospital to get checked out.

You might feel okay right now, but your body is still running on adrenaline. I want to make sure there isn't anything more going on. Is that alright with you?" As quickly as she threw herself into our arms she retreats.

"N...n...no." She stumbles over the word, but when it comes out, it's firm.

"Katy—"

"No." There's no hesitation this time. She's building a wall and is too vulnerable right now for us to lose her trust. "He said, 'No hospital. No police.' H-he had a gun." A tremor rolls through her body, making her teeth shake. She looks at my uniform, and panic flashes in her eyes.

"Y-your..." She tries to slide further back into the wall, but there's nowhere to go.

"No. I'm not here as a police officer. Axel and Spencer called me as a friend. I'm here as your friend, Katy. Nothing else." I extend my hand, offering it to her in comfort. After some hesitation, frightened hand accepts it.

"Katy," Spencer starts. "We need to get you cleaned up. Can we take you home and clean you up there?" Katy scoffs and looks at Spencer.

"You've met her. Nothing has changed. S-she doesn't care about me. I haven't even seen her in a few days."

She? Spencer sees the confused look on my face and mouths, "Mother."

"She can come back to my house." A spark of light illuminates Katy's eyes at Spencer's offer.

"Are you sure?" This is a big deal. We're walking the ethical line, but Spencer only makes calculated decisions, and she would know what is acceptable even better than me.

"I'm certain." There's confidence in Spencer's tone, and

I'm going to trust her.

"Do you think you can walk?" Katy shakes her head once. "Can I carry you out?" She squeezes my hand in response. Tenderly, I lift her into my arms, bridal style, making sure to keep her modesty in her dress.

Spencer, Axel, and I look at each other in a silent conversation, deciding the best way to get her there.

"I'll drive," Spencer offers. I'm grateful because Axel has a pickup truck, and I'd hate to have to lift her into that. However, given her grip on my neck, I'm not sure she's going to release me to drive us.

"Is that okay with you, Katy?" She nods into my chest, and we walk out of the alley. When we step out of the shadows, Katy buries farther into me, and I shush her soothingly, letting her know I have her and she is safe.

Spencer opens the passenger door for me, but when I try to place Katy in the seat, she whimpers and clings harder.

"Please?" I'm not sure what she's asking me.

"What do you need, Katy?" Her body shakes in my arms.

"Don't let go." Her words are muffled and broken in my chest, but I understand her.

"Okay. I won't. Do you want me to sit in the back with you?" She nods again. I look at Spencer, and she closes the front door and opens the back for us. I carefully sit and slide into the back seat, making the smallest movements possible. As I settle us in, Katy's dress lifts slightly, and I see the abrasions covering her shins and knees. This poor child has gone through the unimaginable, and she's being so strong.

"I'll be right behind you." Axel gets in his truck and waits to follow. Spencer gets in the driver's seat and turns to look at us.

"I'll be as easy as I can on the road. Lincoln, do you want help with a seatbelt?" Katy stiffens in my arms at the thought of moving.

"We're okay. Just drive safe." Spencer gives me a tight smile and starts the car.

The drive to Spencer's house is quiet and somber. Katy's body occasionally shakes, and I can't tell if it's from her adrenaline or crying. Either way, I don't let go of her until Spencer shows us to a guest room, and I lay her on the bed. She's reluctant to release her grip on me, but I sit on the edge of the bed, and she curls into my side.

"Katy, we didn't meet out there, but I'm Axel, an ED nurse. I'm going to help you. I'd like to clean you up. Can I start with your hands?" She trembles at my side but adjusts her position and extends both hands to Axel.

I've been on an handful of rape cases in my career and this is usually where my job shifts to try and obtain as many details as possible, but this is different. I don't know if it's because I know Katy or because of her young age. Something is keeping me here, holding her.

Axel cleans her up and bandages a few deeper cuts. He looks at me before speaking gently to her. "Katy, I'd like to take care of your legs. If you're more comfortable, I can have Spencer do it instead." Spencer sits in the corner of the room, texting. I would guess she's letting Justin know how things are going.

"It's okay." She shifts again and moves the throw blanket Spencer used to cover her lower half when we sat. There doesn't seem to be any significant injuries, just more cuts and scrapes like her hands.

Axel takes care of her with gentleness, and I appreciate him more than ever. When I look over at Spencer again, she's staring at me, but not. I can see the glazed-over look in her eyes. I wonder where she is?

6

Spencer

One Month Earlier

It's coffee day. One day a month, I volunteer to bring everyone on shift a cup of coffee. Why do I do this? Because it makes me less awkward when my co-workers can associate me with a normal mundane task. When I hand them a cup of coffee, hide behind my mask, and put on my "work smile," they forget that I don't understand sarcasm as well as my peers or that I might answer a question they haven't voiced because I noticed their microexpressions. Something I've perfected over the years to help me with social cues.

The Hippie Bean is a little shop that personifies its name. It always smells like patchouli with an undertone of coffee. Rainbow tapestries drape along the walls, and I have to avoid staring at them, or they make my mind feel fuzzy with the overload of colors.

The owner, Flower, opens early to complete my order so I can make it to work on time. She knows how much I hate being late. Flower slipped and broke her leg in the store about two years ago, and I was one of the paramedics who came to help her. She took one look at me and proclaimed we were kindred spirits.

The doorbell dings and I glance at my watch before looking over my shoulder. It's still fifteen minutes before opening. No one should be coming in yet.

My eyes connect with a rugged-looking man. He's wearing a cowboy hat and boots in the middle of Chicago. It's not something you see every day, yet he doesn't look out of place. His brown beard shows hints of red, and I can see dark auburn hair peeking out under his hat.

"Thanks for waiting, asshole." The doorbell dings again, and my brain tickles. That voice. Why do I know that voice?

"You're too slow, dickhead." The man in the cowboy hat has a slight drawl to his words. It's subtle and probably not noticeable to the untrained ear, but I pick up on those things.

"Boys, behave." Flower startles me with her reprimand as she stacks the last of my coffees into a large box.

"Sorry, Miss Flower." That. Voice. It's deep and rich and so familiar. It's paired with dark green eyes framed by thick black lashes and hair that reminds me of the color of cinnamon.

"I'm just finishing up with Spencer, and I'll go grab your pastries from the back." The bearded man tips his hat at me and then Flower. "Oh, don't leave yet, Spencer. I want to give you some pastries as well."

"That's not necessary, Flower." She's gone before I've finished my sentence.

"There's no use arguing, Darlin'. Just let her spoil you." Cowboy hat offers his hand to me. "Name's Tucker. I'd like it if you let me help you take this out to your vehicle." He nods to the box of coffees on the counter as I shake his hand.

Handshaking is something that I've perfected. It's a societal norm. Similar to my ability to handle the ambulance sirens when I drive, I can control a handshake's firmness and general length, which makes touching someone bearable. You can also tell a lot about someone's character by their handshake—Tucker's is firm and confident.

"I can take care of it, but thank you." I offer a small smile in thanks. Sometimes, my voice is too monotone, and a smile eases my words.

"No use arguing with me either." Tucker winks and reaches for the box. Once again, the doorbell dings. I freeze. I'm the only one facing the door as the masked man dressed all in black pointing a gun stalks in.

"Nobody move! I just want the money." Tucker stops with his hands inches away from my coffee box, and his friend's entire demeanor changes.

"Alright, boys, I have all of your—Ahhhh!" Flower drops her box of pastries and screams as the masked man steps closer, pointing the gun at her. Tucker wraps his arm around my waist and slowly pulls me behind him.

"I just want the money," the man repeats to Flower. With her hands in the air, she takes tentative steps toward the cash register. Tucker and his friend have a silent conversation, and I hope they aren't planning to do anything irrational. I'm calm on the outside, but my heart is racing like the Indy 500.

Flower opens the register with trembling hands and passes over all the money. The masked man takes it and walks backward with his head on a swivel, watching all of us. When he passes Tucker's friend, he spins on his heels to walk out while shoving the money and gun into his pockets.

As if it were slow-playing on a movie screen, Tucker's friend whips around and tackles the masked man to the ground in a bear hug.

"Lincoln, be careful." Tucker sees the gun fall out of the masked man's pocket and rushes over to...Lincoln? I focus my attention on the two men rolling around when I hear Flower talking on the phone. She must have called the police.

"Yes, Officer Reed has him tackled to the floor. Please hurry." *Officer Reed?* Lincoln Reed. It can't be.

"Miss Flower, do you have any zip ties?" Lincoln's baritone voice booms with exertion from the floor. He's sitting on the thief's back, holding both his hands in one of his, and the other hand is holding...a gun? A quick look shows me it's not the gun that the thief had because that's kicked in the corner. Where was Lincoln hiding a gun?

"Are you okay, Little Miss?" Tucker's hands rub up and down my arms. I watch them and wait for the feeling of unease to wash over me, but it doesn't come.

Sirens outside catch my attention, and two uniformed police officers run through the door. They take over for Lincoln and handcuff the thief, bringing him to his feet and escorting him out the door.

I close my eyes, take a deep breath, and count backward from five, attempting to refocus myself. There's too much unknown going on around me, and I need to concentrate on one thing. Opening my eyes, I can feel them bouncing around the room, attempting to find anything to help my brain regroup.

"Hey. It's Spencer, right?" Tucker grabs my cheeks with his large hands, and once again, I wait for the itchy feeling I usually get when someone touches me. Why doesn't this man elicit the same reactions that everyone else does? Justin is the only other person I've ever felt this instant connection with, that someone's touch didn't bother me. "Little Miss, talk to me. Please."

I look deep into Tucker's eyes. They're blue. I couldn't see them until now because they were hidden by his hat. They're as blue as the color of glass. I can focus on his eyes. My father collects blue glass. Something familiar to focus on.

I grab his wrists to further solidify my connection—to ground me. Tucker's thumbs slowly glide over my cheek, and suddenly, my eyes are closed, and warm lips feather across mine. He's holding his breath, and I realize I am too. I can't tell who got us to this position, him or me. I don't remember moving, but the light brush of his lips turns searing, and my hands fist into his t-shirt.

Tucker's tongue sweeps over my lower lip, asking permission to enter, and I part mine. As our tongues tangle together, I feel his fingertips massage the nape of my neck. I imagine if my hair wasn't in Dutch braids, he'd be running his hand through it, and the thought of that doesn't make me uncomfortable.

"Spencer, are you o—Oh. Okay." I pull away at the sound of Justin's voice. What was I doing? I look down at my hand and release Tucker's shirt.

"Justin, what are you doing here?" My focus hasn't left Tucker's face as I talk to my partner, Justin.

"I-I have to go. Thank you for…" I'm at a loss for words from the smile that radiates on Tucker's face.

"You're welcome. And Spencer,"—He reaches into his back pocket and pulls a card out of his wallet.—"I'm the owner of Midnight Moonshine. If you'd ever like to come by, it's on the house." He leans close to my ear. "That kiss was fucking incredible, Little Miss. Thank you."

Tucker walks toward the door, and Justin steps up beside me. I watch Tucker clap a hand on Lincoln's shoulder as they walk outside to talk to the officers and Flower.

"What the hell was that, Spence? I heard the call come on the radio and knew you'd be here getting everyone's coffees. I got here as quickly as possible to find you playing tonsil hockey with…Who the hell was he?" Justin plucks the business card from my hand.

"No way. Do you know who that is? That's Tucker Bennett. According to his card, he owns Midnight Moonshine. And you just had your tongue down his throat. I'm proud of you, friend." Now I understand the cowboy hat and boots. But…

"Do you know who he was with? Officer Lincoln Reed, I believe."

"Linc? You know him. Lincoln is one of our dispatchers." *Dispatcher. It's him—the* voice I recognized, the one that makes my stomach flutter whenever I hear it on the radio.

"Of course. Why don't you take the box of coffee and bring it back to the station? The police might want to talk to me, and I don't want to leave my car here. Let Chief know I'll be at the station as soon as I can."

"I'll make sure to let Miller know, too. He was freaking out a bit." Crap.

"Justin, what the hell did I just do?"

"Well, my friend. It looks like you just kissed a stranger. Are you sure you don't want me to wait with you?" My fingers gently graze my lips. I can still feel the pressure from Tucker's kiss. It's still dark outside, but I can see his tall frame in the shadows through the doors.

"Earth to Spencer?"

"What?"

"Was his kiss that good?" *Yes.* Justin chuckles when I don't respond. "Okay, I'll take the hint. You sure you're okay here?"

"He's fine."

"Holy shit, Spence." I turn my attention away from the window and look at Justin, laughing.

"What's wrong with you? What's so funny?"

He's laughing so hard he lifts his glasses to wipe away a tear. "You. I just asked if you were okay here, and your reply was, 'He's fine.'"

"I did not."

"You did, but I'll let it go for now. See you at work, Spence."

7

Axel

Sitting in Spencer's kitchen drinking coffee, I look around her house. I've never been here before but I'm not surprised to see how minimalist it is. Everything is black, white, clean and crisp. Her dog, Gage, sits in a corner watching me.

"That's really freaky, Tails?" She turns from her position at the counter, where she's making everyone sandwiches, to see what I'm talking about. "Are you sure Gage isn't a statue?"

"*Kommen.*" Spencer's German shepherd reacts instantly and strides to her. She pets his head and whispers in his ear. Gage walks back across the room and lays down on a dog bed. "He's on alert because of the new people in the house. I told him to relax." She washes her hands before resuming sandwich making. A noise comes from down the hall and we both look.

"She's asleep." Lincoln looks just as exhausted as I feel. Spencer slides a cup of coffee across the counter at him as he takes a seat next to me. He looks up to thank her and I'm vibrating with anticipation...three... two... one.

There it is. His jaw drops as Spencer turns back to her task. When we met her earlier in the alley she was wearing tight jeans and an athletic shirt that was also snug fitting; a typical outfit for her. After Katy was cleaned up and we left her with Lincoln, Spencer went to her room and took a shower.

When she came out I'm sure I made the same face. She looks like every bad decision I've ever made wrapped in a huge bow. Dark green, skin tight leggings cover her to mid calf. On top she's wearing a lighter green color sports bra that's more like a crop top then a bra as it stops mid waist. There's three inches of delicious pale skin on display to tempt every goddamn nerve in my body. I see faint freckles and I want to get closer and connect every one of them with my tongue.

I reach over and lift Lincoln's jaw. I'm not surprised to see he's just as affected by her and I am. Spencer is a mystery to every man in her life except Justin.

"You're both juveniles." Spencer turns with a plate full of gourmet looking sandwiches and places it between us. "I can feel you staring at me. I'm not a fan of clothes and would honestly prefer to be naked but that's frowned upon with company."

Air. I choke on nothing but the air in the room at the bluntness of her comment. Lincoln isn't any better. His eyes are as wide as saucers and his jaw flaps like a fish, unable to form words. I somehow manage to compose myself before him and take the opportunity to make the room even more tense.

"I don't think either of us would mind if you'd prefer to walk around au naturel, Tails. Don't let us disrupt your routine." Spencer knows the attraction I have for her, so my comment isn't anything unusual, but Lincoln? It's clear he isn't impervious to her beauty.

"Would *you* prefer I be naked, Lincoln?"

His hand stops midair grabbing for a sandwich, completely stupefied by her question. The tips of his ears turn beat red as he stammers out an answer.

"I...um..." A scream rings out from down the hall and our heads whip in its direction. "Katy."

Lincoln almost falls off the stool in his rush to get down the hall. Spencer and I follow and find Katy curled into a ball, crying. Lincoln picks her up and settles her into his lap. Katy curls into him, still asleep, but instantly settles. I don't know why she's taken to him the way she has but I'm glad she's found a safe space.

Spencer walks over and places a hand on her wrist, checking her pulse rate.

"Tails, are we sure this is what's best for her?" A darkness flashes over her face before I see her mask snap into place. What's made her guarded?

"She's the victim. She's told us what she wants and doesn't want. She has no real injuries so the law doesn't require us to report the assault."

"But look at her," Lincoln whispers. "She's traumatized. She's just a child." He pulls the blanket over her from earlier.

"I know what her life has been like. She's stronger than either of you men could possibly understand. Her comment about her mother earlier wasn't an exaggeration."

"I knew of Katy at school but she's a good kid so I haven't had much interaction with her. I just want to do what's best for her."

"We all do, Linc." A silence falls over the room.

"You don't have to stay, Lincoln. We're fine here." Spencer and Lincoln have been arguing for the last hour about leaving Katy here alone with her. Spencer can't seem to understand that neither of us are going to leave her or Katy tonight. I already got my shift covered and I'm not taking no for an answer unless Spencer physically forces me out.

"I have complete faith that you'll be fine but I'm still not leaving." Lincoln sits back on the couch and crosses his arms across his broad chest.

A gentle knock sounds on the door and Spencer freezes. Gage goes on high alert and stalks toward the foyer. Spencer pulls her phone out from the pocket of her skin tight pants and taps on the screen.

"Who did it?" There's a slight edge to her voice and I try not to smile.

"Who did what?" Lincoln glances at me and it must be written on my face. "Who's at the door Axel?" Another soft knock sounds and Gage lets out a gentle gruff. Spencer spins on her heels and opens the door.

"I was told there was going to be a sleepover?" Miller holds up a duffle bag in one hand and a case of beer in the other and I watch his eyes roam over Spencer's body. I know they work out together at the firehouse so he shouldn't be as affected by her outfit as we were but judging by the look on his face, he is.

"No," she says. I cover my laugh behind my hand at Spencer's abrupt answer. "The only people sleeping here have vaginas."

Miller gives Spencer his award winning smirk. "I can tuck

it in for you if that gets me an invite." Lincoln almost loses it and Spencer shoots us a look that's deadly.

"I'm going to bed. Don't wake Katy. I don't like any of you in my space." She stalks to her door and walks in. Before she closes it, she calls for Gage and gives us one last glaring look. "I sleep with a gun." With that little nugget of information she closes the door and the click of the lock is audible.

"Fuck she's gorgeous." I have no shame admitting that out loud to anyone, especially a room full of men that I already know admire her too. "Please tell me you brought me shorts or sweats because I can't sleep in jeans and I'm commando under here." I wiggle my hips around in the chair I'm sitting in. Lincoln throws a pillow at me and Miller tosses the duffle bag in my lap.

"There's stuff in there for you too, Linc." Miller's eyes linger a little longer than necessary on Lincoln and it peaks my interest. "So, what do we know about what happened today?"

"I'm going to go change. You can fill him in." I clasp Lincoln's shoulder as I walk past him and nod at Miller. I hear their voices fade as I walk farther down the hall.

We left Katy's door ajar to make sure we could hear her, so I peek in. She looks peaceful. Spencer gave her a T-shirt and shorts to change into earlier but she wouldn't leave the room to shower and other than water we couldn't get her to eat. Tomorrow will hopefully bring her a better day.

I walk into the bathroom and as soon as I see the shower I decide I need to use it. It's been a long fucking day.

I strip and turn the water on. Cold showers build endurance but Spencer must have one of those fancy water heaters because the water is almost instantly hot. After staring at her tempting body for the last hour, I could have used the cold.

I quickly wash my hair and body and sigh when I look down at my semi-hard cock.

I'm naked in Spencer's house. A few hours ago, a simple smile from her would make my day, and now I'm in her guest shower. And fuck, Spencer saw a picture of my dick.

So much for a semi. The thought of Spencer even glancing at my cock has me stiffening. I need to do something about this. I can't go out there with my friends pitching a tent.

Fuck it.

I grab the base of my cock and tug, giving it a long stroke and watching the blood flow to the tip of my piercings. I bite my knuckles to not moan and give away what I'm doing. I stroke myself in long, hard movements because this is more about release than pleasure. There's no time to savor the feeling. The end game is to come and it needs to happen quickly.

I squirt a bit of honey scented conditioner onto my hand to help with lubrication and it allows me to pump my cock faster.

I feel it building. The muscles in my abs starting to spasm, my balls tingling and drawing up. My pace falters as the first wave of pleasure releases. I hold my breath to keep in my noise and eventually let out a ragged exhale as the last pulses of my orgasm subside.

"Fuck."

When I'm done I rummage through the duffle bag, realizing I took the entire thing with me, not leaving Lincoln or Miller anything to change into, and smile. Serves them right. I throw on a pair of sweatpants that are a bit smaller than I usually wear. Miller and I are about the same height but I'm broader than him.

As I exit the bathroom, I can hear muffled voices floating down the hall and see a flickering glow. They must have turned the TV on. Although, as I get closer to the room I don't see either of them sitting on the couch or in the kitchen when I step into the open floor plan room.

A muffled noise comes from the living room followed by a shhh sound. Did one of them finally manage to pin Spencer down? As stealthy as I can manage, I creep over to the couch and see two lying bodies, locked in a passionate kiss. Only there's no red braids or creamy white skin. There's a head of dark shaggy hair with rough hands tugging at the strands.

Miller's hips move over Lincoln's body and another moan I think is Miller's, floats through the room.

"I told you to be qui—wait. Do you? I don't hear the shower." I'm not sure Miller can hear much of anything with his head buried in Lincoln's neck and I'm far enough back that he can't see me over the top of the couch from his position.

"I'm sure he's still in there jerking off. I could help *you* out with that." Miller's hand slides down Lincoln's side and just as it disappears between them I clear my throat.

"Fuck." Miller's hand reappears and he lays his head on Lincoln's chest. Lincoln's eyes dart around the room in panic.

"Is there room for one more?"

Lincoln pushes on Miller's chest but he isn't budging. He's laughing. "Get up." His voice is a pleading whisper. Miller kisses his forehead and pushes up to sit at the end of the couch. Lincoln scrambles to the other end and pulls the blanket down off the back of the couch to cover his erection.

47

"So this is your mystery man, Linc? I'm impressed."

"What? Fuck. What?" He's adorable with his brain short circuiting. Lincoln casts his gaze to Miller who's wearing a shit-eating grin and making no attempt to hide how hard he is. "Why is he impressed?" Lincoln's confused look turns to me. "Why are you impressed?"

"Miller's a fucking catch. Man or woman. You've got a good one." I lean over and shove at Miller's shoulder. "I've been fucking with this guy for years and he's never turned a cheek in my direction." I'm not sure the V between Lincoln's eyes could get any deeper.

"Are you...into guys?"

I give him an honest shrug. "I'm not *not* into them. The right opportunity hasn't risen yet. I could never give up pussy but I can appreciate the male form." I look Miller up and down and linger on the bulge in his jeans. When I look back at Lincoln his eyes focus where mine just were. I bend down and slap Miller on the chest.

"What the fuck?" he protests.

"You saw my cock and freaked out. Now I'm upset. I deserved a better reaction than that."

"I was in fucking shock." A look passes between Miller and Linc. I open my mouth to question what it's all about but I hear Lincoln's name drift from the hallway, stealing our attention.

8

Lincoln

"Lincoln?" Hearing Katy say my name has me jumping off the couch and forgetting that my friend just caught me with *his* friend in a compromising position on the couch. More shockingly, he didn't seem to care.

When I reach Katy, she's standing in the hallway with the throw blanket pulled around her shoulders.

"Hey, sweetheart. Are you alright?" I put an arm around her shoulder and can see the purple under her eyes has faded. She got some much-needed sleep.

"I'm...hungry."

"My specialty." Katy jumps at the new voice as Miller walks toward us. He sees her hesitation and slows his advancement. "Hi, Katy. We've met before. I'm a firefighter where Justin and Spencer work. My name is Miller." After a few moments, recognition dawns on her face.

"Grilled cheese."

I'm confused, but Miller must understand because his lip tilts up in his sexy half-smile, which I love. "And tomato soup.

49

Would you like that?"

Katy nods into my side. Miller turns on his heels, and we stare as he rummages through Spencer's refrigerator.

The brave girl under my arm steps away from me and squares her shoulders. She looks between the three men in the room and then at Spencer's door. Her confidence falters momentarily, and I dip to her level and look into her eyes.

"What do you need, Katy?"

"I'd…um." Her eyes dart between the three of us again. "I'd like to shower."

Axel begins to round the corner of the couch. "I'll wake Spencer to help you."

"No. I don't want to bother her." I open my mouth to protest, but Miller is quicker than I am.

"Hey." His word is firm, but Katy doesn't shy away from it. He puts down the loaf of bread in his hand, and focuses solely on her. "If you listen to one thing, and one thing only, let it be this. There isn't a single person in this house, Spencer included, that will ever think of you as a bother or a burden or anything else negative that you can think of. We all dedicate our lives to helping people. Especially when they're *our* people."

I take her shoulders and turn her to face me. "And just so there's no confusion. You. Are. Our. People. Katy." Her eyes glaze over with tears, and she flings herself into me, wrapping her arms around my chest, and laying her ear on my heart.

Miller and Axel approach us, and we end up in a circle, embracing Katy until her breathing has calmed from her crying.

Axel pulls away first and tilts her chin toward him. "As I

was saying, I'm going to wake up Spencer, Miller will make you food, and mister softy over here can hang with you while the adults do all the work." The sweetest smile creeps across her face, and she whispers, "Thank you." He looks at Miller and then me, and we all nod, agreeing to our roles.

Axel approaches Spencer's door and pauses. I don't think any of us have a clue what she's like if she's woken up. He lightly taps, and Gage lets out a warning ruff. He tries again, and Gage lets out a full bark. It must wake Spencer because there's movement behind the door.

"Go to sleep, you drunk heathens," Spencer's sleep voice chastises.

"I can do it myself, Lincoln. You don't have to wake her." Katy's voice is meek as if she doesn't want to get in trouble.

"Trust me. She'll be more upset if we don't." I pull her closer to me to reinforce my statement.

"Katy needs you." Axel says the one thing he knows won't get any of us in trouble for waking her. The door whips open, and all the air in the room leaves.

"What's wrong with Katy?"

"Fuck."

My thoughts exactly. Axel stares in shock at Spencer's appearance. Her hair is...down. No braids. It's a rich red color and hangs in waves just past her shoulders. The curls beautifully frame her face, making her freckles more prominent across her nose.

"Why are you all gaping at me?" How can she not know how much she affects us all?

"Your hair is beautiful, Spencer." Spencer's eyes find Katy as she says what I'm sure we are all thinking.

"Oh. Thank you." Spencer glides a smoothing hand down

her hair, realizing that's what we're all staring at her for, and I see the faintest of blush on her cheeks.

I already know Miller's fascination with her; it's a mutual one we share. The singular meeting with her in the coffee shop solidified everything that I needed to know about the woman I'd been listening to for years. Always confident and assured when she spoke.

"Katy, what do you need my help with?" Spencer approaches us, and Katy looks at me for approval, and I give her a reassuring smile.

"I'm hungry, but Miller is making me food. But um…I'd like to shower, and they said I need help." Her body stiffens under my arm, and she begins to ramble. "I can do it. I don't really need help. I feel okay." I feel her body tensing, and her breathing increases with panic as I guide her to the couch. Spencer follows and squats in front of us.

"Katy, I'm happy to help. What do you need from me?" She unwraps the blanket, and her hands appear in front of her. She still has several small bandages on her hands and legs, and Spencer understands her meaning without words. "Come with me. We can use my bathroom. It's bigger, and I have everything you'll need in there." Spencer helps Katy stand, and they disappear into her bedroom.

"Fuck." Once again, Axel says what we're all thinking. "Have any of you ever seen her with her hair down?" I shake my head, and Miller not so subtly adjusts himself in his pants.

"What I wouldn't give for my fingers to get lost in her—"

"Fireball." My tone came out harsher than I intended, but I don't want Miller to finish that sentence. I'll admit that a twinge of jealousy surged through me, and I understand the ridiculousness of it because my mind is wandering in the same direction.

"Fireball?"

Fuck. I hang my head, realizing I used my pet name for Miller without even thinking. And using it in front of Axel is worse than a regular slip up. I hold my breath as Axel slides up next to Miller and ruffles his hair. "I like it, big guy."

I puff out the air in my lungs and sit at the kitchen island. "You aren't mad?"

Axel arches a brow. "Why would I be mad?" He slings his arm over Miller's shoulder. "You two are adorable. I don't know why you were hiding it."

"Because you're such a ladies man, Axel. I know you're cool with my sexuality, but I don't flaunt it around you, and I never want to make my friends uncomfortable. I didn't know how you would feel about two of your friends hooking up." I pause and look at Miller. "Um also, when did you see Axel's dick?"

"Hooking up?" Miller shakes Axel's arm off his shoulder and stalks toward me. His hand grips the back of my neck, and he pulls me in for a firm, possessive kiss. When he pulls away, we're both panting for air. "I'm your fucking boyfriend." His statement is firm and growly, and I have to remember we have company in the room because I want to do sinful things to him right now. "And there was an accidental dick pic sent to Spencer that I opened for her while she was driving. It was no big deal."

"Damn, man. You cut me deep." Axel dramatically clutches his chest. "Listen, I may come off as a lady's man, but you two can love whoever you want to love. You be you. I respect you both, so don't keep shit like that from me. And that kiss was fucking hot. You sure you don't have room for one more?"

Miller shoots Axel a look full of heat, and I don't know if it's directed toward him because of his comment or if it's residual from our kiss.

Miller squeezes my neck and kisses my forehead. "I have to cook for Katy."

"Are you going to tell us what that was all about with her?"

Miller shrugs. "I cooked the day her class came to the station for their CPR class. Grilled cheese and tomato soup was on the menu because it's quick, easy, and feeds a lot of people. Katy acted like it was the best thing she had eaten in a while."

We carry on mindless conversation as Miller prepares the meal she requested. The shower turns off in Spencer's room, and we wait for the girls to emerge.

9

Spencer

This isn't the vibrant, lively girl I'm used to seeing. Her body holds the weight of the world as I remove the bandages from earlier.

"Katy, I need to ask you an extremely important question because what you're about to do will change everything. You said earlier you didn't want to go to the hospital or the police, and we will respect what you want. But I need you to know, getting in the shower will remove any evidence of what happened to you."

"That's what I want." Her hand latches onto my arm, and her eyes plead with me.

"I understand you want to forget it ever happened, but if there's any evidence for the police on your body, we're about to wash it away." Her hand on my arm trembles, and she squeezes her eyes shut.

"Please." Her plea is a whisper. There's no conviction behind it, only fear and desperation. I know what she's feeling. The despair, the terror. They manifest into tangible things, when all you want to do is forget a moment in time and leave it behind. I can't fault her for her decisions but I can make sure she knows all of her options because no one ever told me.

"Okay. The water is ready. I want you to be comfortable, Katy. Do you want me to go wait in my room while you shower?" Panicked eyes shoot to me.

"Please stay."

"I'm not going anywhere. I'll sit in here with you." Bending down, I open the bathroom cabinet, take out an antibacterial soap, and hand it to her. "Use this for your scrapes. It will help make sure they're clean. I'll face the wall to give you some privacy."

I take a seat on the toilet and turn. I hear her clothes rustling, and the shower door opens and closes.

"Is the water temperature good?"

"It's perfect. Thank you."

"You are welcome to use any of the products in there. Take your time."

I begin to smell food cooking as I sit and wait. Occasionally, Katy says my name to make sure I'm still with her, and every time I reassure her I haven't left.

Spencer: Katy is doing well. She's shaken up but managing. The Three Stooges are here. Are you free tomorrow? I can come over, and we can discuss things.

Justin: I'll be here whenever you want to stop by. Thank you for taking care of her.

Spencer: I take care of family.

The water turns off, and I stand, waiting with a towel in hand. Katy peeks around the door and smiles when she sees me.

She takes the towel and reappears with it wrapped around her.

"Let's get you dressed." She follows me into my room, and I survey my drawers, realizing I don't have much to offer her. "I'm a fan of tight clothes, but I'm sure you would rather wear something comfortable." I pull a pair of flannel pajama pants from the back of my closet that Nicole left when she stayed with me, but a shirt option is harder to find. "Hold on." I open the bedroom door using my body to cover the line of sight from the opening.

"Gentleman, does anyone happen to have a spare T-shirt for Katy to borrow? My wardrobe is lacking such things."

"There are options in the bag I brought." Miller uses the spatula in his hand to point at a black duffle sitting by the couch. I notice all of the men have changed their clothes and are wearing sweatpants and T-shirts. I don't think I have ever understood the appeal until right now.

Axel's pants are a tad too small and hug his thighs. The shirt he's wearing has the sleeves removed and large cutouts on the side, easily showing off his chest with every move. Miller was already wearing black workout pants and a white shirt when he got here, and Lincoln has traded his navy cargo pants and work polo for a black tank top and dark gray sweats.

"Spencer?" Axel stands next to me, arm extended, offering me the bag. *How did he get here?*

"In case you're wondering"—he leans in so only I can hear him—"none of us mind that you're staring at us like pieces of juicy meat." I feel my eyebrows rise in shock. Is that what I was doing? I take the bag and raise it in thanks before shutting the door.

"Is everything okay?" Katy questions my hasty movements.

"I'm fine. The guys said there should be clothes in here for you. Let's see what our options are."

We join everyone in the kitchen after getting Katy dressed and rebandaging some of her cuts. Dinner was delicious. I'm not sure how Miller managed to make something so simple taste so good, but Katy seemed to savor every bite, making me wonder more about her home life.

"Do we need to contact your mother and let her know where you are tonight?" She stops with her spoon mid-air, and her shoulders slump.

"She won't care. She probably won't even notice I'm missing until the dishes pile up in the sink."

"The fuck." Axel's spoon clinks as he drops it into his almost-empty bowl. "Katy, you're only sixteen. You're saying your mother doesn't care about you?"

"She never has. That's how I met Justin."

I know all about Katy's relationship with Justin, but I'm not sure how much they know. It's not a story to tell right now, though.

The room falls into silence—crunching bread and clinking spoons the only sounds. As everyone finishes, Miller and Lincoln wash dishes, and Katy looks lost as she glances down the hall.

"I...I don't want to be alone." Her gaze drifts to Lincoln, who seems to be her comfort person.

"Do you want to come sleep in my bed with me?" The guest bed is a twin and won't accommodate more than one person, but I have a King-size bed with plenty of room. It's strange to have all of these people in my house, and I'm waiting for my anxiety about needing my personal space to overtake me.

It hasn't yet.

"Um…" I feel her reluctance, and I think I know why.

"Would you like Lincoln to join us?" I see Lincoln's back go stiff, and I know he's shocked by my offer. I'm far out of my comfort zone, but I'm thinking about what Katy needs right now. Her comfort is more important than mine.

"Is that possible?" She's so hopeful. I know she doesn't know any of them or the dynamic we have.

"I wouldn't offer it if I wasn't fine, but it's up to Lincoln as well."

He pauses and finishes drying the dish in his hand before turning around. A look passes between Miller and Lincoln that I don't understand before he accepts my offer.

"If that's what will help make you comfortable, Katy, I'm alright with it."

They finish the dishes, and everyone decides on their sleeping arrangements. Miller on the couch, Axel in the guest room and Katy and Lincoln with me. I've never had this many people in my house, let alone sleep here. And I've most definitely not slept in a bed with someone other than Gage in close to a decade.

Tonight should be interesting.

Everyone settles for the evening. Katy crawls into the middle of the bed, Lincoln gets in on the left with his own blanket, and all that needs to be done is for me to get in. I lift the blanket and slide in, relaxing on my back. I tell Gage to settle, and he lies on the floor beside me.

"Thank you." Katy's meek voice cuts through the silence.

"G'night, girls."

"Night."

I'm hot. Too hot. Why is Gage breathing in my ear? He usually sleeps at my feet. I try to move, but I'm pinned to the bed. Opening my eyes to see what my situation is, I realize it's not Gage pinning me down, it's Lincoln. I forgot I went to sleep with a bed full of people.

Where's Katy?

I lift my head and look around the room. I don't see Katy anywhere, but I hear low noises coming from the living room. Did she get up without me knowing?

Lincoln shifts next to me. His arm drapes over my stomach, and a leg slides over me. Is that… "Lincoln." I shrug my shoulder to try and gently wake him. "Lincoln." I say his name a little more forcefully and try to wiggle out from under him.

"No." The grip on my waist tightens, and he pulls me closer.

"Lincoln, wake up."

"Spencer?"

"Yes. You're in my bed, you're cuddling me, and your erection is digging into my thigh." He wiggles his hips, still half asleep, and the sweatpants he's wearing do nothing to stop his manhood from rubbing against me. His *large* manhood.

A throaty moan escapes him. His already deep voice is gravelly with sleep, and my nipples harden at the sound.

"Spencer."

Now he's moaning my name. What do I do? I'm stuck under this gorgeous man who's dry-humping my leg and moaning my name. Why did my mind just wander to the spectacular kiss I had with his stepbrother?

What is wrong with me?

"Lincoln, please wake up." I shake his shoulder, and he

moans again. "Lincoln." Another shake, and his arm tightens more. He's making it hard to breathe, his grip is firm. "Lincoln."

"Well, isn't this cozy?" I freeze. My eyes drift to the door to see Miller's baby blue staring at me. "He's not usually a snuggly person."

"What?" I'm taken aback by his statement. "What do you mean?"

"Oh. Um…" Miller runs a hand through his dark hair.

"He's my boyfriend," Lincoln's baritone voice hums in my ear. *Now* he's awake. And what did he say?

"Boyfriend? You two are together?"

"Mhmm. He's mine." That's so sweet to hear him call Miller his.

"Miller, you might want to come get your boyfriend. He's grinding himself on my leg, and while I can appreciate his attempt, I'm not a teenager anymore, and I much prefer the actual act of sex."

"Spencer, is that an offer?" Lincoln's hand squeezes my hip. He must be out of his mind.

"Lincoln!"

"It sounded like an offer to me." Miller smirks from his position leaning on the door frame.

"Out. Both of you. Where's Katy?"

"Making breakfast with Axel." Lincoln kisses my cheek before rolling off the other side of the bed, and I feel the heat from his lips lingering longer than it should.

What is going on? The sexual tension in the room is high. I watch Lincoln adjust himself out of the corner of my eye, and the bulge I see is just as big as it felt.

Miller clears his throat. "You might not want to come out

61

here like that and scare Katy."

"Shit. What time is it? I have to get to the school. Is Katy going?"

Miller shakes his head. "You have time, but she's asked not to go. Besides, she has no clothes."

"I'll take care of that with her."

Today, we figure out Katy's future.

10

Spencer

Axel and Miller stay with Katy while Lincoln goes to work, and I head to Justin's to speak with him. She was hesitant, since she knows them the least, but after talking with us, Katy decided she was comfortable enough to stay. If I hadn't felt her comfort level, I would have asked Justin to come over or taken her with me.

I hear Miles crying from the other side of the door as I knock and wait for someone to answer. Usually, I would enter without knocking, but they have a brand new baby, and I respect Nicole's privacy.

"Hey, Spence. Come in." Justin looks a little worse for the wear. His usual buzzed hair and trimmed goatee are overgrown; his glasses are slightly askew on his nose, and...

"Is that vomit or poop on your shirt?"

He looks down, lifts it to his nose, and shrugs. "Both?"

"Fair. Where's my goddaughter?" Justin swings his arm behind him into the house.

"She's somewhere in there causing terror. She's taking full advantage of Nicole and me being exhausted. She was never like this. A perfect angel baby that lulled us into a false sense of security." As I survey the house, I pull my phone out of my pocket.

Spencer: SOS. Justin and Nicole need a break. Can one or all of you come and pick up Hannah? I'll help with the baby. Katy might enjoy the distraction of playing with H.

Axel: On it.

Miller: The three of us are taking a field trip. See you in 15.

"Where's my favorite niece?" I hear a giggle and the pitter-patter of lots of feet. Hannah comes running from her bedroom, followed by Nicole's two dachshunds, Java and Beans. The two little dogs are her best friends.

"Aunt Spender!" She crashes into my legs, and I scoop her up. The affection of children has never bothered me. There was a time in my life when I wanted nothing more than to be a mother.

"Hello, sweet girl. Why are you still in your pajamas?"

"PJ day, ebery day. You like my dress?" She wiggles in my arms to show me the pajama dress she's wearing with princesses.

"It's beautiful but how about we change into a real dress? Do you want to go out with some friends?"

"Yes, yes. Let's go." I put her down before she bounces out of my arms with excitement, and she runs, clapping down the hall.

"What's going on?" Nicole questions as Hannah flies past her. She looks even more exhausted than Justin. Her curly blond hair lacks its usual bounce and is piled high on her head. She's wearing a loose tank top and a pair of basketball shorts that obviously belong to Justin. Miles fusses in her arms, and she bounces him on her shoulder.

"Give me the baby. Nicole, go shower. Justin, help Hannah get dressed for the day and pack her a bag." They both open their mouths to object, and I raise a hand, stopping all protest. "You need a break, and I'm here." Justin happily disappears to Hannah's room.

"A shower sounds spectacular. Are you sure?" Nicole may be asking, but she's already handing a whining Miles over to me.

"I've got him. Go. Shower." She slowly backs away, and her expression is a mix of hesitation and relief. "Go, Nicole." She spins and leaves the room, and I swear I see her skip.

When Justin returns with a smiling Hannah, happily dressed in a purple twirly dress, he's shocked at what he sees.

"What did you do to my son?" I quickly look down, wondering what's wrong. "He's quiet." Miles is asleep in my arms, and I don't understand Justin's reaction.

"Is that a problem? Should he not be sleeping?" Panic washes over Justin's face as I try to stand.

"No. Don't move." His arms fly up in an attempt to stop me.

"Okay. I don't understand what's going on." Justin sits beside me on the couch and slumps back into the cushions with a sigh. I'm waiting for an answer when his eyes flutter shut. I'm more confused than before.

"Brudder noisey. Daddy seepy." Hannah covers her ears to show me what she means, then points at Justin, who has fallen asleep. I think I understand Justin's shocked expression.

65

"Is he? He's sleeping right now, though. They both are. Brother and Daddy are sleeping. Are you ready to go out? Did Daddy pack your backpack?" She nods and runs around the couch. I hear her footsteps leave and then return. She reappears with a sparkly unicorn backpack and a toothy smile.

"I ready!"

Spencer: Text me when you get here. Everyone is sleeping.
    Miller: <thumbs up emoji>

What is the point of an emoji as a response?

I hear footsteps behind me and turn to see a similar shocked face on a freshly showered Nicole.

"You're a baby whisperer, Spencer. How?" Her question is so simple and innocent. She had no idea the pain it causes me to think about the how and the why.

My phone buzzes in my hand, and it's a text from Axel telling me they are here.

"Tweedledee and Tweedledum are here to take Hannah out for a while. They just pulled in." Nicole turns to look at the door and then back at me.

"Um, who?"

"Miller and Axel. And Katy is with them. I thought you two could use a break." I tip my head to Justin, who's fast asleep beside me. She chuckles as if she hadn't even noticed him there. "Will you walk Hannah out and get them settled with a car seat? Then you can go take a nap yourself."

"Yes, oh god, yes. You're a freaking saint, Spencer."

Axel: Package has been procured. Have fun, Auntie Tails.

Spencer: Treat both of them like precious cargo.

Miller: Wouldn't imagine any other way.

Nicole instructs me where the formula and diapers are and wakes Justin from his comatose state so he can nap in their bedroom.

"I've got him. Take a long nap and refresh." Their smiles show all the appreciation I need.

Exhaustion is an emotion I can easily read without the obvious external signs. I've been emotionally exhausted, but on the outside, you'd never know.

One hour. Every nerve in my body is frayed but simultaneously on high alert. I have one hour before Shane gets home from work. The pot roast is in the crock pot. His uniform is clean and pressed for tomorrow. There's a new six-pack in the refrigerator. The house is clean, as always. There isn't anything that he could be upset about.

I stare at the black gift bag with the white tissue paper popping out of it, nervous and excited to show him what we've finally been waiting for. It took longer than we expected, and every month, Shane would get angry, telling me I wasn't trying hard enough or I was eating the wrong foods. I needed to gain weight. Lose weight. I shouldn't sit on my ass so much. I work out too hard.

It doesn't matter anymore. I did it. I'm pregnant.

Miles stirs in my arms, and I realize it's been over two hours since everyone separated. I adjust him and find he's awake and looking around. His navy blue eyes find mine, and he coos.

"Thank you for pulling me out of that memory, little boy."

Checking my phone as I make my way to the kitchen, I texted the group chat with Miller and Axel to see how their outing is going.

Axel: <image> She's spoiled rotten.
　　Spencer: I wonder who made her that way?
　　Miller: Must be Lincoln ;)

I examine the picture of Hannah and Katy eating ice cream at my kitchen counter. Katy is still wearing one of the guy's oversize shirts, and I feel guilty that she wasn't our first priority. I came over here to talk with Justin about a plan, and the state of my friends had me changing my focus.

Axel: How's everything over there?
　　Spencer: Mom and Dad are still sleeping, and Miles is about to eat.

I finish preparing the bottle I was making and leave it on the counter to change his diaper.

Miller: When should we bring the rugrat back?
　　Spencer: Give them another hour and then head back this way.
　　Miller: 10-4 Smithy.

With a clean diaper and a full stomach, Miles lays content in my arms when Justin rounds the couch, looking more refreshed and awake than I last saw him.

"I'm sorry I slept for so long. Is everyone okay?" He sits beside me on the couch and runs a finger across Miles' cheek.

"I want to know your secret, Spence. He must hate us."

"Hannah should be back in the next thirty or so minutes. They sugared her up. I'd say I'm surprised, but it would be a lie. Miles is an angel."

"You're a natural, Spencer." I pass him off to Justin before he can gush at me further.

"I have to take Katy back to her mother's. At the very least, she needs clothes."

"I'm coming with you. I won't let you see that evil woman alone, Spencer. She doesn't care about Katy."

"I expected as much."

"You've got something on your mind, Spence. What's going on?" He's right. I do. I realize the gravity of what I'm about to say to him and how much responsibility I'm taking on.

"I was doing research. Did you know that in Chicago, the age of consent to move out is sixteen? Katy is sixteen. If her mother is as terrible as you both say she is…" I watch the myriad of emotions on Justin's face that my pause has caused. He looks around the room, and I see the panic before I finish my thought. "Justin, I'm asking for me, not you." The panic changes to confusion.

"I don't understand exactly what you're saying."

"I'm saying, what if Katy stayed with me? I know you'd bend over backward for her, but you have a brand new baby and a headstrong toddler. I have a spare room and three men who are apparently as enamored by her as you are. They slept over last night."

"Okay. Wait. That was a lot of information to unpack all at once. I'm going to start with the most shocking things that you said. Three men? Who's the third?"

"Axel, Miller, and Lincoln."

"Our old dispatcher Lincoln? Brother to the guy, you had your tongue down his throat, Lincoln? I didn't know you knew him like that."

"I don't. He's Katy's resource officer at her high school, and Axel's friend. Axel called him to help yesterday." I can see the connections he's making in his mind.

"Okay. That makes sense. And Miller? Where does he play into all of this?"

"Axel called him to bring them clothes last night…and they all stayed."

"Spill it, Spencer." I hate having a best friend sometimes. I'm not entirely sure what's going on. It wasn't my decision to let them all stay, but I didn't object, so in a way, that *was* my decision.

"Katy has taken to Lincoln. He seems to be her safety net right now. She didn't want to sleep alone, so I offered her to sleep with me. She invited Lincoln to join us." If his eyes didn't already convey his shock, his wide-open mouth says it all.

"I'm sorry. Who is this woman sitting next to me? This must be a body double. Where are you hiding my grumpy, leave me alone, best friend?"

My phone dings with a motion alert, and I see Miller's truck backing out of the driveway.

"They're on their way with Hannah."

"Don't change the subject. There's more you aren't telling me."

"When I woke up, Katy was gone, and Lincoln was… cuddling me. Did you know that Lincoln and Miller are together?"

"Woman, you need to stop burying the lead. Lincoln and

Miller are *together*? I had no idea Miller swung that way. And cuddling? Did you freak out?"

I didn't freak out, and that's the biggest shock. Touching isn't necessarily a big aversion for me, but I don't like to be surprised. I don't mind a hug that doesn't linger too long. Handshakes are my preference because I like to get a feel for someone's personality by the force of their grip. But I woke up with Lincoln at my side, and then he draped himself across me and...

"He dry-humped my leg in his sleep."

Justin stands and paces, cradling Miles in his arms.

"That's it. My heart can't take anymore, Spencer. Is there anything else shocking that I need to know?" My phone buzzes with another motion notification, but I ignore it. They must have forgotten something at my house.

"I don't think so."

"So then, what's the plan for Katy?"

"My thought is we ask her mother if we can take Katy off her hands. Convince her that she doesn't need the extra mouth to feed. Hopefully, she agrees, and we can pack up her stuff, and Katy can stay with me. The rest we can figure out as we go. I may need to talk to the chief about getting a permanent schedule instead of a rotating one, but one step at a time."

"If Katy's mom doesn't agree?" This is the part I don't like. I don't know much about Katy's mother other than she's a neglectful waste of space when it comes to motherhood.

"Money talks to people like her. Do you think she'll let her go willingly if we throw money at her?"

"I'll help you with however much you need, Spence." That's not what I was asking.

71

"Justin, I wasn't—"

"I know, I'm offering. You know money doesn't mean anything to me, and if I can help get Katy away from that woman, I'll do whatever it takes. Are you sure you want her to stay with you? We have room here."

"And you have your hands full. I can take care of her."

Justin's phone buzzes, notifying him of motion in front of his house. They must be here. A quiet knock sounds on the door when Justin is halfway there. When he opens the door, Hannah is standing very seriously saying random numbers, trying to convince the guys which ones to punch into the keypad at the door.

"Daddy!"

11

Miller

I want kids. Spending these few hours with Hannah has been incredible. She's stubborn and funny and so innocent and inquisitive. Katy was just as amazing with her as I expected. We stopped for ice cream, and the girls laughed and played with the things Hannah brought in her backpack.

Lincoln has texted me several times to check in on Katy. I know he's eager to get off work and check on her for himself.

When Spencer told us Justin and Nicole needed a break, we came running. We are one big happy family, and taking care of each other is what we do best.

"Are you ready to go home, Hannah? Mommy and Daddy miss you." Her bottom lip pokes out in the most adorable pout.

"Brudder noisey."

"I know, sweetie, but he'll get better." I pack up her small toys into her backpack and look around the room to make sure we haven't forgotten anything.

"Did you two want to stay here while I bring her back?"

Axel and Katy look up from their spots on the couch.

"I'd like to go so I can see Justin, if that's okay. And the new baby." Of course she would. I have no idea why I even suggested it.

"Absolutely. Let's head out." Spencer has a complicated alarm and lock system at her house, and we got a Nobel Prize-worthy lesson on how to lock everything properly when coming and going. I have no idea what she's hiding in here that requires such security, but a woman living alone can never be too careful, I guess.

I already know she keeps at least half a dozen guns in various places around her little pool house, which kept me on high alert watching Hannah's every move.

When we get to Justin's house, he has a locking keypad similar to Spencer's. Hannah starts spouting random numbers, giving me a stern face when I ignore her and knock.

"Free, six, twoo, seben. Daddy!" Justin opens the door, holding Miles, and I take the baby so he can scoop up Hannah.

"Hey, baby girl. Did you have fun with your uncles?"

Axel swiftly steals Miles from me with a big grin and pushes his way past us into the house. I let Katy go in before following behind the crowd. Justin gives Katy a side hug, and I can see the concern on his face as she walks farther into the house. He puts Hannah down, and she runs to look for Nicole.

"How is she?" I know the "she" he's referring to is Katy.

My shoulders heave with my sigh as I reflect on the last hours we've spent together. "She's avoiding, deflecting. Acting like nothing is wrong." I haven't had many interactions with Katy over the two years she's been back in Justin's life, but we've all had enough to know her personality. She's usually a happy kid despite her home life. She puts on a brave face, but I can tell underneath she's scared.

"Has Spencer told you her plan?" Justin keeps his voice low as we step into the kitchen. His living room and kitchen have an open floor plan, but the rooms are large enough to have a quiet conversation without being overheard.

"She has a plan?" While that doesn't surprise me, the look on Justin's face makes me pause. It must be something big for him to look concerned over Spencer's decision. She's always calculated and confident when she decides something.

"She wants to take in Katy."

Okay, now I understand his concern. I look to the couch where Axel cradles Miles, and Katy and Nicole play on the floor with Hannah. Nicole looks much more refreshed than when I saw her earlier.

"As in, have Katy live with her? What about her mother?"

"Yeah. She said you, Axel, and Lincoln would probably help out, but—"

"Without a doubt. I'm here to help with Katy in any way I can, and I know Axel and Lincoln will feel the same. What do we need to do?"

"I guess we make a plan."

"Are we sure this is the best plan?" I look up at the dilapidated apartment building. It's hard to believe Justin used to live here. Although that was close to a decade ago.

"It's the only plan we have." Justin doesn't look comfortable being here. I know this is where his life both ended and began when he tried to take his own life, and Katy saved him.

Spencer, Justin, and I all exit my truck. We decided to leave Nicole and Axel with the kids at Justin's house. Katy has been through enough in the last twenty-four hours, and if her mother is anything like Justin has described, she doesn't need to be subjected to any more negativity.

If I had my way, we would have left Spencer as well, but it was hard to argue with her valid point. Even a crappy mother would, or should, hesitate if two full-grown men show up at your door saying they want to take your daughter. At least with Spencer here, it lessens the blow that she wants to live with another female. We can just be the muscle to move Katy's belongings.

"You've thought of everything, haven't you?" Spencer did her research. She's carrying with her a folder containing a document for Katy's mother to sign stating that she's giving parental consent for Katy to move out and live with her. I also overheard a hushed conversation that they are willing to throw money at her mother if that's what it takes to get her to agree. We all know that Katy is better off with any of us than being here with her absentee mother.

"Katy deserves better, and if this is what it takes to make it legal, then I'm crossing all of my T's and dotting all of my I's."

"It's that one up there. 3F." The three flights of stairs we ascend are dirty and unkempt. Paint chips from the brick and cobwebs decorate every corner.

Spencer knocks on the door when we finally reach it. There are loud noises from a TV coming through the thin door. We agreed to let Spencer take the lead, with Justin backing her up since Katy's mother would probably remember him.

The door opens, and a woman with bottle-blonde hair who looks far older than her years looks back at us.

"Who are you? I ain't got no money for whatever you're selling."

"Ms. North? Barbara North?" The woman's eyes sweep over the three of us, trying to figure out who we are and why we know her name. She stops and pauses on Justin.

"It's Babs. Why do I know you?" Her eyes scrutinize Justin.

"I used to be your neighbor when Katy was little."

"Katy? You know my useless daughter?"

My hands involuntarily bawl into fists. How could she say that about that sweet girl?

"We all know your daughter, Ms. Nor-Babs." She glares at Spencer.

"Oh yeah? Well, she isn't here, and I have no idea why you three are. What do you want?"

"Katy," Spencer says flatly. Her mask is on. It's the first time I've seen it in the last two days, and I don't miss it.

"Listen, lady I already told you she wasn't here." Babs' voice rises with agitation.

"I'm aware she isn't here. She's at my house, and I'd like your approval to keep her there." Babs steps back as if she's been slapped.

"You what?"

"I'd like to house your daughter at my residence for the foreseeable future. The age of consent to move out is sixteen, which Katy is. I have a document right here for you to sign, giving her permission to move out. I'll just need…" Spencer continues to talk, but I can see in Babs' eyes she's tuning her out.

"Babs." I know I agreed to be quiet, but this isn't getting

us anywhere. "We want…Spencer here wants Katy to live with her. She will take care of all of her finances. You don't have to do anything but sign the paper saying it's okay." I can see the shimmer in her eyes at the loss of responsibility, but something quickly changes.

"What do I get out of it? I have chores that need to be done. You can't just expect me to hand you my daughter."

"We just want what's best for Katy—"

"Two grand." I gape at Justin. They talked about money being a last resort. I was hoping she would do the right thing for her daughter.

The corner of her lip tilts up, and she stares Justin down. "Ten."

Did she just counteroffer him? She's really putting a price on her daughter? This is disgusting.

"Three. We just want to get Katy's things, and you won't have to worry about anything else regarding her."

"If you want her and her things, I want five grand." My heart is breaking hearing this piece of shit woman barter her daughter for money.

"Four thousand. You sign the papers, keep all Katy's stuff, and we walk away."

I can feel the rage coursing through me as this piece of shit woman auctions off her daughter, and I want to punch something. I don't think I've ever been so repulsed by another human in my life. We are doing more for Katy than I could have even imagined.

"Forty-five hundred."

This bitch. I have no idea how Justin is keeping his cool, but I'm done.

"We'll give you six grand if you add onto the paperwork

that Spencer has full guardianship of Katy, and when we come back with real paperwork, you sign it, no questions asked." Justin and Spencer look at me due to my outburst, but I don't care. I need to get Katy as far away from this evil woman as possible. If *I* have to request guardianship for her because Spencer can't or won't do it, I won't bat an eye.

Babs concentrates on my offer for far longer than is necessary before smiling an evil smile.

"Where do I sign?" I take the paperwork from Spencer and add my addendum. Spencer initials what I've written and hands it to the worthless woman to sign and initial. We tell her we'll be right back with the money, and she smiles like she's won the lottery. I'm sure in her mind she has, but in reality, it's Katy and it's us. Katy is getting out from underfoot of a woman who never treated her like a daughter and we are gaining a wonderful woman whose life is about to change for the better.

There's silence between us until we get back into my truck.

"Fuck!" I take my aggression out on the steering wheel with a few quick jabs until Spencer puts her hand on my forearm, stopping my next punch.

"We got our girl." I take her hand and rest my forehead on the steering wheel.

"Justin, I'm sorry. I'll give you the difference. I just couldn't listen to her for another second, treating Katy like she was property to be sold."

"Miller, money means nothing to me. You got more than we came here to get. I don't want anything from you." Justin clamps a hand on my shoulder and squeezes.

"Do you realize what you just did?" Spencer's question catches me off guard. She takes her hand away and turns

79

in her seat to face me. "You got her mother to essentially sign her rights away. That means we can help Katy get emancipated and truly leave her mother."

"Really?" I had no idea. I just reacted.

"I'll contact my lawyer in the morning and see what needs to be done." Justin squeezes my shoulder again and sits back in his seat. "Let's get to the bank and finish this. Katy needs a new wardrobe and Nicole would love an excuse for a shopping spree."

12

Lincoln

Today has been the longest day. Despite all the updates about Katy, I need to get eyes on her. My protector instinct took over the moment I saw her in that alley.

Miller told me they were on their way back from Justin's house after Nicole, Spencer, and Katy had a small shopping trip for essentials for Katy.

I arrive at Spencer's first, and since it's a nice afternoon, I get out and wander around the pool between the houses. When I'm lapping back to the front of the house, I see a large envelope with her name handwritten on the front, leaning against her door. As I bend down to pick it up, I hear the crunch of gravel behind me and the distinct feeling of a gun barrel in my lower back.

"Stand up, slowly." I make no sudden movements and slowly rise with the envelope in my hand. I already locked up my duty gun in my glove compartment, but I have my personal piece on my ankle if I need it. "What's in the envelope?"

"I have no idea. I was picking it up to look."

"Who are you, and what are you doing here?" The gun digs a little farther into my back, and I do my best to keep my balance while my hands raise in surrender.

"My name is Lincoln Reed. I'm a friend of Spencer's. I'm waiting for her to come home." I'm wearing my navy tactical pants and department polo, but whoever this is can't see my shirt. I have the upper hand at the moment since he doesn't know who I am or the training I have.

"My daughter doesn't have any male friends other than that kid with glasses, and you aren't him." Daughter? Is this Spencer's father?

"Sir, my name is Officer Lincoln Reed. I'm with the Chicago Police Department. I'm a friend of Justin's as well." I feel the pressure of the gun relax for a moment before it's back.

"The envelope. Hand it over." I carefully shift my arm back, and he takes it from me. I hear a phone ring from behind me, and Spencer's dad adjusts to answer it.

"Spencer, do you know an Officer Reed?"

"Dad, get that gun out of Lincoln's back. He's a friendly, Detective." Detective? Was her father on the force?

I hear gravel from tires coming up the driveway, and the gun moves from my back. When I turn, Miller's truck is parking, and Spencer is jumping out before it comes to a full stop.

"What are you doing, Dad? Put the gun away. That's not necessary. You'll scare Katy." Her dad's gaze turns to the teenager climbing out of Miller's truck wearing real clothes. I'm glad to see she's no longer wearing a combination of everyone else's.

"Spencer, who are all of these people? He was standing here with this envelope. Do you trust him?" Spencer sighs and pushes past us to unlock the door. Miller and Axel, who had been hanging by the truck waiting, come over with several shopping bags in hand.

Miller approaches and extends his hand to Spencer's father. "Miller, sir. I work with Spencer at the fire department." They shake, and it's Axel's turn.

"I'm Axel. I know your daughter from the Emergency Department. I'm a nurse there." As Axel walks into the house, I turn and extend my hand.

"Officer Lincoln Reed, I work as a school resource officer at Katy's school." I motioned to Katy, who hung back outside.

"And who are you, child?" Katy's eyes shift to me, and I nod, giving her an encouraging smile.

"I'm Katy." She offers her hand, and his face softens. He clasps both his hands over hers and smiles.

"Nice to meet you, Katy. My name is Eddie. Eddie Hall."

"Detective Edward Hall? I thought Spencer's last name was Coble?" He smiles at Katy and directs her to go inside. When the door closes, he turns back to me.

"You know my name, I see. Spencer's mamma kept her last name, and so did our daughter. You know how dangerous this job can be. We thought it would be safer." I understand his reasoning. Eddie Hall is a decorated detective who retired with honors. I had no idea Spencer's father was one of my idols.

"It's a pleasure to meet you, Detective."

"I don't want any of that bull shit. Just call me Eddie. But Lincoln, was it?" I nod. "Do you plan on sticking around here?"

"For as long as your daughter will allow me."

"You and I need to talk. There are some things I need to tell you in confidence. She'll be madder than hell if she finds out, but I won't be around forever." Now, my curiosity is piqued.

"Understood. Should I bring this to her?" I motion to the envelope he's still holding.

"Shit." Realization dawns on him that he's still holding it under his arm. "You didn't bring this here?" I shake my head, not understanding his concern. "No one drove up the driveway after I saw your friend's truck pull out. Someone walked this here."

"Any idea who?"

He assesses me. Trying to figure me out.

"Who are you to my daughter?"

"I'm just a friend, sir."

"You know she's a special woman, right? Her life hasn't been easy. I...I blame myself for a lot of it." A cloud of guilt washes over his face. Spencer is a strong, independent woman. I can't imagine her being anything other than who she is.

"I'm sure you did the best that you could."

The look he gives me is haunted. There's a story behind it that he wants to tell me.

"Take my number, son. We need to talk." He looks at the front door and then back at me. "Soon." He hands me the envelope and I give him my phone. "I'm passing this torch to you. I have a feeling I know what's in here. Look at them with her alone, and I hope she'll tell you her story so I don't have to." His words are cryptic, and coming from a fellow officer that puts me on high alert.

84

"Eddie, is Spencer in danger? Katy will be staying here for the foreseeable future, and I can almost guarantee that one or more of us will be here with them. Is there anything we should be worried about?" His eyes quickly flash to the envelope.

"Just be vigilant and take care of those girls. We'll talk." With those last words, he slaps me on the back and walks toward his house.

Shifting the envelope in my hand, I bounce it up and down, feeling the weight. The shape makes me think there are pictures inside. Should I open it before I show Spencer? The cop inside of me wants to, but the person wants to respect her privacy. She didn't seem concerned when her father showed it to her, so maybe I shouldn't be either.

As I walk into the house, Katy is showing off some of her outfits to the guys. Spencer sits at the kitchen counter on her laptop, and when I approach, I see she's looking at furniture.

"Doing some shopping of your own?"

"Katy needs a proper bedroom. There's enough space in my room to move my desk there. She needs a place for her clothes. Maybe a vanity. Does she need a shoe rack?" Spencer seems a little on edge, which is uncharacteristic for her. Placing a gentle hand on her arm, she looks at me with furrowed brows.

"Why don't you ask her?" Her face lights up as if she hadn't thought of that.

"Lincoln, did I make a colossal mistake? I don't know the first thing about raising a teenager." She's worried. I can't help but smirk, seeing her frazzled.

"Spencer, you aren't alone. You've made an incredible decision to help Katy. It may be sudden, but I think I know you well enough to know you don't make any decisions lightly. We are here to help. Use us." Hmm. Why did her cheeks flush?

I place the envelope on the table next to her and she assesses it. Turning her attention back to her laptop, she sighs.

"What did my father tell you?" She looks over her shoulder at the fashion show and then back to me with curious blue eyes.

"Only that I should show you these alone, and he hoped you would tell me your story."

She nods and stares off. "Not now, okay?"

"Whatever you need, Dream Girl." I walk away before yet another nickname slip-up can be questioned. Although I may have only officially met Spencer a month ago, this woman's voice on the other end of the radio has haunted my dreams for far longer.

My hand caresses her body from her hip to the side of her breasts. She's so soft and awakens nerves in my body that haven't been roused in ages. I lean over and take one of her rosy nipples into my mouth, sucking and licking until it becomes hard. Her sounds turn me on.

My hand trails down her body, reaching the heat I long to bury my face into until she comes on my tongue. Her breathing increases under my hands, and I feel her panting breath on my face as I continue to alternate between her luscious breasts. Her back arches under my caress as my fingers brush over her clit.

Her moans spur me on, and I increase the speed and

pressure of my fingers. I want to feel her pulse around my fingers as she comes.

Fingers tug at my hair. The bite of pain makes me want to pull her pleasure from her even quicker.

"Lincoln." Her breathy moan of my name sounds fucking incredible, spilling from her lips. "Lincoln."

"Mmm. Tug harder, Dream Girl."

"Lincoln. Wake up. Fuuuuck."

"Mmm, you like that?"

"Oh god. Oh fuck. I'm…I'm…" She sounds even more beautiful than I imagined when she comes. What does her face look like? I have to open my eyes and see.

Open my eyes.

Open.

"Oh fuck!" I scramble up from my position, practically laying on top of her. That was…I thought. "I was dreaming. Spencer, I'm so fucking sorry." She lays panting below me, and I hear clapping.

"That was spectacular to watch."

"Fuck Miller, get out." I just violated Spencer in her sleep. I thought I was having a fucking wet dream with my Dream Girl. It wouldn't be the first time Spencer was the star of a late-night fantasy for me.

"Nuh-uh." He steps further into the room and closes the door behind him. "I heard Spencer moan and had to see what was going on. What *is* going on in here?"

Tentatively, I look over to Spencer.

"I'm so fucking sor—" Spencer grabs my shoulders and pulls me into her, crashing our mouths together. Her lips move and coax mine to open in my momentary state of shock.

She's kissing me.

Spencer is kissing me.

I feel the bed dip, and a hand smooths up my back. "Kiss her back, Babe. Live out your fantasy."

The feeling of being pressed between the two of them encourages me. I slide a hand into Spencer's hair and revel in the feel of her soft locks. Miller's lips caress my neck as Spencer's tongue caresses mine.

I must still be dreaming because there's no way my boyfriend is kissing my neck while I'm half lying on top of my dream girl with my tongue down her throat.

My cock is rock hard and pinned against Spencer's leg. I lift my hand and slide it along her bare stomach, and feel the goosebumps pebble under my fingers. Miller's mouth alternates between nips and licks along my bare shoulder as my hand reaches Spencer's breast.

Knock Knock. "Breakfast."

Spencer quickly pulls away at the shock of hearing Axel's voice through the door. The lust fog in the room quickly dissipates. She touches her lips, and her eyes bounce around the room.

"Where's Katy?" Spencer looks at Miller as if she's looking through him before he responds.

"She fell asleep on the couch while the two of you were in here talking last night. We took her to her room. Axel and I slept on the floor. That rug is comfortable."

"Okay." Spencer nods her head, remembering the details. "We all have work today, right?"

"Axel is tonight, but yeah." I'm glad Miller can think straight to answer questions because right now, my mind is mush.

"Good. Okay. Let's get ready." She stands and disappears into her bathroom, leaving Miller and I both sitting in her bed with raging hard-ons.

"What the fuck was that all about, Linc?" I can't form words. I stare at the bathroom door, my hands flexing at the memory of her velvety skin.

Miller grabs my wrist and sniffs my fingers. "Fuck she smells good on you. Her orgasm was...fuck." He shifts next to me and adjusts himself.

Grabbing Miller's hand, I shove it down the front of my joggers and rub it over my aching cock.

"I need you to take care of this. Can we slip past them to the other bathroom?" I feel the groan in his chest as he wraps his fingers around me, giving my cock a quick stroke.

"I'll make it happen. Let's go."

13

Miller

I hear moaning coming from behind Spencer's door, and my curiosity is piqued. I motion to Axel, who's in the kitchen making waffles with Katy, that I'm going into the room, and he nods and goes back to his task.

When I open the door, my jaw hits the ground. Spencer's face is twisted in pleasure as Lincoln's fingers bring her to orgasm over her tight pants. They're both clothed, and I'm not entirely sure either of them are fully awake.

Lincoln sits up quickly, his face racked with guilt, but I can't stop myself from clapping. He got the girl first—the one that the three of us have been tripping over each other just to get an ounce of her attention.

Last night, he asked to speak to her in private and brought the envelope that we had been eyeing all night. I know it had something to do with Spencer's dad, but when I asked Lincoln about it, he told me, "Not now."

Spencer grabs Lincoln, pulling him into a kiss and me out of my musings. He's frozen in shock, but I'm not allowing a second of this opportunity to be missed. Kneeling on the bed behind Lincoln, I whisper in his ear.

"Kiss her back, Babe. Live out your fantasy." That's all the encouragement he needed. I'm not sure if his hesitation was shock, guilt for what he had done to her in his sleep, or maybe even me. We've been exclusive for a while, but he's the only man I've ever been with. We never took adding a woman to our relationship off the table, but we also never put it there.

I feel their connection. Their bodies vibrate with the adrenaline of the situation. Lincoln's hands begin to wander as I taste and lick his bare shoulder.

Knock Knock. "Breakfast."

Dammit Axel! I shift uncomfortably, adjusting the growing erection in my basketball shorts. They're doing nothing to hide my bulge, and neither are Lincoln's joggers.

Spencer makes conversation as if the last few minutes hadn't just happened and then leaves us both hard and wanting, to get ready for the day.

"What the fuck was that all about, Linc?" He doesn't answer me. I can't blame him. I'm a little lost as to what just went down. I see his fingers twitch, and I grab his wrist. He brought her to orgasm, rubbing her with these fingers. I bet she soaked her pants. I bring his hand to my face and inhale. "Fuck she smells good on you. Her orgasm was...fuck."

He grabs my hand and shoves it down his pants, rubbing it along his cock. I take the hint and give Lincoln a long stroke.

"I need you to take care of this. Can we slip past them to the other bathroom?" I can't stop the groan that rises in my chest. *Fuck yes we can.*

"I'll make it happen. Let's go." I reluctantly take out my hand and grab his. I silently open the door and gesture a hand in the air to catch Axel's attention. He's back in the kitchen with Katy at the island. He sees me and smiles, but before he can speak, I put a finger to my lips, stopping him.

I can do this. I'm a pro at charades. I motion between Lincoln and me and then down the hall to the bathroom. Then I point a finger at Axel and two fingers at my eyes and rotate them toward Katy. I feel Lincoln moving at my back and turn to see he's using his fist to pump at his cheek as his tongue bobs in and out the other side, mimicking a blow job. I shrug and smile because that's exactly the plan.

Axel smiles and engages Katy in conversation as we quietly pass through the living room into the bathroom.

As soon as the door closes, Lincoln has me against the wall with a firm hand in the middle of my chest. He looks at his watch and smirks.

"We have twenty minutes to both shower and get off. Think we can do it?" His already deep voice is thick with lust, and I shiver at the intensity.

"Will you tell me about it? I want to know what she feels and tastes like." Lincoln steps away from me and turns on the shower. We strip the little clothes we have on, and as soon as he's naked, my hands are on him.

I thread my fingers through his cinnamon-colored hair while the other goes straight to his cock. He twitches at my touch, and I smile as I take his mouth.

"Tell me. I'm dying to know." I'm not giving him much time to answer. My hand has set a steady rhythm stroking and pulling his cock.

"Get in the shower and get on your knees." I don't need to be told twice. I get in and wait for him to follow. The floor is cold and hard on my knees, but the anticipation of making

Linc fall apart from my mouth is a high that outweighs the discomfort.

The moment the shower door closes, I grab his ass and pull him into my mouth. I feel the vibration of his low moan through my body. He grabs my hair and sets the pace.

"I thought I was dreaming. I've dreamt about her before. What it would be like to do to her exactly what my body was doing in its sleep. I'm still not entirely sure what was real and what I made up, but I know her orgasm was real." I moan around his cock at the memory of his fingers rubbing between her legs.

"She smelled fresh and clean. Like a spring day. Her hair... fuck, to run my fingers through her wild, silky hair was a dream come true."

Spencer lives in her double braids. Until yesterday, I had never seen her hair any other way. Lincoln's hands flex in my hair as he remembers. I suck harder, drawing him further into my mouth. The taste of his pre-cum drips on my tongue, and I have to adjust my legs, widening my stance.

"Your poor knees. Up." He tugs at my roots, and I reluctantly pull my mouth away and stand. "We need to hurry." Lincoln attacks my neck with his mouth and grabs my cock. I hiss at the pressure he uses. Between the show I watched of Linc and Spencer, our little make-out sandwich, and having his cock in my mouth, I'm ready for release.

I mirror his movement and hastily stroke him. We both need this.

"Tell me more," I breathe into his neck between kisses.

"Her skin is velvety soft, her lips are plump, but her tongue demanded my submission. Gentle yet controlling."

I'm so fucking close.

"Show me." I crush my lips to his and let him take over. Lincoln kisses me like he described, and I moan as I imagine her kissing him like this.

I reach down with my free hand and cup his balls. If he's as needy as I am, we both need this release. Now.

"Fireball." There's eagerness behind his whine as he throws his head back. I bite down on Lincoln's shoulder, giving him what he needs to come. It causes him to squeeze me harder, and we both succumb to our orgasms.

Hot warmth coats our hands and stomachs, and the air around us heats from our panting. I press my forehead to his and look down at the mess we've made of ourselves.

"This will be an easy cleanup." I swirl my finger around the mess on Lincoln's abs as the shower water washes our come away.

"Fuck." He kisses my forehead and turns toward the water. "We need to finish up and get to work."

Axel thought ahead, and when we get out of the shower, wondering what to do now, I find our bags right outside the bathroom door, waiting for us.

"We should buy him dinner." Lincoln pulls out a clean, navy Chicago PD uniform from his bag as I take my similar navy Chicago FD uniform out.

"Just give him the details of what happened in Spencer's bedroom, and he'll be more than happy."

Lincoln sucks in a breath as he pulls on his pants, and a look of guilt flashes across his face.

"Fireball. Are you upset with me? We haven't talked about doing anything like that, and it just kind of happened."

Is he serious? I grab his hips and pull him close.

"The only reason I'll be upset is if that doesn't happen again.

Spencer is...Spencer. I don't know how to describe it, but I know that we both feel the same way about her." I sigh heavily, my chest heaving between us. "We do need to talk to Spencer today, though. I'll feel her out and see if she's okay with everything. Although, based on that kiss, I think she's more than okay." A light blush crosses Lincoln's cheeks, and I kiss his nose before pulling back. "We have to go, or we'll all be late.

When we exit the bathroom, Axel is wearing a shit-eating grin. Spencer sits at the counter dressed for work, braids firmly twisted on her head.

Katy sees Axel's face and spins around, smiling at Lincoln and me. "You two are the absolute cutest. And please don't hide yourselves around me. I'm sixteen, not six. I see the way you look at each other." She pauses and swirls her head to glance at the four of us. "I see the way you *all* look at each other. Please live your lives, and don't let me stop you. Except...maybe not in the living room. Bathrooms and bedrooms are fair game, though."

Shock. That's the look on the faces of all four grown adults in this house right now. You could hear a pin drop with the silence after her declaration.

"Katy, there isn't—"

"Sixteen, not six. And I'm not blind, Spencer. You're like the juicy steak being salivated over by a Golden Retriever, a Labrador, and a Bloodhound." Axel chokes on the cup of coffee he's sipping. Katy leans down to pet Gage behind the ear, who's sitting between her and Spencer. "Sorry, boy. You don't compare to them. You have better training and are fully housebroken."

"That's insulting," Axel says, recovering from his coughing

95

fit. "But I have to know who's who. Miller's the Lab, right? Oh no. Would that make me the Golden Retriever? I'm not sure I like that. Linc is definitely the Bloodhound."

Katy gives an innocent shrug, and I can see Spencer trying to hide her smile behind her coffee mug.

"A Golden Retriever. Why can't I be a Pitbull or a Rottweiler? I'm more than a happy boy who wags his tail and follows his owner around all day." As Axel rants, he cleans the counter and adds breakfast dishes to the sink. He refills Spencer's coffee without her asking, and the room erupts into laughter. Axel looks at all of us like we're crazy until he realizes what he's done. He huffs, making us laugh harder. "Okay, fine. I'll be the Golden Retriever."

Katy stands and rounds the corner to Axel. She dramatically pats him on the shoulder.

"Good boy." It's my turn for my jaw to drop. "Lincoln, I'll be in your truck." She saunters to the front door, grabs her backpack, and leaves.

"I like her. She can stay. Let's go, Miller, or we'll be late." Spencer stands and places her empty cup in the sink. "You *are* a good boy, Axel." I can see his brain turn to mush as she leaves the words hanging in the air.

Taking Lincoln's hand, I pull him into me. "I guess a little PDA is acceptable." I give him a chaste kiss and grab my bag to leave.

"What are you up to today besides a nap before work, Axel?"

"Apparently, this good boy is on delivery duty. Katy's new furniture is arriving today, and Spencer asked if I could accept it."

Lincoln fakes a cough while saying, "Golden Retriever,"

and I laugh my way out the door.

14

Spencer

Chaos. My life has become chaos, and not the organized type. Absolute insanity. I'm not used to sharing my life, house, and especially not my bed with anyone else but Gage. At times in their lives, Justin and Nicole have stayed at my house for temporary placement, but I just agreed to keep Katy. And apparently, along with Katy comes three sexy men who…all want me?

How did this happen?

As much as this morning was a complete shock to wake up to, I let it happen. I let it happen because it never does. Lincoln's hands and mouth on me felt, well, if I'm being honest with myself, it felt right.

"Should we talk about it?" There's an edge of nervousness to Miller's question.

"What 'it' are you referring to?" He knows full well I know what he's asking about.

"Okay, Smithy. Let's be coy. We can talk about the kiss between you and my boyfriend. The fondling between the three of us. Oh! Or how about the orgasm that my boyfriend gave you? Where would you like to start?"

I'm surprised he waited until two hours into our shift before he started interrogating me. Can I confess things to him? Of the three guys, Miller and I have the strongest relationship. He fills in for Justin as my partner when my best friend does things like spend months in rehab or has not one but two babies and takes twelve weeks off each time. I rarely wear my mask around him anymore, and I consider him a good friend.

"I don't sleep much."

"Okay? That's not where I thought this conversation would go. Do you want to talk about *that*?" I stare out the front window of the ambulance as we drive aimlessly.

"The past two nights, I've slept. I haven't had any nightmares. When Lincoln and I went into my bedroom last night, he wanted to show me what was in the envelope left at my door."

"What was in it?"

"I don't know. I guess we fell asleep. We talked for a while about Katy, and then I woke up to…well, you saw." I'm not embarrassed by what happened. I'm not even sure I can say I'm surprised. Katy wasn't wrong when she pointed out the obvious tension between us. While being physically around Lincoln is new, I've been attracted to his voice for years.

"I'm not sure I understand why you're telling me this, Smithy."

Besides Justin, no one knows much about my past, and I like it that way. I have rough obstacles to hurdle in my everyday life. Being seen as a victim is not something I want to deal with.

I may not know exactly what's in that envelope, but I know

the handwriting that my name is written in.

Shane.

I've felt his presence a few times. I wasn't all too surprised when my father saw him sitting down the street. Shane doesn't scare me anymore. I've built my life around making sure I never had a reason to fear him. He's the reason for the locks and security system—why I have so many guns hidden around the house. Gage.

"I think Lincoln has helped me sleep. Although, he seems to be a heavy sleeper with wandering hands, so I'm not quite sure why."

"I happen to like his wandering hands." I glance at Miller, and he winks at me.

"What should we get for lunch?"

"Spencer, it's barely ten in the morning. I'm not thinking about lunch yet. What are you avoiding?"

I'm avoiding a lot, but it's not just me.

"What are *you* avoiding, Miller?" I hear his chuckle

"I'm jealous. I've been pining after you for years, and within days, my boyfriend gets to have you before me. I'm wounded, Spencer."

"Why?"

"Why am I wounded?"

"No. Why me? I've seen you with other women over the years. Why have you been pining over me for so long when you could have your pick? I have the same question for Axel. He *does* have whatever woman he wants."

I'll admit at first, I was oblivious to Miller and Axel's flirting. They're both ladies men, and I took their flirting as over-friendliness. I've seen how they treat other women and that's not how they treated me. I've never felt like I was a woman for them to conquer.

"Are we really doing this right now? Could you at least pull over so I can look at you and not your profile." I dip my head and switch lanes. It's a reasonable request that I can grant.

I pull into a shopping center and back the ambulance into a spot at the rear of the parking lot.

Turning off the rig, I shift in my seat to face Miller. He's massaging his forehead with his hand, deep in thought.

"I'm sorry. I didn't realize that would be a stressful question."

"That right there, Smithy. That's part of it." He peers at me with a look of awe in his eye.

"I don't understand."

"Exactly."

I feel lost in a conversation that's barely started. My apology is a reason he feels emotions for me?

"Can I hold your hand while I tell you all this?" He extends his arm, palm up, allowing me to accept or reject it. I see no harm and slide my hand into his.

His panty-melting smile appears, and I wonder if it was a mistake to touch him until his thumb brushes over the top of my hand, and my body lights up under his touch.

"Smithy, Spencer. There are few genuine surprises in life. Every day we clock in, and as different as each shift can be, it's a job that I do. Sure, there are surprises from each call, but that's my duty. *You*? You constantly surprise me. Your neurodivergence has never been an issue for me. It intrigues me in ways that make me want to know you better.

"When Justin announced Nicole was pregnant again, I was counting down the weeks until I would get to ride with you. Working with you is a competition for my brain. WWSD.

What would Spencer do? You make me a better person."

"I didn't know you thought of me like that. You flirt with everyone."

A guilty look flashes over his face. His thumb continues to caress the top of my hand and my nerves ache to feel his touch in other places.

"I'm not as comfortable with my sexuality as Linc is. Hell, I've never been with a man other than him."

"Are you gay? Bisexual? Experimenting?"

He chuckles and squeezes my hand. "God, this is why. You are exactly who you are, Smithy. There's no ulterior motive. There is never any hidden meaning behind your words. What am I? I have no idea. I'm Lincoln's boyfriend. I have been for over six months. I'm not experimenting." Miller's eyes take a slow perusal over my body, and I feel the heat of them on my skin as if I were naked. "I'm definitely not gay. I'm Lincoln's, and he's mine."

"And this morning. Were boundaries crossed?" Miller's boyfriend participated in sexual acts with me. I can't imagine they've ever spoken about it before since it happened while Lincoln was asleep.

Realization dawns on me and I worry if I unconsciously crossed a boundary. "Oh no. Is Lincoln okay? I'm not a man."

"Thank fuck for that." He lifts my hand and kisses my knuckles. This is wildly inappropriate behavior for co-workers, and we are on duty in our workplace.

"Lincoln and I were both very okay with what happened. You've been the subject of many of his fantasies that he got to play out in his sleep this morning."

I have no idea where things are going with any of these men, but it's quickly becoming evident that they aren't going anywhere. If they will be around, I owe them a version of my truth, even if it's just for Katy. Since Katy isn't going anywhere, I don't think they are either.

"I need to send a text." I remove my hand from his and feel the loss of his warmth.

Spencer: I need to talk with my three admirers. It's time. Can I bring Katy to you for a few hours after work?

Justin: Of course. She's always welcome. When did they become YOUR anything, Spence?

Spencer: They may not even be my friends after they hear about my past. I'll drop her off around six. Thank you.

Justin: You have nothing to be ashamed of, and those three aren't going anywhere. Good luck. I'm here if you need me, and I come with free baby puke.

Spencer: Thank you but I think I'll pass on the baby puke.

Justin: Your loss. See you when you get here.

Spencer: Hello, Annie. Is there any chance you have time for coffee today? I'm on duty but could meet you somewhere close to your building.

Annie: Of course. I have a light day. I can meet you somewhere. Blake is here as well. Is this a business or social meeting?

Spencer: Social. Bring Blake.

"I need to call a house meeting tonight before Axel goes to work. But first, I have to have a quick lunch date."

Miller looks confused but agrees.

15

Spencer

I text Annie to meet at a sandwich shop down the street from her building. Miller and I got there before her and ordered our food. I asked him to sit on the other side of the shop so I could have my meeting with Annie and Blake, and he agreed without hesitation.

The front door opens, and all attention turns to the gorgeous blonde in a black pantsuit who commands attention in every room she enters and her equally beautiful brunette companion wearing a flowy burgundy dress accentuating her baby bump.

Blake bounces to me with a huge smile and hugs me around her belly. Annie follows with a more proper greeting, a handshake. She has more of a social persona to uphold than Blake, and I can understand her formality.

"Sit with Spencer, Baby. I'll grab our food. We called ahead so it would be ready." Blake turns toward the counter, and Annie takes her elbow before she walks away.

"Darling, you sit. You've been on your feet all morning. I don't know how you're six months pregnant and still walking in those heels."

"How about you both sit, and I let my Labrador get the food."

Blake giggles, "Your what?" She turns to see me flagging down Miller. "Oooh. Yummy."

"Miller, can you listen for their food and bring it to us when it's ready?" He nods in agreement, and we settle into the booth.

"Please tell me that hunk of a man belongs to you." Blake gasps and her hands fly to cover her mouth. "Spencer, are you blushing?"

I groan and wonder if I've made a mistake asking to speak with them. Blake is the perfect amount of bubbly insanity to balance Annie's seriousness. Once Annie's submissive, their relationship shifted when they added Cole, Nicole's brother, into it.

Annie was a patient of ours after she was involved in a major motor vehicle accident that involved two fatalities. Justin developed a friendly relationship with them, meeting Cole's sister. Nicole was the best thing to ever happen to Justin.

My relationship with Annie, Blake, and Cole is nowhere near as personal as Justin's, but the type of relationship they have is as close as I can get to what is currently happening in my life, and I need some advice.

Ignoring her blushing question I answer her other inquiry. "Yes. He's one of the reasons I asked to meet you both."

"*One...of*. Is there more than one *he* that we need to talk about?" Blake is entirely too excited for this conversation.

"Three."

"*Three?!*" Blake whisper-shouts and looks over her shoulder at Miller. "Tell me they all look like that?" She does a double take and stares at Miller a moment longer. The barista calls Annie's name from the counter, and Miller stands to retrieve their food.

When he brings it to the table, Blake has stars in her eyes. Annie has been suspiciously quiet throughout the entire interaction.

"Ladies." Blake swoons as Miller walks back to his table, but not before giving me his panty-melting smile. By the time Blake manages to form words and say thank you, Miller is seated again.

"Do I know him? Baby, do we know him? He looks so familiar. Is he one of Justin's friends?" Blake rubs her protruding belly. "I swear this little one is sucking every last brain cell from me. My memory is terrible lately."

"We do. And yes he is a friend of Justin's. A co-worker. We met him at the dinner that Justin and Nicole hosted where she… Well, that was the past. Spencer, the other two men in question, are they also co-workers?"

"You're very perceptive, Annie. Miller is a firefighter, Axel works at the ED as a nurse, and Lincoln is a police officer with the Chicago PD." It doesn't surprise me that Annie has already picked up on my reasoning for asking them to lunch. While Annie, Blake, and Cole had their struggles in the beginning, they have a very successful polyamorous relationship with twins already and another baby on the way.

"How long has it been going on?" Annie is a business-woman who deals in facts. I hear mine and Miller's name called from the counter, and he nods at me, letting me know he'll get my food as well.

"It's not quite going on as of yet, but I feel the signs are there for a potential relationship."

"With all three?" Blake whispers as Miller approaches the table and gives me my food.

"Do you need anything else, ladies?"

"No, thank you. I appreciate your help, Miller."

"Anything for you, Smithy."

Blake squeaks at his nickname for me. "I need all the juicy details."

I spend the next twenty minutes giving them any relevant details, including my situation with Katy and her blatant acceptance of whatever is going on in my house.

Annie listens with a stoic expression while Blake oohs and ahhhs. I don't know anyone else in an unconventional relationship, and while our situations aren't exactly the same, I'm confident that they have a unique view to share with me. I have three men vying for my attention. Annie and Blake were an established couple who added Cole to their relationship.

I've only had one experience with a relationship in my life, and it's not something I ever want to repeat.

"So let me make sure I'm up to speed." Blake takes a long sip of her strawberry lemonade, then sits back, getting comfortable with her hands on her baby belly, to review our conversation. "Hottie back there has a boyfriend who gave you a happy ending in your sleep. You kissed him in some Oreo cookie make-out session before you were interrupted. Where does guy number three come in?"

"Axel is the biggest flirt of them all, and while he's never quiet about his feelings for me, it wasn't until recently that I became aware his comments are more than just harmless flirting."

"While my wonderful, fairytale fiancé here will tell you to

jump in with two feet, you wouldn't have asked us here if you didn't have reservations." And this is why I came to Annie. She won't sugarcoat anything for me.

"I'm a complicated person when it comes to feelings. I don't typically trust easily, but these three men have had my trust and respect professionally for years. Is it irresponsible of me to let those feelings cross?"

Annie nods in understanding. "I see your reservation now." Cole had been Annie's dog walker before their emotional relationship started. Similarly, she trusted him as an employee before a lover.

"Trust your heart, Spencer." Blake's statement rings with hearts and butterflies.

"*Listen* to your heart, but trust your gut. If the two align, you'll have the right answer." Annie's advice is sensible and reasonable and I respect it.

I clean up my area and stand to throw away my trash. We haven't had a call all morning, and I feel we're on borrowed time, and I want to be prepared.

The front door opens and a gust of wind almost blows the napkin off my plate. Backlit by the afternoon sunshine is a pair of boots, dark denim jeans, and a cowboy hat.

My breath ceases in my chest as my body instantly recognizes the man in the doorway. I'm frozen, standing at the garbage can.

"Everything okay, Spencer?" Blake places a hand on my back, trying to understand what's happening. Does she not feel his presence? This man commands a room just by walking into it. His charisma and charm most likely manifested the perfect sunray as his backdrop when he walked in.

"Tucker." I'm not aware I say his name out loud until his head turns in my direction. Or maybe I didn't, and he heard the thoughts roaring in my head because right now, all I'm hearing is a freight train.

The man in question recognizes me and, without skipping a beat, comes barreling toward us. The trash I'm holding falls to the floor as one hand wraps around my back, and another firmly grips the back of my head.

The moment his lips touch mine, and the roughness of his beard skates across my cheeks, I'm brought back to the coffee shop a month ago. The kiss took me by surprise, both at the suddenness of it and the intensity that two strangers could share.

He draws me in closer as I hear gasps from Blake or Annie. As our tongues tangle and I melt further into this man who is still very much a stranger, I hear a loud crash behind Tucker. I can't bring myself to pull away and find out why, but moments later, Tucker is ripped away from me, and the sound of flesh hitting flesh brings me out of my fog.

Blinking several times, I realize that Miller has Tucker on the ground, and the men are wrestling and throwing punches.

"Who the fuck are you? You can't assault my woman and get away with it."

"*Your* woman? Fuck. Shit."

Miller throws punches as Tucker deflects the best he can from his prone position.

"Spencer?" Blake snaps me back into reality. "He looks familiar, too. What is going on? I need to drink your water. These men are hot for you. Is that Axel?"

"No. That's Tucker. He-he owns Midnight Moonshine."

Tucker gets the upper hand and rolls Miller to his back, pinning his hands above his head.

"Shit, that's how I know him. Why is that so fucking hot to watch?" And this is a prime example of Blake being the opposite of Annie. She speaks her mind. But I also have to agree, and so does my body; it's hot.

"What the fuck is your problem, asshole?" Tucker's southern drawl has my stomach fluttering and my core clenching. Miller tries to buck under Tucker, but the man is solid and doesn't move. His attention turns to me, and his eyes soften.

"Are you okay, Little Miss?" Those are the exact words he asked me in the coffee shop the morning of the attempted robbery. I can feel my face flush as his attention is directed to me.

"Who the fuck are you?" Miller growls as he continues to struggle under Tucker.

Everyone's attention turns to the door as the sirens sound, and two uniformed officers charge through. They draw their guns when they see the position of the two men on the floor.

"Hands up. Stand up slowly. Don't make any sudden movements."

One of the employees, a mousy-looking young brunette, slides up behind us. "Are you ladies okay? The cops got here as soon as they could." I can hear the trembling in her voice and understand why she called the police.

Tucker and Miller shout slurs at each other as the officers put handcuffs on them.

"Fuck. Miller? What the hell, man?" I see Officer Westbrook clicking Miller's hands behind his back. "Let's go, gentlemen. You're getting a free ride to the station, so we can sort this out."

As Miller looks at me and says, "Call Linc," Tucker turns to the officer pushing him out the door, and I hear him say, "Call Officer Lincoln Reed."

Miller's head whips to Tucker as quickly as mine. I forgot Tucker was Lincoln's stepbrother, and it's clear Miller has no idea who he is.

16

Lincoln

My walkie crackles at my hip. "Officer Reed, you have a phone call."

"On my way." I hasten my walk to the office. No one would call me at work unless it were an emergency.

When I enter the office, the receptionist points me to a phone, and I pick it up, tapping the blinking line.

"Officer Reed."

"Lincoln, man. What have you done? You have a brother?"

"Axel? I have a stepbrother. What does that matter? Why are you calling me at work?" He's laughing, and I'm a bit frustrated at his humor and lack of explanation for calling.

"Your boyfriend and stepbrother had a brawl in a sandwich shop downtown, and both are down at the PD asking for you. Spencer called me when she realized she didn't have your number." *Shit.* How could I not have exchanged numbers with her? Orgasm? Sure. Phone number? Nah.

"What the hell happened?" I cover the mic on the phone and let the receptionist know I have a family emergency and need to leave. Axel's laughter booms again, and I want to pummel him through the phone.

"According to Spencer, your stepbro kissed her, and Miller went all caveman on him. There's a story I'm missing, and I want the gossip, Linc."

"Fuck." I look apologetically around the office for my slipped curse. "I'm heading to the station. Let me know if you hear anything else. Is everything good over there?"

"Yep. Furniture is in and moved around. It's a teenager's dream."

"See you soon."

"Thanks, Westbrook." I double tap my knuckles on the counter after signing the paperwork for Miller and Tucker's release. Shortly after Axel's call, Westbrook called to let me know that they were asking for me and giving each other the stink eye, trying to figure out how they each knew me. For the station's entertainment or my aggravation, they were kept at opposite ends of the room so they couldn't talk.

"Anytime, Reed. You owe me a drink and a story. These two were going at it pretty good."

"I got you." I walk into the room and nod to the rookie in charge of watching them. Miller and Tucker are each handcuffed to a bench, glaring at each other.

"This is rich guys." I walk to Tucker, who's closest to the door, and uncuff him. He rolls his shoulders and rubs his wrists. I watch him lick at a cut on his lip as he eyes Miller across the room. "Tucker, meet Miller, my boyfriend." His eyes fly to mine and are as wide as saucers. "Miller, meet Tucker, my stepbrother."

"Stepbr—Fuck, I'm sorry, Linc. I had no idea. Not that it makes kissing Spencer any different." He shoots a death glare at Tucker, and I sigh. I cross the room and uncuff Miller. He gives me his boyish smile, melting my insides.

"Tucker, why must you instigate things? Didn't you satisfy your childish antics by kissing her the first time?"

"The what?! There was a first time?" Miller's eyes shoot daggers at Tucker.

Shit. I never thought to say anything about the kiss to Miller because it was such an isolated incident. Spencer never contacted Tucker, so I thought the entire thing was a random fluke. I also never thought I'd find myself in a situation where I'd be kissing the same girl my brother had, or my boyfriend wants too for that matter.

"There sure was. It's hard to forget the sweet lips of my Little Miss. Tell him, Linc."

I place a flat palm on Miller's chest and feel it heave. He grabs my wrist and stares me down.

"You knew about it?" I see the hurt and confusion in his baby-blue eyes.

"I was there, but I promise you it was consensual. Spencer actually kissed him first."

"Bullshit. Spencer doesn't go around kissing random guys." He pushes my hand away and paces the length of the wall.

"Fireball, look at me."

"Aww. What's wrong, *Fireball*? Are you afraid of a little healthy competition? I heard you refer to her as *your woman*."

I wish Tucker would just shut up and stop stoking the fire. Although I've never seen Miller act this protective. I'd be lying if it wasn't turning me on.

"*Our* woman."

Fuck me. I guess we're putting all our cards on the table in the middle of my PD.

"Our? Are you holding out on me, little brother? If I had known you were up for sharing, I might have asked to join."

I have no idea why my usually mild-mannered brother is acting like a huge dick right now. He's throwing all his Southern gentlemanly charm out the window to goad Miller about Spencer.

"Tucker. I'm respectfully asking you to shut the fuck up. It's not too late for the sub shop to press charges."

"Your boyfriend here threw the first punch. I was just kissing a beautiful woman, who, by the way, was kissing me back."

"Lincoln," Miller growls my name, and I really need my cock to understand this isn't the time and definitely not the place.

"Miller, I hate to side with him, but I saw it with my own eyes the first time." His shoulders deflate as he digests my words. He takes a few deep breaths before he perks up.

"Hey Tucker, family meeting tonight. You got plans?" His smile is wicked and I don't like where he's going with this.

"Miller. That's not a great idea." Putting them in a room together again, after their already volatile encounter, doesn't seem like a fun evening for me.

"I think it's a great idea. Spencer can clear the air. We can all figure out what's going on." Miller speaks with conviction as he stares Tucker down.

"I'll be there. Send me the information, little brother. Am I free to go? I have a business to check on since I'll be unavailable for a few hours tonight."

"You're all set, Tuck."

"It was nice meeting your beau. See you tonight." He tips his imaginary hat and leaves the room."

17

Axel

Everyone left for work and school this morning to have a seemingly mundane day. I planned to sleep until the movers arrived with the furniture, but they were early. I spent two hours rearranging the rooms for Spencer, finding not one but three hidden guns. We will definitely be having this conversation soon. Katy may be sixteen, but gun safety is important at any age.

When I finish all the moving, I have just enough time to nap for a few more hours, except when I'm about to lie down again, my phone rings.

"Hey, Tails. Do you miss me already?" She sighs, and before I can retract my words for annoying her, she shocks me.

"Miller was arrested along with Lincoln's brother—"

"Linc has a brother?"

"I tell you one of your friends has been arrested, and you question the stranger in the scenario?" *Shit. She's right.* But in all the years I've known Lincoln, he's never mentioned a brother.

"Sorry. Squirrel brain. What happened, and what can I

do?"

"I need you to contact Lincoln. They're both asking for him but I realized I don't have his number."

How is that possible?

"I can do that. What caused the fight?" Silence. Other than the commotion in the background she doesn't say a word. "Spencer?"

"I'm here."

"What caused the fight? Miller is usually a gentle giant. Is he okay?" I hope her silence doesn't mean something terrible happened. She said he was arrested but that's all the details she gave.

"Me."

"Tails? Did you just say...*you* caused the fight?" I hear the whoosh of air as she blows out a breath.

"Tucker walked in and saw me. He came up and kissed me and Miller didn't appreciate it."

"Huh. I don't know who I'm more proud of, Miller or you. I can't wait to get the gossip tonight. Are they taking him to the PD?"

"Yeah."

"I'm on it."

When I call the school to get in contact with Lincoln, he's as confused as I am.

The sound of the front door slamming wakes me, and Miller and Lincoln's angry voices flood the room.

"Nothing good will come from my brother being here tonight?"

"You didn't see—wait, yes you did because this was the second time he's kissed her." I peek my head up from the couch as Miller flings open the refrigerator and pulls out a beer.

"Morning love birds." They both glare at me and I throw my hands up in surrender. "What's going on?"

"Miller invited my brother to our family meeting tonight. He feels Spencer and Tucker should explain themselves to us."

There's an us? I know there was a moment between them and Spencer this morning, but an *us*? I love the sound of it but I've never gotten my hopes up when it comes to Spencer.

"Forgive me if I feel like I'm owed an explanation. Linc, I didn't even know you had a brother. We've been dating for over six months. Family is something I should know about by now. And they've kissed. Your brother has kissed the woman we've all been chasing around like the puppy dogs Katy accused us of being."

"Speaking of Katy, I need to go pick her up from school." Lincoln spins his keys around his index finger and gives Miller a hopeful look.

"I need to call my Chief and get my ass reamed out." In three long pulls, Miller empties his beer and grabs for another. His frustration is palpable and I can't blame him.

Lincoln nods in defeat, kisses Miller tenderly on the forehead, and leaves despite their current argument.

"Do you want to talk about it?"

"No. I'm going to shower." He stalks down the hall.

"If you need a hand just yell."

I guess there's no point in going back to sleep now. Everyone will be home soon and I need to take my pill before

I get truly squirrely.

As the afternoon progresses everyone slowly pours back into the house. I haven't felt the lack of space in Spencer's small pool house until now. Everyone tries to keep to their corner of the room. Lincoln brought Katy directly to Justin's house from school per Spencer's request via her newly acquired phone number, thanks to me.

Anxiety rolls off Miller's shoulders as he counts down the minutes until Lincoln's brother arrives. The animosity between the two of them hasn't changed.

Outside, we hear the crunching of gravel in the driveway. Spencer comes out of her room, and all eyes turn to her. I wish she was wearing more clothes, knowing we're about to have company, but also, goddamn, does she look edible. Her skin-tight workout pants are a dusty blue color, but her already barely there black sports bra has what looks like three strings holding up one side of her shoulder.

"Smithy, don't you want to put on more clothes for our guest?" She scoffs at him as she continues to the door. His use of her nickname reminds me that I still need to ask her about the guns I found. I hear a growl and don't know who it comes from, but I agree with the sentiment. Spencer momentarily disappears in the foyer, and I hear the door open.

"Welcome, Tucker." I hear a thud, and I'm on my feet in seconds, Lincoln and Miller following me.

"Little Miss." Tucker has Spencer backed into the wall, hovering over her.

"Stop. *Bleiben.*" Her tone is stern and every man in the room instantly freezes. I hear Gage growling next to me and realize her command was probably to him, but she got the entire room's attention. Only Spencer has that kind of authority because I see the determination in Miller's eyes to finish what he started this afternoon.

Lincoln steps in front of Miller, smoothing his palms down his chest, trying to calm him.

"Get the fuck off her. Did you not get your ass kicked enough earlier?"

"Tucker, be smart," Lincoln urges his brother without taking his eyes off Miller.

"Down boys." Spencer easily ducks under Tucker's arm and I swear I see him pout through his beard. "Today is about me... and the pictures that were delivered." If she didn't already have our attention it's all on her now.

Lincoln looks confused and concerned. "You opened the envelope?"

"I did. I had a feeling I knew what they would be, and unfortunately, it's much worse than I thought." There's a crack in Spencer's usual stoic face. Her mask is on which is something we haven't seen much of in the time we've been invading her home.

The air in the room shifts. The rage and anger switched to concern and curiosity.

"Can everyone please sit?" This is pre-Katy Spencer and it's not my favorite.

18

Spencer

Today is one of the most unpredictable days in my life. An orgasm, another random kiss, a fight, and now Tucker is sitting in my living room. Tucker smartly chose an armchair while the other three sat on the couch.

Having Tucker here changes things. My mask is on, which it would have been for this conversation anyway, but my guard is also up. He knows nothing about me, and I'm about to reveal the most intimate side of myself.

The most confusing part about this situation is that everything about it feels right. Even Tucker's presence feels like a piece of the puzzle I was unaware I was missing.

"Tails, talk to us. You're making me nervous. What was in the envelope? What were the pictures?"

"Me..." They all stiffen, and I pause before sharing the most significant piece of the news. "And Katy."

"What the fuck."

"What's going on?"

"Who sent them?"

"Are you in danger?"

The last question is from Tucker. The playful, flirtatious attitude he's given me since we met is gone. Fury mars his features. He's still wearing his cowboy hat, but his blue eyes are hooded.

"Are you and Katy in danger, Dream Girl?" I want to lie and tell them no, but that won't help the situation. Instead, I add fuel to the fire and retrieve the envelope filled with pictures. I hand it to Lincoln since we were supposed to look at them last night, and of the four, he's the most qualified to handle this situation as a police officer.

"Holy fucking shit. How far do these go back?" Lincoln continues to flip through the pictures and the rest lean in to look.

They haven't gotten to the one with the note yet. I know the explosion is coming. I'm preparing and bracing for the outbursts when they do. I intentionally left it on the bottom of the pile.

I see it in their eyes the moment before it happens. Miller isn't in the picture because he hadn't arrived at my house yet, but it's a close-up of me unlocking my front door, Lincoln carrying Katy, and Axel following. The words SHE'S MINE are written across the picture in black marker.

Loud roaring erupts in the room as they all talk over each other. I can't make out anything they're saying. Despite being prepared for the noise, it's getting to me. Sirens, baby cries, screams of pain—I can handle those. The rage and anger of four very different voices as they paw through the pictures, hands, and arms flailing in every direction, is too much.

I slowly retreat toward my bedroom door when firm arms

wrap around me from behind in a bare hug. My body instantly locks up before I smell rich leather and Tucker's calming voice in my ear.

"Shh. It's alright, Little Miss. I've got you." His drawl is husky through his whisper as he gently rocks me in his arms. Without even knowing me, he read me. He knew what I needed.

One by one, the rest see what's happening and quiet down. They each approach me and place a gentle hand on my body.

"We're sorry, Tails. We didn't mean to upset you. You're important to us, and seeing those pictures of you and Katy… well, I know I'm fuming." There are grumbles of agreement around me.

"I'm okay. I just…can I have a moment?"

"Yes."

"Of course."

"Whatever you need."

"Are you sure you're ready for me to let go?" Tucker tightens his bear hug ever so slightly to let me know he's here if I need him.

"I-I'm overstimulated and need to do…something to help me compose myself again." I trail my gaze to Miller and then to Lincoln. If any of them understand, it would be those two.

"Whatever you need, Little Miss." Tucker slowly removes his arms, and I take a few deep breaths as the air around me prickles my skin.

"There are some—" If I'm going to do this, I have to be honest. "There are many things about me you don't know." I take a few steps forward and squat in front of the coffee table. Reaching under the lip, I remove my 9mm Glock Gen 19.

"There's more?"

"More?" I give Axel a puzzled look.

"Yeah. I, um, found a couple when I was moving around the furniture earlier. I was planning to ask you about them at some point." He nervously runs his hands through his perfect curls, and I find myself wondering what they would feel like between my fingers.

I set the gun down on the kitchen counter and move to a hall closet to retrieve the box with my cleaning supplies. When I sit at the counter and open the box, Lincoln approaches me.

"May I?" He motions toward the counter, and I nod. He lifts his left leg and rests it on the bottom rung of a stool, pulling up his pant leg to reveal his off-duty weapon. Removing it, he sits next to me at the counter and begins mirroring my motions.

Remove the magazine.

"Right out of high school, I met a recruit during my father's annual department BBQ fundraiser. He was handsome and charming and despite my...flaws—"

"Smithy, don't talk about yourself like that."

I smile at him in appreciation. "As a naive eighteen year old who didn't fully understand how I was different from others, I felt I was flawed. But Shane never acted like that mattered."

Check the gun barrel for bullets.

"I was the center of his world. My father thought I had found a fantastic man. He'd made his career in the police force and knew I would be well cared for by a fellow brother-in-arms."

Remove the slide.

125

"At nineteen, he told me he loved me, and I gave him my virginity. He had always been so patient with me about wanting to wait until I felt ready. A year and a half later, when I was almost twenty-one, he asked my father for his blessing to propose."

Disengage the recoil spring.

"Without a doubt in his mind, my father said yes. I don't know if Shane applied before or after he asked me, but two months after he proposed, he was offered a job in Indiana with more pay and room for advancement."

Remove the gun barrel.

Lincoln's hands copy every movement I make and at the same pace. He understands that this is therapeutic for me. It's calming my nerves and helping me get through my story.

"Since we were engaged to be married and my EMT certification was national, it was only logical I move with him. Being alone in a place I didn't know was intimidating for me, but I was in love, and Shane was my future. I would go where he goes. Once again, with my father's blessing, we moved."

Clear the carbon and any debris.

I take the cleaning rod out and screw on the brush tip. I only have one rod, and Lincoln waits his turn while I run it through the barrel.

"Thirty-seven days. That's how long it took before I began to notice gradual changes. Things might have started sooner, but we were both in a new place, starting new jobs, and life was stressful. On that thirty-seventh day, he yelled at me. He knew my sensitivity to sudden loud noises." I hear a throat clear and a sigh. "Please don't beat yourself up for tonight's outburst. I understand your reasoning and was prepared.

Your reactions were just a bit more intense than I planned for."

I hand the rod to Lincoln so he can use it to clean his barrel.

"Once Shane realized that raising his voice elicited such an extreme reaction, it continued. If dinner wasn't done before he got home, his uniform not being properly pressed to his liking, he yelled. Despite his knowledge of my sensory issues with clothes, he decided one day that I needed to cover up my body, even while I was in the house. He made me wear baggy clothes from then on."

Repeat previous step with a clean cloth.

Lincoln finishes and hands me back the rod. I switch the brush to the clip and add a cloth, to ensure the barrel is thoroughly cleaned.

"While I was there, I didn't make any friends. I was never brave enough to ask if I could go out when my co-workers invited me. Shane kept asking me when we were going to get married, but I didn't want to anymore. He must have seen the fear in my eyes and made the decision that if we weren't getting married right away, we were going to start a family."

I pass the rod and a new cleaning cloth to Lincoln when I realize he's holding his breath. In fact, they are all looking at me and hanging on to my every word.

"I was never raped."

"Thank fuck, Dream Girl."

"Sorry I gave you that impression. I still loved Shane, or at least I thought I did. He threw away my birth control. At the time, I was willing to do anything to keep the peace and him happy."

Oil the moving parts.

While Lincoln resumes his cleaning, I use a new cloth and

oil to lubricate all the mechanics.

I close my eyes for a moment and take a few cleansing breaths. This next part hurts.

"It took me several months to get pregnant." I hear their reactions to this news, but I need to keep going. "Once I did, things with Shane went back to normal. We were happy again. He wasn't intentionally doing things to overstimulate me anymore. He stopped talking about getting married and talked about the son he was going to have. Only the blood work I had around ten weeks told me I was having a girl."

Reassemble.

I put down all the tools and slowly put my gun back together. Lincoln stares at me, no longer worried about his.

"I didn't tell him. I was too afraid to disrupt our newfound peace. I didn't know until it was too late that he was coming with me to my next appointment. There wasn't a chance to warn anyone not to mention the sex of the baby. When the doctor walked in, she cheerfully asked if we were excited about the news of our little girl. I wanted to act ignorant, but I couldn't. I had told him the test was inconclusive, and he believed me."

Without realizing it, the four men surround me in a comforting way. They're listening and absorbing my words despite the war of emotions on their faces.

"He kept his calm the rest of the appointment and the entire ride home. Once we were home, that's when it all started. He knew I had lied or, at the very least, had kept the truth from him. He locked me in the spare bedroom upstairs for two days before I saw him again. I had a bathroom and running water, but he didn't bring me any food." I stand and replace the gun back in the holster under the table.

Moving around the kitchen island, I open the lower cabinet on the other side, reach under, pull out another identical gun, and begin the cleaning process again.

"At the end of the second day, he brought me a hot dinner and apologized profusely. I was scared and starving, and I accepted both without hesitation. I had no one but him. I didn't have many other people in my life, and my father thought Shane hung the moon. I felt ashamed that I couldn't give him the son he wanted."

"Smithy, you can't blame—"

"I know this now. I know a lot of things *now*. Back then, not so much." I turn my attention to Axel. "Can you bring me all of the guns you found today?" He wanders the house and brings me two more. He retrieves one from my bedroom and one from the guest bathroom. Four of the nine I keep hidden. I continued cleaning for a few minutes, building strength and courage to continue.

"At my twenty-week ultrasound, he came with me to confirm the baby still wasn't a boy. Several times during the appointment, the technician asked if I was okay because I was trembling so badly. I told her it was nerves and I was cold, but in reality, I was scared. I didn't want to be locked back up again. Things had already escalated. He would grab me roughly, causing bruises on my arms or hips. Shane talked about wanting to put the baby up for adoption because a girl was useless to him."

"Fuck," Axel curses under his breath, and I give him a tight smile.

"I was having a perfectly healthy pregnancy. My daughter looked beautiful on the scans and despite everything Shane was putting me through, I was excited to be a mother. I had hopes he would come around. Shane gave me a week of that hope after our ultrasound. I thought he had made peace with having a baby girl. The man he was when we lived here was back. He was sweet and attentive. He even took me out on a date. I was certain he was turning a new leaf. Until…" My hand trembled, making the gun rattle.

"Fuck this." Tucker grabs me from behind in his bear hug again, but this time, he carries me to the couch and sits, planting me firmly in his lap. I adjust so I'm sitting across his legs and rest my head on his shoulder. Miller sits at my feet and lifts my legs into his lap. Axel joins us on the other side of Tucker and rubs my hip. Lincoln lowers himself to the floor between Tucker, and Miller and runs a soothing hand on my thigh. These men give me strength in their touch to relive the worst days of my life.

This is wrong…but it isn't. I allowed Tucker, a man I know nothing about, to control me and my body. He carried me across the room, and I willingly took his comfort. I'm taking all of their comfort, and I feel…fine. It's calming me. I don't feel itchy or the need to crawl out of my skin. I feel content. And I need to finish my story.

"It was a Tuesday evening."

19

Tucker

I have no idea what it is about this mysterious woman that has me so captivated, but I'm hers. It's as simple as that.

Earlier, when I saw her retreating from the other guy's reactions, I moved out of instinct. My mother had panic attacks when I was a child. Deep pressure is what helped calm her. Though I never saw any evidence of abuse, they stopped when my father died from a farming accident.

I was entranced watching Spencer clean her guns one after another. She knew exactly what she was doing with complete comfort and ease. When I saw the shake of her hand, I knew she needed more. I have yet to learn what the relationship is between her and the three other men in the room, other than Miller referring to Spencer as his. Right now, it doesn't matter to me.

As I carry her to the couch and settle her in my lap, I already feel her stress ease. The guys follow me and each hold a piece of her to give their own comfort and strength. I have a feeling we are about to hear the hardest part of her story.

"It was a Tuesday evening. Shane made me Shepherd's pie. He knew it was my favorite. After a nice dinner and conversation, he told me to take a bath and relax. I was overjoyed at the idea. I soaked and rested and felt refreshed. I stayed in the tub until my fingers and toes were like prunes." She absentmindedly rubs her thumbs over the pads of her fingers, remembering the feel of it.

"While I was getting dressed, he came in and told me he had another surprise for me and to come downstairs when I was finished." Her body becomes rigid in my arms, and looking at everyone's faces, they see it, too.

"When I took the first step to go downstairs…I fell."

That's not the truth. I can feel the fear radiating from her.

"Little Miss, I'm gonna need you to be honest with us. I can promise you right now that not a single person here will hurt you. And before you protest, that's what your dipshit ex made you believe; I want you to listen to me right now." I tilt her chin so she's looking into my eyes. They're glossy, and I want to find this Shane asshole and make him pay for every tear she's ever shed for him.

"Spencer, I know you don't know me from Adam, but you can ask my brother here. I'm a man of my word. You looked real pretty cleaning your guns, and I'll say I'm impressed. But if any of these men ever lays a hand on you in anger, I'll put a bullet in his brain and not think twice." I shift my gaze to Lincoln, "And if I ever lay a hand on her, I expect you to do the same, brother." Lincoln gives me a curt nod, and I know he believes my conviction.

"Why?"

Who the fuck knows. Chemistry. Fate. Fucking God. A penny I made a wish on and threw into a fountain when I was six. I'll give her the only truth I know.

"Because you're worth it." She gasps at the enormity of my statement, but they're the most honest words I've ever spoken. "Tell us what happened, Little Miss. The truth this time."

"When I took the first step, I was...pushed down the stairs." I tighten my grip around her, feeling the shudder go through her body.

"Fuck, Dream Girl." I heard Lincoln call her that earlier, and for the first time, I realize that every single man in this room has a sexual attraction to Spencer. Even my little stepbrother, despite his boyfriend being right next to me. What an interesting dynamic this woman has orbiting around her.

"We lived in an older house. The stairs were wood and steep, with a landing in the middle. I fell all the way to the bottom. I must have passed out because I don't remember getting to the bottom floor, but..." Her body recoils inwards, and I brace myself for what she's about to say next. "I came too, when Shane was kicking my stomach. I was only an EMT then, but I knew whatever marks he was creating could be swept under the rug as part of the fall."

Every one of us is ready to search out and kill this man. It's written plain as day on our faces and the heavy breathing containing our rage.

"I lost consciousness again, and when I came around this time, I was alone. Alone and in excruciating pain. I knew if I was going to leave, it was my only chance. Beaten and broken, I got into my car with only my wallet and willpower. I had broken ribs, most likely a concussion, and bruises lining my body. But none of that mattered to me. He completed the task he set out to do. Despite my discomfort during the four-hour drive, I waited and waited. She never moved. My baby girl never moved again. I drove straight to my father's house. I knew the only way he was going to believe me was if he saw it with his own two eyes."

She's been through so much, and my heart breaks for her. I want to fix every one of her worries and dispose of anything and anyone that's ever caused her pain.

"Because of what happened, it put a strain on the relationship between my father and me. He blames himself. He couldn't believe he missed every sign of the abuser that Shane was. He drove me to the hospital, and we told them I was mugged. They confirmed she had passed and..."

"Shhh. You don't need to say anymore, Little Miss." I want to cocoon her into me. Taking a bold risk because I know nothing about this woman other than what she's told me and the immense pull I have toward her, I tug on the hair tie at the bottom of one of her braids. It slips from her hair, and I gently unravel her braid from the bottom to her crown until her copper hair flows in waves. She sighs, and her body melts farther into mine. I repeat the process on the other braid until my fingers can freely flow through her locks. I can tell she needed this extra stimulation after the confession she just made to us.

Us.

I almost forgot we were surrounded in a room together. As I massage Spencer's scalp, a soft moan escapes her. I will my cock not to respond to her noise, but it isn't listening because she continues mewling.

"Little Miss, I need you to stop making those sounds. I'm trying to be respectful, but you're making it difficult." I'm not sure she's even listening to me; too lost in the feel of my hands in her hair. I feel a growl at my side and realize Miller isn't happy with me.

We need to talk about what those pictures mean, but right now, she seems like she's had enough. She's shared her unimaginable truths with us, and I won't ask for more than she can handle. Spencer moans again and I can't take it anymore. My body reacts before my brain can catch up, and I fist her hair and pull her head back. Sealing my lips to hers, I kiss her gently. She returns my offering, and I drink her in. Her soft lips caress mine, and I want to deepen the kiss, but she's in charge.

"Tucker." My name is a growl on Miller's lips. I care fuck all about his opinion. If Spencer wants to kiss me she can kiss me.

"Fireball, let them be."

"Are we going to just let him do that? She barely knows him." I ignore them and continue kissing my girl. I feel the couch dip next to me, and any protest Miller has, dies on Lincoln's lips as he kisses him. I hear their heavy breathing but get distracted as Spencer shifts in my lap and straddles me.

"I want her lips," Miller whines, and I open my eyes to see Lincoln kissing his neck. I pull away from Spencer, and her lips drift to my neck. Reaching my hand across the couch, I grab Miller's chin and pull him to me.

"If you want her lips, you can taste them on mine first." I wait for his reaction. I'm not willing to take something he doesn't want to give. I see his chest heaving and know he's turned on. Whether it's from his previous activity with Lincoln or the thought of kissing me, I'm not sure.

135

"Kiss him, Fireball." That must be the permission Miller was waiting for because he lunges forward, crushing his lips to mine. Miller tries to dominate our kiss but he's about to learn his place.

"I don't think so, Bruiser. I'm in charge." I lower my hand to his neck and push him back so our lips hover an inch apart. "Lincoln, you better control your boy toy before I do." Miller's Adam's apple bobs under my hand, and I watch his pupils dilate. He likes that idea. Why do I like the idea of sharing my brother's boyfriend?

Axel pulls Spencer away from me, and if I wasn't in this tense staredown with Miller, I'd protest, but I have a situation that needs to be dealt with at the moment.

"Linc?" He hasn't answered me, and I don't know if it's a good or bad thing. I know Lincoln and I both have particular tastes when it comes to the bedroom. Our flavors of sexuality have always danced on both sides.

Reluctantly, I release Miller's gaze to look at my brother. He's watching our interaction with lust-filled eyes. He wants this, too.

"On your knees, Miller." The room goes silent, and Axel and Spencer's make-out session comes to a halt. Miller has a choice to make, and I feel like this is a line in the sand he needs to decide to cross or walk away from. Either answer is fine with me.

His eyes give everything away. He wants this but is hesitant. Lincoln has mentioned Miller to me a few times, and I know this is his first relationship with a man. Right now, he's probably wondering if he can handle both of us. The answer is no, but we could ease him into it.

"The choice is yours, Fireball. You can obey or say no.

No one will fault you for your decision." I give Lincoln an appreciative nod. He could also tell me no—Miller belongs to him. He doesn't have to share with me. It's not something we've ever done before. But I really fucking hope he says yes.

20

Miller

What the fuck is happening? Kissing Tucker was not in the plans for…well, ever. This afternoon I sucker-punched the guy, and now my tongue is down his throat, and fuck, I like it.

"On your knees, Miller."

Fucking hell. I wouldn't call what Lincoln and I have a dom/sub relationship, but I let him dominate most of our sexual activity. He's more experienced, and I enjoy listening to him tell me what to do to give him pleasure. But Tucker's words, with his intense tone, has me second-guessing everything.

I don't know what to do. I want to do as I've been told, but he's not Lincoln. In fact, he's Lincoln's brother—the man I wanted to kill a few hours ago. I need Linc to decide and tell me what to do.

"The choice is yours, Fireball. You can obey or say no. No one will fault you for your decision."

Holy shit. This feels like a big step. It is a big step. If I give in to this and allow whatever is about to play out happen, things will change. Hell, things are already changing.

My mind whirls with the trauma Spencer shared with us and the kiss I shared with Tucker. Am I in the right mind frame to make a decision like this?

Tucker's hand flexes on my neck, reminding me it's still there and that he's waiting for a response—my choice.

"I want to kiss Spencer."

"I don't think that was an option. You got to taste her on me. Do you need another taste before you decide?"

Fuck yes, I want to kiss him again. I want to do more. I have a feeling the world that Lincoln has opened up to me has just been a taste of what it could be. Tucker strikes me as a man with more sexual knowledge than I could even comprehend.

"Please." I'm so fucking turned on I don't even know what I'm begging for. Tucker, Spencer, an answer. I don't fucking know. I want it all.

"Fireball, look at me." I give my beautiful, green-eyed boyfriend my undivided attention. Fuck he's gorgeous. The smirk he gives me tells of all the dirty thoughts running through his mind. "Do you want to stop and walk away?" Fuck no. I vigorously shake my head. "Good boy." He runs a hand through my hair, and if I were a cat, I'd be fucking purring.

Tucker pulls my attention away as his hand around my neck slides down my chest.

"Eyes on me, Miller." Fuck I love Linc's dominant voice. It's impossibly deeper than his usual cadence. "If your apprehension is me, stop. I've never shared with my brother before, but if you'd like to try, my answer is yes. You are asking to share, correct Tucker?"

"I am." I shiver as Tucker runs a finger across my nipple. I bite my bottom lip, and Linc quickly pulls it out.

"I think you like the idea. Do you want to share what's holding back your answer? What's making you hesitate?"

Nothing.

Everything.

Fuck this is confusing.

My eyes slowly drift to everyone on the couch.

Lincoln, my boyfriend, that even though I haven't said the words yet, I'm in love with his handsome, broody ass.

Spencer, my elusive mystery woman who keeps me on my toes and calls me out on my bull shit. I want to kiss her so fucking bad. I need to know what she tastes like, but I don't have the option right now.

Axel, my best friend, whose face is currently buried in Spencer's neck. I'm jealous he's getting to taste my girl but not jealous of him. Should I be?

Finally, Tucker. I can still feel the coarseness of his beard on my face. I want this. I want more.

"He scares the fuck out of me." I can't believe I confessed that out loud. Tucker's hand smooths over my chest again, and I see the understanding in his blue eyes.

"Give me a safeword, Bruiser. I don't want you to be afraid of anything."

"Fucking shit, guys. You're getting me hard over here, and I have a beautiful woman in my lap. Code Blue. The safeword is Code Blue, which goes for everyone under this roof." Axel has spoken and gone right back to his assault on Spencer's neck.

"Alright, you heard the man. Does that work for you? If it does, you were told what to do. So, safeword or… Get. On.

Your. Knees." Lincoln moves off the couch so I have room to make my decision.

I've already made it. Sliding to the floor, I present myself to Lincoln and Tucker. I sit awkwardly on my heels, not knowing exactly what I should be doing. I flick my gaze between them. One looks hungry and the other satisfied. Both looks are equally arousing. My cock strains against my jeans at the sheer anticipation of what's to come.

"Do you wanna watch the show or join in, Tails?" I hold my breath at Axel's question. I wait for her answer, but I don't dare move a muscle. I'm still waiting for instructions.

"Will you watch with me? I don't want to interrupt their dynamic. They have things to work out." My Smithy can watch me all day long.

"Please let me kiss her." I'm fucking done for. I'm eager to get my lips on the woman who frazzles my every goddamn nerve. I'm the only one in this room who doesn't know what she tastes like, and it's driving me mad.

"Earn it."

"What?"

Tucker's grin is devious as he stares down at me. He shifts to the edge of the couch so his knees surround me.

"I said, earn it. Hands in your lap."

Fuck. We're doing this. I link my hands and place them on top of my thighs. I hold my breath, waiting. What will he instruct me to do next?

Lincoln and I have never done anything this formal before, especially with an audience. Tucker grabs my chin and my attention.

"I know we've established a safeword, but I need to know where your head is. Are you comfortable with this, and how far would you like to go?"

How far? I may not be in control right now, but he's giving me the choice.

"You can trust us, Fireball. I'd never do anything out of your limits. I know we've talked about them, and I'll make sure Tucker knows them as well."

"I trust you. Completely." Lincoln and Tucker exchange a look. Without words, I can't comprehend their expressions, but they understand each other and come to a nonverbal agreement.

"Before you can earn Spencer's lips, I want you to show me that your mouth is worthy of hers." My eyes watch his fingers as they unclip his belt.

"Do it for him. Take him out, Fireball."

I swallow down the nerves threatening to spill out and rise up on my knees. My hands shake, but it's pure adrenaline coursing through me. The rush feels like the same high I get when my pager goes off at the firehouse. The excitement and anticipation motivate me to open the button of Tucker's pants and unzip his fly. His light gray briefs stare at me, and he lifts his hips, urging me to lower his pants.

Lincoln lowers himself next to me and runs his hands along the hem of my shirt. His fingers graze my sides as he lifts my shirt and removes it. He runs soothing circles on my back as I slip my hand into Tucker's briefs and pull out his already hard cock.

"Prove your worth, Bruiser." I kind of fucking love that nickname. It's his acknowledgment of our fight, but it doesn't feel condescending.

I squeeze my hand around his length using the pressure I know I like and stroke. My experience with men is limited to Lincoln, but we've done plenty of exploring, and I'm confident in my blow job skills.

My limits are non communication. As long as I understand what's happening, if it's something new, I'm willing to try. I just don't want any surprises.

I alternate my hands, pulling his cock between my palms, and feel him harden. The vein underneath bulges as his tip darkens in color from the added blood flow.

"I'm ready whenever you are. Show me how good you treat my brother." His words feel like a challenge that I'm willing to accept. Leaning forward, I leave one hand at the base of his shaft and swirl my tongue around his tip.

Once, twice, three times is all it takes before the first moan rumbles in Tucker's chest. That's the noise I was waiting to hear. Inhaling a deep breath through my nose, I dive into his lap, taking as much of him as I can. As I pull back, I use my tongue to trace the now prominent vein under his length. I quickly suck him back in and set a pace going farther and farther each time.

Lincoln and I have practiced this particular skill because a blow job is sexy, can be done in small spaces, and, if done correctly, can be quick and dirty.

My angle isn't quite right, so I shift my legs to get closer to Tucker. As I'm about to pull Tucker into my throat, a deep, velvety whisper pauses my action.

"Fireball. Can I take your ass while you take his cock?" I try to nod my approval, but Tucker fists the front of my hair, pulling me off him.

"Be respectful and answer him." Lust and fire burn in his eyes, and it's a heady mixture that has my cock twitching in my pants.

"Yes, please."

"Please, what? Use your big-boy words, Bruiser. Tell us what you want."

Tucker turns my head to look over my shoulder at Lincoln, and I take a moment to admire his toned, tattooed chest. I have no idea when he lost his shirt, but I approve.

"Please fuck me while I suck off Tucker."

A beautiful smile creeps up Linc's lips. "Good boy."

Tucker releases the grip on my hair and runs his fingers over my scalp, easing the burn he caused. I glance next to us to check on our spectators.

"Are you good, Smithy?" She's turned in Axel's lap, facing out and watching our interactions directly. Axel's hands roam up and down her arms and legs while he peppers her neck and shoulders with kisses.

"I'm excellent. Are you enjoying yourself?"

Fuck. Lincoln's hands undo my pants, and he palms my cock, using the heel of his hand to run along my length. I hear Spencer giggle, and it's music to my fucking ears.

"I'll take that as a yes," she purrs.

"You're lips are my fucking prize. Prepare for an epic kiss." She smiles, and her eyes roll back into her head as Axel sucks on the sensitive spot behind her ear.

I half help to remove my pants, and Lincoln pulls my hips back to adjust me for a better angle. I hear the opening of the lube packet that we both conveniently keep in our wallets for times like this. Cool gel runs through my ass cheeks, and Lincoln's fingers scoop it up and rim me to prepare to take him. I lean down to put Tucker back in my mouth, and he stops me.

"Let him get inside you first." Tucker languidly strokes

himself while he waits. I feel the first sensation of pressure as Lincoln slips a finger in, and I suck in a breath. Tucker's free hand returns to my head, and he resumes his scalp massage. Now I understand why Spencer was so mesmerized earlier. This feels like fucking magic.

Lincoln and I have an active sex life, and it doesn't take long before I'm ready to take him. There's a part of me that likes pain, and I enjoy the burn as I bear down and allow Lincoln entrance into my body. I rest my head on Tucker's thigh to stabilize myself as Lincoln pushes further into me.

"Alright, Fireball. I'm all the way in. Now take him." Tucker's hand moves, and I replace it with mine. Once again, he stops me before I take him in my mouth.

"Are you going to let me come down your pretty little throat, or do you want me to pull out? I need to know now before we continue."

"I'll happily swallow." A devilish grin appears, and he thrusts his cock to the back of my throat at the same time that Lincoln pulls out. I choke but eagerly take what he's offering. There won't be any deep-throating him with both of them using my body.

They quickly find a rhythm with me rocking between them. My body accepts the pleasure they're giving me. I want to be a more active participant, but both men are moaning and grunting with pleasure, so I know they're enjoying themselves, and I sure as fuck am.

"Fucking shit. Fuck, Tails. Please tell me you're as turned on as me right now. I feel like I could explode just watching them." I don't hear if she answers him because Lincoln reaches around and grabs my aching cock. Thank fuck because I'm ready to explode but won't get there without a little help.

It feels like a race for who comes first, and at this point, I'm in such pleasurable bliss I couldn't fucking care less.

"Are you ready for me, Bruiser?" I hum my approval, and Tucker thrusts deeply into my throat. His hot come spills into my mouth and I greedily swallow him down and relish in the sounds he makes as he comes. I gave him this pleasure.

I'm one step closer to kissing my girl.

I feel the last twitches of Tucker's orgasm and lean back. He shifts his arm between our bodies and pushes my back to Lincoln's chest.

"I've got this, Linc." For just a moment, both of them have their hands on my cock, stroking. Fucking ecstasy.

Lincoln releases me and brings his other hand around my chest, grabbing my shoulder. My knees are killing me from the position, and I'm sure we'll both have rug burn, but this experience is worth it.

"Are you ready for me, Fireball? I'm about to fill your ass with my come." This man could make me come reading a fucking grocery list. His voice is sex on a stick.

"I'm ready." And I'm definitely ready. He readjusts his angle, and his cock rubs the sweet spot that almost has me seeing stars. Our bodies slide against each other with the sweat from our exertion.

Needing something to do with my hands, I slide them under Tucker's T-shirt and feel the curves of his abs. I'm mad he kept his shirt on while Linc and I are naked. Next fucking time.

Lincoln's grunts become louder, and with a final thrust and a corresponding tug from Tucker, we come. Lincoln spills in my ass while I fill Tucker's hand, and I feel dirty, satisfied, and loved.

I collapse into Tucker's lap as Lincoln collapses onto me. Spencer stands and comes back with wet towels and tissues.

We thank her and untangle ourselves while we clean up. I catch movement out of the corner of my eye and turn my gaze to see Tucker licking his fingers. No. He's savoring his fingers. The ones I just spilled my come into. He's licking me off of him. Fucking shit.

"Well, brothers. Did the poor sap earn a kiss from the Princess?"

Thank you, Axel.

"Fuck yes, I did." I take a step in her direction and a flat hand splays across my chest.

"Me first." Tucker pulls me into his chest and nips at my bottom lip. "Thank you." Before I can respond, our lips seal together in a kiss filled with the gratitude he expressed. He pulls away before I get lost in him again and turns me toward Spencer. "Go get the girl."

Spencer stands, and I close the few steps between us. Her cheeks are flushed a beautiful pink, and her shoulders rise and fall with her labored breathing. I bring a hand to her face and run the back of my knuckles across her cheek.

This is it. This is the moment everything changes. Axel's relationship with her has always been flirty and professional. She hasn't had many interactions with Lincoln, and Tucker might as well be a stranger. But me? Us? We are co-workers, partners, and friends. Kissing her crosses a new threshold—one I've wanted to cross, but it seemed more like a fever dream.

"Did you enjoy the show, Smithy?"

"Very much so."

"May I kiss you?"

She nods. "You've earned it." I slide my hands into her hair, holding in the groan that the feel of it between my fingers elicits. Tilting my head, I lower my lips to hers.

"Are you sure? There's no turning back from this?" I need her to know she has a choice. She'll always have a choice with me.

Her answer comes in a kiss as she presses her lips to mine. They're soft and full, a stark contrast to the roughness of a man's kiss. Spencer presses her body to mine, and she melts into my arms. Bending down, I grab the back of her thighs and lift them. Her legs wrap around my waist, and I deepen our kiss.

"Miller." I can't decipher Axel's tone, but he's interrupting my moment, and I don't like it.

21

Axel

This is the sweetest torture. I have a stunning woman in my lap. *The* woman. The one that I've teased and taunted for years, never thinking there was a chance she could be anything but a pipe dream.

"Don't they look hot together?" My voice is hoarse with lust, and my cock strains in my pants from her rocking in my lap.

"It's beautiful."

I watch them clean up Miller's interaction with Tucker before he approaches Spencer. I know this moment is monumental for him—it's been monumental for all of us. When they finally kiss, I see the sparks fly. There's no jealousy, only pride—pride that my boy is getting his woman. At the moment, we've *all* got the girl.

Miller lifts Spencer into his arms, and as much as I want to see where things go, we have a sixteen year old that still needs us, a plan to make about a potential stalker, and I have to get to work soon with a raging boner.

"Miller." I need him to stop. I don't want any of this to

stop. I need to fucking come. "Miller." I don't intend it, but there's an edge of desperation in my voice.

"Fuck off, Axel. I'm busy." I know. I fucking know. Clearly, I'm not going to get through to Miller. I gently rub a hand down Spencer's spine and imagine what it would be like to have her sandwiched between the two of us.

"We need to get Katy." Their kiss pauses, and I see Miller's shoulders fall. He knows I'm right. He pulls away and rests his forehead against Spencer's. Spencer sighs and closes her eyes. This is a big adjustment for her.

"I'll get her," Spencer offers. "Do you want to come with me, Miller?"

He's hesitating. I would jump on the chance to have one-on-one time with her right now.

"Axel, do you need some help with that?" Miller's eyes shift to the tent in my pants.

"Me?" I thought I would just end up suffering with blue balls all night or rub one off before I left.

"Yes, you." He kisses Spencer on the forehead and steps up to me. He rubs his hand down his face and huffs. "Fuck. I guess tonight is an honest free-for-all. I haven't been able to get your dick pic out of my mind since I saw it." Oh fuck. I completely forgot about that with everything that's happened.

"Little Miss, I'd love to go with you to pick up Katy. You can tell me all about her." Miller and I stare at each other in silence, which is quickly becoming awkward as Spencer and Tucker leave.

"Fireball, why don't you take a step back and let Axel think? What you're offering him is different from what we just did." His body shifts as his leg moves to step away, and something inside me snaps. I grab Miller's bicep, and he stops. His blue eyes fall to my hand then up to my face. The corner of his lip twitches and it only takes a second to understand what's going on behind it.

"I can fix this." Miller's hand grazes the front of my joggers, and my breath hitches. "I'm dying to see your piercings in person." A desperate groan leaves my throat without my permission.

"I've never..."

"Neither had I until Lincoln. He's a good teacher." I feel the relief of pressure as his hand slowly strokes my cock over my pants. My hand flexes around his arm. My hesitation isn't that it's a guy offering to blow me. It's Miller. I'll have to look at him after, tomorrow, and every day going forward. And Lincoln. The three of us are friends.

"Linc, you're good with this?"

"I'm good if you let me watch. I'll be even better if you let me join." A shiver runs down my spine at his deep voice so close to my ear. I feel the warmth of his body as he steps up to my back. His naked body. *Their* naked bodies. Miller and Lincoln have me sandwiched between them. Linc may not be touching me, but I feel the heat radiating between us. I have a decision to make, and I have seconds left before my hormones take over.

"Okay, okay. Fuck. Shit." I spin out from between them, flustered and turned on but needing a moment to think.

"Hey, no pressure, Axel. I'm sorry. I didn't mean—"

"Mills, you're good. I just need a minute." I need seven hundred of them actually because I'm about to make a decision that will definitely change our relationship.

"Fuck it all to hell." Grabbing Miller's arm again, I pull

him forward, causing him to stumble. When our mouths crash together, it's with more force than anticipated, and Miller bites my lip. I taste the copper in my mouth as our tongues battle. And battle we do. I can't imagine what we look like as our hands pull at each other's hair, and hands grope anywhere they can touch.

Miller fists my curls, adjusting my head to deepen our kiss and he grabs the hem of my shirt, lifting it up my chest. Our mouths part only long enough to lose my shirt, and our hands are as greedy as our mouths. His course, calloused fingers are a shock to my over-sensitive nerves as he explores my body.

"Is that a yes, Axel?" Fingers trail down my body until he's rubbing me over my pants again.

"Yes. Fuck. Okay, yes." I push down on his shoulders because now that I've made the decision, I don't want to wait.

He chuckles. "Is someone eager?"

"You made me an offer that I couldn't refuse. Now pay up."

"Gladly." Miller spins us and pushes me onto the couch before falling to his knees. I've never been more excited about elastic-waisted pants as he easily pulls me from my joggers.

"Fucking hell, Axel." My eyes snap up to Lincoln, staring at the head of my dick. "That had to fucking hurt."

"Like a bitch, but I get lots of compliments." My magic cross piercing consists of two barbells through the head of my cock.

"May I?"

I make a sweeping motion over my lap and widen my legs. "Be my guest." Lincoln drops to his knees next to Miller.

I know I should probably find this obscene, my two best friends staring at the most private part of my body. Instead, seeing them both on their knees is nothing short of erotic.

I close my eyes and take a deep breath to calm the butterflies in my stomach and the hummingbird in my chest. Their fingers gently glide around the head of my cock, exploring my piercing.

"Shall we share, Fireball?"

"What?" I sit up and snap my eyes open. "Share? As in, both of you sucking on my cock?"

"And stroking, licking, nipping. Whatever it takes to get you to come." This isn't real. I'm dreaming. This is some crazy erotic wet dream, and at any moment, I'm going to wake up in my bed humping my pillow and be severely disappointed.

"Axel? Code Blue?" Lincoln questions.

No.

"No fucking way. If you both want to take me, do it. I'm along for the ride."

"Take you, huh?"

Oh shit. Miller arches a brow at me. That was the wrong thing to say.

"Look, I'm up for the idea of exploring, but...baby steps."

Lincoln's deep laugh vibrates through my body and warms me from the inside out.

"Like this?" Miller licks a line from balls to tip and sucks my head into his mouth.

"Fuuuuuck. Just like that." I saw him do something similar to Tucker and wondered what it would feel like. Now I know.

Metal clinks on Miller's teeth as he pulls away.

"That's going to take some getting used to."

Lincoln grabs the base of my cock and performs a similar move so pleasurable my hips lift from the couch. His suction is stronger than Miller's, and fuck if this isn't going to be the shortest blow job of my life.

They take turns doing all the things Lincoln promised. Their hands are everywhere. Caresses to my thighs, abdomen, balls, every place imaginable, they touch me.

"Jesus fuck. Fuck. I'm going to fucking blow. Shit." Miller's hand tightens around my base, and he moves to the side, allowing Lincoln to take over. Lincoln sucks deep, hollowing his cheeks while his tongue caresses the sensitive spot under the head. Someone's hands roll my balls, and my body convulses. My abs constrict as my cock jerks in Lincoln's mouth. Come coats the inside of his mouth, and he swallows every drop.

Flopping back on the couch, I suck in gulps of air. I grab a handful of Lincoln's hair and pull him off me. He smiles up at me and swipes his thumb across his bottom lip.

Miller grabs the back of Lincoln's neck and pulls him in for a kiss. His tongue explores and tastes me in Lincoln's mouth, and again, I find myself being more turned on than put off like I think I should be.

My watch beeps, pulling my thoughts away from the hot makeout session between my legs. Time to get ready for work.

22

Spencer

The dynamic in my house has shifted—my very small house, which is never quiet, and I'm rarely alone.

There are times when I need solitude, and they understand when I take Gage into my bedroom and lock the door. A hot bath with Epsom salt and lavender relaxes me and helps calm the environment around me.

There has been no further sexual activity in my house. Well, none that has involved me. I wake up most mornings with Lincoln smashed to my body and Miller behind him. Every night they crawl into my bed makes me want to tell them to leave, but I know, come morning, when I awake from a dreamless night's sleep, I'm thankful. Something about not sleeping alone takes the nightmares away, and after years of little to no sleep at night, my body feels more relaxed and at ease than it has since my teenage years.

Axel is returning from work when we're leaving but on the nights he's off my threesome in bed becomes a tight foursome.

Tucker has never spent the night. He comes over mornings

or afternoons in between work. Running a successful club takes up a lot of his time. Of all the men, he's the most affectionate. He doesn't shy away from showing how he feels with small touches and caresses.

Katy has been here a few weeks and is thriving. I'm a bit nervous as Miller and I start our month of night shifts in a few days. With Justin still being out on leave, switching shifts wasn't an option, but I tried.

There have been no more appearances or sightings of Shane, but I won't be lulled into a false sense of security. I haven't lived my life on high alert all these years to let my guard down because there are more bodies here. The increased presence of people that are important in my life has heightened my awareness.

One of the most challenging conversations I've ever had, apart from telling my father about Shane, was telling Katy about him. We all sat down and discussed precautions. It was hard for me to give up part of myself, but everyone now knows the codes to get in and out of my house, as well as the location of all nine of my guns.

When I left Shane, I expected him to come after me. I didn't know if he thought he had killed me and left me for dead at the bottom of the stairs or just our unborn child.

I waited and held my breath. I saw him in every man who walked past me for the better part of a year. My fascination with guns came from my therapist, who told me to try and find a hobby. Collecting and maintaining firearms wasn't quite what she meant, but it was something that I had complete control over. There's no gray area, only black and white.

My father later told me he drove to my old house and

threatened Shane. I don't know what he told him, but I thought he had left me alone—at least until my father saw him parked down the road and I saw the pictures he left. He's been watching me. For a while. I had to warn Justin and Nicole as well since there were pictures that included them. Justin is aware of my past, and everyone is being extra vigilant.

Lincoln and Tucker have agreed to stay with Katy while Axel, Miller, and I are on night shifts. I trust them implicitly, but I'm still on edge. Night shifts have never bothered me, but I've also never had another human being to worry about while I'm not here.

"Little Miss. Katy is going to be fine." Tucker runs an understanding hand down my arm, and the goosebumps that appear aren't from discomfort.

"You've never spent a night here before. Are you sure this is something you want to commit to?" I'm still unsure where Tucker fits into this strange family we've created, but he seems unphased by everything happening.

"I'm here for you and Katy. You've got a cop and a country boy here to watch over her."

I explained to him our unique relationship with the feisty teenager and the trauma she went through. He fell easily into his role as another protector.

"Come here." Tucker pulls me into his chest, giving me a unique hug that is individual to him.

"You ready, Smithy?" Miller exits my room with a wet mop of hair, smelling clean and spicy from his body wash. He sees me in Tucker's arms and immediately understands what's happening. "Katy is in good hands. There's no need to worry."

"Yeah, *Mom*. I'll be fine." Mom. That's the one thing we didn't tell Katy about. She didn't need to know all of the traumatic details of my past—only ones that directly affect us now.

Tucker's hold increases around me when he feels my body stiffen from her innocent words.

"Back to your pre-calc, Katy." Lincoln, sitting next to her on the couch, attempts to redirect Katy's attention to their task. He seems to be a math wiz and enjoys helping her with homework.

"She meant nothing by it." Miller's warm body heats my back as he whispers in my ear. They envelop me in their joint embrace, radiating their strength. "It was just harmless teasing."

"I know. Thank you." I've never had anyone in my life so attuned with my emotions. Justin has always understood me more than anyone, but there were still things I kept masked away. I don't know what it is about these four men. Even on my best days, when I think I'm hiding a particular feeling or a bad memory, one of them sees it. They don't allow me to hide. I both love and hate it.

"I'm ready, Miller." With reluctance, both men let me go, and while I feel their absence, I feel their lingering strength more. "Lock the doors and arm the security system. Don't open the door for anyone. If someone knocks, they don't belong here. Everyone who needs it has the codes to get in. Gage's German commands are written on the note attached to the refrigerator." As I'm rambling, Lincoln joins us in the kitchen.

"Dream Girl, your feelings are valid, and we hear you. We will protect Katy at all costs, no matter what. I promise."

Lincoln rubs his thumbs across my cheeks and kisses my forehead. I know if Axel weren't already at work, he'd be right here in this mini-huddle with us.

Miller threads his fingers into mine and smiles.

"Okay. I've got the girl. Give me the kisses, and don't make us late." Miller leans toward Lincoln, making kissy lips. Shocking myself and him, I lean in and steal the kiss from him.

There's a moment of pause as he acclimates to lips he wasn't expecting. When he kisses me back, I realize how much I miss the connection between us. It's easy for me to compartmentalize my emotions when I need to, and I've done my best to contain the lust I have for these men.

I can't process everything they make me feel all at once without feeling overwhelmed. It's not them that overwhelms me. I won't even say it's the emotions themselves that do it. The magnitude at which I feel for them is what tries to overpower me.

"Dream Girl, are you going to let me say goodbye to my man before you steal him away for the night?" Miller laughs into my lips as he slows the kiss.

"That was unexpected, Smithy."

"Should I not do it again?" Miller grabs me around the waist and pulls me into him so I can feel the effect of our kiss against my stomach.

"You can kiss me anytime you want." His boyish grin lights up his face.

"Except right now because he's mine." Lincoln pulls Miller away and locks their lips together.

"Can I get a goodbye kiss like that, Little Miss?" I turn to see Tucker running his hand over his beard with anticipation in his eyes. He's older than the others by at least ten years. His hat usually hides the salt and pepper streaks along his temples, but as he's gotten more comfortable here, he's been hanging it up in the foyer when he comes in.

"I didn't offer. I took what I wanted."

"Ah, I see." Seconds later, I'm dipped back in a soul-shattering kiss that has my heartbeat whooshing through my ears. Tucker pulls me upright, and I sway in his arms from the quick movement. "Have a wonderful evening at work."

"Since we're taking what we want…" Once again, I'm pulled into a firm chest, and Lincoln's lips devour mine. My head spins from the lust engulfing the room.

"Is it too late to take back my love is love speech?!" Katy makes gagging sounds from her spot on the couch.

"Don't be a brat, Cupcake."

I arch a brow at Miller. "Cupcake?"

He shrugs. "She's obnoxiously sweet."

"Oh my GOD. Goodbyyyyyyyye." We all laugh at Katy's exasperation.

23

Lincoln

My mind wanders most of the night, thinking back to the kiss we all shared. I've caught Tuck a few times staring off and wondering if he's thinking the same. Katy went to bed early and I've been sitting in uncomfortable silence next to my brother for over an hour.

Tucker is a decade older than me. His mother married my father when I was fourteen. We didn't have much of a relationship at first because I was an asshole kid who didn't want to share his time with his father. He was a twenty-four year old college graduate making his way in the world and didn't want to waste his time playing nice to his stepbrother.

I'd like to say things got better as we got older, but we never had a great foundation for a relationship to develop. We saw even less of each other when he invested in a dive bar and turned it into Midnight Moonshine. He was busy running a business, and I graduated high school and joined the police academy.

I never told Miller about Tucker because he's extremely family oriented and I always felt less-than having a minimal relationship with Tucker. Despite the type of relationship we may or may not have, he's always called me his brother, never step.

Fuck. We shared Miller. Shared *my* boyfriend. I should have some kind of feeling about that, right? Something more than it was incredible, and I want to explore it more.

"I can smell your gears burning, Linc. What's up?" I must be in a real spiral for him to notice my overthinking.

"Where did you come from?"

He chuckles. "Well, you see. When two people love each other very much, they —"

"Fuck off." I push his shoulder, and he barely gives from the shove. "How did you weasel your way into Spencer's arms so easily? Miller and Axel have been throwing themselves at her for years. You swoop in at a moment of crisis and sweep her off her feet."

"And you?"

Me?

"What about me?"

"How long did you pine after her, little brother?" Longer than I'd care to admit. How I could want a woman from her voice alone is beyond me.

"I met her the same day you did."

"That's not what I asked." *Shit.* I thought I could deflect the question. If I admit the truth, I'll sound like a stalker. "How long?"

"Long enough." He turns and lifts his leg onto the couch to face me.

"How. Long? I don't understand why you're avoiding the question." I sink into the couch, hoping it will swallow me. Why is this so hard to admit? Is it him? He's always been so bold and confident. I've had to work on it for a long time. It helps that my voice is deep and automatically gives off an air of authority. "Linc."

Tucker puts a hand on my thigh to grab my attention, and it burns. His touch feels like it's pure fire. That's new.

"Unofficially for about three years."

"Explain."

I drop my gaze to my lap, trying to look like I'm thinking, but my eyes stare at his hand, which is now heating my entire body. Tucker's hand flexes and I have to bite my lip to stifle the moan that threatens to bubble out.

"I…" *Shit*. I shift on the couch to mirror his position, and he moves his hand away. Thank fuck. "I've been listening to her on the radio for years. When I was dispatching on light duty, I got to interact with her often while working. I've known *her* for a long time. I recognized her voice immediately in the coffee shop that morning. But then…"

"Then I kissed her first." I nod. "To answer your question, I didn't weasel my way anywhere. I saw something I wanted and took it. Did any of you ever shoot your shot?"

"No. At least not that I'm aware of." Why does that seem like such an easy answer? Just go for what you want.

"Well, that little brother"— he leans over and taps my cheek twice—"is the reason it took you so long to get the girl."

I grab his wrist, and his eyes flash from my hand to my eyes. I see his jaw twitch and wonder what he's thinking.

"Are you jealous? You can kiss me too if you want." The fact that I'm not turned off by that thought should be a red flag, right?

"I…"

He rubs a thumb along my jaw, and my eyes flutter shut. I

feel the couch dip, and the air around me heats.

"You need to learn to take what you want, Lincoln."

His lips are right in front of mine. I feel his breath fanning across me, and the urge to close the distance is strong.

"Miller." I pull away from his touch. When I open my eyes, he looks...proud?

"You're a good man, Lincoln. We may have shared your boyfriend, but he never gave permission to share you. He will."

His statement holds such confidence.

When my alarm goes off, I stretch and nearly fall off the couch. I've gotten used to sleeping in bed with Spencer, but I offered it to Tucker last night and made myself comfortable in the living room.

As I roll myself off the couch, my phone buzzes on the coffee table.

Spencer: How was the evening?

I told her what time I set my alarm for, and she waited an entire sixty seconds before texting me. I bet she's been on the edge of her seat for hours waiting to send that. She's nothing if not punctual.

Lincoln: Katy finished her homework, I slept on the couch and almost fell off, and Tucker almost kissed me. Or I almost kissed him. I'm not sure.

As soon as I hit send, my phone rings.

"I had a feeling I'd get a call, Dream Girl."

"Explain yourself." Oh. Not Spencer, and I'm clearly on speakerphone.

"Morning, Fireball. How's your shift?"

"Explain, Linc." His voice has an edge of annoyance. I scrub my hand down my face, barely awake for this conversation, but I started it, so I have to finish it.

"Nothing happened. We were discussing Spencer and talking about taking what we wanted. He asked me if I was jealous and told me I could kiss him."

"But you didn't?" His annoyed tone now sounds hopeful.

"I didn't." If there was any doubt in my mind about whether I had made the right decision, it's gone now. "*You* stopped me, Fireball."

"Lincoln?"

"Spencer? Where did Miller go?"

"I think you broke him. He's staring out the window with a weird grin on his face. We'll be home shortly."

Chuckling, I say goodbye and start my day.

Katy, Tucker, and I are sitting at the counter eating breakfast when Spencer and Miller come in. Spencer breathes a sigh of relief when she sees us, and my boyfriend charges right for me.

Miller spins me in my chair, grabs my cheeks, and kisses me with more passion and heat than is appropriate for the current occupants.

"I love you."

He-He loves me?

"Why?"

A sharp elbow hits my side. "That's a shit response,

brother."

Tucker is right. *Why*, isn't usually what you say in return when someone professes their love to you. I can't help it though. I'm in shock.

"Maybe you missed what I said." Miller's hand drifts to my chest, and he lays it over my heart. "I said, I love you, Lincoln Reed."

"Ugh. I'm going to finish getting ready for school. I think I prefer the making out to this sappy stuff." Katy's protesting huff makes us all laugh.

Tucker stands and grabs Spencer's hand. "Let's give them a moment, Little Miss." I hear Spencer's bedroom door close behind me and exhale a long breath.

"You love me?"

"I. Love. You. Not gonna lie. I'm a little confused about why you're questioning it, but I also don't want you to feel pressured to say it in return. I just couldn't hold it in any longer."

I reach my arms around his waist and pull him closer. "That was the reason for my why? Why now, randomly in front of everyone, after a night shift? Did something happen?"

His hand roams from my jaw to the back of my neck and into my hair.

"I'm going to pretend I'm not insulted. You think something had to happen for me to tell you how I've been feeling for a while? No, Lincoln. I've just been too chicken shit to share them."

"No. I know. I understand. It just came out of nowhere. God, Fireball. I've wanted to tell you, but I've been too worried I'd scare you off. I know all of this is new to you. Fuck. I love you too."

166

Miller smashes our lips together. The kiss starts heated and needy but quickly slows to sensual. The admission between us is almost a tangible feeling on our lips.

"Oh my gooooood. There's too much sucking face in this house."

Miller and I pull away and connect our foreheads as we laugh at the teenager complaining.

"Can we pa-lease go to school now, Lincoln?"

"Better get going before she combusts." Miller kisses my forehead and turns toward Spencer's door. "Spencer, the coast is clear."

Tucker exits the room, holding Spencer's hand. Her hair is wild and unbraided, and I'm beginning to realize it's something he does to her every chance he gets.

"Alright, Katy. Let's get going. I'm planning to stop by the store after work. Does anyone need or want anything? Axel, do you need any of your special hair products?" I'm tired of living out of a bag and want to pick up basic toiletries to keep here. It's been a few weeks, and I don't see us going anywhere anytime soon.

"No, dickhead. Do you need to pick yourself up some tampons?"

"Would you pick me up some conditioner? I'm running low. I can send you a picture of the specific brand. Katy, do you need any sanitary products? I'm not sure what you brought when you came."

Katy's brows crease. She stares at the floor, and I see her fingers twitch as if she's counting. Probably to figure out when her next cycle is due.

When she looks up, her eyes are shifty, and her features have an edge of panic. I imagine it's slightly nerve-racking as a teenager to ask a non-related male to buy you pads or tampons.

"Um. I'll pick something out while we're at the store." She hikes her book bag higher on her shoulder and walks to the door. "I'm ready."

24

Axel

I t was such a long night. I missed everyone coming and going this morning. I wanted to get home in time to see them off, but my relief was late.

As I'm pulling out of the parking lot, a text message pops up on my dashboard monitor.

Katy. I need to talk to you as soon as you're free.

Axel: Is everything okay?

Katy: I'm not sure, but you're the one I want to talk to.

Axel: After school?

Katy: Can you come by at lunchtime? 11:45?

Axel: I'll be there.

What could be so wrong that she can't or doesn't want to talk to Lincoln, who's right there in the building with her?

I huff and drop my head back on the seat as I wait for the traffic light to turn green. I guess I'm not getting much sleep today.

When I arrive home to Spencer's house, that we've all taken

over as ours, I notice something tucked under the windshield of her small SUV.

"Fuck." As I approach her vehicle I recognize the handwriting scrolled on the back of a picture. I spin around, looking at every dark and hidden corner of the yard. Is he still here somewhere, watching?

I quickly run to the front door. Using my body to hide the keypad, I get inside and close the door behind me, locking it.

My mind is in a tailspin as I rush to her room and fling open the door. No sooner do I spot her figure in bed, she's sitting up aiming a gun at my head, half braced over a body next to her. I forgot Miller was here and she wasn't alone.

"Oh shit." I thrust my hands in the air and step back, slamming into the door frame. "Spencer. It's Axel. I'm too pretty to die this young."

"Dammit, Axel." She drops her hand to the bed, and I lower my arms. I want to pretend their quivering is muscle fatigue from holding them in the air, but it's the spike of adrenaline coursing through me. I bend and brace myself on my knees, catching my breath.

"What's going on?" A groggy Miller sits up, assessing the situation. "Shit"

"I'm…sorry…Tails." My panting breath is labored. Maybe there was a touch of fear mixed with the adrenaline. I puff out a long breath and stand straight.

"What's wrong? Why did you barge in here like that? Are you just getting home?" Her gaze flicks to the door, trying to see what brought me into her room in such a frenzy.

"Wow. So many questions. Yes, I just got home. I barged in because I forgot you weren't here alone, and there's a picture on your windshield." Her fingers wrap tighter around the handle of her gun.

"Relax, Smithy. You're safe." Miller eases a hand from her elbow down to her fingers and she relaxes with an exhale.

"What is it? What is the picture of?" She pushes the blanket off and swings her legs to the floor. I'm momentarily transfixed by the length of her toned legs. Her biker shorts crept up in her sleep, exposing their entire length. She stands and pulls them down, and I'm probably about to drool when she snaps her fingers.

"Axel. Focus now. Gawk later."

Miller chuckles behind her, and I shoot him a glaring look.

"Sorry, Tails." I shake my head and give her my full attention. "I didn't touch it. I only saw the handwriting on the back. It says, DO YOU KNOW WHO I AM YET?"

"What an asinine remark. Of course, we know who he is." As simple as the word asinine is, she never curses and has twice in this conversation alone. "What time is it?" She lifts her cell phone and swipes her screen. "I have no unusual motion notifications. How did he get past my security?"

"This fucker is unreal. Let me grab the picture now that I know you're okay." I nod at Miller and stalk out of the house on a mission. This guy is getting bolder, and although it's just pictures right now, stalkers always escalate.

My mind is singularly focused on Spencer's windshield, and I miss the figure standing near her passenger door.

"Which one are you?" I whip around and see Spencer's father staring at me, eyes squinted, gun at his side. What is it with everyone around here having guns?

"I'm Axel, Sir. I'm the nurse." He may be retired, but he's just as intimidating with his high and tight haircut, which is more salt than pepper. His dark brown eyes assess me, and I can only imagine how someone felt on the opposite side of an interrogation table with him.

He grunts and tips his head toward Spencer's window. "Another one?"

"Yeah, the first since the big envelope." I pull it off and read over the message. It's written hastily in black marker.

He shakes his head and looks toward Spencer's door. "It's not. I've got half a dozen in my house. I've been grabbing them off before she sees."

What? "There's been more?" I flip the picture over, and I'm stunned. "Holy fuck." Mr. Hall snatches the picture from my hand.

"It's not the first like this either."

It's a similar picture to the previous one with the note, but this one is of Lincoln carrying Katy out of the alley by the school.

"He was there? Is he always watching her?" He opens his mouth to speak, and the door opens behind us.

"Axel, what's taking—Oh, hi Dad. What's going on out here?" Mr. Hall turns his back to Spencer and hides the picture.

"She already knows about it. I told her I saw it when I got here. I went right inside to check on her." He mumbles, "dammit," and turns back around.

"Let's go inside, Spencer. We have to talk." He walks toward the door when Miller appears behind Spencer. "You're the...not the normal partner. That's Justin. He just had another baby with the blonde. But I've seen you leave and come back with my daughter."

"I'm Miller, Mr. Hall." He extends his hand out, and Spencer's dad takes it.

"Eddie. Please, call me Eddie." I can tell there's a firm shake going on between them based on the colors their hands are turning.

"Dad." Spencer's warning tone lets everyone know she sees it, too. "I promise I keep good company. Miller is a firefighter and a paramedic filling in for Justin while he's on paternity leave." Their hands release, and we all walk inside.

Eddie's head is on a swivel as he takes in the room.

"You've done a lot to the place. It looks nice."

Has he not been here? I got the impression there were some troubles between them, but I didn't think it was this bad.

"Thank you, Dad. Have a seat, everyone." Spencer opens a cabinet and pulls out a bag of coffee and the filters. Coffee sounds amazing. My adrenaline is officially gone, and the lack of sleep from working all night is starting to get to me. If Katy didn't need to see me in a few hours, I'd be crashing until I have to work again tonight.

"Is the cop here?"

"Lincoln is at work, as is Tucker?" Spencer answers him without even turning around.

"I don't know Tucker. Is he the one who always dresses like a cowboy?" Miller laughs from across the room.

"Yes, Dad. Tucker owns a club. Midnight Moonshine. It's a country line-dancing bar."

The coffee pot begins to brew, and the smell makes my mouth water. I grab several mugs, the sugar container, and the milk and creamer from the refrigerator. I begin to make my mug sans coffee, and Miller eyes me with a puzzled look. The moment the hot, heavenly liquid is done, I'm finishing my cup.

"So which one are you dating, or are they all like your bodyguards or something? Can't say I'm upset that you and that child aren't ever here alone."

Miller and I look everywhere but in Eddie's direction. I have no clue where to even begin to answer that question. There hasn't been any talk of titles or relationships. There wasn't even talk about us basically moving in here. It just happened, and that was it.

"They are all my partners." She drops that sentence like saying the sky is blue. There's confidence and a matter-of-fact tone.

All my partners.

"All, huh? Well, you're a special girl, and it takes a special man, or sounds like men, to give you what you need. Now, let's talk about this asshole."

That's it? No grilling or arguing? No accusatory speeches about monogamy? It seems he's just going to let it go and move on to another topic. Alrighty then.

"I have a confession, and don't be mad at me, Spencer. I've been taking pictures off your car for a bit now. This isn't the first one." Spencer puts the pot of coffee on the island and looks at her dad. No, she's looking through him. I want to give them their moment, but every nerve in my body is begging me to grab the coffee pot and caffeinate my tired body.

Eddie sighs and looks away first, and *thank god*. Their trance is broken, and I eagerly reach for the pot to fill my cup, wishing I could IV the caffeine straight into my veins. I haven't even changed out of my scrubs yet or showered, and I'm feeling every inch of the grime and sickness of the Emergency Department that lingers with me.

"What are the pictures of?"

"All of you. Individuals of you all doing various things. This is the first one with a note, though. Well, other than the original one." Spencer nods as she listens and takes in all the information. Miller seems just as awake as I feel, and he nurses his coffee like a lifeline. All three of us were on night shift last night, and they couldn't have been asleep for long before I barged in. How Spencer looks so awake and alert is beyond my comprehension.

"Should we call the police? Other than Lincoln." No one has even mentioned contacting them at any time during all this.

"There's no point. They will protect their brothers in blue. It's why, despite any physical marks I ever had, I never reported him."

"Spencer..." Eddie says her name with so much emotion. It sounds like years of torment and sorrow.

"Detective, we've been over this time and time again. I don't blame you, and you shouldn't blame yourself either. It's in the past."

"And it's coming back to haunt you, dammit." He slams a fist on the counter and Spencer doesn't flinch. It's a testament to the trauma she's endured, and it cuts me in fucking two. No one should be that conditioned to not react. She lifts her coffee and takes a sip, ignoring her father's outburst. I want to wrap her up in my arms and hide her away from all of this, but that's not who she is. Spencer faces her problems head-on and with confidence.

"What do you propose?"

"I don't know." He sinks back in his seat, defeated. "I don't fucking know. Pictures aren't proof of anything. Have your cameras caught him?"

"Not that I know of. I'm not getting any strange notifications on my phone. He's somehow alluding my cameras and I don't like it." She takes another sip of her coffee, and I admire her tenacity.

"This is fucking ridiculous." Miller perks up from his outburst. "I thought we were on the good side. Why does a dirty cop get all of the privileges?"

"Because brothers in blue protect their own. Ask Lincoln; he'll tell you the same. It takes a lot for them to turn their backs on each other." Eddie sounds guilty again, and he glances at Spencer in his peripheral.

"So we just do nothing and let him taunt us until he escalates? And then what? It sounds like we're stuck with no solution." There has to be more that we can do. My exhaustion is turning to frustration.

"That's exactly what we're going to do. Nothing."

I can't help my jaw dropping at her statement. "But how? Why?" I don't understand.

"Because he wants a reaction. We have to keep living our lives and hope he gets bored."

"Are you kidding me, Tails? How far back do some of those pictures go? It's obvious he hasn't gotten bored yet, and now we've just given him more things to be interested in."

"Yes," she sighs. "Yes, I realize that too." Her index finger taps along her mug. She's beginning to feel overwhelmed or out of control, and I don't blame her.

I lock eyes with Miller and motion to Spencer's hand so he can see what I'm seeing.

"Hey, Tails, I need to take a shower. Would you like to join me?"

Before she can respond, her father stands.

"I don't want to impose any more than I already have. I'll be more vigilant at keeping watch on your house. I'll speak to the neighbors as well. He has to be coming in from the back or the side." He gives each of us a goodbye nod, and Spencer walks him out, locking the door behind him.

Miller meets her as she reenters the living room and pulls her into him. It's the type of hug we've seen Tucker give her when she's on the verge of falling apart.

"How about the three of us all take a shower, and you let Axel and I take care of you?"

That's the best idea Miller has ever had. He doesn't wait for an answer. He spins her toward her bedroom, which has a large stand-up shower, and guides her toward the doorway.

"You game, Axel?"

I don't need to be asked twice. I'm already stripping off my scrub top and undershirt and following.

I turn on the shower while Miller undresses himself and then Spencer. She's trusting and allowing us to take care of her, which I know is a weighty step for her. I undress and test the water temperature and signal to Miller that it's good. I step in first and extend my hand to her. Miller holds the small of her back as she joins me. There are shower heads on both sides of the walls, allowing us to all enjoy the hot water.

I pull Spencer into me, and she rests her head on my chest and closes her eyes. I can feel her body relaxing when Miller steps up behind her. We stand under the stream of water, cocooning her between us.

I can tell when she feels in control again. Her body radiates the confidence that we're used to seeing. Her mask is off, and she isn't hiding. Her body slides between us, and she lifts on her toes and pulls me down for a kiss. It's slow and sensual, and I can feel her appreciation in each stroke of her tongue.

"Tails, that's not why we're in here."

"I know. Just kissing." I won't say no to that.

"Smithy, can I wash your hair?" She nods against my mouth, and Miller reaches around us to grab the shampoo bottle. She sighs in contentment as his fingers massage her scalp. "How about you, Axel?"

I pull back from Spencer, tilting my head. "Me?"

"Can I wash your hair, too?" *Oh.*

"Um…" The mood in the room wants me to say yes, but I momentarily panic, thinking how my special hair products are in the other bathroom.

Don't ruin the moment, dumbass.

"That sounds nice." I spin Spencer so her back is to the stream, and as I tilt her head back to rinse her shampoo, Miller's fingers run through my curls. "Oh fuck."

I feel the air on my shoulder as he huffs. "Problem?" Miller's lips scale across the back of my neck, and I feel the heat from his mouth. It somehow burns hotter than the water.

"N-no. Your hands feel incredible. I've never had anyone but a hairdresser touch my hair." He kisses feather-light lips across my shoulder, occasionally sucking in my flesh. "Miller?"

"Shh. Just kissing. That's what Spencer said."

"Just kissing," I mumble through the pleasure of his massage.

We readjust in the shower so I can rinse my hair and Spencer can wash Miller's. We play this dance until everyone has been shampooed and conditioned, and by the time we're ready for soap, there are two very prominent extra members in the shower with us.

"You can't blame us for this, Tails. You're a temptress on a good day but wet and soapy and add in kissing; you're a fucking Goddess."

"I'm not complaining."

25

Miller

This morning is turning out completely different than I had planned. I told my boyfriend I loved him, and he reciprocated. I fell asleep with Spencer in my arms but was soon woken up by her covering my body with a gun in her hand.

I'm supposed to be protecting her so that was a small bruise to my ego. Although, I can't deny the heat that spread through my body when I saw that gun in her hand. So fucking sexy. Especially when I saw it was only Axel and not an actual intruder that caused her to draw her gun.

I can't say that I'm happy to learn that her ex is still sending her, or rather us, regular pictures, but we are here, and we aren't going anywhere.

Axel didn't have to point out that she was beginning to spiral. I noticed her body slowly tensing throughout the entire conversation. The mug tapping was the final straw. I didn't know what I wanted to do, but Axel identified how to fix the problem quicker than I did, and that's what makes us all a great team for our special girl.

I've been dying to get my hands on Axel's curls, and this was the perfect opportunity. As the three of us wash hair and trade kisses, there's nothing sexually charged behind our actions. Every move is for comfort. When Spencer melted between us, I felt powerful knowing I helped relax her. We all do. We're slowly becoming her safe space, and the more she relies on us, the more burden we can take from her, for her.

"You can't blame us for this, Tails. You're a temptress on a good day but wet and soapy, and add in kissing, you're a fucking Goddess." Axel's assessment is spot on as I maneuver my hips to not smack her in the stomach with my erection.

"I'm not complaining." She runs a soapy hand down our chests, over our abs, and down to our protruding lengths.

"Smithy," I warn. "Only kissing, remember. We aren't here to play." There's zero conviction behind my words as her soapy hand glides over my cock, and it twitches.

"Fuck, Tails. Don't tease me. I'm already struggling to hold it together." I watch her hand squeeze him from root to tip, and the head around his jewelry turns an enticing shade of purple at her pressure.

"You made me feel better; now let me make you feel better."

Who the fuck is going to say no to that.

"It's really okay, you don't have to—" I'm silenced by Axel as he grabs the back of my neck and kisses me.

I don't hesitate and kiss him back. Spencer makes room for us to get closer without releasing our cocks. In fact, I'm pretty sure her hand tightens, and the groan that melts into my mouth from Axel leads me to believe she's doing the same to him.

"It's so sexy when I see any of you kiss. I like knowing you enjoy each other the way you enjoy me."

"We like to enjoy you too." I reach a hand up and start at her hip, slowly drawing a line up her midsection. When I reach the bottom of her breasts, I swirl my fingers around but don't touch her nipple where I can tell her body is aching to be played with. Stiff peaks brush against my arms, and I want to take them in my mouth and worship her, but she steps away from my hand before I can move any higher.

"It's not my time right now, it's yours."

Axel's mouth moves down my jaw to my neck, and I lean into Spencer and kiss her. She matches the rhythm of her tongue with her hand, and I know I won't last long.

"Fucking shit, Tails. Your hands are goddamn magic. I'm so fucking close."

I guess I'm not the only one.

"Are you boys going to come for me?" I pull back and look at the vixen in front of me. She's never talked dirty before, and I fucking love it.

"We certainly fucking are." I smash my lips back to hers and take over the kiss. I place my hands over both of hers and help bring Axel and me to orgasm. It only takes a few strokes, and I come, followed by Axel.

Unintelligible curses pour from our mouths as we coat our hands and stomachs with our joint releases. The stress I didn't know I was holding melts away as the last bursts of my orgasm leaves me.

My lust takes over, and I push Spencer up against the wall. She inhales sharply as her back presses against the cold tile. My mouth is on her neck, nipping and licking away the water droplets that fall from her hair. I cup the underside of her breast, fingers twitching to feel the weight of them in my palms, and she covers my hand.

"Miller. This was about you. I'm alright. Let's get out and get some sleep." I drop my forehead to her shoulder and groan. She's so fucking selfless. Axel chuckles behind me and smacks my ass.

"Come on, big guy, listen to our lady."

"I don't wanna," I whine in my most childlike voice, making us all laugh. "Fiiiiiine." I press one last kiss to her lips, and as we step out of the shower, I smack Axel's ass in retaliation.

I hear a low buzzing on the nightstand and peer behind me. Axel's phone alarm chimes and a glance at the time shows me it's only eleven. We've barely been asleep, why does he have such an early alarm?

Doing my best not to disturb Spencer, I shake Axel's arm, and he pops open one eye.

"Your alarm is going off."

"Shit." He rolls to his back and scrubs a hand over his face. He groans as he lifts onto his elbows and looks at the time.

"What's up?" He doesn't look happy to be awake.

"Katy asked me to meet her for lunch. I got the feeling something is wrong. I can't bail on her."

Shit. Why wouldn't she talk to Lincoln? He's right there in the school with her.

"Need some backup?"

He looks down at the sleeping beauty between us then back at me. "I don't want to leave her alone if we don't have to."

I understand his apprehension. I feel the same way, but I know if push comes to shove, she has enough of an arsenal here to protect herself. If Katy is in trouble, she's our responsibility, and we have to do everything in our power to protect her.

"I'll text Tuck, and we'll let her dad know before we leave." He thinks for another moment, his eyes roaming over Spencer's sleeping form. I understand what he's feeling. We've wanted her for so long, and the thought of anything happening to her is scary as fuck. She's ours, finally. She called us her partners, and while I don't know exactly what the extent of that means to her, it's enough of a title for me. She's mine, and I'm hers. And I guess the other merry band of dickheads that are under this roof all belong to each other now too.

"Okay." He runs a hand through his hair and freezes. It's a sight to see. His curls stick up at every angle. I stifle a laugh because I've never seen his hair so unruly before.

"Don't laugh at me, asshole. You washed my hair without my special products, and then I laid down with wet hair. It's definitely a ball cap day."

We carefully untangle ourselves from Spencer, although if I know her as well as I think I do, she's not actually sleeping. She trusts us with Katy and respects her enough that if she came to Axel specifically, she'll let him deal with it.

"So what's up? Why are we going to have lunch with Katy?" He hasn't given me any information, and this entire thing puts me on edge. I don't like to keep secrets from Lincoln. We base our relationship on trust and honesty. And to be honest, I'd like whatever this is going on between all of us to be the same.

"She didn't tell me. Just said I was the one she wanted to talk to."

"Should I text Lincoln?" I watch his shoulders fall.

"I've been wondering the same thing. But Katy reached out to me for a reason. I'm taking a leap bringing you along. Let's not push our luck too much further."

"Okay." I understand, but that doesn't mean I have to like it.

Axel hands me his phone as we pull up to the school at 11:40 and tells me to text her that we're here. A few minutes later, Katy walks out and pauses when she sees me standing outside his truck. Her head dips lower, and she shrugs her book bag further up her shoulder before continuing toward us.

"Hey, Cupcake." I pull her in for a hug. "I hope you don't mind me crashing your lunch date with this ugly mug." I shoot a thumb over my shoulder and feel her laugh. "You have us a little worried."

"Yeah, sorry about that." She gives me a guilty look as I take her book bag and motion for her to get in the passenger seat. Axel leans over and hugs her as I climb in the back.

"Okay, Katy girl, you got me here. What's going on?" She glances over her shoulder at the school and back at Axel.

"Could we go somewhere, anywhere else?" Now I'm worried. Is something going on at school? With Lincoln? Fuck no. Not him. Everyone in our house is good.

"Sure." Axel puts the truck in drive and heads to a strip mall down the street. Axel parks his truck and turns to face Katy. "Spill it, girl. Your lunch is only thirty-five minutes."

Her shoulders tremble, and I reach around the seat to place a soothing hand on her arm.

"Whatever it is, we'll figure it out or fix it." My words don't seem to help her feel any better. "Do you want us to call

Spencer?"

"No. God, no." She looks at me with sheer panic in her eyes. "She'll be so disappointed if…" She stares at her hands as she picks her cuticles.

Axel leans over the seat so his face is even with hers. With his index finger, he tips her chin up so she's looking at him.

"If what? What is it, Katy?" The concern in his voice mirrors my feelings.

She turns her head and looks out the passenger window. Her dark hair is pulled up in a ponytail, and she has a black bow tied at the top. It makes her look younger than her sixteen years, and I mourn the loss of her childhood with the life she's already lived. I vow right here and now to myself that we will give her the best life she could possibly have.

She shocks us both by opening the door and jumping out of the truck. Axel and I scramble to catch up with her as she walks toward the stores. In the area she's heading, there's an ice cream shop, a hairdresser, and a pharmacy. Does she want ice cream?

"Where are we going, Katy?" She ignores me and beelines toward the pharmacy. Axel and I exchange a confused look but diligently follow as the automatic doors open, and she walks in with a purpose.

We watch in silence as she looks up at the signs hanging from the ceiling, telling her which aisle products are located. When she makes her decision, she picks the row she needs and walks toward the back of the store. As we file behind her, I can see her steps becoming heavier.

Axel and I exchange another look. The aisle we're approaching has condoms, personal items, pads, and tampons. She told Lincoln this morning that she'd pick out what she needed when she went shopping with him later. What would make her ask Axel to come for lunch? She didn't even ask us to bring her here; it's just where we ended up.

"Katy?" I soften my voice still not understanding why we're here and hoping she'll give us an explanation soon.

She ignores me.

She slows down when we reach the tampons but doesn't stop. When she does, I'm confused. Axel grabs my forearm and squeezes. I try not to wince at the force of his grip but don't question it. He must realize something I don't.

"Katy?" When she looks at him, her eyes are glazed over with unshed tears. "Are you late?"

Late? She nods, and tears stream down her face as I realize we've stopped in front of the pregnancy tests.

"Fuck." I pull her into my chest as she sobs. "Axel, grab what we need, and let's take her home. I'll text Linc."

I walk Katy out to Axel's truck, and a few minutes later, we're on our way to Spencer's house with me in the backseat and Katy silently crying into my chest.

26

Tucker

Miller: Axel and I need to run an errand. If you are able, can you swing by the house and stay with Spencer so she isn't alone?

Tucker: Of course. Be there soon.

I had been gone for barely three hours when the text came in, and within thirty minutes, I was letting myself in the front door and crawling into bed next to my queen. Her hair was damp, and she smelt freshly showered as she curled into me.

I've barely dozed off when I hear the front door open. A soft knock taps on the door, and Axel's head peeks around. They all worked the night shift, and it's barely lunchtime. I know they have to be exhausted.

He gives me a weary smile and tilts his head toward Spencer's sleeping form. "We need her out here. Can you wake her?"

"What's going on? Is everyone okay?" I can't imagine what's happened in the few hours since I left this morning.

"They will be. Katy...needs Spencer." He gives me a half

smile and closes the door.

Brushing a gentle finger across Spencer's cheek, I kiss her forehead and whisper, "Little Miss, I need you to wake up." Her body sighs, and I have a feeling she heard the entire exchange between Axel and me.

"I'm not going to get any sleep today, am I?" I'm not sure what she's talking about, but it only adds to the guilt I was already feeling for having to wake her so soon.

"Axel said Katy needs you."

"Katy?" Maybe she wasn't awake. Spencer rolls and looks at the time, then her bedroom door. "Isn't she in school?"

"I have no idea. Axel just poked his head in and said to wake you and that Katy needs you."

"Wait. Why are *you* here and not them? Why isn't Katy in school? What's going on?" She's coming apart with all the unknown. I pull her into a bear hug and relay the information I know.

"Miller texted me and said he had an errand to run with Axel. They asked me to come stay with you so you weren't alone. That's everything I know. Take a few breaths for me, and then we can go out there together and see what's going on." Her chest expands against mine, and I loosen my grip and inhale with her. When she exhales, I do. We repeat the breathing two more times before she relaxes in my arms.

"Okay. I'm ready."

"Good Girl." I kiss the top of her head, and we climb out, getting ourselves appropriately dressed before we see what's waiting for us on the other side of the door.

I link my hand with hers before we enter the living room, and Miller is sitting on the couch with an inconsolable Katy. He looks weary at his inability to console her.

Spencer releases my hand and drops to the floor in front of Katy. I lock eyes with Miller, trying to read anything about the current situation, but there's nothing. His gaze is vacant.

Spencer takes Katy's hand, and she flings herself into her arms. I hear muffled "I'm sorrys" through her tears, but I still don't see a reason for all her emotions.

"Katy." Spencer pulls her away by the shoulders and dips her head down to try and catch Katy's attention.

"I fucked up. I'm so sorry. I don't want to go back. Please don't send me back to her. I l-love it here. You're all so incredible to m-me. Shit. I'm sorry. This is all so messed up. P-please don't hate me." Her shoulders shake from the force of her sobs, and Spencer pulls her back into a hug.

Spencer's eyes dart between Miller and Axel, and she mouths, "What's going on?" The tension in the room is thick. Katy's crying becomes so intense she's hiccuping. Axel crouches down next to them and rubs her back.

"Tell Spencer. Don't be afraid, Katy girl."

After a few deep breaths and sniffles, Katy pulls back. She's still staring at the floor when her tiny voice whispers to Axel. "Show her." Axel looks at Miller, who nods in agreement. He bends over and takes something off the side table next to the couch.

Axel doesn't try to hide the pregnancy test as he hands it to Spencer. She takes it, and I instantly see the wall come up. Her mask is on. Why?

"I need a moment." Spencer places the test on the table and untangles herself from Katy's grip. Despite the pleas and apologies Katy is crying to get Spencer to stay, she isn't here. Spencer has mentally checked out. When the bedroom door shuts, Katy collapses. Miller scoops her back into his arms on the couch and attempts to console her.

"What the hell just happened, Axel?" I try to keep my voice low so the conversation stays between him and me.

"Katy is pregnant."

"I figured that much out. Why did Spencer just close off and disappear?" He sighs and the look he gives me is thick with sadness.

"Spencer deals with her emotions differently than others. She said she needed a moment so we're giving her a moment."

"Fine. I'll go talk to her myself." I can't believe they let her walk off without going after her.

Axel grips my forearm with such force that I wince. "I suggest you release me, Axel."

"And I suggest you walk in there with the gentlest of fucking kid gloves, and don't force her to say anything she doesn't want to. You're here because she feels a connection with you, but we've known her for years. Don't fuck things up."

I grab the wrist holding my forearm, and look Axel square in the eyes. "I respect you for that warning, but as I said before, shoot me dead if I ever hurt her. And that means mentally as well as physically." He releases my arm, and I release his wrist.

When I approach Spencer's door, I knock lightly and walk in. I don't want to give her the opportunity to reject me. She's sitting on her floor with Gage at her side, emptying her magazine bullet by bullet and replacing them. Her guns are her safe place.

"May I approach you, Little Miss?" Entering the room is one thing, but invading her space when she has a gun and a very protective dog is another.

She pats Gage's head and whispers a command in his ear. He rises, moves to the corner of the room, and lies in his dog bed. I take that as an answer to my question and join her on the floor.

"You got another one of those for me?" She reaches into her nightstand drawer and pulls out an identical Glock to the one in her hand. We empty and refill the magazines a few times before she pauses and looks at me.

"Have they told you anything about my diagnosis?"

"No ma'am, and even if they tried, I wouldn't have allowed them to continue. Your past is your story to share, and I'm ready to listen whenever you're ready." She slumps back against the mattress and tells me her past about a brave young girl and her lifelong struggles. How she's adapted and overcome them to become the woman I'm more than proud to call mine now.

"Does Katy know your story?"

"Some, not all, and I'm sure she's out there thinking the worst of me right now because I abandoned her, but...I needed backup that none of you could understand right now."

"Lincoln?" He's the only one not here of the four of us.

"No." She sits up and begins reassembling her gun. "My best friend, Justin. Katy has a special place in his heart, and I need him to help us navigate this."

I've heard of Justin, but we haven't met. I know he's her usual partner, and Miller is a firefighter.

"Is he on his way?" She nods and checks her watch.

"Any minute." She must have gotten a notification because the front door opens, and I hear Katy gasp and screech Justin's name.

Spencer stands next to me and offers her hand to help me

up. I chuckle and take it but stand on my own. I pull her into me as the sound of commotion starts in the living room.

27

Justin

I finally feel like I'm getting the hang of life with two littles. Hannah has settled back into her routine, and Miles is getting more on a daytime schedule rather than being up half the night.

Spencer: I have a Katy situation, and we need you.

Well, fuck. Spencer wouldn't reach out if it wasn't urgent. I stand up from the couch with a sleeping Miles on my chest. Walking to his room, I flag down Nicole, who's playing with Hannah on the floor. Once I lay Miles down in his bassinet, I show Nicole the text from Spencer.

"Go." She encourages me without question.

"Are you sure, Pumpkin?"

"Yes, I'm positive. I'll call Cole and see if anyone wants to hang out. If Spencer texted you, it's urgent. Go. We'll be fine." She kisses my cheek and pulls out her phone, typing a text while sitting back on the floor next to Hannah.

Justin: On my way.

I kiss Hannah and Nicole again before I leave. When I arrive at Spencer's house, I notice all the vehicles in the driveway and wonder even more what the problem could be. Miller and Axel are here, and another truck I don't recognize, but she's very much not alone inside.

I let myself in and find Axel pacing and Katy sobbing into Miller's chest on the couch. I don't see Spencer anywhere.

Katy gasps when she sees me and screeches my name, burying herself further into Miller. I charge into the room, and Axel stops me with a hand to my chest.

"Why are you here, Justin?" Who the hell is he to question why I'm at my best friend's house? And Katy, the teenager whom I consider my savior, is crying her eyes out, and I need to know why. Right. Now.

"Spencer told me to come. Where is she, and what's going on?" I don't mean to raise my voice, but my mind is everywhere now, trying to determine why everyone has such high emotions.

"I'm right here, Justin." Spencer walks out of her room, followed by a man older than us with a beard and slightly longer hair tucked behind his ears. It's Tucker, the cowboy she kissed at the coffee shop.

Spencer raises her hand for me to come and I gladly accept. Stepping up to her, I pull her into a hug, and she whispers into my ear. "We have a situation."

"I'm here to help, whatever it is."

She pulls away and looks around. "Can we have the room with Katy?"

"We'll go wait outside to let you have your privacy, Little

Miss." Cowboy kisses her on the top of her head and offers me his hand.

"Tucker. Can I assume you're Justin?"

I take his hand and appreciate the firm shake. "I am."

"Well, Justin, thank you for taking care of our girls until they found us. I promise we will take good care of them for you." He claps my shoulder and nods toward Axel.

When Miller tries to stand, Katy clings to him harder. She's afraid of something, and the hairs on the back of my neck rise. There shouldn't be a reason for her to be afraid of anyone in this room.

"Katy, please relax." Miller smooths a hand over her ponytail that's barely hanging on. She's a disheveled mess, and my anxiety is creeping up. "It's Justin and Spencer. It will be okay. We'll be right outside."

"O-okay," Katy hiccups out. She releases her grip on his shirt, and he slowly stands.

"Go easy on her." What the fuck is going on. I'd do anything for the two women in this room. Just as much as I'd do for Nicole or Hannah.

Katy curls herself into the smallest ball possible. Her knees hiked up to her chin, and her arms wrapped tightly around her legs, holding herself together.

"Katy?" I sit next to her on the couch and rest a hand on her knees.

Muffled by her legs, I barely understand her when she speaks. "I'm sorry. I'm so, so sorry. I can't do this alone. Please help me. Please don't abandon me."

"Katy, I don't know what's going on. No one's told me anything but I'd never abandon you. Ever."

"Oh god." This I hear clearly as she pops her head out and

196

stares at me. She turns to Spencer, shocked. "You didn't tell him?"

"It's not my news to tell." Spencer reaches around and twines her hand through Katy's. "I'm sorry I left earlier. Please know it was my own demons that I had to deal with before I could help you."

My confusion is turning to annoyance the longer I'm left in the dark. Spencer walked away from Katy? Is that why she was hysterical when I came in?

"Can someone please fill me in on what everyone is so upset about? I can't help unless I know what I'm working with."

Katy's gaze drifts to Spencer, who nods, giving her the strength to speak. Katy releases her fingers and drops her legs off the couch. Her chest rises as she inhales a deep breath, gathering her courage to tell me what's going on.

"I'm... I'm...pregnant." She whispers the last word, but I hear her loud and clear. She's pregnant.

"From—"

"Yes."

I grab her cheeks more forcefully than I mean to and quickly apologize. My adrenaline at her confession got the best of me, but I need her to hear me loud and clear.

"Katy. Spencer and I are here for you. There were no conditions put on our offer when your piece of shit mother signed you over to us. You're ours, and we are here for you. We'll take care of you. I owe you the debt of my life, and I'll never forget that. What do you need from us?"

She melts into me, and I wrap her in my arms. Spencer rubs her back, and we share a long, silent conversation over Katy's shoulder.

Half this baby belongs to her rapist. Whatever avenue she chooses, we will be here for Katy every step of the way. There's no other choice for either of us. If I know Miller, Axel, and Lincoln as well as I think, they will be onboard as well. And as little to nothing that I know about Tucker, if Spencer is letting him be around with everyone else here, she must trust him with the same.

"What would you like to do?" Spencer asks the question that's weighing heavy in the room.

"I-I can't..."

"Katy, if you listen to nothing else I ever say, I want you to listen to this right now." She turns to face Spencer and wipes at the wetness on her face. "In this house, we believe in choice. *Everyone* who has stepped foot in this house over the last several weeks believes in choice." Spencer rests her hand on Katy's stomach. "If the end of your 'I can't' sentence is you can't keep it, we'll find a doctor to take care of it for you. If the end is I can't get rid of it, we'll find you the best obstetric doctor. You're safe here. You always will be. It's your body and your choice, and although the initial choice was taken away from you, it's all yours now."

I've never been more proud of Spencer. I've seen so many changes in her since Katy moved in. They're good for each other. I know things can't be easy for her with the guys always being here, but if she wanted them gone, they would be.

I agree with everything Spencer just said. Katy doesn't deserve to be in this situation, but every decision she makes from here on out is hers. There's power in choice, and I hope this can give Katy some of her power back.

"It's also your choice when you decide." I reach out and

grab Katy's hand. "There's plenty of time if you want to think and weigh your options. Either decision is a big one, and we'll help you every step of the way."

"But how can I? I have nothing."

"Katy." She jumps at Spencer's curt tone, and if I'm being honest, I do too. "You have four men that"—she sighs—"live in this house because of you." I do my best to stifle a laugh, but I fail, and Spencer glares at me. "You have that fool next to you, and you have me. You have *all of us*. Justin's lawyer is working on guardianship, emancipation, adoption, whatever it is, we need to make it official that you never have to go back to that good-for-nothing woman that birthed you."

Katy's eyes widen in shock, and her head swivels back and forth between us.

"Adoption? I didn't know that was an option." She puts a hand over her stomach, and I think she misunderstood what Spencer was referring to.

"Not your baby, Katy. You. Although adoption for your baby is also a choice you have."

"Me? Adopt *me?*" She's processing the information we just gave her.

"Yes, Katy, you. Remember, you don't have to decide anything right now." Her head absently bobs. "I have an idea. Want to come hang out at my house for a couple days? Miles might help you make a decision." I bump her shoulder to try and lighten the mood, and I see her lip twitch. "You can talk to Nicole about what pregnancy was like."

I see Spencer stiffen at my last sentence, and I reach behind the couch and rub her shoulder. She closes her eyes for a second and nods at me when she opens them. She understands I didn't mean anything negative toward her or her experiences.

"Um. Is that-can I, Spencer?"

"Of course you can. Do you want to wait until Lincoln gets back, or would you like us to talk to him?"

Shit. I know the bond she shares with all these men, but Lincoln, in particular, seems to have a special place in Katy's life.

"I should tell him. Can someone take me after he gets home?" She doesn't seem confident in her decision, but it's the right one.

"Katy, you come over whenever you get everything settled here. Should we have mac n cheese for dinner?" Her face lights up, and so does my heart. I kiss her forehead, not needing an answer to my question, and stand. "I'll send the calvary back in. I can hear them pacing outside."

"I'll walk you out, Justin." Spencer rubs Katy's arm. "We'll be right back."

Spencer follows me outside. Miller, Tucker, and Axel see us and immediately start to talk at once. She raises a hand, and they stop.

Very interesting. She holds a lot of power over them.

"Katy is fine. She's trying to decide what she wants to do. She knows it's her choice, and *we* will support her, whatever her decision is." Her words dare any of them to object, but they won't. Everything we said to Katy was the truth. "Go spend some time with her. Once Lincoln gets home and she explains everything to him, Katy is going to go hang out at Justin's for a bit. She can talk to Nicole and see what it's like being around a newborn."

As they file past Spencer, they all kiss her. Forehead from Miller, nose from Axel, and Tucker goes in for a passionate kiss on her lips.

"You're incredible, Little Miss." She blushes as he walks inside.

"Damn, Spence. I might be jealous if I didn't have a woman that meets and exceeds my every need."

"Jealous of four penises?" She gives me a knowing look, and I try to keep a straight face but concede way too quickly.

"Well, when you put it that way...no thanks."

"How is everything going with the lawyer? I didn't mean to say anything that would get her hopes up if it's not possible."

"It's all a possibility. It's just a matter of what avenue we want to take and what her mother is going to sign for. Best case scenario, she signs Katy's rights away, and we can proceed with adoption."

"Pay her whatever she wants. I'm good for it." At least we agree on that.

"My lawyers are taking care of everything. She has to do it willingly, and we need to stay above board so she doesn't contest it later. And you know I'd never take your money."

"Justin, who?" A woman of little words and lots of meaning. Who is going to adopt Katy?

"Nicole and I have talked about it. We would happily take her into our home. We already love her like our own, but we think she would be better with you." Shock is not an emotion I see often on Spencer, but that's exactly the face she's wearing right now.

"Why me over you? You're already parents. You are more experienced than I am to handle her." I chuckle as I give her a sideways look.

"I have a two year old and a newborn. Katy is sixteen. And think about it, if she keeps the baby, you'd be the hottest grandma?"

"Goodbye, Justin. Someone will bring Katy over this evening."

"What? Too far?" She turns toward the door, ignoring my joking. "Wait, can I ask one question?" She pauses and turns back to me. I smile as she glares. "What's going on in this brothel of yours?"

"I wish I knew."

28

Lincoln

One more hour. I have no idea what's going on, but Katy wasn't at lunch. I worried when I didn't see her. It brought me back to picking her up in the alley, and I've been on edge. When Miller texted me to say he was taking Katy home without further explanation, I wanted to get in my truck and leave.

I chose to be responsible. I stayed, knowing she's in good hands. I've missed several days of work already and want to remain in good standing here. That doesn't mean I'm enjoying my decision.

Lincoln: Please tell me everyone is okay? I'm on the verge of panic over here.

I look at my phone for the hundredth time, and still, no one in the group chat has answered. Something must be wrong.

"Dammit. Why won't anyone answer me?"

"Officer Reed? Is everything okay?" *Shit.* I spin around to see Meghan, a Junior who I know from seeing her interactions with Katy, looking at me with concern behind her green eyes. It's the middle of eighth period, and everyone should be in class.

"Hi, Meghan. Shouldn't you be in class?" Her long, strawberry-blonde hair sways as she holds up a piece of paper—a bathroom pass. That makes sense.

"Officer Reed. Is Katy okay? She didn't come back after lunch. She was acting strange this morning, and I know she usually carpools with you."

"Strange how?" I didn't notice anything on the ride in this morning. Did something happen once she got to school?

"Um, well. She looked really distracted and kept staring off in class." Meghan and Katy have Art and Science together, two of Katy's favorite subjects. She wouldn't be wandering off unless something was on her mind.

"Did she say anything to you?" I need information, and apparently, I'm desperate enough to try and get any scrap possible, even from the petite sixteen year old in front of me.

"No. Katy mentioned she wouldn't be at lunch, but nothing more than that."

Fuck. I squeeze the phone in my hand, willing any of the other five people attached to the text I sent to respond.

"Thank you, Meghan. Finish up and get back to class before we both get in trouble. I'm sure Katy is fine. She went home after lunch." I fake a smile, and she returns it.

I continue down the hall and walk into a janitor's closet. I'm calling everyone until someone picks up the phone.

"Hey, Linc—"

"Dammit, Fireball. Don't 'Hey, Linc' me. What's going on? I'm in panic mode over here, hiding in a closet, making calls in the middle of my work day because no one could pick up the phone and answer a simple text. What's going on? What's wrong with Katy?" He sighs. There's so much behind the sound, and I know he won't give me any information.

"I'm sorry. There's been a lot going on. Katy needs to talk to you when you get home."

"Miller, what's going on?"

"It's not mine to tell. She's waiting for you when you get here." I need *something*. This is pure torture.

"Please just tell me she's okay." I bang my head against the closed door and silently beg him for information.

"She's not in any danger. She's here waiting." That will have to be good enough to get me through the next forty-five minutes.

"Okay. I mean, it's not, but okay. I'll be home in an hour."

"We'll see you soon." There's silence, but he didn't say goodbye. I pull the phone away and see we're still connected.

"Miller?"

"I love you." Ah, now I understand the pause. His confession this morning is new for both of us and will take some getting used to.

"I love you, too, Fireball. See you soon."

Fucking high school boys. I got stuck for an extra hour at work because some seventeen year old boy got caught kissing a girl that wasn't his girlfriend, and she slapped him. I had to wait for their parents to show up, making me leave later than usual.

As I pull up to the house, Spencer opens the door. An instant feeling of calm washes over me as I look at my Dream

Girl. She looks tired but beautiful. Her usual braids are in, but they're loose like she threw her hair up haphazardly. Black cropped leggings and a tight pale pink top cover a body I'm dying to worship.

She's standing at my door when I step out of my truck, and I don't have an ounce of restraint. I grab her waist and push her against Tucker's truck next to us. My hand is on her neck, and my lips on hers before I even register I'm doing it. She kisses me back with all the passion I'm giving her.

I pull away from the kiss and rest my forehead on her shoulder. "Fuck, you're perfect."

"That was unexpected."

"Sorry, Dream Girl. I'm a little stressed not knowing what I'm about to walk in on." I pull back and search her face for any information. It's pointless because her face is blank. She's not quite masking, but…shielding, maybe. She's giving nothing away.

"Please go in there with an open mind. You're the last one Katy needs to talk to, and next to Justin and myself, you're the one she's most nervous to tell."

"Justin? He knows what's going on? Spencer?"

"Go talk to her, Lincoln."

I stare at the door for a long moment before my feet move. I open it and allow Spencer to walk in first. When I step in behind her, I see Katy's suitcase waiting next to the door, and my panic is back in full force.

"What's this all about? Where are you going, Katy?" My tone is more forceful than I expect, but my adrenaline pumps at the thought that she's about to tell me she's leaving us. It may have only been a few weeks, but Katy and I bonded that day in the alley, and I plan on being a part of her life for as long as she lets me.

Katy stands from the couch, not quite understanding my outburst. As I take long steps to reach her, Miller steps in front of me, but I don't take my eyes off Katy, whose brows are furrowing at me.

"Calm down. She isn't *going* anywhere but to hang out with Justin and Nicole for a few days." I exhale and look at Miller, giving him a sweet smile.

"Hi, Fireball. I missed you." I lean in and kiss him tenderly, feeling him smile into our kiss.

"Can we talk, Lincoln?" Katy's voice drips with apprehension, and I hate that I may have caused it.

"Go talk to her," Miller whispers into my lips.

"Hey, kiddo. Want to go for a walk around the pool?" She looks to her left, and a silent question passes between her and Spencer. They nod at each other, and she turns back to me.

"Sure."

Miller squeezes my hand. "Listen to her."

A feeling of dread sinks heavily in my stomach as I follow Katy out the front door. I have no idea what she's about to tell me, but I don't like the way anyone is acting. She looks like she's been crying. The holey jeans and v-neck yellow T-shirt she left the house in this morning have been replaced with loose cotton shorts, and a shirt that I'm pretty sure belongs to one of us guys by the way she's swimming in it.

Katy stops halfway around the pool and steps in front of me. She nervously tucks a lock of hair behind her ear, opens her mouth to speak, but closes it again.

"Katy, nothing you say will change anything between us. You're safe here. You're safe with me." She sighs, and as she

207

sucks in the next breath, it's broken as tears begin to fall down her cheeks. I pull her into me and rub her back, trying to comfort her.

"Lincoln... I'm pregnant." *Oh god.*

"Oh, Katy, I'm so sorry." I hug her tighter trying to hold us both together.

"I-I think I want to keep it. I'm not sure. I'm going to go spend some time with Miles and Nicole and see what it would be like." Now I understand why she's leaving for Justin's.

"That sounds like a perfect idea to start with. You know that no matter what decision you make, it changes nothing for any of us, right? We're here for you." I hope I never make her feel any other way. Spencer said she was nervous to tell me. She must feel the bond like I do.

"I do. I didn't at first. I begged Justin and Spencer not to send me back to my witch of a mother. I feel like such a failure."

No. I grab her shoulders and pull her away from me.

"You have failed at *nothing*. It's so brave that you told us as soon as you figured it out. You're the bravest person I know, next to Spencer. Has she told you any more of her story?" Katy shakes her head, and I pull her back into me. "She will. When she's ready. Let's get you to Justin and Nicole's. Sounds like you have some babysitting to do."

29

Spencer

I need…I have no idea, and that feeling alone is unsettling. I'm tired but wide awake. My mind is whirling a mile a minute, but I can't pin down a single thought. I haven't eaten, and I'm not hungry, but I find myself aimlessly looking through cabinets in the kitchen.

I always pride myself on being in control, but so much has happened today that I can't figure out where to begin to process everything.

Warm hands run along my stomach from behind, and I smell Tucker's unique leather scent. He wraps his arms completely around me, pulling my body flush to his.

"Tell me what you need, Little Miss. I can see the tornado over your head." He always sees. They all do, but he's usually a step ahead of the rest. Could it be his past experiences or his age? Whatever it is, I appreciate him—I appreciate all of them. "Do we need to clean some guns?"

"No. I need to process but there's more things to sort through than usual."

"It's been a long day." He kisses the back of my head, and

I hear him inhale the scent of my hair. A low hum escapes him, and I smile.

"Let me tell you something that might help take a little off your plate." I spin and wrap my arms around his back. "Hi, there."

"Hi. What do you have to tell me?"

"I've been spending a lot of time here and away from the club." I open my mouth to apologize and tell him he doesn't need to jeopardize his work for us, but he stops me with a simple look. "Good girl." He kisses my forehead, and the words make my stomach flutter. "As I was saying. I've been *happily* spending a lot of time here and realized I've been enjoying myself. I've never had a reason to do anything other than work, but I suddenly find myself with…other interests."

"Tucker."

"Let me finish, Little Miss." I nod and rest my cheek on his broad chest. It's my turn to inhale and enjoy his scent. "I have an amazing team at the club and decided it was time for some promotions. I've run the club alone for so long and need to let others spread their wings. In a week or two, once I'm confident that everyone is settled in their roles, I'll have plenty of free time for you and for Katy. And I guess the gaggle of other men in your life as well."

"You know I already appreciate everything that you do. You don't need to change your life for any of this." I don't understand why they've all dropped everything for us.

"You're correct, I don't need to. I want to. You've given me a reason to get my head out of my ass or the asses of drunk idiots that flood through my doors. It's been too long since I've had another person to care for, and you've given me two."

"Or five?" I feel his groan vibrate on my cheek.

"Four and a half. I'm still on the fence about Axel."

"I heard that asshole." I bury my laugh in Tucker's shirt, careful not to scratch my face on the buttons. His usual attire consists of jeans and a button-down dress shirt, and I love how he still looks rugged and handsome.

"Four and a quarter now because of the insult." Tucker looks over his shoulder and flashes Axel a smile. I hear the couch rustle and footsteps approaching us.

My hair is swept off my shoulder, and gentle kisses pepper my neck. I've almost always worn my hair in braids. It was easy and convenient, but Tucker is obsessed with unbraiding them the moment he sees me. The others seem to enjoy being able to run their fingers through my copper strands, and I enjoy it, too, so I've begun taking the braids out as soon as I come home.

"Little Miss, how about we have a family meeting and talk about everything."

Family.

It's a foreign concept for me. It's never been something I've felt I had. I had my parents, and they loved me out of obligation. I don't think Shane ever loved me. The closest I've ever come, other than Justin, who I consider a brother, is when I was growing my daughter inside me. I saw a future where we lived our lives together as a pair.

"That sounds nice."

Axel takes my hand and laces our fingers together. Tucker reluctantly lets me go as I'm led to the couch. Axel sits and takes me with him, and I get comfortable on his lap.

"What's going on?" Miller questions as Tucker sits next to us on the couch.

211

"Family meeting." Tucker's hand wraps around my thigh, giving it a squeeze. "Today has been a lot, and I think we could all use some talk therapy to discuss what's going to happen from here on out."

"Family meeting. I like it." Lincoln sits in one of the chairs, and Miller sits on the floor between his legs.

I like this. This feels right.

There are a few moments of silence, no one quite knowing where to start. Lincoln clears his throat, and all eyes are on him.

"Katy's news was…a bombshell. But it's nothing we can't all handle. She confessed to me that she's leaning toward keeping the baby." This information doesn't shock me.

"I expect that is what she'll decide to do. Does anyone here have a problem with that?" As I knew there would be, there's silence with a few grumbled no's. "Good. Then, let's assume she is until she tells us otherwise. Axel, do you know a good obstetrics doctor? Katy would probably be most comfortable with a female."

"Why are you asking me? Don't you have a lady doctor?" He looks genuinely confused.

"Well, I've caught you with your pants down in the linen closet more times than I care to recount. I thought maybe you were swapping more than bodily fluid in there and had some insider information."

My body is in motion before I realize what's happening, and I'm straddling Axel's lap. One hand is firmly planted on my hip, and the other holds my chin, preventing me from looking anywhere other than his deep brown eyes.

"Tails, you listen to me right now. There wasn't a single woman I didn't compare to you in every way. Nothing ever went any further than what you saw in the closet. I like making out, and I like getting blowjobs. I'm a bit of a pig, and I know it. If you ask around the hospital, I bet most women would tell you I'm a tease. They would leave satisfied, but it was never anything more than my hand despite many protests. My eyes have been on you for years."

His words make the butterflies in my stomach flutter, and I feel his cock hardening under me.

"I'm happy to ask around the hospital for a good OB doctor, but I do not, in fact, have any secret knowledge other than this." He leans forward and nips the spot just below my ear, and I'm almost embarrassed by the sound that escapes me.

"Shit, Axel." I have no idea who said that because my brain has gone to mush. I reasonably understand that it's not physically possible, but it certainly feels like it is.

"Axel," Lincoln warns. "We need to finish talking. If she makes that sound again, my dick might explode from my pants."

"I'd pay to see that." Axel dives back into my neck, and I brace myself on his chest to hold him back.

I'm being thrown around again like a ragdoll, and before my mind can connect with the motion, Tucker has swooped me into his embrace, my back to his chest, whispering calming words into my ear.

Axel grumbles, and Tucker shoots him a warning glance.

"You can't be trusted right now, young man. Let's finish talking first." Axel's face sours at his chastising, but suddenly, there's a glimmer in his eye. He reaches over and pats Tucker's shoulder, his grin growing wider.

"Okay, Daddy Tucker. I'll behave."

Oh my.

"Don't sass me, little boy, or I'll show you what *Daddy Tucker* can really do." I see Axel gulp and back down.

"On that note, can we discuss this morning's incident or almost incident?" I don't think any of us are quite sure what exactly Miller is referring to, and he can tell. "The almost kiss between you two."

Axel sits up quickly, his head whipping between Miller and Tucker. He loves gossip.

"Wait. There was an almost kiss? I want details. Damn, I miss the good stuff getting stuck at work."

"How about I address this." There's so much testosterone in this room right now, and a wrong word could make it explode. "As I told my father this morning, you are all my partners. I know we haven't discussed relationship roles, and other than Miller and Lincoln, nothing has been established."

"Tails, if you didn't understand what I just said to you, I'm all yours and no one else's."

There's a round of agreement in the room, and I huff. "Yes, I understand you're all obsessed with me. I don't think that's the issue at hand. We need to establish other clear boundaries. Lincoln, Miller, since you're the ones in an established relationship, I think I'll revert this back to you two. I'm willing to share and...be shared." There are groans and several adjustments of pants. "You're thoughts?"

Miller sits up straighter and sighs. "I know I went all 'that boy is mine' this morning, but I don't really feel that possessive when it comes to you guys. The fact that Lincoln thought about me enough to stop something that we hadn't consented to was enough to make me realize I like what we all shared that night, and I'm comfortable repeating it." I watch in amusement as Lincoln grabs a chunk of Miller's hair and pulls his head back, slamming their lips together. It would appear that Lincoln appreciated his confession.

"Fuck, I'm down for anything with the people in this room. Let's have our cake and eat it too." Axel's smile is wide and mischievous as he shimmies in his seat.

"I'm happy if you're happy, Little Miss. Whether that's watching or participating, I just want to see you enjoy yourself." Tucker's hand slides up the nape of my neck, and his fingers massage my head. I contain my moan this time, knowing things are already getting heated in here.

"Hey loverboys, we need an answer from you." Miller pulls away from Lincoln and glares at Axel.

"You want an answer? You want to know if we're okay sharing each other?" My pulse quickens as Miller leans over and crawls across the floor to Axel.

"Holy fuck." I inwardly agree with Axel.

Miller reaches Axel and sits up on his knees. Reaching up he grabs a handful of Axel's shirt and pulls him in, smashing their lips together. Their kiss is demanding and forceful as they battle for dominance. I'm so entranced with the men making out next to me, I don't notice Lincoln has crossed the room to us. I shiver at his deep voice directed toward Tucker.

"I think we have some unfinished business, brother." Lincoln bends down, bracing both hands on the back of the couch, his chest hovering over mine. He leans across my shoulder, and kisses Tucker.

I began to laugh—to myself at first—but slowly, the sound creeps out and becomes louder, disturbing the makeout sessions around me. The silence is deafening as their moans stop, and the only thing to be heard is my laughter.

"Problem, Dream Girl?" Lincoln angles his head and kisses across my collarbone.

"I'm entertained at the idea that I can be the only female in the room and not the center of attention."

That was the wrong thing to say...

30

Tucker

Hearing Spencer laugh is a magical sound I want to listen to for eternity. Hearing her say she isn't the center of attention makes me want to take her over my knee and show her how much we can worship her if she allows it.

I must not be the only one with that opinion, as growls are heard throughout the room.

"I didn't mean it like that."

Ah, listen to the scared little rabbit trying to backtrack her words. I like this vulnerable side of her.

Lincoln stands, pulling Spencer up with him, and spins her to face us. He steps up behind her, and I watch his hips rotate.

"Do you feel that, Dream Girl? That's all for you. Look at these three men. Look at their cocks standing at attention, straining against their pants. Our tongues may be on each other, but our minds are on you."

Damn, Lincoln's coming in with the smooth words that couldn't possibly be more perfect.

"Are you ready to let us worship you, Tails?" Spencer holds her breath, and I'm worried we're overwhelming her.

I stand, sandwiching her between Lincoln and me, and gently kiss her, trailing my mouth against her jaw until I reach her ear.

"Everything is always your choice. There's a safeword for a reason. If you get uncomfortable or overwhelmed, Code Blue stops everything, and no one here will ever fault you for stopping." Her body relaxes between us, and she exhales long and slow.

"I... I'm scared," she confesses. A confession I'm sure is hard for her to make. "I haven't been with anyone since Shane, and there are many more of you than me. I understand the logistics, but the practicality of the matter is there are still more of you than holes in me."

"Don't worry about that, Dream Girl. We can entertain ourselves and you at the same time. Shall we move to the bedroom to be more comfortable?"

She's considering her options, and I don't fault her one bit. We've all been itching to get our hands on this incredible woman, and I'm sure all of us will need to use a great deal of restraint.

"Okay."

Axel stands and removes his shirt while kicking off his joggers. He stands naked as a jaybird before us and shrugs.

"I'm ready to get this party started." He has no shame as he walks to Spencer's room, full ass on display, and stands at the door, waiting. He motions to himself and wiggles his hips. "Well, it's not going to suck itself."

"Don't be a pig, Axel."

"Is that an offer, Daddy Tucker?" *It is now.*

218

"Excuse me, Little Miss. I have a boy to deal with." I kiss her temple, and in three long strides, I'm standing over Axel. I only have a few inches on him, but that's all I need right now.

"You've got a smart mouth, you know that?" His lip twitches, and I want to bite it.

"I've been told. Are you going to do something about it?"

"Yeah. You can't talk if your mouth is full." I knock the ball cap off his head, which I've never seen him wear before, and grab a fist full of his hair. It's flat, having been hidden under the hat, but holy fuck is it soft.

"Well, Axel. It's not going to suck itself." I see the amusement in his eyes as the tables turn, and he slowly sinks to his knees, never breaking eye contact. With my free hand, I undo my belt and pants and pull my engorged cock out. It bobs in his face, and he grabs the base and sucks me down. I have to lean forward and brace myself against the door frame so my knees don't give out on me.

"Fuck, Axel. Your goddamn mouth." I'm watching my length dip in and out when I hear Spencer moan. I turn my head and find Miller, Spencer, and Lincoln walking toward us, hands roaming over each other's bodies.

"Excuse us, brother. It seems like you have something to work out here. We'll just go work things out over there." Lincoln points to the bed, and I move over, giving them room to pass us in the doorway.

"Holy fucking christ." Axel tugs on my balls while hollowing his cheeks, and I have to start thinking about cleaning horse stalls as a kid to stop myself from coming too soon.

My eyes follow the trio as Miller helps lay Spencer on the bed and tells her to move to the middle. They strip to their

219

boxers, and each takes a side of her gorgeous body. Their mouths and fingers trace the exposed skin around her neck, shoulders, midsection, and upper thighs.

It takes me a moment to realize Axel has stopped moving, and he's watching them just as intently as I am. I run a hand through his hair and watch his eyes flutter closed as I fall from his mouth.

"Are we going to let them have all the fun, Axel?"

"Fuck no." He launches to his feet and jumps on the bed, causing everyone to bounce.

"Children," I mutter.

"Aww, don't be salty, Daddy Tucker," Miller teases. I glare at him and stalk toward the bed.

"Someone's in trouuuuuble."

"Axel, you have another hole I can fill if you can't keep your comments to yourself." Axel closes his mouth quickly at my threat.

I grab Miller's ankle and pull him down the bed until his body is at the edge. I bend down, hovering over him, and put our chests together. "Bruiser, do you need another lesson in respect like Axel just had? I thought I'd already taught you that, but we can try again if necessary."

"It won't happen again, Tuck. I promise." He lifts his head and nips my bottom lip. I drop my arms and put all my weight on him, locking our lips together, and he grunts. I smile into our kiss and take what I want. When I lift up, I smack him twice on the cheek, just hard enough to sting.

"Good boy. Go pleasure our girl while I get undressed." Miller scrambles back toward Spencer and whispers something in her ear. She briefly thinks over what he said, scanning the room, and sits up. She raises her arms, and

Miller carefully removes her top.

My mouth goes dry as her full breasts with dark pink nipples spill out. She's impossibly more gorgeous than I could even imagine. Spencer's eyes watch my fingers as I unbutton my shirt. She's focused on my hands and not what the other men do to her. I like having this power.

Lincoln's mouth wanders lower on her body, and I watch his mouth surround her nipple. The pleasure takes her, and Spencer's eyes flutter closed. I remove my pants, letting them worship her like they promised. I take in her every moan and whimper. Catalog every twitch and gasp. I'll remember everything she likes when it's my turn. Until then, I watch.

Axel's lips sweep across the band of her pants, and her stomach sucks in at his touch. Is she ticklish?

"Tails, can I take these off?"

"Yes."

There's no hesitation or contemplation this time. She's firm in her decision to allow him to remove her clothing.

Axel carefully peels off her pants, and all eyes are on her. We wait with bated breath as a small red landing strip of hair appears. She's neatly trimmed and seems to not be wearing any underwear.

"Fuck me, Dream Girl." Lincoln runs a gentle hand over her pubic hair. "You were hiding this from us? I didn't know what to expect, but this is...mmmm."

"Well, now we all know that the carpet matches the drapes." Axel winks and Spencer lightly kicks him in the chest.

"Child. You're a child, Axel." I roll my eyes, and his smile brightens.

"Hey, you know you keep me around for the comic relief." He leans down to Spencer's leg, and his mouth leaves a path of wetness as he kisses her from ankle to knee, her sweet moans spurring him on even more. "And my mouth."

"I'll allow the excuse."

Spencer's body bucks as Miller and Lincoln each take a nipple, and I stroke myself over my briefs. I could stand here and listen to her moan all night. She's incredible as she writhes under them.

Lincoln's hand dips lower, and Spencer parts her legs to allow him access. I'm the only one currently getting the view of her engorged pussy, and I want to come right here and now. Linc's fingers easily slide between her lips, and I see her arousal coat them. I groan at the same time Spencer moans and crawl onto the bed to watch his fingers play.

Pulling my cock out, I lazily stroke myself in time to Lincoln's fingers. He massages Spencer's clit, and her moans of pleasure are a drug to my system.

The temperature in the room rises as everyone pants and moans. Axel has pulled Miller out and is vigorously sucking his cock while Miller makes out with Spencer. Lincoln's fingers have picked up speed while he pulls at her nipples with his mouth.

I watch. I love to watch. Their pleasure is just as much mine as it is theirs. My free hand strokes Spencer's creamy inner thigh and I see the smattering of freckles over her body that isn't visible unless you're as close as we are right now.

I watch in anticipation as Lincoln's fingers lower to her entrance, and he teases her with circles before dipping in slowly.

Spencer's body stiffens, and a split second before I'm about to use our safeword, she pulls away from Miller's mouth.

"Code Blue."

Immediately, everyone moves back. My chest fills with pride at her and them for their quick response. I pick up a throw blanket that fell on the floor and lay it over her. She gives me a shy smile, and I return it with a reassuring one.

No one touches her as we wait to see what happens next.

With the gentlest voice possible, I wait until she makes eye contact with me. "Spencer, would you like to talk to us?"

Her body language is closed off as she adjusts and sits up against the headboard.

"I...he..." I can see the emotions running across her face. I extend a hand to her in an offer of comfort. She stares at it before her delicate fingers appear from under the blanket.

I take her hand in mine and gently massage her palm and wrist to ease some of her tension. Something Lincoln did triggered her based on when her reaction occurred and the single word "he" she muttered.

The three guys look nervous and guilty as their eyes dart between Spencer and me. She did the right thing and used her safeword when she felt uncomfortable. I can understand their emotions, but right now, our focus needs to be on Spencer.

"I have to tell you the rest of my story before we go any further."

31

Miller

This is what fucking heaven feels like. If I die right now, I'd be a happy man. My tongue tangles with Spencer's, my hands wander between her body and Lincoln's, and apparently, Axel sucking my cock is one of my new favorite things.

Lincoln shifts his arm, moving lower on Spencer's body, and she turns away from me.

"Code Blue." *Fuck.*

Without hesitation, everyone moves back. Spencer used her safeword. Something made her uncomfortable, and I feel like shit that we pushed her to that edge.

Tucker grabs a blanket and covers her. She scoots to the top of the bed and rests against the headboard.

Tucker speaks first, the three of us looking at each other dumbfounded. "Spencer, would you like to talk to us?"

"I...he..."

Which "he" is she referring to? Fuck. This is torture. A safeword is a precaution, but I never thought we'd need to use it. I'm so fucking proud she did, but we need to figure out what we did and how to never make her feel like this again.

Tucker extends his hand, and she takes it. We may joke and call him Daddy, but he somehow always knows what Spencer needs, just like a father would.

"I have to tell you the rest of my story before we go any further." There's more? How could there be more? She's been through so much.

"I didn't just lose my daughter that day. There was extensive damage done to my entire abdomen. When they did the ultrasound and confirmed there was no heartbeat, they also found internal bleeding. I had to have a full hysterectomy. They could have tried to save some of the reproductive organs, but I didn't want any long-term effects, so they took it all. I can never have children. I needed you all to know this before we go any further. You deserve to be with someone who can have children if that's the future you want. I'll understand if it is."

Holy shit. Spencer's been through so much. I didn't see any scars on her. How did I not notice? My eyes flash to her abdomen, and of course, I can't get anything past her.

"There are scars. My father demanded the best plastic surgeon, and I was diligent with my aftercare routine and everything I could do to eliminate the scarring as much as possible."

"Smithy—"

"Don't, Miller. I didn't tell you this for pity. I want you to have full disclosure of the burden that comes with me."

"No." Everyone jumps at Tucker's firm and demanding tone. "I will not allow you to talk down about yourself for circumstances that you couldn't control. My desire to be

225

with you has nothing to do with your ability to reproduce. Birthing a baby doesn't make you more or less of a mother. There are plenty of ways to make that happen, *if* having children is what you still desire. I can't speak for anyone else, but you're enough, Spencer. I'll take you exactly how you are. Reproductive organs or not."

Damn. Tucker always knows what to say.

"Smithy, we have Katy. She's more than enough of a handful for us. And if she keeps the baby, we will have him or her."

"Dammit." Axel is using his fingers to count, and I give him a puzzled look. "That's a lot of fucking people. We're going to need a bigger house." Axel's absurd statement makes everyone laugh, lightening the mood in the room.

"Dream Girl?" Spencer turns to look at him. Lincoln is the youngest of us, and although we haven't talked about it, I know he would make a fantastic father. "I can tell you that I've always seen children in my future. I know it's not something boys usually think about, but I've always imagined being a father and growing old with my kids."

"I understand."

"You don't. Listen to me. I feel a bond with Katy, exactly how I feel like a father/daughter bond would feel. I can't imagine anything being more real than that. I love that little snot but don't tell her I said that because she'll tease me. The only thought that scares me more than losing her is losing you. I'm in. I was in when you were just a voice on the radio. Call me a hopeless romantic. I don't care." Lincoln has tears in his eyes, and I want to console him, but it will have to wait.

"Hold on!" Axel's face lights up, and somehow, I don't think what he's about to say will be as insightful as the rest of us.

"What's wrong, Axel?"

"If Spencer can't have babies, then we don't need to use condoms." I slap him upside the head and hear Spencer hiding her laugh behind her hand. Cautiously, I remove her fingers one by one.

"Don't cover your laughter; I love hearing it." Spencer's eyes search each of our faces looking for any hint of a lie. She won't find any. We meant every word that we said—even Axel's excitement of unprotected sex.

"Is everyone clean?" Is she considering Axel's question? "Well, I guess that question actually falls to you, Tucker. The rest of us get tested regularly for our jobs."

Tucker squeezes the hand he's still holding. "Yes, Little Miss, I'm clean. It's been…well, let's say it's been a while since I've been with anyone, and I was tested at my last physical."

"So it doesn't bother any of you that I can't carry children?"

"Nope."

"Not at all."

"Not me."

"You're enough."

"There's one more thing." *Please. No more things, Spencer.* "Well, two. I've never done anal sex, and eventually, with this many partners, one or more of you are going to want to explore. We can work up to it. And two, I have a very sensitive gag reflex. I don't mind giving blow jobs, but there won't be any throat fucking because gagging overstimulates me, and I'd hate to kill the mood like this again."

"You're fucking incredible, Tails." It *would* be Axel to find anal sex and gag reflexes incredible. I'm in awe at her bravery and a little tickled at her use of the word fucking. "Can we get back to the fun stuff now?"

"Oh my god, Axel, you really are like a puppy."

"Yep. I'll cuddle you and lick you and love you forever." He bats his eyelashes at me and rubs against my arm.

"I said dog, not cat. Get off me." He glances down at my semi-hard cock and smiles.

"That's not what you were saying a little while ago." *Well, fuck. I can't argue with that.*

"Okay, children, the adults would like to play." Tucker gingerly kisses Spencer's knuckles and watches for her reaction. She seems receptive to his advances as he continues his line of kisses up her arm, slowly crawling up her body until he's hovering over her. "Are you alright, Little Miss?"

She shakes her head. "No, I'm ravenous." She wraps her arms around his neck and pulls his body down on top of hers. I'm about to reach over and grab Lincoln when I'm pushed onto my back, and Axel wraps his swollen lips around my cock. I press my head into the pillow and moan at the delicious feel of his tongue.

"Hey Fireball, you keep making those noises, and I might think you're trying to replace me."

"Linc. You need to feel his *fuck* his mouth to understand. *Shit.*"

"I want to feel you, Little Miss. Can we get rid of this blanket?" She hums into his kiss and he rolls toward Lincoln to remove the blanket.

I get the first look again at her gloriously naked figure, and I want to look for the scars she told us are there but quickly decide I don't give a fuck; she's stunning with or without them.

"Dream Girl, you really are a sight to behold." Lincoln runs a finger across her collarbone, and she shivers. A surge of lust courses through me seeing my boyfriend touch my… girlfriend?

"Hey, Smithy? Can we call you ours? *Fuck*, Axel. Give me a second." He chuckles as he pops off me. "I want to shout it from the rooftops that you're ours, but if you're not comfortable with that, I'll silently lust after you from the shadows." Her eyes pan the room and see the hope shining on everyone's faces.

"There are a lot of you and only one of me. Society doesn't always accept polyamorous relationships. Are you alright with accepting criticism?"

I brush my thumb across her cheek and kiss her lips gently. "I'm happy to call everyone in this room mine." I look up at Tucker, still hovering over Spencer. "Even this guy. He's not all that bad."

"Watch that mouth, Bruiser." I give him a mischievous grin, letting him know I'm aware of exactly what I'm saying.

"Then shout it from the rooftop if that's what you need to do."

"Yesssss. I have a girlfriend!" Axel fist pumps the air, and I can't help but chuckle at what a goofball he is. He grabs my cock and shoves me entirely into his mouth until I hit the back of his throat. I flop back on the bed with a loud moan.

"Fuck! Smithy, you don't have to worry about your gag reflex. Apparently, Axel doesn't have one. He's got you covered."

32

Axel

Hot fucking damn. I must have saved a lot of kittens in a past life because this one is perfection.

Did I ever think I'd find pleasure listening to my best friend moan because I'm sucking his cock like a Hoover? Not at all. Do I find his noises just as arousing as Spencer's? Yes, the fuck, I do.

"God dammit, Axel. Go show our woman some attention. I need a minute to breathe before you suck out my soul." I chuckle around Miller's cock as it slides from my mouth. I climb halfway up his body so I can reach Spencer's amazing tits.

It was torture in the shower having to be a nurturer and not the hormonal teenager that my body wanted me to be, but damn, it was worth it to get to this moment.

As I stare into Spencer's beautiful blue eyes, a sharp sting radiates across my ass.

"Get off me, you beast." Miller shakes his hand in the air with a sour face. "Why is your ass so hard?"

"I work out, baby. It's all the squats I do."

Tucker rears his arm back and smacks my other ass cheek. His sting is different from Miller's. The pain is more pleasurable somehow, and I moan.

"Axel?" Spencer's fingers dance across my cheeks. "Look how turned on you are. You like that, don't you?" There's no judgment in her question. It's honestly not even a question. She can see it. My face is heated, and my heart is racing.

Tucker's warm breath fans across my shoulder as he comes closer. "We can explore that another time. Right now, this is about our girl." He's right.

I take Spencer's nipple into my mouth and swirl my tongue around the peak. She's so responsive to all of us. Lincoln moans next to me, and I look over to see Tucker kissing his way down Lincoln's abdomen while still running his hand up and down Spencer's thighs. The man can multitask. Miller captures Spencer's lips, and I feel like my eyes are on sensory overload. I want to watch everyone all at the same time.

I follow Tucker's idea and kiss down Spencer's body. When I reach her patch of hair just above my goal, I nuzzle my nose in it. Most women shave entirely, and I thought I liked it. I was wrong. Something about this little patch of hair makes her seem more like a woman. *My* woman.

"Tails?" Miller releases her lips so she can acknowledge me. "I really want to taste this pussy."

"Manners, Axel."

"Sorry, Daddy Tucker. Spencer, may I please taste this gorgeous cunt of yours?" Tucker groans, and I don't know if it's because of my statement or the fact he just took Lincoln's cock into his mouth.

"Yes." Her response is breathy as Miller worships her tits, but it's still a yes.

I lower my body the last few inches and widen her thighs to get better access to my prize. Because Spencer Coble is a fucking gold medal.

Her pussy is pink and glistens with her arousal, and I want to dive in and taste her, but I know how long it's been and how evil her asshole ex was to her. I want her to enjoy every second of pleasure I give her.

I kiss her inner thigh, and she giggles.

"Do it again, Axel." Miller stares down at me, waiting. I kiss her again, swirling my tongue, and the beautiful sound fills the air. "Okay, now make her moan."

"With pleasure." I swipe my tongue from her entrance to her clit, and Spencer sucks in a breath and releases a throaty moan. It's music to my soul.

"Dream Girl, that was sexy as fuck." Everyone has their hands on her again. Miller has a nipple, Lincoln has her lips, and Tucker massages her other breast. Spencer is in heaven.

I begin my focus on her clit and try to listen for sounds and watch movement to see what brings her the most pleasure. I want to be the first to taste her come when she explodes. Revel in the thought that I made her fall apart.

I lift a finger to her entrance and carefully draw circles, giving her time to stop me. When she doesn't, I slowly slide a finger inside, moaning into her pussy at the feel of her warmth surrounding me. She's hot and wet and feels like silk. I slowly pump in and out, again listening and watching for reactions. She constricts my finger with her pussy walls, and I wonder if she's getting close.

Gently, I slide another finger in. She's tight, but her body accepts me beautifully. I don't think I can decipher what sounds she's making because of me or them. She's

232

continuously moaning and whimpering, and it's intoxicating.

"I...I." She's panting now. "I don't want to safeword, but I need a moment." I pull back and prop myself on my elbows, staring up her body. With everyone's hands removed from her, I have an unobstructed view of her face.

"Talk to us, Little Miss." Tucker rests his head on Lincoln's stomach and gently runs a hand on Spencer's arm.

"I don't want you to think anything is wrong because it isn't." She turns her head to the side and looks at Lincoln. "What happened that morning, when you were asleep, it was a fluke." Lincoln looks at her, confused.

"What do you mean by fluke?"

Her cheeks pinken as she gathers her thoughts. "I don't... orgasm easily. It's never been something that comes naturally to me. I know that's the goal of your desires, but I don't want you to get your hopes up."

"Little Miss, can you get yourself to orgasm with your hands or a toy?"

"No. I have on occasion, but it's been rare. I stopped trying because it's easier not to frustrate myself. I've spoken with a therapist before, and she thought I'm just stuck in my head and don't ever allow myself to relax." She sighs and closes her eyes. "I want you to know that everything you're doing feels incredible, but if your end goal is an orgasm, we might need to move on to another activity that's more suitable for your orgasms, not mine."

"I like a challenge." Tucker smacks me upside the head this time.

"You've been warned to behave, Axel. Little Miss, you have had an orgasm before, right?"

"I'm not inexperienced to the pleasure the body can

experience through release. I understand the mechanics of it."

"Smithy, that's not an answer."

Please, oh please, say you've never had an orgasm before. It would be the highlight of every man in this room to be able to own every ounce of her pleasure.

"Well, things were pleasurable with Shane in the beginning. There were highs and lows to my sexual enjoyment."

Tucker places his hand on her lower abdomen, just above her tuft of hair.

"Have you ever had a tingly feeling that started here and grew? A feeling that turned into tiny little fireworks exploding inside. Maybe your fingers and toes tingled? The sensations took your breath away and made this pretty pink pussy flutter and constrict." Tucker moves his hand to cup her with his palm.

"Oh."

Oh? Oh, what? I need to know. I'm practically salivating to know if she's ever experienced a true orgasm.

"I've never experienced anything quite like that. Except for the morning I was half asleep with Lincoln."

"Fuck." Miller buries his head in Spencer's neck and growls.

"Dream Girl, I'm not sure you realize what you've just done."

She doesn't. She has no fucking clue. A look at each of them tells me they are just as feral at the thought as I am. All of her pleasure belongs to us. This almost feels like too much power to hold.

"Alright, children. I need y'all to keep it in your pants." Spencer burst out in uncontrollable laughter. Tucker leans over her and stops inches from her lips. "What's so funny, Little Miss?"

I don't think I've ever seen Spencer so carefree. I love this side of her. She's letting loose and living in the moment.

"You… you're the…only one…wearing p-pants." She barely gets her words out through her laughter. When we all realize what she's said, the room roars. Tucker is indeed the only one wearing any clothes. It may just be his black briefs, but he has the only "pants" to keep himself in.

"Tails. That's totally a joke I would make. Am I rubbing off on you? I mean, I'd rather rub *on* you or rub one *off* on you, but I'll take what I can get." I know it's coming this time, and grab Tucker's hand mid-air. I take his index finger and suck it into my mouth. When I hear the low rumble of his groan, I smile, knowing he's remembering my lips on his cock.

33

Lincoln

How the fuck did I get here? Physically, mentally, everything. I'm stunned speechless by Spencer's confession. How does a woman this incredible get to be in her thirties and never experience a real orgasm? She admitted her struggles, and I believe they're real. But I also have complete faith we can relax her enough and get her out of her head to repeat that dream-like orgasm I made her have.

I. Made. Her. Have...*Fuck*.

Had I known that was truly her first pleasurable orgasm, I might have felt more guilty. Or maybe less guilty? Is that why she ran away and showered? Did she not understand what her body had just gone through?

As I watch Axel suck on Tucker's fingers, I think of all the ways I'm going to make this woman come again.

"Do you trust us, Dream Girl?"

"Of course." Her answer comes without hesitation.

"Then let us make you feel good. You lay here and relax, and we'll do all the heavy lifting."

The excitement and anticipation in the room is palpable. Everyone slowly resumes what they were previously doing and she was enjoying, except Tucker.

"Little Miss, can I sit behind you? I want to help you relax your mind while they relax your body." She nods at him, and he moves to the head of the bed. They rearrange so her back is leaning on his chest, and he massages his fingers into her hair.

Miller and I give our full attention to her luscious breasts while Axel continues his work between her legs. Knowing what we do now, we're all more purposeful with our actions— slower strokes, gentler nips and sucks. We'll be the tortoise in this race.

I can tell the difference in her moaning. While her moans earlier were eager and needy, these are breathier and gentle. The same underlying tone of pleasure creeps into her noises, but the softer sounds show more enjoyment. Tucker whispers words of praise into her ears that's making my already aching cock throb.

"Close your eyes, Little Miss. I don't want you to look. I just want you to feel. Take a deep breath for me. Good girl."

Tucker's voice grows huskier as he describes what she's feeling.

"Let me be your eyes. Do you feel the boys worshiping your pert rosy nipples?" She hmms her answer. "Do you like the little nips and licks, or would you prefer they get a little rougher? Lincoln, show her the difference."

Hell, fucking, yes.

I suck her into my mouth deeper and flick my tongue eagerly. Before I pull away, I graze her with my teeth, giving just the tiniest bit of pain. Miller likes a nip to his nipples, and

I thought Spencer might too. Something that could cause pleasure but also keep her slightly grounded to reality. If her corresponding moan means anything, I guess my assumption was correct.

"Oh god. Yes, that."

"You heard her brother. Whatever you just did, keep doing it. Wonderful job. Tell me what you like. Now, do you want Miller to continue what he's doing, keeping his slow gentleness with his mouth, or would you like Lincoln to tell him how to mirror his actions? I know how soft and skilled his tongue is. It feels incredible, doesn't it.?"

"Stay." Her word is a passing breath on her lips. This is the sweetest torture. I know what she's feeling. He does have the softest, most skilled tongue, and it's fucking hot that Tucker knows it too.

"Alright, one more. I want you to feel their mouths, but can you tell me what you feel Axel doing? Don't focus on any one sensation. Just tell me what you feel." Spencer tilts her head to the side and looks up at Tucker.

"Kiss me." He groans and takes her lips. I have to reach down and adjust myself. I'm trying my best not to hump the bed, but I'm getting close to losing that battle.

Tucker pulls away from the kiss and places a soft hand around her neck. His fingers push deeper into the side—he's checking her pulse.

"Stop distracting me, you siren. Tell me what Axel's tongue is doing to you." Her eyes close, and she adjusts her head so she's centered on his chest.

"His tongue is hot and slippery. Or am I the slippery one?" I feel her shift as she opens her eyes and leans forward to look at Axel. He feels her movement as well and pops his head up, smiling.

"Tails?"

"Am I that wet?"

"It's like a slip and slide down here." I can't take another second of this. I can see her arousal glistening on Axel's face, and I need to know what she tastes like. I grab him by the throat and launch myself down Spencer's body. When my lips touch his, I shove my tongue in his mouth and swirl, looking for any remnant of her essence. It's there. They taste like nothing I've ever experienced before, mixed together. He battles his tongue with mine, not for dominance but to make sure I get as much of her taste as I need.

I release my hold on Axel's neck and drop my forehead to Spencer's stomach. "Fuck, woman. You're heaven inside and out."

I pivot my head to look at her, and she smiles at me. "I could say the same about you. Any of you."

"I need you to relax, Little Miss. We have a job to do." Tucker's hands move up to either side of her head, and he threads his fingers through her hair, starting at her temples. She moans and melts into him. "I have a question for you since this seems to have been the catalyst of your stress both times. Can Axel put his fingers inside you, or would you rather he just use his tongue?"

"In. Inside. I'm sorry I keep stopping you—"

"Shhh." He puts a finger over her lips. "Never apologize for telling us your comfort level." She opens her mouth to speak, and I surround her nipple with my tongue, drowning whatever she was about to say. Miller chuckles and runs his hand through my hair. My moan vibrates across Spencer's chest, and she giggles. I love her giggle.

"No more stalling, ma'am. Close your eyes." I turn my head to watch Axel, whose shoulders dips as he adjusts his position and enters Spencer. She gasps, and we all pause, wondering if she's okay.

"Don't stop, No one stop."

"Are you feeling the tingle low in your stomach? Maybe it's a fluttering?"

"Y-yes. Butterflies."

"Good Girl. Now listen to me. Don't think about it." Tucker is whispering now. I'm close enough to hear him, but he wants to make sure she knows this conversation is just for them. "I want you to think about when you and I sat on the floor right next to this bed. Do you remember what you were doing?"

"Loading ammo."

Ammo, not ammunition. Her mind is already beginning to melt for us.

"Is that soothing? Centering? Does it help you drown out the world around you?"

"Yes."

"Go there. Take your mind to the place that soothes you." Tucker's hands leave her hair and trails a path down her shoulders to her wrists that lay limp at her sides and back up. Her hips buck, telling us she's getting closer. Tucker's hands trail back down and stop at her palms, rubbing circles in them.

"Little Miss, how many rounds are in a standard magazine for a Glock 19."

"Fifteen." Spencer's knowledge of firearms has always been a turn-on for me.

"In your mind, I want you to imagine loading an empty

clip. Count them out loud."

Without hesitation, she begins to count.

"One....Two..." A look passes between Axel and Tucker. "Three... Foo-ooh."

"Four. Keep going," Tucker counts for her.

"Four," she whispers. "Five." Her stomach muscles jump, and I know she's almost there. Does she? "S-six....Se-EVEN."

"Seven. Good girl," Tucker purrs in her ear.

"Eight." That number was purely a moan. A moan different than any one I've heard yet from her. "Ninetenelev—"

"Nine. Ten. Keep going."

Her breathing is quick and shallow. Her fingers wiggle. She's feeling the tingling.

"El-el-elev. Oh god. Of fuck. Tucker." Spencer never curses. It's happening.

"It's okay, Little Miss. Eleven. Listen to my voice. Twelve." She reaches up and grabs handfuls of his hair, and by the look on his face, he loves it.

I need to be selfish. I want to watch her fall apart. I lean back and replace my mouth with my fingers, rolling and pinching. Miller sees me and does the same; his fingers make gentle circles around her nipple.

"Thirteen." Tucker barely gets the words out when Spencer's toes curl, and her mouth drops open. She stops breathing just as her legs try to clamp around Axel's head. I grab her thigh and open it back up. Miller takes her other leg, and together, we spread her open as she bucks and her orgasm rushes through her body.

Axel places a firm hand over her pubic bone to try and keep her in place. Tucker whispers in her ear, but I'm transfixed on Spencer's face. She's silent with her mouth agape. Small squeaks pass her vocal cords. When she finally lets go, the moan that she produces is a feral scream of pure ecstasy.

"Please. Please." Her eyes pop open, and she stares down at Axel. Spencer's blues are swimming in a pool of tears as Axel sits up on his knees with a giant smile.

"I-I-I..." She's overwhelmed, overstimulated, but sated. She doesn't know how to react. Tucker senses it and pulls her hands out of his hair. He crosses his arms over her chest and hugs her close. Miller and I surround either side of her, and Axel leans up and lies gently on her chest.

Together, we form a barrier as she cries. Orgasms can be many things: relieving, cathartic, an escape. In Spencer's case, knowing her history, I imagine this was a trauma dump for her. She was convinced she couldn't orgasm at all. She had resigned to the fact that she couldn't relax enough to make it happen. We proved her wrong, and her system needs a moment to process all that emotion.

As proud as all of us are right now, that's on the back burner. Spencer's mental security is our top priority. She needs to feel safe, and it needs to be with us.

We hold Spencer, our limbs tangling together. Tucker whispers words of praise and encouragement in her ears again. Daddy Tucker to the rescue.

Spencer's tears stop, but none of us move. Several minutes pass, and her eyes flutter closed. She must be exhausted—we all are. It's been a long, sleepless day for most of them.

BEEP-BEEP. BEEP-BEEP.

"Nooooo," Axel whines from his space between Spencer's breasts.

"What's wrong?"

"It's the alarm. The three of us have to get ready for work,

Babe." Miller deflates as he says the words.

"And we're all going to have the worst case of blue balls all night." Axel looks up at Spencer. "But god, was it fucking worth it. You did incredible, Tails. Thank you for the honor. I don't take it lightly." She wiggles a hand out of Tucker's grip and runs it through Axel's hair.

"It was a group effort. Thank you. All of you. How about the three of us shower quickly to wake up?" She gives Axel and Miller a sweet smile.

"No fair." I pout my lip and bat my eyes at them. Axel punches my arm.

"First, talk to me in the morning after you've gotten a good night's sleep. And second, do you see this hair? If I don't shower and tame this mane, I'll scare all the small children tonight."

I lean over and kiss his forehead, then Miller's. "Both good points. Go shower." I kiss Spencer and linger a little longer before sitting up and watching them all walk to the bathroom.

"I could get used to this, Tuck."

"Me too, little brother. You're sleeping on the couch." With a thud, I land on the floor, Tucker having pushed me off the bed.

"Asshole."

"Love you too."

34

Spencer

It's a good thing my body is used to little sleep and that I prefer to drive. I've spent half the night watching Miller's head bob forward. One time, it fell to the right, and he hit the window. He was awake for a little while after that.

"This is nice, Smithy."

"I thought you could use some fresh air." We're sitting in the back of the ambulance, swinging our legs with coffees in hand, looking at the stars over the water.

"Yeah. I'm sorry I'm being a terrible partner tonight. You know nights are hard for me on a normal day when I can sleep between shifts." He leans his head on my shoulder, and I kiss his forehead. The gesture surprises him, and he lifts back up and looks around. I'm just as surprised as any public display of affection has never made me comfortable.

"I think you've broken me."

He rests his head back on my shoulder. "I think I like you broken, Smithy."

Pulling into the station after what felt like the longest night ever, I'm ready to go home, shower, and sleep. We only had one call last night, and it was a car fire. Our only purpose was to be there "in case" we were needed, which we weren't. The lack of activity made the night drag on, but the perk is that there's nothing to restock or count for the next shift. Miller has the post-shift checklist done by the time we're backing into the bay.

"Coble, come up here a minute," Chief Wetli bellows for me from the Eagle's nest, the open balcony that oversees the entire fire station. The short, broad, and recently balding man waits until he knows he caught my attention and scoops his hand through the air for me to join him.

"Smithy?" Without saying the words, he's asking if he should join me. I shake my head and climb the stairs. I don't and haven't done anything wrong to need backup.

I approach the Chief's office and knock on the door frame of the open door.

"Come in. I won't keep you long." I step inside and stop right in front of his desk. "This was delivered for you here around five a.m. One of the recruits"—he mumbles dumbass under his breath—"was outside running suicides and said a guy dropped this off for you." He pulls a generic white envelope from his desk with my name in familiar letters handwritten across the front. My mask is already on. It always is in this building. He doesn't see any change in my expression or demeanor because there isn't one for him to see.

"Thank you, Chief."

"Anything I need to worry about, Coble?"

"No, Sir. I'll be sure to tell you if or when there is." He's an intelligent man. He doesn't believe me on pure suspicion but has no proof or reason to question it.

"Dismissed. Get some sleep. And tell Miller he looks like shit."

"Will do, Sir."

As soon as I see Miller's truck, I let my mask fall. He jumps out of the driver's seat and charges toward me, stopping a few feet away. We need to have a genuine discussion about our workplace roles, and I appreciate the space he gives me right now.

I put out my empty hand, and he stares at it for a moment before looking back at my face.

"Keys, I'm driving. You're a walking zombie."

"You want to drive my...yeah, fuck it." He hands me the keys and I hand him the envelope.

"No fucking way. Here?" My thoughts exactly. Shane was here. *Here.* My place of employment. He's escalating. "What's in it?" He flips the envelope and realizes it's still sealed.

"Let's go. We can open it without the possibility of other eyes when we get home."

The drive is silent. Mostly because Miller fell asleep before we got down the block, but my mind is also quiet. I don't know if it's because there's so much to think about, my brain has shut down, or because, for the first time in my life, I feel safe.

I've always felt safe at home. It's the place where I can be myself without judgment. My parents always made sure I knew that. But once I walked out the front door, there was an entire world that would judge and criticize me for being different.

My father taught me how to embrace some of my "talents"

as he called them. When he realized that I had a photographic memory, he helped me learn to mentally catalog everything I see instead of it sitting in a mess in my head.

When I became obsessed with facial expressions and wanted to learn every micro expression that everyone could make, we worked on what was deemed an appropriate amount of time to look at someone without staring. One of my favorite things to do that summer was go down to the station with him, and he'd let me sit in his office and watch the other officers at their desks. That's where I believe I got the best training. Police officers are trained to keep their faces neutral. When they knew I was there watching, they would try extra hard and then talk to me afterward to see if I figured them out.

I miss my father. I've given him space, too much space, to wallow in his guilt, and it's time to reconnect.

When I stop at a red light, I pick up my phone and open his contact.

Spencer: Dad, can you meet me in 10 minutes at my house?
   Dad: See you soon.

I'm not surprised to see him already waiting outside when we arrive, although I am surprised that my phone didn't get any motion sensor alerts.

"What's wrong?" My father approaches me as I step out of Miller's truck and must see the concern on my face.

"Take ten steps to your left." Without hesitation, he follows my instructions and I wait for the alert that doesn't come.

"No wonder."

"No wonder what, Spencer? What's going on?" I show

him my blank screen, and he stares at it momentarily before putting the pieces together. He helped me install the alarm and cameras out here and knows where they all point. We're standing in the middle of the driveway and should be seen by at least two different cameras. Neither of which seem to be working properly.

I hear the passenger door close, and a half awake, Miller rounds the front of the truck.

"Why didn't you wake me, Smit—Oh, hi Eddie." Miller extends his hand to my dad, and they shake. "What's wrong?"

"The cameras aren't working right. It explains how I've been plucking pictures off your cars without you knowing."

"*Fuck*. Sorry, Sir." Miller rubs the back of his neck, and my dad shoos his comment off with a hand wave.

"This situation requires a fuck. Let's get inside and figure out what's going on." I reach in the truck, pick up the new envelope, and hand it to my dad. He takes it with a confused look. "Where's this from?"

"It was delivered to the firehouse around five a.m. while we were on duty."

"God dammit. Your work? The fucking bastard." His opposite hand balls into a fist. I want to take his pain away, knowing he feels in part that some of this is his doing.

"Let's get some coffee and see what's inside."

When I open the door, Gage greets us, letting me know that at least someone in the house is awake.

"Hey, Dream Girl, *Daddy Tucker* and I were just thinking— Oh! Hi Eddie. Um, sorry about that." The tips of Lincoln's ears turn red when he realizes Miller and I aren't alone.

"What you kids do behind these doors is none of my business. Let's chat." He motions toward the kitchen counter, and everyone listens.

There's already a full pot of coffee, and as I'm pulling down mugs, a warm presence steps up behind me.

"How was your night, Little Miss?" I turn my head over my shoulder and smile up at Tucker's blue eyes. He bends and brushes a kiss over my lips. "Do you have any regrets about yesterday?"

"None. And our night was quiet and slow. I'm ready for some sleep."

"How about some chamomile tea instead of caffeine then?" I sigh as his fingers graze my arm, and I lean back into his chest.

"That's probably a better ide—"

"I'm fucking exhausted!" The front door swings open, and Axel boisterously announces his entrance. "Where's my girrrrr-hey, Eddie. How are you?" He looks at me and mouths, "Sorry."

"Listen, boys, this is the last time I'll address this. You're all grown adults. I may be an old man, but I ain't no prude. I've never seen Spencer so touchy-feely, so you all must be doing something right." He peers at Tucker, holding me, and smiles. "Treat my girl right, and we'll be fine. Speaking of girls, where's the feisty one?" He looks around for Katy.

"She's with Justin and Nicole for a few days." I hope he doesn't ask any more questions. If she decides not to keep her pregnancy, there's no reason to ever bring it up with him.

My dad smirks and huffs a laugh. "Can't say I blame the child with all the hormones in this little house. I don't know how you're all managing to fit in here...never mind." He picks up a mug and extends his arm for me to fill it.

Once everyone has their beverage of choice, we gather

around the kitchen counter. My father pulls out the newest envelope, and the guy's responses are various degrees of anger.

"What's in it?" Lincoln's deep voice sounds menacing as he eyes the writing.

"We're about to find out." My father slips his finger through the fold, and the tearing sound cuts thick through the tension in the room.

"When was this?" He flashes the picture toward Miller and me.

"What the fuck?!" Miller grabs the picture of us sitting on the back of the ambulance the moment I kissed his forehead. "This was tonight. Fucking hours ago. He was watching us? Is there anything else?"

He pulls out another photo and a note with familiar handwriting on it. The picture shows Miller, Axel, and Tucker outside on the day we found out Katy was pregnant. It must have been when Justin and I were inside talking to her.

"Eeny, meeny, miny, moe. Which one of your men should I catch by the toe?"

"How the fuck is he getting near the house? It has security and cameras." Lincoln's rage is palpable.

"They aren't working."

"They what? How is that possible?" Axel runs a hand through his hair in frustration.

I walk into the living room and grab my laptop off the coffee table. I type in my password for my security app and see that all the cameras are working properly.

"They look fine," Miller says with disbelief in his voice.

"Wait. Keep watching. The left corner." Lincoln makes a

circle with his fingers, and we all stare and wait. I don't see anything out of the ordinary, and I'm about to give up when he yells, startling all of us. "There. Did you see it, Detective?"

My father slaps Lincoln on the back. "I sure as shit did, son." I must have blinked at the exact second of whatever they saw.

"What did I miss?"

"Are you slipping on me, Spencer? You missed the shadow of the bird that flew by? I saw it the first time but didn't realize it repeated until your man pointed it out. The video is on a loop."

"I'll call my guy." Tucker has a guy? "My security is top-notch at the club. He'll have this figured out and fixed before you leave for work tonight." Tucker kisses my forehead and pulls me into his side. "I'll let you sleep for a while, and I'll be back around two with Chip."

"Sleeeeeep." Axel's head drops to the counter with a thud, and I can't agree more with his sentiment. I'm still in my work clothes.

"Alright," my dad claps his hands, startling some of us. "I'll let everyone get settled for the day. We'll start with fixing the security system. Tucker, stop by and get me when you come back later, and I'll help you out since I helped put the system here in the first place."

"Sounds great, Sir."

"Eddie. None of that sir crap."

Tucker extends his hand. "Alright, Eddie. I'll see you this afternoon." They shake, and my father makes his exit.

As soon as the door closes, warm bodies swarm me with gentle caresses.

"You know I'm not fragile, right?"

"You're a fucking flower, Tails. Some of us missed you. Just let us get some lovin.'"

"Could we have a morning that's not full of stress?" Miller kisses my temple, and I wholeheartedly agree with his question.

"Tonight is your last night shift for two days, right, Little Miss?"

"Thank fuck," Miller replies for us.

"Last night was mine. Not to brag or anything."

"Shut up, Axel." Lincoln pushes his shoulder.

Somewhere in the room, an alarm goes off. I don't know whose it is but I'm sure it means it's time for someone to leave for work.

"Duty calls, Dream Girl. Justin is bringing Katy to school, and I'm bringing her back to his place afterward." Lincoln pushes the other guys aside and wraps an arm around my waist and the back of my head. He licks his lips then presses our lips together. He doesn't have to wait for a response as I open for him, and our tongues dance. He deepens the kiss, and I can almost taste his need and the protection he's trying to convey to me.

"Lincoln."

"I know, you'll be fine. I just worry about you anytime you're out of my sight. Get some sleep." He kisses the tip of my nose, passes me off to a waiting Tucker, and steps over to Miller.

The ends of his hair are damp as they wisp around his ears. I can smell his all-too-familiar scent of leather, and it comforts me. Tucker sweeps his lips across mine, making me smile. This man makes me feel like I'm home whenever I'm in his arms. I wonder if he makes the others feel the same.

252

"I'll be back at two. Will you be alright with Miller and Axel?"

"Yes, I'm a good babysitter." I look over my shoulder and see the two eyeing me for my comment. They know I'm teasing them. I also know Tucker was asking if I want him to stay as well.

"Be safe, and don't leave the house alone."

"I'm a big girl and have been taking care of myself for far longer than any of you have been around."

"And now you don't have to, and we *want* to take care of you. Promise me, Little Miss. At least for today until we get these cameras fixed and in order." I could argue, but he only wants what's best for me, and I know that.

"Hey, Dream Girl. Keep Gage on high alert in case he's tampered with the security system, too."

"Good idea, brother."

There's another round of kisses between everyone coming and going, and as I walk to my bedroom to finally take off my work clothes, I'm cornered against the wall, taking my breath away.

35

Tucker

he protectiveness I feel over this woman should not be as intense as it is for such a short time, but it is, and I'm not fighting it. Lincoln and I say our goodbyes in the driveway, and I let him drive away before I stop at the main house and approach the front door. The white house with black accents is well-kept, but you can tell it lacks a woman's touch.

I ring the doorbell and hear footsteps approach before the door opens.

"Tucker, everything alright?"

I take my hat off out of respect and nod. "It is. Might we speak a moment?" He steps back and allows me inside.

The living room opens to the kitchen. Everything is neutral tones, and like the front of the house, it's not quite a bachelor pad, but you can tell a woman doesn't live here. I pause at a picture of a pretty middle aged woman with auburn hair and blue eyes.

"My Heather, Spencer's mother. We lost her when Spencer was in middle school. Died of cardiac arrest in her sleep. We never saw it coming. I believe it's what pushed Spencer to become a paramedic."

He walks past me to the refrigerator and pauses. "Water? Coffee? Whiskey?"

"How about coffee with a splash of whiskey?"

His head dips. "A man of my own heart. I think I'll join you."

Eddie pours our mugs of coffee and spirits and motions for me to follow him. He opens a door off the kitchen to a three-season porch with several chairs, a couch, and dark-tinted windows.

"Take a seat." I sit in a dark green recliner, and he sits beside me. With his mug, he points to Spencer's house, that's in full view from the porch. "I've spent many hours out here watching over her from afar." He takes a sip from his cup and gives me an earnest look. "I don't have to do that too much since you boys came around." I smile over my mug. "I appreciate all that you're doing for her. But you didn't come here for small talk, so tell me why you did, Tucker."

I respect a man who gets down to business.

"I'd like to get the pictures you've been collecting. I've hired a private investigator to look into what's going on. The pictures, along with any knowledge you have, would greatly help him."

He takes another swig of his drink, but I can tell this sip goes down harder.

"How much has she told you?"

"As far as I know, everything. I know about the proposal and the verbal and physical abuse. Spencer informed us about the baby and, recently, the hysterectomy. Bless her loving heart, she told us so we had the opportunity to step away if wanting kids was something we needed in our lives."

His brow arches, and he rubs his palm up and down his leg. "And you all stayed?"

"Eddie, I promise you we all have good intentions with your daughter, and her ability to birth children isn't a condition for any of us to leave."

"The cop, he's your brother?"

"Step. We didn't grow up together. We're ten years apart and I was already a man when our parents married. We didn't even have a real relationship until nearly a decade ago."

"Are you *all* together?" He's being very deliberate with his questions. I can tell they are out of genuine curiosity and not judgment.

"This is probably a conversation you should have with your daughter. Yes, we are, but I promise you, Spencer is our main focus. We're all pretty selfish when it comes to her." He nods, thinking over my words and his next question.

"And the little one, Katy. Where does she fit in with your little family?" *Family.* That word causes a warmth to bloom in my chest. Without realizing it, that's what we've become.

"Katy is Katy. She had a bad home life, and Spencer rescued her. We consider her ours and will treat her as such. She isn't going anywhere." He stares off at Spencer's house. After several minutes of silence, I assume the conversation is over and finish my drink.

"Would it be possible to get those pictures from you?"

"She won't like my offer." I think about his statement in relation to my question and can't put the pieces together.

"Offer?"

He looks at me with a serious expression. "I want to trade. You need it more than me. There are five bedrooms and a larger bonus room that could probably fit the size bed all of you big men need." Wait. Is he talking about the house? I glance behind me through the window into the kitchen.

"The house. Eddie, are you saying you want to trade houses with Spencer and…us?"

"Yes, son. I thought you were smarter than this. What else would I be talking about? You need this big house for all six of you. I'm one man. The pool house is the perfect size for me. I can't keep up with it and all this space is going to waste. She won't accept it from me, so you need to convince her. I see the way she looks at you. Spencer likes those other boys, but you're different. She respects you and every word that comes from your mouth. If you promise me you'll do everything in your power to convince her, you can have all of my knowledge of that asshole bastard."

"Deal." We shake hands and head back into the house. He opens a drawer in the kitchen and hands me a large, thick envelope. "He put all of these on our vehicles?"

"Unfortunately. Don't show them to Spencer unless you have to. I know she got that big envelope a while back, but some of these are worse. Katy has been appearing in them more often. There's even one back when Spencer first met Justin. He's hanging on to his life by a thread as they get him into the ambulance."

I don't know Justin's story, so I simply nod my acknowledgment. I'll have to ask one of the guys at some point.

We exchange numbers, shake hands, and as soon as I get in the truck, I call Chip.

"What's up, Boss?"

"Chip, I have a security job at my girlfriend's house. I want the works. Price isn't an option. I need a two-bedroom pool

257

house." I think for a moment and make up my mind quickly. "And a five-bedroom house, both on the same property. I need you ready at one-thirty."

"Got it. Can I ask a question?"

"Of course."

"Girlfriend? Is this new?" I had a feeling that's what he was going to ask. Let's see how he responds to my answer.

"Yes, and a few boyfriends. We're a big, happy family. Oh, and Chip, if you look at any of them sideways today, you're fired."

Without hesitations, he answers, "Wouldn't dream of it, Boss."

I hang up the phone and dial the next number.

"Montgomery."

"Monty, it's Tucker. I have pictures for you and someone to interview who has inside information."

"Perfect. When?" This is what makes him a good P.I. He's all work and no bullshit. "He's my girlfriend's father, the ex's almost father-in-law. They worked together. He's willing to tell you everything you need. I'll drop the pictures and his number into your P.O. Box in twenty."

He hangs up, and I head to the post office. When I arrive, I use my key to drop the envelope of pictures into the box along with a piece of paper with Eddie's information on it. I thought long and hard about looking at them before I dropped them off, but that's Spencer's past. I'll be patient and let her tell me whatever she feels comfortable with when she's ready.

As I'm walking out, my phone rings. I take it out of my pocket to see an audio message from Miller. Quickly, another comes through, and another. By the time I get to my truck, there are five audio messages. Is something wrong? I click the first file and listen. I hear lots of rustling and muted sounds. Is that Spencer?

"Pweeese. Oh god." The message ends. I hit the next one, and again, there are more muted voices.

"No. No." What the fuck is going on. Is Spencer in distress? I turn the truck on, throw it into reverse harder than necessary, and whip it out of the parking space. I'm ten minutes from her house but can get there in eight, maybe seven if I don't hit any red lights.

The next two messages are completely muffled and I can't make out any distinguishable sounds. There's one more audio left, and my adrenaline is pumping so hard my hands are shaking. I struggle to hit the button on the last one, but I'm only a few blocks away, so I say fuck it and reach under my seat for my gun.

Flying into the driveway, I barely put my truck in park before jumping out and checking my clip to confirm it's loaded. It always is, but it's a habit to check. As quietly as possible, I unlock the door and turn off the alarm. There's yelling coming from the bedroom, and my body is so amped up I don't realize the noises are pleasure and not pain until I swing the door open and find Spencer on all four, head in Axel's lap, and Miller balls deep in her pussy.

"Get the fuck off her." I press the gun to Miller's head, and he freezes.

"Chill, Tucker. Put the gun down." Miller's hands slowly raise.

"I said. Get. The fuck. Off. Her." I'm seeing red. I realize I'm being irrational, but I feel like I've been taken over by a raging bull, and nothing is stopping me right now.

"Okay, man. I'm pulling out." Miller gently sits back on his knees, and his cock bobs on his stomach, glistening with Spencer's arousal. When he steps off the bed, I grab the barrel of my gun and offer it to him. He hesitantly takes it.

"Put that away and take care of Axel before you both get another round of blue balls."

I'm on autopilot. Everyone in the room is watching me, and all I can do is stare at the goddess on her knees, where she doesn't belong. My pants land on the floor at the same time my shirt does, and I shrug out of my briefs.

"Fuck yeah, Daddy Tucker putting us all to shame. I love how you hide that anaconda in those tighty-whities."

"Axel," Miller warns. "I wouldn't mess with him. Look at his eyes." My eyes? What could he see in my eyes?

"Move, Axel." He shifts from under Spencer's head, his glistening cock telling me at one point, he had her glorious lips on his cock.

I gently place my hands on Spencer's hips and push her forward so she's lying on her stomach. Rolling her over, I lift her to the top of the bed and press a kiss to her forehead.

"You should be treated like a Queen. May I bow down to you?" I rub a thumb across her jawline so she's looking at me. She nods several times, not knowing exactly what I mean but trusting me. My hand moves from her chin and follows the length of her body. Her breathing is shallow with anticipation.

Adjusting my hips, I grab the base of my cock and line up to her soaked entrance.

"Are you ready for me, Little Miss?"

"More than ready."

TUCKER

36

Miller

With a smile, I watch as Axel pins Spencer to the bedroom door. He entered the room before she did, waiting for her to come by. I know how horny he is because he texted me several times throughout the night whining.

"Hey, Tails." His nose nuzzles her neck, and she tilts her head to give him better access.

"Axel. You startled me. I'm inclined to be upset, but…" Her voice trails off, and I see his hand sweep gentle fingers over her nipple.

I'm aching for this woman. My cock was semi-erect all night. When she kissed my forehead, I thought my cock might explode from that simple touch.

"I want you, Tails. So fucking much. Please. I'm begging you. You're all I ever think about. I think your name is tattooed on my cock with as much as I've been chanting your name when I jerk off."

I scoff behind them. "That's romantic, Axel." His foot swings back to kick me, but I deflect him.

"Can we...can we pause and shower...shower off the work day?" Her words come out staggered between gasps and moans as Axel continues the assault on her neck and breasts.

"Axel, be a good boy and listen to her." He whines into Spencer's neck. I step up behind him and run my hand up the nape of his neck and into his soft curls. I love his fucking curls. When I reach the crown of his head, I close my fist and pull his head away from her neck. His eyes meet mine from his upside-down angle. "Don't you want to be a good boy?"

"Fuck. Why does that do something to me?"

"Because I think you like the praise. Now, kiss Spencer once more and be a good fucking boy and go turn the shower on like she asked." I watch his Adam's apple bob, and I lick his neck, feeling his moan vibrate under my lips. "Go." When I release his hair, he stumbles back into my chest, and I smile while he regains his composure.

As he walks backward toward the bathroom, he blows Spencer a kiss and winks before turning and jogging the rest of the way.

"He's an animal on the best days, isn't he." Spencer's cheeks and chest are beautifully pink, and her pupils are blown with lust. She's turned on, and I like her like this.

I reach over her shoulder and grab the end of a braid. Carefully, I pull out the tiny clear rubber band and shove it in my pocket before I start the unbraiding process. I keep eye contact with her—the act being as sensual as anything physical we do together. My fingers massage her scalp as I reach the top and start again with the other braid.

Spencer is putty in my hands by the time Axel returns, telling us the water is ready. With her hand in mine, I guide her toward the shower. I'm feeling as feral as Axel's words to her, but I'm maintaining my composure by a thread. The last time we showered together, she jerked us off, and as amazing as that sounds right now, I want her, not her hands.

Despite the obvious need and want between us, everyone keeps their hands to themselves. Although the combined lust swims in the air, and eyes wander everywhere.

"Fuck, Tails. You're... you're beyond words." Axel steps up behind her and wraps his arms around her chest, cupping each breast in his hands. I want to scold him, but we've done all the needed washing and are about to get out.

I'm enjoying the show, watching his fingers knead her nipples in slow circles. I grab his wrist so he doesn't move and surround his fingers and her nipple with my mouth. My lips suck on Axel's fingers while my tongue flicks Spencer's nipples. They moan their satisfaction, and it's precisely the sound I was looking for.

"I'm so fucking hard it hurts. Let me have you, Tails. Please don't make me wait another second." I'm not sure who the vixen is between us, but she wiggles her ass into Axel's cock, and I see the second he snaps. "Hold on to Miller's shoulders." Spencer looks at me, and the corner of her mouth tips up. She knows exactly what she's doing.

I grab her arms and place them around my neck while Axel takes her hips and pulls them back toward him, getting the angle that he needs to enter her.

"You have no idea how much I've fantasized about this ass." His hands make circles over each cheek, and he squeezes, causing Spencer to moan. I feel it in my chest, and it's hard not to moan myself.

Axel slides his cock between her legs and thrusts up and down, teasing her. I take Spencer's lips in mine and know the moment he stops teasing.

"Oh fuck." Spencer's swear is muffled by my lips. She never curses unless it's an extreme situation.

"How do those piercings feel, Tails?" Shit, how could I forget about the piercings? Maybe this wasn't the best idea.

"Are you okay, Smithy? If you need him to stop, just say it. Safewords don't apply right now. Stop is stop." She's panting, and her eyes scrunch closed. Axel isn't moving, waiting for her answer. He's about halfway in, but he isn't small, and add the piercings, I imagine she's feeling a lot.

"I...he feels so good. Big. Good. Amazing." The lines on her forehead relax as she rocks back into him and moans.

"Maybe you're setting the bar too high for the rest of us, Axel."

"It's hard to compete with the cross." Axel is so cocky, but it's part of his charm.

"If you're done comparing dick sizes, I'm ready for the promises you've made."

Axel slaps his chest in horror. "Did those filthy words just come from your pretty mouth?" She's about to answer when he slams his hips, causing her to rock hard into my chest. I have to take a step back to brace myself from falling.

"Be careful man. Precious cargo and a slippery floor. Warn me next time."

"Here's your warning." He firmly grabs her hips and thrusts in again. I carefully watch Spencer's face for any signs of discomfort, but all I see is pure bliss. Her mouth parts as the sounds of pleasure escape her. The creases on her forehead and between her brows are gone.

Axel's pace is deep and even, and I share my time looking at them both. I find myself mesmerized, staring at where they connect. Watching him dip in and out of her, my hips begin to move with his rhythm.

"Like what you see, Mills? Think you could handle me?"

No.

"Yes. Easily." The thought of his piercings in my ass both terrifies and excites me. "Maybe one day."

Axel continues to pound into Spencer and their sounds of pleasure echo off the bathroom walls.

"How you doing, Smithy?"

"Shhhh. Busy." I chuckle at her response and reach under and take her swinging breast into my hands. I want to try and give her another orgasm, but right now, in the shower, isn't the time.

When I glance up, I can see that Axel is getting close. His abs constrict as he pumps into her, and he's taking deep, shallow breaths.

"Tails. I'm almost there. Can I come in this tight pussy, or would you rather I pull out?" I'm shocked he's coherent enough to give her the option right now. He looks completely lost in lust. "Decide quickly, beautiful."

"In. Oh god. In." Axel's hand slides up her back, and he braces on her shoulder, thrusting harder and deeper. Their moans echo around the room, and it's the most incredible music I've ever heard.

"Fuck. Oh fuck, Spencer." With one last, hard lunge, Axel's forehead tenses, and he spills inside her. His orgasm face is just as incredible to watch as Spencer's was. When he's done, he tickles his fingers down her back and slowly pulls out. She tries to stand, but Axel holds her down to my shoulders.

"Just give me a minute to watch my come drip from your pussy." He swipes his fingers through her, coating Spencer's lips with his release. "Fuck this is… it's fucking erotic."

I can't even see it, but I know his description is accurate.

"Hey, at least with shower sex, there's easy cleanup." His hand disappears again, and Spencer moans.

"Let's get you cleaned up, Smithy. Do you think you can take another round?" She lifts on her toes and kisses my jaw.

"I certainly can."

We finish our shower and dry off in the bathroom. Hands and lips wander everywhere, making the task difficult but fun, as Spencer giggles at our playfulness.

When we stumble into the bedroom, someone's phone is dinging with a notification. It must be Axel's because he grabs his phone from his discarded scrubs and tosses it on the bed without looking.

"I need to charge that. It's almost dead."

"Good call." I take my phone from my work pants, and Spencer does the same, plugging hers in. Axel rounds the bed, picks up his phone, and plugs it in on the opposite nightstand. I extend my arm, about to ask Axel to plug mine in as well, when Spencer drops her towel, completely distracting me. Despite having just been naked with her in the shower, she still stuns me with her beauty. And now, knowing what her body has been through and healed from, I have an even greater respect for her.

Axel jumps onto the bed like a dog, and my phone falls from my hand. He reaches out and pulls Spencer on top of him, tickling her.

"Please. Oh god." She shrieks, and Axel stops.

"What's the matter, Tails? Is tickling a limit? We haven't talked about limits yet. It's probably something we should all talk about together." He tickles her sides, and her giggles get louder.

"No, no." They're rolling around on the bed, and it's so nice to see her carefree, but I want her, and the need keeps rising.

"Axel." He stops tickling her, and he must see the desire in my eyes because he kisses her quickly and turns her toward me.

"I think someone wants his turn, Tails. He's waited long enough. Don't keep him in suspense for too much longer." She crawls on her knees to me at the end of the bed, and I might as well be drooling at the sight before me.

"Smithy, I'm on edge. I'm going to do my best to take it easy with you, but holy fuck, I could devour you right now."

"Miller, I've told you before. I'm not a fragile flower. Do your worst. I know my safeword." I grab her chin and look into her blue eyes. I want to make sure she understands what she's saying and isn't just trying to appease me. I know I won't find anything. She's confident in every decision she makes, even this one.

"Okay, I'll trust you because I know you trust me." She smiles, and it's sweet with an edge of sass to it.

Oh, Spencer, I'm about to take the sass right out of you.

I pull her in for a passionate kiss and try to convey exactly what I'm about to do to her. I don't let the kiss linger long before I pull away and grab her shoulders.

"Turn around and get on all fours. I want to stare at this ass while I take you." She looks as eager as I feel and turns and presents herself to me. Axel sees an opportunity, sits at the head of the bed, and pulls her into him.

"If you feel so inclined, I'll gladly take your mouth on my cock. Otherwise, I'm here for you to lean on and save your arms. No expectations." I see the sly smile she gives him before she opens her mouth and licks him from base to tip.

"Fuck me." Axel slaps his hand on the bed and fists the blankets. She sucks his tip into her mouth, and I'm fucking green with jealousy until I remember I have her pussy ready and waiting for me.

Lining up behind her, I pull her cheeks apart to see exactly where I'm sinking into. When my cock finally inches in, she's tight, and her heat surrounds me like a hug. I slowly pump my hips, sinking farther and farther. When I bottom out, Spencer gasps, and Axel's cock falls from her mouth.

"Miller."

"I know. I feel it, too. I can be easy."

"Don't be easy. Please." The words rush out of her, and I know she means them.

"You got her, Axel?"

"Go for it. I've got her."

I grab her hips and take one last look at her body. I see the faint pink marks near my fingers where Axel's hands were previously. I feel a rush of possessiveness but also excitement. My first thrust is controlled, and a moan of relief escapes me. It feels like coming home. Like somewhere I'm meant to be.

I begin a steady rhythm, increasing slightly with each thrust. I want to make sure she's comfortable despite her telling me to do my worst. I'd also love for her to orgasm, but that will probably be something we have to work on after I'm done, and I have no complaints about that.

Her moans of pleasure float through the room, and I grunt with every thrust. She's being cautious and only taking in Axel's head so she doesn't accidentally go further than she's comfortable with. Either way, he's definitely enjoying himself.

"Get the fuck off her." Suddenly, there's a gun pressed to the back of my head. I recognize Tucker's voice, but there's an edge to it.

"Chill, Tucker. Put the gun down."

"I said. Get. The fuck. Off. Her." He's on edge and has a gun to my head. I'm not messing around with him.

"Okay, man. I'm pulling out." I sit back on my knees and gently pull out. My cock bobs, and I feel the loss of her heat. I step off the bed, not making any sudden movements, and Tucker takes the barrel of the gun and offers it to me.

"Put that away and take care of Axel before you both get another round of blue balls."

37

Axel

Tucker storms into the room and, in a flash, has a gun to Miller's head. My adrenaline pumps through my body, and my heartbeat whooshes in my ears. I see Miller and Tucker's mouths moving, but all I can do is watch and make sure Spencer is safe.

"Put that away and take care of Axel before you both get another round of blue balls."

I'm totally down for that.

Tucker stares at Spencer as he strips his clothing. When he finally removes his black undies, my jaw actually drops.

"Fuck yeah, Daddy Tucker putting us all to shame. I love how you hide that anaconda in those tighty-whities."

"Axel," Miller warns. "I wouldn't mess with him. Look at his eyes." He's right. There's a fire in Tucker's eyes that I haven't seen before.

"Move, Axel." I may have joked with Tucker a minute ago, but I've learned my lesson. I give Spencer's cheek a gentle swipe and slide out from under her. Tucker takes her hips and readjusts them until she's at the top of the bed, and he hovers over her.

"You should be treated like a Queen. May I bow down to you?" He rubs a thumb across her jawline so she's looking at him and nods several times. Tucker's hand moves down the length of her body as I feel a hand glide up my chest.

"Tucker told me to take care of you, but I know you already came once. Do you need another round?" Miller tugs at my cock, and the sensation is so much different than Spencer's soft tongue.

"No, I'm good, but let me take care of you." I reach for his engorged cock, and he stops me.

"Watch." He motions toward Spencer and Tucker next to me.

"Are you ready for me, Little Miss?"

There's so much reverence in his question. She's precious to him in a way that is different from the rest of us. We each have our own relationship with Spencer but his is on a deeper level. I'm not mad or jealous. I'm in awe.

"More than ready." Spencer spreads her legs wider to allow him entrance, and he slowly slides his cock into her.

"I know I'm big, and I'll do my best to make it as painless as possible. If Miller hadn't already prepared you, I'd have done that first. It might burn, but tell me if it's too much."

The whole "with age comes wisdom" thing must be true. Either that, or it's a Southern gentleman thing because he worships her like none of us can.

"Will you let me take your ass?" Miller squeezes my ass cheek, and I instantly clench my butt.

"I've obviously never—"

"Neither have I. I'm a bottom for Lincoln. If you're willing to try, so am I?"

Am I? That's a big step. Looking over to Spencer and Tucker, I think of what a monumental step she's taking, putting her trust in four men she's known for various lengths of time. Miller has been my best friend for years, and if I'm going to experiment and try new things, he seems like the best candidate.

"You'll go slow?"

"Of course. And you have your safeword. I'll start with my finger, and we'll go from there." I nod and hear the nightstand drawer open. I'm not surprised to know he has lube hidden in there. "Let me get a towel. I'll be right back."

As he walks across the room, I stare at his gloriously toned ass. Whispered words from Tucker grab my attention.

"You're more beautiful than a sunset over the lake at my parent's cattle ranch. You take my breath away every time I see you. Your body was made from the heavens to fit me perfectly." He begins to hum a tune I don't recognize, but if I had to guess, it's a country song.

Miller returns with a smile as he stares at Tucker and Spencer.

"Aren't they nice to watch?" I hum my response but don't pull my eyes away. He lays a towel down on the bed, and I look up at him over my shoulder with a puzzled look.

"What's that for?"

"I don't want this to be impersonal, Axel, lay on your back. We don't want to get any lube on Spencer's bed."

"Isn't that so nice of you?" I really need to think about my snark sometimes.

"If you want to be a brat, I don't have to be nice?"

Yeah. Definitely need to think more before I sass the man who's about to put something in my ass. I can't help myself.

Sometimes my mouth works quicker than my mind.

I lay on the towel and get comfortable on the pillow. I angle myself, so I have a full view of the sex going on next to me. I'm not sure I've ever seen such intimate lovemaking, and I don't want to miss a moment if I don't have to.

The clicking of the lube cap brings my attention back to Miller. For a split second, I'm brought back to work and the hundreds of rectal exams I've seen and done. Miller must see something in my face change, and he closes the cap and leans over me.

"We don't have to."

He read me wrong.

"I couldn't help but think of the exams I do at work. My mind flashed there for a moment, but I promise I wouldn't say yes if I didn't want to." Miller's smile tells me he understands, and he dips down, taking my lips in his. I get lost in his kiss. His lips are thinner than Spencer's but just as soft.

Miller must have already applied lube to his fingers because his one hand is hovering oddly between us, and I appreciate him taking this time to help me get out of my head. When his hand moves, I feel the cool gel rimming me. It's an odd sensation. One that my brain is struggling to compete with. I know what he's doing *isn't* wrong, and it feels better than I could have imagined, but a small doubt in the back of my brain tells me I shouldn't be doing this.

"Relax, Axel. You're breathing heavily. I haven't even done anything yet."

"Sorry."

"Don't be. Get out of your head and just feel. This was new to me not that long ago as well, remember? Lincoln talked me through it, and I'll do the same for you."

274

He's right. They've been together less than a year, and as far as I know, Miller had never done anything with a guy before Lincoln. And he's never done anything like this with any guy. He's trusting me with this new experience as well.

I take a deep breath and close my eyes. My body relaxes, knowing this is my best friend, and he wouldn't do anything to intentionally make either of us uncomfortable.

"Watch them." I happily turn my head back to Tucker and Spencer. I was trying to be present for Miller and not pay attention to them, but with permission, I happily take in their beautiful sight.

A light layer of sweat has formed on Tucker's forehead. I know the restraint he's holding back to be slow and gentle with her. He's a better man than Miller and me. He told her she was a Queen and should be treated as such. I fucking agree, and there's a part of me that feels guilty. One for taking her in the shower for the first time and two for not being gentle. I wouldn't be surprised if I left a bruise or two on her hips.

"How does that feel?" I turn back to Miller, brows crunched. It feels just as good as it did...*oh*.

"You...I didn't even feel it." I was so entranced with my viewing party, I hadn't realized Miller had slipped his finger in. It's strange and a little uncomfortable, but now I can understand how this is enjoyable. Miller alternates his finger from shallow pumping to small circles to stretch me out. I know there are plenty of nerves there, but I've never had anyone explore before, and when the first moan leaves my lips, it surprises me more than anyone else.

A smug smile crosses Miller's face, and I pull him in for a kiss. I take the lead with my tongue, and he lets me. I'm overloaded with the sounds and sensations around me. Miller whispers, "Breathe," into our kiss, and I feel the pressure and understand his warning.

A second finger slides into my ass and the pressure increases, but so does the pleasure. I feel needy and don't know how much more I can take. I want this.

"Please, Miller." My hips rock involuntarily onto his fingers, and I want more. I want him deeper.

"I'm bigger than two fingers, Axel."

"I don't fucking care. Please." He chuckles into my neck as he pulls his fingers out and nips my shoulder.

Miller sits up on his knees and grabs the bottle of lube again. He puts a generous amount of the gel on his hand and slides it up and down his shaft. He's right. He's definitely thicker than his two fingers, but at this point, I'm over the edge of horny. I'll truly beg if I need to, but I need him now.

"If you're comfortable, I'd like to stay in this position. If you'd rather turn over, I'm okay with that too." I widen my knees in response, and he smiles and looks down at my cock. It's ready and standing at attention. He takes his lubed hand and strokes me a few times, and my hips buck off the bed. "Stroke yourself and watch Spencer while I get settled. The first entry will be the hardest. Take any distraction you can."

"No. I want to watch you. I don't need a distraction; I trust you." I cup my hand around his, and for a few pumps, we stroke my cock together. I release the pressure so he can move his hand, and he adds more lube to his fingers and pushes them inside me one last time before taking his base and lining up.

I tell myself to relax and take several deep breaths. Miller takes the breaths with me, and on the third one, he pushes in as I exhale.

"Holy shit." That's…I don't fucking know.

"Shhh. You're doing good. Keep breathing." Miller runs a hand up my chest, and I concentrate on the feel of his fingertips, and they trail across my body. He pulls out and pushes back in, the discomfort turns to pleasure with every inch he rocks into me.

"My god, Miller." My muscles relax the further he sinks in.

"It feels good, doesn't it." He's not asking me, he's telling me. He knows what I'm feeling, and that makes this even better.

"What about you?" My question comes out between pants and moans. I want to know if this is just as enjoyable for him as me.

"Fuck, Axel. It's incredible. I may need to see if Lincoln will let me top him."

"Thinking about another man while your dick is in my ass. Foul play, Mills." He reaches up and grabs my hair. It stings more than it should because it's still damp from the shower.

"Trust me. I'm right here with you. But imagine this. I'm here in your ass, and Lincoln's behind me in mine, pounding into us both."

"Oh fuck." I like the sound of that way more than I should. New kink unlocked. "Let's call him. Let's leave a voicemail."

"Or you could send him an audio file like you did to me." Miller and I snap our attention to Tucker.

"What?"

Tucker turns to us, not stopping his lovemaking with Spencer, and smiles.

"Did you not wonder why I came in here, guns a-blazin'? I got several audio files through text but couldn't make them out and thought Spencer was in trouble."

What the hell is he talking about? My phone is plugged in on our side. Spencer's is plugged in on hers and...*Shit.*

"Miller, where's your phone?"

"My...oh shit. You knocked it out of my hand. It's gotta be somewhere here on the bed." We feel around, and neither of us comes up with his phone.

"Fuck it. Send him an audio on mine. It'll be an even bigger surprise." I reach my phone and unplug it, laying it on the mattress next to me. "You're in charge of the sound." Miller flashes me his panty-dropping smile, and I clench down on him.

"God dammit, Axel." He huffs and closes his eyes. I like his reaction and I laugh and do it again. He gasps and smacks a hand to my chest. "If you want to enjoy this for longer than three more seconds, you'll be a good boy. Stop that."

"Holy fuck." I melt at his words. He smiles and brushes his lips against mine.

"That's what I thought."

Spencer giggles next to us and grabs our attention. I reach over and run my palm along her breast and she arches into my hand.

"Something funny, Tails." She moans out the word no, and I swear Miller and Tucker have a silent conversation. They slam into us, causing the noise in the room to erupt into animalistic moans. Tucker is no longer being sweet with Spencer.

"Axel, can you reach between us and play with Spencer's clit?" Daddy Tucker wants help?

I look at Miller, who nods, and we shift lower on the bed so I don't have to strain to reach. Tucker shifts from his elbow to his knees so there's better access for my hand. A long, high pitch sound escapes Spencer when I touch her sweet spot.

"Now it's a party."

Miller and Tucker smile at each other, and Tucker grabs him by the neck and pulls him in for a kiss. I thought the shower sex with Spencer was going to be the highlight of my day, but damn, is Lincoln going to be mad when he gets home.

I glance at Spencer, and she stares at them in awe, making out.

"They're hot together, aren't they? All muscle and brawn."

Tucker takes out the aggression he's been holding back from Spencer on Miller's lips.

"Let's send Lincoln some video to go with the audio."

Spencer reaches down and hands me my cell. Turning the camera, I pretend to be the world's greatest porn director and aim the video on their locked lips. I pan down to my hand, strumming on Spencer's clit and up her body to her face, where she's biting her lips and moaning. Finally, I move it to my side of the bed and focus on where Miller and I are connected.

I'm watching Miller pound into me through the screen when he thrusts so hard I drop the phone.

"Whatcha doing?" He narrows his eyes at me and glances at the phone, picking it up. It must have stopped recording when I dropped it because Miller pushes the button and begins recording me. He moves the cameras between Spencer and me, and I know he has a better angle than I did, and this video will be so much better.

"Who do you think will come first, Tucker? Everyone has a twenty-five percent chance."

Shit. Miller is trying to kill me. I may have already come in the shower, but I'm hard as a rock, and he keeps rubbing my prostate. If he wants to, he can make me come at any time. I'm at his mercy.

"Let's focus on our Queen. She's the most important." Spencer's moan is one of appreciation, and we all agree with Tucker. "Miller, take over for Axel so he can focus on her beautiful breasts. I think she's relaxed enough to give us her pleasure. What do you think, Little Miss?" He pushes on her pelvis just above my hand. "Are you feeling that tingle deep down? I can feel your pussy walls fluttering.

"Yes. I feel it. Oh god."

"Shhh. Don't think, just feel." Tucker runs his hands up her inner thighs.

We all focus our attention on Spencer. Her pleasure is our primary goal and we are taking it very seriously. Miller hasn't stopped pumping into me, but it's more of a leisurely pace, as his new goal is to make her come with his fingers. I involuntarily moan as I think about my mouth on her pussy, and how fucking amazing it was to have her come on my tongue. With my free hand, I stroke my cock, trying to give myself some relief. Spencer sees and reaches over.

"Let me." She replaces my hand with hers, and the contrast is almost shocking. Her touch is gentler and softer than mine or Miller's hand. She watches herself as she pumps me, a small smile creeping on her face.

Out of the corner of my eyes, I see her legs start to quiver, and when I look at Miller, there's a smile of determination on his face. Tucker adjusts his position, lifting Spencer's hips, and she screams. She wasn't prepared for her orgasm to take her yet, and as her body convulses her hand on my

280

cock tightens. Between her sounds, her hand, and Miller's hardening thrusts, I lose any control I had left and come. Ropes of hot liquid squirt from my tip, coating my stomach and Spencer's hand.

"Fucking Christ, Tails. Oh god. Fuck." There's so much going on around me. Spencer releases my cock just as Miller lays on top of me. I hear panting, and I'm not sure if it's me, him, him, or her. Maybe it's all of us.

Miller's thrusts are deep and slightly erratic, and I know he's about to come. He lets out a loud moan and quickly sits up, pulling out and stroking his cock feverishly. He spills on my stomach, adding to the mess I made of myself, just as I hear Tucker cursing and spilling his orgasm into Spencer. Miller falls on the bed next to me and flops back. Tucker and Spencer make out next to us and I don't think I've ever felt more content than in this exact moment.

I pick up my phone, realizing that at some point, Miller hit send and dropped it. I wonder how much of a show Lincoln got.

Suddenly, laughter bursts next to me, and Miller is hysterical.

"What's wrong with you?"

"Looks like we're all going to need another shower." He swirls his fingers through the mess on my stomach, and everyone joins in on the laughter.

"Little Miss, I have something to tell you. Well, all of you, really."

"Alright." She gives him a skeptical look, and I'm right there with her.

"We're moving into the big house, and your father is taking over the pool house. I won't take any arguments. It was his suggestion, and I agree."

38

Lincoln

It's strange not driving Katy to school. I didn't realize how used to our morning chats I had become. There isn't a lot of one-on-one time in that tiny house, but those fifteen minutes alone with her are always nice.

Katy sees me in the cafeteria as I walk in and comes right to me. Her bright smile warms my heart. I miss her bratty humor around the house.

"Hey, Lin—Officer Reed." Her eyes quickly dart around to see if anyone nearby heard her slip up. I informed the school of her new home situation, but I can understand Katy not wanting her peers to know too much.

I greet her with a warm smile in return. "Hey, Katy girl. We miss you at home. How is Casa Webb?"

"Hannah is a handful, and Miles is adorable. It's great." I place a hand on her shoulder, something that looks inconspicuous, and give her a squeeze. She understands my gesture and grins.

"And Justin and Nicole?"

"Wonderful, of course. How long am I staying?" I can't

tell from the tone of her question if she's asking because she wants to stay or she's ready to leave and come back to us.

"You're old enough to make that decision, Katy. There's no pressure to stay or leave. You can come home with me today, or I can take you back to Justin's. If you need more clothes, we can get those for you, too."

"Oh, clothes aren't an issue. I'm actually coming back with far more than I left with. Nicole is giving me half her wardrobe because it either doesn't fit anymore, or she says it isn't very motherly of her to wear, now that she has two kids."

That sounds like a Nicole statement.

"Well, that's awesome. The decision is yours when you want to come home. Justin extended an open-ended invitation, but I'll tell you this, Axel misses having someone around on his level."

She looks at me and tilts her head. "I don't know if that's an insult to him or me."

"Definitely him. Now, go eat breakfast and get to homeroom. Oh, how are you feeling?" For a moment, her face falls, and I regret asking. She readjusts her book bag on her shoulders and plays with the end of her hair.

"I feel fine." She lowers her voice and looks around again to make sure no one has come any closer to our conversation. "Should I be feeling fine? Is something wrong? I expected to feel nauseous or something."

Poor thing. We haven't talked much about her positive test, and it sounds like she hasn't talked to Nicole yet, either.

"It's still early, and not everyone gets mo—feels sick." I realize saying morning sickness out loud might not be the best thing, just in case anyone does happen to eavesdrop.

"Okay." She nods and seems a bit more relieved.

"Whenever you make a decision, just let us know. There's plenty of time."

"I know. I will." She smiles and heads to the cafeteria line to get her breakfast.

I wish I could pull her into my arms and hug her until she feels whole, but it's not the time and place.

Most days are uneventful for me. While it's not as fulfilling as being a street cop, I'll take what I can get. I couldn't retire. I love the job too much, but being shot in the leg close enough to my knee to cause problems solidified my future. It was either desk work or this, and I'm not a desk jockey.

As I'm walking the halls, my phone buzzes. I pull it out to check, and there's a message from Axel. No, it's a video. I click on it and quickly fumble to turn the volume off. I shove myself into a corner so no one can walk up behind me and watch Tucker and Miller making out.

That's pretty fucking hot. The camera lowers down Tucker's body, his very naked body, where he's connected with Spencer, and a hand is between her legs. I quickly lock the phone and look around. The halls are empty, but this is absolutely an inappropriate video to watch out in the open, or even in a school building, for that matter. But I'm a fucking cat, and curiosity is getting the better of me.

I radio the office and give them the code for using the bathroom in case they need me. It's not necessary, but I don't like them to worry if something happens and it takes me a little longer to get across the school in an emergency.

As soon as I lock the bathroom door, I turn the vent fan on, open my phone, and click on the video again. I turn the volume up the tiniest bit just so I can hear over the fan, but not enough that anyone outside the door could. The screen follows the line of Spencer's body, and all I can think is my brother is one lucky bastard. Spencer is moaning and biting her lip when the camera moves again. I inwardly protest until I see a very familiar set of abs pumping into an ass.

"Fuck me, Fireball. Who knew you had that in you?"

Miller pumps hard into Axel, and the phone falls, ending the video. The wave of heat coursing through me changes to disappointment until I see another video waiting to be played. It had to have come in while I was watching the first one.

I eagerly press play and notice the angle is different. Axel must have had the phone for the first one because this angle shows a naked Axel with Miller's cock thrusting into him. That's fucking hot and infuriating. Why am I missing this? Why didn't I know Miller had interest in being a top?

"Who do you think will come first, Tucker? Everyone has a twenty-five percent chance."

Fuck. Me. Sideways.

"Let's focus on our Queen. She's the most important." Spencer must like the sound of that because her moan is intoxicating. "Miller, take over for Axel so he can focus on her breasts. I think she's relaxed enough to give us her pleasure. What do you think, Little Miss?"

Oh, I fucking hope so. Am I going to get to watch Spencer come again?

I rub my rapidly growing cock over my pants. I absolutely will not jerk off in the school bathroom, but I need the relief of some pressure.

I can hear talking, but I'm more focused on what's going on. Axel has her breasts, Miller has her clit, and Tucker is

286

holding her legs. Everyone's attention is on Spencer, and she's enjoying herself completely.

The camera is shaky but shows me glimpses of everyone's hands and connections. Axel takes his cock and starts stroking in rhythm with Miller's thrusts, and Spencer's delicate hand reaches over and takes it for him.

I pause the video to calm myself down. My heart is racing, and without realizing it, I'm rubbing my pants in time with the video. I need to calm the fuck down. *Now.*

No. What I need to do is put the phone down and somehow finish the rest of my day. I know how the end of the video is going to go. They're all going to come, and I'll probably come with them. I'm not a teenager and don't want to be walking around with jizz in my pants all day. I need to put it away, then go home and rail Miller, and make sweet love to my dream girl…After I take Katy back to Justin's.

Shit. What if she wants to come home? I love Katy, but my blue balls require her to spend at least another day at Justin's house.

With every ounce of willpower I have, I put my phone in my pocket. I think about sending a warning text to Miller, but he doesn't deserve the heads up. He'll get what's coming to him. I think of the aftermath of getting shot to will my cock down before I leave the bathroom, and it works. I still have to get through the rest of the day, but I can come up with a plan that's suitable for the offense.

"Is everything okay, Linc? You seem…antsy." From the moment Katy got in my truck and confirmed she was spending the night with Justin, all I've been able to think about is dropping her off and getting home.

"Sorry. Just have a lot on my mind. Everything is fine." She puts her hand over mine on the steering wheel, where I'm tapping my fingers.

"Seriously, what's up?"

What's up? My boyfriend sent me a racy sex video with everyone involved but me, and if I don't stick my dick in someone soon, I might explode.

Yeah, let's not say that out loud.

"Like I said. A lot on my mind. Just anxious to get home and...talk to Miller."

"Ohhh, I get it." She gets it? What does she get? "You're horny, and since I'm not there, you guys can have all the grownup fun time you want."

Air. I need air. I feel the tips of my ears flaming as I roll down the window, hoping the wind will help cool me down. It doesn't. Hearing Katy laugh at me doesn't help either.

"Did I embarrass you, Linc?" She holds her hand over her mouth, trying not to laugh out loud.

"No. Yes. Shut up, child. I can't talk about this stuff with you." Her laughter spills over, and tears stream down her cheeks by the time I pull into Justin's driveway.

The front door opens, and Katy practically spills out of the car in hysterics. Justin runs over, not realizing her crisis is laughter and not another ailment, and she crashes into his arms.

"What the hell is going on?" Justin looks between the two of us, wearing completely different expressions.

Katy's arm flails out, and she points at me. "He...he..." She takes a deep breath and spews out the words. "He's embarrassed to talk to me about sex."

"Um. O-kay." He draws out the word, still not understanding what's going on.

"He wants to get home to Miller and get some. He's practically vibrating with excitement. Let's not hold him up. I don't want to see him explode in your driveway."

Groaning, I drop my head to the steering wheel, convinced I'm as red as a tomato.

"You good, Linc?" Justin sounds amused at my sheer mortification from this conversation. "Do you want to come in and have a dri—"

"Nope, gotta get home. Bye, Justin. Bye, brat. Close the door. Don't let it hit you on the way out." Katy grabs her book bag from the truck and wiggles her fingers at me before closing the door with a shit eating grin.

She manages a sarcastic, "Have fun. Use protection," before I leave Justin's driveway. I'm at the edge of my limit. Using the Bluetooth in my truck, I call Miller.

"Hey, Babe. You on your way home?" All I can do is growl as his voice instantly brings me back to the videos I watched earlier. "Lincoln, you okay?"

"No. I'm not fucking okay. I got not one but two fucking sex tapes today that I had no involvement in. I had to use every ounce of willpower not to jerk off or blow my load in a public school FULL OF CHILDREN, MILLER. Did you forget that I work with kids? Then, as I'm driving *our* kid to Justin's house, I'm so fucking on edge that she calls me out on being horny and wanting adult time. She laughed in my face when I got embarrassed and gave me a bratty sendoff, telling me to *use protection*. I'm not okay, and *you're* about to not be okay."

"Our?" *What the fuck?*

"What?"

289

"You called her *our* kid."

"Are you fucking kidding me right now. I just vented all that to you and warned you what was coming, and you hyperfocused on the fact that I called Katy *ours?*"

"Yeah. I'll take whatever punishment you're about to dole out, but you called her ours. That's a big deal, Babe."

Fuck. He's right.

All the fight leaves me. I'm not sure when I started thinking of Katy as ours, but she is—just as much as Spencer is ours, but in a different way. We've created our own little, well, I guess big, family.

"Dammit. How am I supposed to continue to be upset when you say shit like that?"

"Hey, Babe, did you watch both videos? Did you see how well I fucked Axel? He loved every second of it, and we want to repeat it with you fucking me while I fuck him."

"Fuck, Fireball." I'm not even sure the words are decipherable through my growl. "I'll be home in five, and you better be waiting for me."

"Of course. Love you."

"You're not my favorite right now, but I love you too." I hit the end button on my steering wheel and punch the gas a little harder.

39

Spencer

My alarm wakes me at one forty-five, and I attempt to roll over, but I'm stuck between two large bodies. I momentarily panic until I open my eyes and find Miller and Axel on either side of me, still sleeping.

Someone needs to wake up for Tucker and his alarm friend, and by the looks of these two sleeping beauties, it's going to be me. As I'm peeling an arm off, Tucker walks in the door, looking refreshed and handsome. I don't know when he left the bed, but I fell asleep after cleaning up.

"I've got it, Little Miss. You can go back to sleep if you'd like. Chip is starting at the big house to give y'all more time to sleep. I know the last two days have been rough."

"Tucker."

"I wouldn't listen to any arguments earlier, and I won't listen to them now. Let me ask you this, is there enough room for five grown adults in this pool house?"

"No." It's the truth. We are cramped here. The guys are living out of duffle bags, and we do laundry daily because of it. And some days, I feel like I need a second refrigerator with how much they eat.

"Is there enough room for a teenager and her baby?"

"No." The spare bedroom has barely enough space for Katy's bed and the dresser I bought. There's no way a crib could fit in there as well.

Logically, I know the switch is needed and helpful, but that's the house I grew up in, where my mother died, where I ran when my life fell apart after Shane. Despite holding so many good memories, the bad outweighs them in my head.

"Little Miss, can you give me a single, *good* reason why we shouldn't take your father's offer?" I can not, and that's the problem. Tucker takes my silence as his answer. "That's what I thought." He runs his knuckles across my cheek. I know he does it because he likes tracing my freckles. "Sleep more. I'll come and wake you when it's time to start here. None of you got much sleep yesterday."

I smile at him sweetly and try to get comfortable under all the man muscle around me. Gage's ears twitch across the room when the front door closes. He sniffs the air then lays back down. He's been oddly accepting of all the commotion around the house despite it being completely different from the life we had before all this chaos.

It feels like I've just fallen asleep when a phone rings that isn't mine. Miller's arm flails around, searching for it aimlessly before he finds it and sits up.

"Hey, Babe. You on your way home?"

I take the opportunity to pry myself from the bed and sneak off to the bathroom. I'm sore from the morning's activities. A soreness that's different from any gym workout I've ever done.

Checking the clock, it's already after four p.m. I feel a little disoriented because I never sleep this late. Sleeping at all at any length is still new to me. Having warm bodies in my bed seems to have taken away the nightmares, or if I'm still having them, I'm not remembering.

I relieve my bladder, brush my teeth and hair, and go into the closet for clothes before reemerging in black biker shorts and a sports bra. When I step back into the bedroom, Axel is awake, and Miller is sporting a wide grin.

"We're in trouble."

"Trouble? How so?" I can't imagine what I've done to constitute being in trouble. I'm a grown woman. I don't do things to "get in trouble."

"Lincoln watched the videos while at school. He told me to be ready."

Alright, I can understand how we could be in trouble. Well, them at least. I was just a bystander.

"Oh good, you're all up." Tucker comes over and embraces me in a toe-curling kiss. I'm breathless by the time he pulls away. "Chip and his crew are ready to start on the outside of the house. I was coming to wake y'all."

"How are you so chipper, Daddy Tucker?" Axel appears to be sticking with that name.

"Because I'm an adult that has to function no matter how much sleep I get."

"Miller said Lincoln is on his way home and isn't too happy with any of us." There's more excitement in Axel's tone than there should be, but I presume his meds have worn off and part of his enthusiasm is his ADHD.

Tucker's lip tilts as he looks down at me. "Is that so? I guess we'll see what happens."

We're all standing in the kitchen when the front door

swings open.

"Fireball, Spencer, Axel, bedroom, now." As he comes into view from the foyer, there's determination and fire in his eyes. "I don't give two shits about who hears what outside these windows. You don't get to tease me and get away that easily." His voice is huskier than normal with lust, and my stomach flutters at his demanding tone.

"What do you need Axel and me for if Miller is the one in trouble?"

Lincoln strides toward me, wrapping one hand around my waist and the other through my hair. He gets inches from my lips before looking into my eyes.

"Because, Dream Girl, they're going to watch as I make love to you. And then, when you're satisfied and sated, I'm going to fuck Axel while Miller watches. I'm going to pound him until I find my release, but neither of them are going to be allowed to come.

Tucker chuckles from the other side of the room, and Lincoln's head whips toward him.

"Don't think I haven't forgotten about you. I know you left when I did this morning, so I'm not exactly sure how you got involved in their escapades, but you need to deal with the new alarm system while I deal with them."

"I look forward to it, brother. May I offer some assistance?" Pure mischief radiates off Tucker. He gestures toward the bedroom, and we all follow. "Where would you like them to watch from?"

Lincoln looks around the room to see what his options are. He pulls over my desk chair and drags over an armchair from another corner.

"Excellent. Sit down, boys." With quizzical looks, Axel and

Miller take their seats.

"I think voyeurism is pretty hot," Axel boasts as he sits in the desk chair and spins.

Tucker offers me his wrists, showing me the black cuffs he always wears. These are the source of the leather I always smell when he's around.

"Will you unbutton these for me, Little Miss?" Two black snaps hold each cuff in place. When I unbutton the two on his left wrist, I expect it to come off in one piece. Instead, it unwraps several times around, showing five individual strands of wrapped leather.

"What's this?" I look at the twelve or so inches of cuff in my hand, and he takes it from me, offering his other wrist. This one unwraps the same, but he lets me hold it while we turn to Axel.

"Give me your hands." Axel hesitantly lifts his arms, and Tucker holds his wrists together. With the leather wrap, he twines it around Axel's wrists and snaps the cuff closed.

"What the fuck? You've been walking around, casually wearing handcuffs this entire time. Fuck yeah, Daddy Tucker!"

Tucker ignores him and looks back at me. "Would you like to learn how to wrap them?" I'm mesmerized by the leather in my hands. I gently pull the strips apart, and I can't help but bring them to my nose and inhale.

"Leather. You."

"Me?" Tucker places his hands over mine, and I watch as he begins to twist the cuff around my wrist, eventually closing the clips and binding my hands together.

"You always smell like leather." Lifting my hands to my nose, I inhale again and close my eyes. "Now I know why."

As easily as he wrapped my wrists, he unwraps them and cuffs Miller's together.

"They're all yours, little brother." Tucker claps Lincoln on the shoulder and exits the room with a wink and a tip of his hat.

Miller and Axel look feral as they assess their situation.

"Dream Girl, may I make love to you?" Lincoln offers me his hand, and I stare at it.

Every moment with these men chips away at me. None of it is bad, per se. I spent years carefully crafting a home for myself and Gage, a schedule and routine that not only worked for me but wouldn't inconvenience anyone around me. I'm used to making people uncomfortable, wearing my mask, and walking through life with my head down.

These four individual males in my life watch over and protect me physically and emotionally. Sometimes, they know what I need before I do, and it's unnerving.

"I…" I take a step back from his offered hand. Lincoln looks confused and drops his arm.

"Spencer?" That's not what he calls me. I hear the confusion in my name, but I'm his Dream Girl. Or do I want to just be Spencer? Maybe that's the problem. I'm Tails, Smithy, Little Miss, and Dream Girl. Am I Spencer anymore?

"Code Blue." I barely hear the words as they hiss over my lips.

"Okay, Spencer. What do you need?"

Spencer. Spencer. Spencer.

I don't know who asked the question because whoever it was didn't use my nickname.

Miller and Axel stand from their seats, no longer handcuffed. I can tell by the looks on their faces that they see my panic. Maybe they feel it. It feels tangible to me—something I can cling to or push away.

I look at my hand and find myself rubbing my wrist. It's a nervous habit I started after my baby girl died. I wore the hospital bracelet for weeks. I would spin it around my wrist until it was raw. My father begged me to take it off, but I couldn't. I wouldn't. One day, when I fell asleep on the couch, I woke up, and he had cut it off. For me, it was a comfort. He saw it as an obsession and a reminder of his guilt. I moved into the pool house the next day.

My. Pool house.

"Get out." I don't even recognize my voice. It's horse and laced with pain.

"Smithy? Let us help you." I cover my ears, not wanting to hear the nickname. My hands tangle into my hair, and I quickly pull them away. I haven't braided my hair yet, and the feeling of it on my neck suddenly makes my skin crawl.

My hair ties are in the bathroom, but I have to walk past Miller to get there. I have spare ones in my car. I can sit in my car, braid my hair, and have a moment of solitude.

Will they follow me? They can't. I need space. I used our safeword. Does that work for non-sex-related things? Lincoln wanted to have sex, so it must work the same way.

"Stay." I hold my hand up to the three men, who have a myriad of emotions on their faces: scared, confused, worried. I'm feeling them all as well. I take a few steps to the nightstand and pick up my phone.

"Gage, *Kommen.*" He's instantly at my side, and I step backward out of the room. I hear their hushed words as they try to decipher what just happened. I walk straight to the front door, slipping on sandals. When I step out, a plain white van is parked right in front of the door, and I drop to my knees.

"He's here." Burying my head in my hands, I rock, waiting for Shane to take me away. My hair falls in my face, and again, my skin crawls. Gage growls next to me, and I can't appreciate him more.

"Okay, Gage. *Ruhig.*" I chuckle to myself at someone trying to tell Gage to be calm when he's protecting me. He won't respond to anyone else right now. "Little Miss. What's wrong?"

Tucker? It's Tucker. It's not Shane; it's Tucker and his alarm friend. The van belongs to his friend.

Tucker steps closer despite Gage's warning growl, and I stand. "Don't touch me." His arms are already outstretched. He's trying to give me a bear hug to calm me like he always does when I get overwhelmed. It could work. It probably would, but it's not what I want right now. I need to pull my hair out of my face and get some fresh air to breathe.

"Okay. I won't come any closer. What happened? Are you alright?" He looks behind me through the still-open door and shakes his head once. I look over my shoulder to see the three men I left behind staring back at me.

"I-I have to go."

"Go where, Little Miss? We're right here for you." Although I'm sure his quiet tone was meant to be soothing, it only sounds condescending.

"That's the problem!" Did that loud noise come from me? I can feel my eyes, wide as saucers, frantically looking everywhere except at Tucker. "I have to go. Don't follow me."

"Spencer, what's wrong? Please talk to me." No. Not

Tucker, too. My name from his lips sounds like nails on a chalkboard.

"I...have...to...go." Each word is a struggle to breathe, and I manage to stagger my way to my car. Gage and I get in and make it to the end of the driveway before the tears fall.

My mind races, unable to pinpoint a single thought other than my hair. I never leave the house without my hair braided unless it's a special occasion. My body must know what I need more than my mind can comprehend because I unconsciously find myself in Justin's driveway.

"Gage, get Justin." He understands me, despite my lack of a German command. He trots to the front door and barks a few times before Justin appears. The panic is almost instant on Justin's face when he looks around and doesn't immediately find me.

Gage jumps down the front steps back toward me, and Justin hastily follows. Based on the look of panic on Justin's face when he approaches my door, I must look like a mess. He swings the door open and embraces me in a hug.

"Spence, what's going on? Is everyone okay?" He's what I needed for comfort. My body knew, but there's one more thing I need that he can't provide.

"Nicole. Is Nicole home?" He cups my cheeks and looks into my eyes. I see the worry laced on his face, but I'm already feeling infinitesimally better.

"Yeah. Let's go inside." I walk in with Justin's arm to support me, both mentally and physically. The last thirty minutes has taken a toll on all aspects of my body.

"Hey, Spe—Oh my god, what's wrong?" Justin guides me to the couch where Nicole is holding a sleeping Miles.

"Please braid my hair."

"Braid your…"—her confused expression darts back and forth between Justin and me several times—"Sure. Justin, will you take the baby, and I'll get the supplies I need?"

I sit on the floor in front of the couch and wait for Nicole to return. When she does, she has a spray bottle, a brush, and a pouch that I assume holds hair ties. I move forward so she can sit on the couch behind me, and she straddles her legs around my torso.

"Please tell me what you're doing before you do it."

"Of course. First, I'm going to brush and part your hair. I assume you want your two braids?" I nod. "After I have it parted, I'm going to wet it a bit. It looks like you might have gone to bed with wet hair. The water will help tame the kinks from sleep. Does all that sound okay?" I nod again.

At the first pass of the brush I feel my anxiety ease even more. She's gentle, almost reverent, as she untangles my knots. Knowing my hair is about to be off my neck from hanging freely, slowly melts away the panic I'm feeling. It wasn't a conscious decision to come here. I know Nicole is a hairdresser. Despite everything else going on around me, my hair was my first priority to feeling better. It's something I can control, even if I don't have the capacity to do it myself right now.

Justin comes into view with a cup of coffee. I take it from him with a small smile, confident it's exactly how I like it.

"I'm going to start braiding the left side now."

"Thank you. Where's Hannah and Katy?" I just noticed there is no exuberant toddler running around, and a pang of guilt hits my stomach at my relief. I'm glad not to have to deal with her emotions at the moment.

"They walked down to the park. Do you want to talk?"

Instantly, my panic spikes again.

"Alone? Justin, they aren't safe. Shane is always watching. We need to get them right now. There has been more pictures." I try to stand with Nicole's hands half in my hair, and Justin places a firm hand on my shoulder.

"Never alone, Spencer. I hired someone to hang around when the girls go out."

"You hired...a bodyguard?" While that thought shouldn't shock me, I'm impressed he would do such a thing.

"The guys have been keeping me apprised of what's happening. I'm so sorry you're having to deal with all of this."

"Spencer, I'm going to do the other braid now. And you don't need to worry about Katy being here. We will always keep her safe." Nicole's words smooth my edges. They're safe here.

"I know you will. I know." And I do. My rational thoughts are coming back. Having my hair off my neck is clearing my mind. I take another sip of my coffee while Nicole finishes.

"All done. It's been a while since I've done braids. You're probably more of a pro at them than I am, but I hope this helps." She runs her hands down my hair and stops at my shoulders, giving them a reassuring squeeze.

"Thank you. It's perfect." I pick myself up off the floor and sit next to her on the couch. She looks more refreshed than the last time I saw her. So does Justin, for that matter. They must be getting the hand of parenthood with two.

"I'm sorry." I feel ridiculous. I have four extraordinary men who are at my beck and call and willing to do anything I ask of them, and I just ran away to barge in on two overtired parents so I could have my hair braided like a child. This feels like an all-time low.

"Spencer, whatever you feel like you need to apologize for, don't. You came here in need, and we are always here to help. Can we do anything more? Would you like me to leave so you can talk to Justin alone?"

"No. I just need…" What do I need? I needed air and space, but I came here. I retreated to a house full of kids. Well, a house that should be full of kids, it's just not at this moment. Did I only come here to have my hair braided? I could have easily done that myself. "Can we go out?"

"Are you asking me or Justin?"

"You, Nicole. Maybe we can see if Annie and Blake can join us? I think I need some female time. I've been swarmed with testosterone lately. No offense, Justin."

He tips his head. "None taken. You ladies go out. Although you might want to put on more clothes, Spence." I look down and realize I'm still wearing only a sports bra and biker shorts. It's not necessarily inappropriate, but more clothing would be better.

"You can borrow a t-shirt to throw over that if you'd like. Or you're welcome to anything in my closet. I know you're particular about your clothing choice." Nicole smiles at me sweetly. Justin has always accommodated my idiosyncrasies, and Nicole has followed suit. I've never felt uncomfortable around them or my choices.

"If you have a plain cotton shirt, I'll be fine."

Justin grabs my knee and stands from where he sits on the coffee table. "I'll grab you one and call Cole. He can bring the kids over, and you girls can go out. As he leaves the room, I finally feel like I'm back in control of my body and my emotions.

"Thank you for the braids, Nicole. Are you sure you can

get away? Miles doesn't need you? I don't want to be selfish with your time."

"Oh god, no. I've been dying to get out but have felt too selfish to ask. Justin can't say no to you. It's the perfect excuse, and I get to put on real clothes. Seeing Annie and Blake makes it even better." Her smile stretches from ear to ear.

My phone buzzes, and I'm almost afraid to look. I haven't heard from any of the guys since I left, which I appreciate. But a part of me is also a little upset. I'm an oxymoron. They are giving me what I asked for, but checking to make sure I'm alright would still be comforting.

Reluctantly I look at my phone, half dread and half hopefulness. I'm pleasantly surprised to see the text is from Blake, and I can hear the bubbliness in her message.

Blake: Coffee and s'mores with my girls!!! See you soon. :)

There's no need to respond as I see the three dancing dots appear and realize it's a group message, and a glance at Nicole shows me she's already typing back.

Nicole: I'm excited for a PSL and some girl chat. Can't wait.

PSL. Nicole is obsessed with everything Pumpkin, especially her pumpkin spice lattes. Her love of the fruit is the reason Justin lovingly calls her Pumpkin and why Annie makes sure that S'morgasm, the coffee shop we're going to, keeps the ingredients stocked year round, just for her. Being a billionaire has its perks.

Justin returns and hands me a buttery soft, white v-neck

shirt. He knows me well. Nicole excuses herself to change before we leave, and I step into the kitchen to wash my now-empty coffee cup.

"I called them." I look over my shoulder and arch a brow at Justin. "The guys. I called them and told them you were here and safe and that you're going out with the girls. They were blowing up my phone, panicking. They demanded to come over and talk with you, but I told them you needed time, and they could come over once you've left. What happened, Spence?" I heave a heavy sigh and turn to face him, leaning on the sink.

"I'm not sure. It's been a long time since I've been in a relationship. I don't believe I've ever been in a healthy one, and now I have four men who treat me like I hang the moon. I need to talk to the girls about everything. I got overwhelmed. Being treated well is new. For the longest time, I lived in fight or flight. I panicked at being treated like a decent human being. No. That's downplaying it. They treat me like I'm their queen."

"As they should."

40

Katy

I'm not a burden. I'm not a burden. I'm. Not. A. Burden. Why can't I convince myself of these words no matter how much I try and how much everyone keeps telling me. It's hard enough being sixteen and living under someone else's roof. They aren't obligated to provide me with anything, yet they all happily do it.

Why?

And now, I'm pregnant. And I want to keep the baby. Is that selfish of me? What can I provide a baby if I can't even provide for myself?

"Higher, Katy!"

"Okay, hold on tight." Hannah giggles as I push her higher on the swing. I can imagine myself doing this, pushing my own son or daughter on the swings.

Without the bodyguard, of course. I don't know exactly what's going on, but I know whatever it is has escalated. The conspicuous man standing under the tree sticks out like a sore thumb, but I appreciate him and what he's doing.

It's also hard not to appreciate him as a man. He has at

least a foot over me, the bushiest eyebrows, and thin lips that seem to be in a permanent scowl. When he looks at Hannah, I've seen his silver-blue eyes soften when he thinks no one is looking. He looks more Viking than man with his dirty blonde hair pulled back in a tight man bun.

I'm daydreaming about the man so vividly I don't even hear him approach.

"Miss Katy, it's time to go. Mr. Webb just texted and asked for us to return."

"Shit, Dempsey. You scared me. Don't be so sneaky." The corner of his lip twitches. Did it amuse him that he snuck up on me? Probably.

I have to turn my head away as I feel my cheeks heat. I don't know what kind of middle school girl crush my hormones are trying to have, but they need to stop. At least he isn't old. I'd guess early twenties. I'd never ask, though. He doesn't seem like the sharing type. Nor does he seem like someone who could possibly ever be interested in an underage pregnant girl.

"Sorry, Miss Katy. You should be more aware of your surroundings." His gruff voice chides me, making me feel even more like a child in his presence.

"Isn't that what you're here for?" I snap back. There's that lip twitch again. I guess I'm just that entertaining.

"We should go." He disregards my comment like yesterday's trash.

I grab the chains and slowly stop Hannah with little protest. Justin told her that Dempsey is in charge no matter what. She knows better than to argue with him, even at close to three years old.

"I've been informed to tell you that the twins are coming

over for a playdate if you need any incentive to return home, Hannah." I don't think Hannah understood a word he said other than twins and playdate. Her face lights up, and she takes off across the park lawn.

"Better catch up with her, Miss Katy?"

"Me? I'm the pregnant one, and you're the one who got her all excited. Why is this my problem?"

"I'm only here to keep you safe and stop any danger. The only danger she's in is a skinned knee if she trips, and that's your area." He tucks a lock of hair behind his ear that's fallen across his face and I yell at my stomach for doing a backflip.

He's about to be in danger for making me run after this toddler.

"Fine, but if *I* get a skinned knee, you're carrying me home."

"Of course."

Chasing after Hannah makes our walk home shorter than necessary. I finally catch up to her, panting for breath. Dempsey reaches us a few strides later, not a hair out of place or a labored breath.

Bastard.

Hannah crashes into the front door, banging at the locked wall in front of her.

"Daddy, we's home. Open up!"

Before I can punch in the door code, it opens, and Axel greets us with a huge smile.

"Hannah Banana. You're home." He scoops her up and gives her a big hug. Axel kisses my forehead as I slip past him into the house as he extends a hand to Dempsey.

"Axel. Thanks for what you're doing."

"Ignore him," I tell Axel. "He's just my muscle."

Dempsey scowls at me, and I stick out my tongue before

307

giving him my back.

"Dempsey. It's nice to meet you. It's my pleasure. The girls are *lovely*." I don't miss how he emphasizes the last word, but I ignore it in search of my other favorite men.

"You're home. Great. Cole and I are leaving." Justin slings an arm around Cole, who doesn't look convinced about going anywhere.

"Are you sure about this? The twins can be a handful." Cole's twins, Ruby and Rory, only a few weeks older than Hannah, run past us chasing Nicole's dachshunds.

"So can Axel. He needs a taste of his own medicine."

"What's going on?" There are a lot of men standing around, and Spencer and Nicole are nowhere in sight. My question is ignored for other instructions.

"Dempsey, the ladies are all at S'morgasm. They are awaiting your arrival. They have about a ten-minute head start on you. I don't need to tell you how important their safety is."

"On it, Mr. Webb." Dempsey turns on his heels and leaves. I'm so confused as to what's going on.

"Alright, if you need us, we're going…out. Not sure where yet, but anywhere other than here. For the next two to three hours, you all get to be the dads, and we're going to be men. Your only job is to keep them alive and don't burn the house down. I like it. Bottles are premade in the refrigerator for Miles. Just heat it in warm water. He's not picky about the temperature, just not too hot."

"What about me? Do I get to go out, too?"

"Nope. This is a crash course in parenthood for all of you and a few hours of normalcy for us. Or however you want to look at it."

"Justin. Look at this." I sweep my hand across the room. "This is chaos. You can't leave me here with them."

He kisses me on the forehead as he walks past me. "Sure can. Have fun." The closing of the front door sounds like the lock on my coffin. When I turn to face the room, all I can do is laugh.

"How did this happen?" I must ask the wrong question because every one of their faces fall. Something *did* happen. Holy shit. "What's wrong?" The silence in the room surrounding the loud kids is deafening. "Linc, what happened from the time you dropped me off to turning back up here? You were in such a good mood." His face is etched with guilt, and I'm getting nauseous. This feeling is dread, not baby-related. I don't like the way any of them look.

"We aren't sure," Miller confesses. "I think we overwhelmed Spencer to the point she needed space. She came here, and the girls went out." I've seen Spencer on the edge, and the guys are always able to bring her back. But if they were the reason she was there, I can understand her needing space away from them.

"Did something specific happen to make her that way?" Their eyes dart between each other, and I instantly know it's something they don't want to tell me. It's the look that Miller and Lincoln share that tips me off. "Oh."

"Oh? What does 'Oh' mean?" Tucker grabs a twin as she runs by, scooping her up. He holds her in front of his face. "What's your name, cutie?" She giggles and squirms.

"I Ruby. Who's you?"

"I'm Tucker." She reaches up and grabs at his hat.

"C'av your hat?"

"My hat?"

"Pweeeese." He sets her down, making sure she's stable before letting go.

"Sure, Little Bit. Here ya go." He places the oversize cowboy hat on her head, and she looks adorable.

"Tank you!" She runs off yelling, "I cowgirl, I cowgirl."

"The other brunette is Rory, and the curly blonde is Hannah. Oh, and the baby is Miles."

"There's another one?"

I always forget that Tucker is new to the inner circle. The rest of the guys were friends before kids came around, and as they were born, they folded naturally into the family.

"Listen, Daddy Tucker, it's fine." Axel clasps a hand on Tucker's shoulder and is met with a returning scowl. "Don't look so afraid. There's four little kids and four grown men plus a completely capable teenager. We've got this."

We definitely did not "got this."

"I was told they were all potty trained!" Miller's horrified screech echoes down the hall. Rory told him he had to potty, and Miller happily followed him to the bathroom.

My head ping-pongs between the frantic conversations going on around me.

"You still have to wipe their asses."

"Axel, watch your mouth."

"Sorry, Daddy Tucker. I'm panicking right now. I can't get it out. Where did these kids get gum? It's stuck in my hair."

"Why is it blue?! Poop shouldn't be blue. Is he an alien? It sure smells like it in here."

"Sorry, Miller. We made cupcakes yesterday with blue

frosting." I try not to laugh at the chaos.

Hannah perks up from her spot next to me on the floor. "Cupcakes?" Crap. I shouldn't have said the C word.

"Not right now, Hanny." She pouts and looks toward the kitchen counter where the cupcakes in question sit in their container.

"I thought I was good with babies. There must be some-thing wrong with this one." Tucker bounces in place with a whining Miles in his arms.

"He's been gassy. Skin-to-skin sometimes helps. I've seen Justin do it," I offer.

"Skin to what?" He looks horrified. "Has anyone seen my hat? Or Lincoln and Ruby?"

"Last time I saw them, they were in a standoff about the color of a cup, I think? Something about pink versus orange. But can someone please tell me how to get gum out of my hair? It's my pride and joy."

I'm internally laughing at all of this. Any doubts I had about wanting to keep this baby are gone. Even though we are in complete survival mode right now, not a single one of them has stepped back from the challenge. They'll be here for me. Here to help me care for and raise my baby.

Decision made.

41

Spencer

I have never had girlfriends before. I can't say I'm overjoyed about having them now, but with my current situation, I can understand the need for females to get together and talk about their male counterparts.

The idea of sitting around and complaining about a situation you've willingly put yourself in seems preposterous to me, but here I am.

My eyes keep wandering to Blake's extremely large belly. She's ready to give birth any day. Will this be Katy's future? Will I be jealous? I was never envious of Annie or Nicole, and there hasn't been any with Blake, but I'm not as close to them as I am Katy.

"Oh my goooooooooood. This is better than sex." Nicole sips on a fall-scented latte that smells like it has more flavor than actual coffee.

"Alright, Spencer. You got us all here. It's time to spill all the details of your four-way sex-a-thon that you have going on at your house." Blake practically vibrates in her seat with anticipation.

"Darling," Annie scolds Blake. "I'm sure Spencer doesn't want to talk about what goes on behind closed doors."

"Oh, don't be a prude, Annie. You know you're curious, too. I definitely am." Nicole curls her feet under her, getting comfortable for the information she's sure I'm going to confess.

"I walked out on them tonight. This morning, I had amazing sex with three of them, and this afternoon, when Lincoln wanted his turn, I...I left. It wasn't anything Lincoln did, and I know he feels like it was. I need to fix it."

"Justin said all the guys looked torn up when they arrived." My eyes drift to Nicole in shock.

"What do you mean? Where are they?" The three burst into laughter and I can tell I'm on the outside of some joke.

"Oh, please let the pregnant woman tell her. I need all the goodness I can get with my ankles the size of Texas." Nicole bows her head to Blake and gestures for her to continue. Blake clasps her hands together, giddy to tell me what's happening.

"So, Cole went over to Justin's with the twins, and the guys came over after we left. Weeeeell, Cole, and Justin decided to give the guys a crash course in fatherhood, and they went out, too."

"Where's Katy? She was at the park with Hannah." A panicked feeling bubbles in my stomach again.

"Relax." Nicole rests her hand atop mine. "Dempsey made sure they got home safe, and then he came here." She arches a brow over her shoulder, and I see a tall, viking-looking man standing in the corner. He sticks out like a sore thumb.

"That grown child over there? He's your bodyguard? If he shaved, he would look twelve."

"Trust me. He's plenty skilled."

"ANYway," Blake huffs out. "So your men and Katy are watching the kids—all four of them." I still don't quite understand the amusement of the situation.

"Wanna see?" Nicole waves her phone between us.

"OMG, yes. Gimme." Blake bounces like she doesn't have a full-term baby in her body. Nicole pushes a few buttons on her phone, and a screen of cameras appears. She clicks on one of the views, and we watch. "Oh no. Lincoln is trying to give Ruby an orange cup."

"Not orange. He's in trouble." Annie leans closer to get a better look. "Is there sound?"

"Oh, yeah." Nicole pushes another button, and the background noise startles us all. Miles is whining, Miller is screaming, and Axel is...crying.

"I want peek. No ow-inj."

"Ruby, it's just a cup. The juice tastes the same. See." Lincoln sips from the orange cup, and Ruby's face twists.

"Oh no." Blake covers her face as we watch the tiny brunette's mouth open, but no sound comes out. "Here it comes. Get ready."

A shrill scream pierces the air around us through the speaker. *"Miiiiiiiiiiiiiiiiiiine!"*

"Rory, come back here." Miller's voice booms from somewhere outside the camera view. A moment later, Rory, with no pants on, comes running into the room.

"Sissy, you K? Shhh, no cry." He wraps his tiny arms around Ruby, and collectively, we all aww.

"Dude, is that blue shit on your shirt?" Axel points at a spot on Miller's shirt, and although we can't exactly tell what it is, the quickness that Miller removes it from his body tells us it

most likely was blue poop.

"Blue?" Annie questions.

"Katy and Hannah made cupcakes, and we sent some to your house. I guess the twins enjoyed them." Annie eyes Nicole, who mouths "sorry" and tries to look innocent.

"Watch your mouths and get some pants on that kid." Tucker appears on the screen from the corner, holding a now-sleeping Miles. He sits in the rocking chair, and I hear a sniffle next to me. Turning to Nicole, I give her a look that expresses, "What's wrong with you?"

"Tucker is doing skin-to-skin with Miles. Katy must have told him about his tummy issues the past few days. What a sweet man. He's a keeper, Spencer." I can't stop myself from staring at this broad, gruff cowboy of a man holding a tiny baby bare-chested.

Guilt tries to rear its head again, knowing that what I'm seeing is something I can never give them, but then I remember our conversation and everything they said to me.

They want to be with me, barren womb and all.

"My father offered to switch houses and went to Tucker about it. He said we need the room, and it's just going to waste. That's what overwhelmed me. Moving makes all of this permanent, and I don't feel worthy of everything they're offering."

There's a round of objections from them, and I listen and consider what they're saying.

"You deserve the world."

"You need four men because you're a woman with a big heart."

"You're incredible. Stop thinking negatively about yourself."

I let it sink in. These are all things the guys have told me or some variation of it.

"I need to tell you all my story. It's not a pretty one, but one I want to share. Although the guys all know and are supportive, you are all mothers and will understand more than they ever could. I want to tell you about my daughter…and how I lost her."

When I finish, all the girls are crying, and I find my cheeks wet as well. Dempsey brought us napkins a while back, and they are almost gone. I never realized how much keeping my situation locked up inside me was festering and holding me back. Every time I allow someone else into my inner circle, it's both terrifying and heartwarming.

I've always expected to see pity in people's eyes if I opened up, and although I see sadness, I also see awe. Awe at the strength they keep telling me I have, that I survived a terrible situation and made it out on the other side better than before.

All the words they say to me are things I've said to or thought about Katy. Maybe that's why I feel so drawn to her.

"I'm ready to go. Thank you all for your time and kind words." I need to talk to the guys.

The ride back to Justin's house is quiet. Nicole plays soft music to fill any silence. Annie and Blake asked if they could take another hour, and we told them it was fine. As we pull up to the house, I expect to feel dread, but I don't. I feel more confident than when I left. Then I have been lately. The men inside that house want me for me, and I've already let them farther into my life than I ever thought was possible.

"I'll take the kids in the backyard with Katy and let you all talk."

"Thank you, Nicole. You and Justin are the best friends I could ask for."

She squeezes my hand and leaves the car, giving me a few minutes before I have to face my future.

When I gather my remaining strength, I take the path to the front door. As I reach the steps, the door opens, and a shirtless Miller walks out.

"Hey, Smithy." He's handsome. Thick dark hair frames his blue eyes and tanned skin. His chest and expanse of muscles draw my eyes down, and when I bring them back up, he's smiling.

"Hi, Miller. I see you survived the blue poop."

He rubs his bare chest. "How did—cameras. I should have expected Justin to have security here. Did you enjoy the show?" He continues down the stairs until he's standing at the bottom with me.

I stare up into his eyes. He wants to touch me. I can see the micro muscles twitching as he holds himself back.

"You can kiss me, Miller."

"Thank fuck." He pulls me in for a kiss that I expect to be hot and searing, but it's gentle and almost chaste. The passion that he puts behind his kiss is more telling than anything else. He's apologizing when he has no reason to. It's my apology that needs to be heard.

I pull away and open my mouth to do just that when he pushes a finger to my lips.

"No. You have nothing to be sorry about. We pushed you. Lincoln is torn up about it. He doesn't need your apology either, though, just your acceptance of his."

I sigh into his chest. I don't want them to make this easy on me, but I should expect nothing less.

"We were all at fault. I should have spoken up, but I didn't know I was having those feelings until it was too late."

"And what feelings are those, Smithy?" He tips my chin with his finger so I can't look away.

"Unworthy. Inadequate. Overwhelmed by all of the goodness that was surrounding me."

"Spencer, listen to me."

"Don't call me that." My hands fist into his non-existent shirt.

"Don't call you Spencer? That's your name." I close my eyes and shake my head.

"You're correct. It's my name, but it's not who I am to you. I'm your Smithy. I used to hate it—all the nicknames you all call me—but I become a different identity when you call me your terms of endearment. I like that identity."

"Okay, Smithy. I like that identity, too. I like *you*. A lot."

"The feeling is mutual. What's going on in there?"

"Nicole told us you were back and wanted to talk to each of us individually. We rock, paper scissored for first dibs. I won." He flashes his panty-dropping smile and kisses me again. This time, with the passion I expected. A kiss that shows more emotion than his words express. I have a feeling this is the first of similar kisses I'm about to share.

42

Tucker

We survived. I didn't think we would, but Nicole walked in the door, stifled a laugh, grabbed the kids and Katy, and took them outside. Before leaving, she warned us to be easy with Spencer's heart, and she would probably want to talk to each of us individually.

Miller and Axel jumped at the chance to be first, which ended in a rousing best-of-three rock, paper, scissors contest. Miller won with a triumphant grin, and Axel pouted like a toddler and whined about the gum in his hair.

Lincoln's guilt is festering. He's put on a smile while here, but I know my brother well enough to see the feelings he's hiding. Spencer used her safeword again. While we are all proud of her for using it, both times she did it was in relation to Lincoln. Not anything that he did specifically, but whatever he was doing at the time brought up feelings that caused her to panic. I've tried quietly reassuring him that he's done nothing wrong, but it hasn't helped. I can't say I'd feel any different if I were in his shoes.

Everyone is antsy without the kids to distract us, minus

Miles, who's still asleep on my chest. I imagine it feels like we're all waiting for our turn at the firing squad.

The front door opens, and our attention turns to the woman who holds our hearts. It's there, in our eyes, our postures: the way Axel's fingers twitch to touch her.

When I hit my forties, and no woman or man had caught my eye, I thought Midnight Moonshine would forever be my mistress. One morning, in a random coffee shop, when an asshole pointed a gun at a complete stranger, my heart changed. Even if I had never seen her again after the moment we shared—the kiss—I was changed.

Spencer approaches Axel first. He's the next logical choice after Miller. I don't know the full extent of what happened in her room after I left but I know Miller and Axel were cuffed and bystanders to the scene unfolding.

"Hi, Axel." Like a lost puppy finding its home, he scoops her into his arms, and she practically disappears into his chest. "Oxygen is necessary to live, and you're constricting mine." His arms relax, but he doesn't let go.

"Tails, I know you're not a fan of apologies, so I won't give you one." He kisses the top of her head and inhales the scent of her hair. "Communication is important in any relationship, but you're extra spicy sometimes, and you have to give us a minute to take a sip of milk."

"That's…"

"That sounded way better in my head. Speaking of which." He bows his head and shows her the wad of gum sticking through his strands.

"I thought I smelled mint. Come with me."

Axel playfully swats her butt as she walks toward the refrigerator. They talk in hushed tones as Spencer uses a combination of ice and, oddly enough, peanut butter to remove the gum. I've never seen him smile so brightly when she tells him it's all done. Axel pulls her in for a swoon-worthy kiss, and I look away to give them their moment.

Two down, two to go.

I appreciate that she's on a mission to speak with us individually, but I'm not owed anything from her. She felt uncomfortable with the situation in her bedroom and used her safeword. She did the right thing.

I feel her presence before she reaches me. My body is always aware of hers, like two magnets being pulled together.

"That's a good look on you. Newborn baby is your color." She smiles down at me, but I can see the guilt she's harboring.

"Miller called me the baby whisperer. I think I just ended up with the easiest of the four."

"Tucker…" Her pause speaks a thousand words in its silence. "Are you sure?" The question is open-ended, but I know what she's asking. She's looking at me, holding a future she can't give me. It makes me wonder how much Axel calling me Daddy Tucker affects her.

"Little Miss, a baby isn't endgame for me. You are." I cradle Miles in my arms and stand. I need to touch her.

With the baby between us, I rest my hand over her heart. The words racing through me are too soon to be spoken out loud, but she understands. Instead, I go for the next best words. "I'm so fucking proud of you for speaking up. I apologize for trying to stop you from leaving. I didn't know at the time you had used your safeword. Do you want to tell me what happened to make you leave?"

"It doesn't matter now. I worked through it. Everything piled up all at once. Little things I didn't realize were bothering me all came to a head."

"Did coffee with the girls help?" I sweep a stray strand of hair away from her face. Her braids aren't as tight as usual, and wisps have fallen out.

"It was enlightening and entertaining. They appreciated your shirtlessness." She sees my confusion and points at a camera mounted near the ceiling.

"I shouldn't be surprised. I'm sure it was extremely entertaining. Do you happen to know where my hat went?" She giggles, and my heart splits open. It's an incredible sound.

"Have you seen Gage?"

Come to think of it, I haven't. "Not lately."

"Gage, *Kommen*." Gage appears from a corner I didn't know he was in. I throw my head back and laugh at the ridiculousness. Gage is wearing my hat with a bandana wrapped around his collar.

"Which one?"

"This was a Hannah masterpiece. Katy helped her."

I lift my hat off the dog and place it back on my head, chuckling. "He's a good boy."

"The best." Spencer's eyes bore a hole in the ground. She has one more of us to talk to, and it's clear he's weighing heavily on her mind. "Where's Lincoln? I need to talk to him, too."

"Little Miss, there's something you should know that I don't think you realized." Miles stirs in my arms, and his little eyes flutter open with a coo. Axel hears and offers to bring him to Nicole. With my arms empty, I can finally wrap them around Spencer's waist, and I know she needs the connection, too, when she sighs into my hold.

"What's wrong with Lincoln?"

"I'll remind you that I'm so proud of you for communicating and using your safeword when you needed it, but both times you've used it was with Lincoln." Her sharp inhale of breath is paired with a quiver of her lip. I see the panic begin to rise and pull her closer. "He is just as proud of you, Little Miss. I promise. He's just very cautious. When you speak to him, you need to be delicate. Lincoln *is* a flower right now."

Spencer understands my comparison. Lincoln is strong and confident, but for her, he's her chaos, and I'm her calm. I won't pretend that I don't notice the difference her father was talking about. Whether it's wisdom or age, I don't know. My simple, or rough when needed touch, can calm Spencer no matter what the situation is. I felt defeated when she walked away from me earlier, but I didn't have all of the facts. I didn't know she had used her safeword. My approach would have been different, or not at all.

Her comfort level with Lincoln is different. Despite not knowing each other any longer than she's known me, they've had a long-standing verbal connection on the radio. The relationship between emergency personnel and their dispatcher is a deep-rooted trust—one that I'm sure neither of them has even realized. That's why, in those two situations, she felt confident telling us to stop.

"Where is he?"

"He followed Nicole outside with the kids and said he needed some air. She told him about a path through their yard that leads to a gazebo. I imagine that's where he headed."

"Thank you for...being you."

"Always, Little Miss." It's my turn for the kiss that seals the apology. The unspoken apology that neither of us needs but our minds want. Our lips speak words that don't need to be said out loud. We're sorry. We're scared. This is tricky. It's too much and not enough. The I love you's that are too soon but, when finally spoken, still won't convey the try depth of our emotion.

I wish her hair wasn't braided so I could run my fingers through it and massage her scalp, which is my secret melting Spencer weapon. Instead, I massage the back of her neck with my fingers while my tongue massages hers. It seems to have the same effect because when we finally part, her eyes are glazed, and she looks more relaxed.

With a final kiss to her forehead I send her to go find my brother and complete the puzzle of our family.

Just as she's about to walk out the back door, she turns. "Switching houses is a good idea. Thank you."

"No, thank you, Little Miss."

I see her pass Axel before she stops to talk to Nicole, who's now holding Miles. He comes back inside with a weary look.

"That was torture."

"The babysitting or the gum in your hair?" He rubs his head, where a greasy spot awaits for his next shower.

"I'd shave my head if it meant never having to see her look that tortured again."

I understand his sentiment wholeheartedly.

Nicole points to a worn path that leads to a lush part of their backyard. I hope when she finds Lincoln, they listen to each other. His heart is just as entangled with hers as the rest of us but the trust they have—that's unmatched.

"How did it go?" Miller squeezes my shoulder and follows our gaze as Spencer's white shirt retreats into the bright green backyard.

"She got the gum out of my hair."

"She gave me my hat back."

Miller huffs. "I guess we wait to see if she gets the boy, too."

Spencer's form finally disappears, and I hope to god she gets the boy too.

43

Lincoln

I need air. She's here. Spencer is here, but I'm so torn up inside, I can't talk to her yet. Axel and Miller salivated over who got to see her first, and all I felt was dread.

"I'm taking all the underage ones outside so you guys can talk. Katy, grab a kid." Nicole grabs Hannah, and Katy groans and takes Ruby's hand.

"I'll help." I pick up Rory and can tell Nicole is about to protest. "I need some fresh air. Please." When she tries to take Miles away from Tucker, he waves her off. She nods in understanding and I follow her to the back door. "We have a gazebo through the trees if you need some alone time."

All the kids run directly to the swing set when we get outside. Katy follows to push them on the swings.

"She's going to make an excellent mother. Age has nothing to do with it." I look on in awe at her ease with the kids.

"Has she decided to keep the baby? Did she tell you that?"

"As far as I know, she hasn't made a final decision. Katy told me she was leaning toward keeping it, but there hasn't been a concrete statement about it."

"She doesn't have to. Look at her, Lincoln. She's in love with motherhood. It's so natural for her. I've seen her rubbing her lower belly and whispering to herself." She turns to face me with an earnest look. "I'm only going to say this once and then never again. The four of you man-children need to figure your shit out. Stay, walk away, I don't care. Spencer won't leave that little girl now that she's claimed her. I know you love Katy, too, but she will always have a bigger piece of Spencer's heart. Katy and her baby need a stable home life. It's something she's never had before, and she deserves it. She doesn't need to see "Mom and Dad" arguing all the time. You guys need to be all in or walk away. And that's for both of them, not just Spencer. All or nothing."

"I love them both." She's not surprised by my statement, but I am. Those three words have been floating through my head, but I haven't said them out loud until now. They feel right.

"I know you do, but love isn't always enough. Justin loved me, too, but he wasn't all in because he was putting me over his mental health. He had to love himself again before he could love me or the baby I was growing."

"I've been told." I wasn't present then, but I've heard all about it from Axel and Miller. Nicole got pregnant on their first date, and when Justin found out, he put her above all else. He became obsessive, eventually forgetting to take his anxiety and antidepressant meds, and his mental health declined. He stepped back. He committed himself, and even then, when he was healthy and back on his meds, he watched her from afar, still not feeling worthy of her.

I know that feeling.

"Tell me she's okay, Nicole. Did she say anything while

you were out?"

"I can't tell you anything that you shouldn't hear from her yourself. Talk to Spencer, Lincoln." She's right. I know she is. It doesn't mean I wouldn't have loved some direction or insight.

"You mentioned a gazebo?" She points to a path that disappears into the woods, and I thank her and wander away. I follow a path through the trees that's well worn but starting to overgrow. They most likely haven't been back here much since the baby was born.

The sun is still high in the sky, and there's plenty of light peeking through the trees. My lungs appreciate the crisp, fresh air, and the smell of moss and wet dirt surrounds me. It's precisely what I need.

A large, well-maintained gazebo appears through the trees. It's painted in a pale green color to blend in with the greenery around it and there's a bench swing in the middle.

"Because, Dream Girl, they're going to watch as I make love to you."

Was that what scared her? Me making love to her? The love part? The cuffs? The threat of fucking Axel?

There were no signs. What did we miss? What did *I* miss?

Sometimes, I forget that Spencer isn't black and white. She's all of these magnificent shades of gray. Every one imaginable. It's what has always attracted me to her, even on the radio. She was composed and confident, and unless you listened, really listened, that's all you heard. But I listened. I could tell when a particular call would affect her more than others. Her slight pitch difference when she would be in the back of the ambulance if there was a child patient.

Spencer always drives the ambulance, and Justin does

patient care. That is, unless the patient is a child, in which case she would ride in the back. Her cadence is smoother and slightly higher with children.

When she's truly driving an emergency and navigating the roads with sirens, her tone is lower, concentration thicker, and her register deeper.

I *know* this woman. How did I miss her panic in the bedroom? Were there signs?

"Fuck." A startled bird flies away at my expletive, and I sigh when I hear a twig snap behind me.

She's here. She's found me.

I wasn't sure how much time I had or how long she would talk to the others before she came to me, but I knew she would.

"Dream Girl." Her footsteps are slow and calculated as she ascends the three wooden steps into the gazebo. "Sit with me?" I pat the empty space on the swing, but she doesn't accept. I hear the wood creek as she sits on the benches that line the octagon frame.

I understand her hesitation. Well, I honestly don't because I still don't know what happened.

I bend over, leaning my elbows on my knee, and fist my hair. I've never felt so conflicted in my life. I want to grovel at this woman's feet and beg her for forgiveness. Forgiveness for famine, for cancer, for world peace. Forgiveness for the rain in the fucking clouds and the worms in the dirt.

I can't wear the brave face I've worn all day because there isn't an ounce left inside me. I'm scared. I'm terrified. I feel broken and I still. Don't. Know. Why.

I stand because I can't do *nothing*. I can't sit here in this silence and pretend. I keep my eyes cast to the ground and walk to Spencer. When I see her flip flop covered feet, I drop to my knees and bury my head in her lap.

She can reject me—she always has the option to reject me. After agonizing moments of waiting for her to say anything, there's still silence. I run my hands up her thighs and slip the tips of my fingers into her shorts.

The simple feeling of her warm skin under my palms smooths some of the frayed edges of my nerves. My body vibrates with anticipation of what comes next. Spencer moves, and I hold my breath, expecting her to push me away, but she doesn't. Her fingers thread through my hair, and she pets me. She does it again, and I swear the moan that escapes my throat might as well be a purr.

Spencer shifts more, and her finger sweeps across my cheek. I'm... I'm crying. I had no idea.

"Shh, Lincoln. I'm here. I'm not going anywhere. I'm here."

"Fuck." I pull my hand out of her shorts and spread her legs so I can crawl between her thighs. I need to be closer. I wrap my arms around her lower back and rest my head half on her upper thighs, half on her stomach.

"I'm sorry. I'm so sorry, Dream Girl. Please forgive me. I'm so sorry, Spencer."

"Lincoln."

"No. You don't need to say anything. Tell me how to make it better. I'll do anything. I'm all in. I'm all in for you and Katy. Tell me how to make it better." I feel the heat from the tears this time. What has this woman done to me?

"Look at me." I can't deny her anything, so I lift my head and look into the most sincere blue eyes. She takes my cheeks into her hands and smiles. She fucking smiles as her thumbs brush my tears away.

330

"Thank you, and I'm sorry."

I want to simultaneously puff out my chest and deflate because I don't know what any of those words are for.

"I don't understand." My voice trembles as I look up at her.

"Thank you for being my safe space, Lincoln."

I must have heard her wrong. "That's not me. Tucker is your safe space. We all see that."

"No, Tucker is my calm. *You* are my safe space. I can't imagine the burden I must have put on your soul having used my safeword twice on you. I hadn't realized it until Tucker pointed it out. That's what I'm sorry for. I'm sorry because it gave you the impression it was directly related to you. I can see in the tortured expression on your face that you do. But it's *because* you're my safe space, I was comfortable enough to feel my discomfort. There's no mask on with you. You see me, all of me, Lincoln. When I'm with you, I feel things that hide. Things I don't know are there until my guard is fully down when you're around."

"Your...safe space." I hear her words, but they sound unbelievable. Not that I don't believe her; I just had no idea she felt so at ease around me.

"Yes. I was fine with everything happening in my bedroom. It wasn't the thought of the sexual acts that were about to happen that made me use my safeword. When I opened myself up to letting it happen, other things crept in. Mostly doubt."

"What were you doubting?" It's hard to imagine Spencer anything more than confident.

"Myself. There's no world in which the woman who was abused and battered both physically and mentally, who had no self-worth and was living each day to pass to the next one, now has four men who worship her. Four men who adore all the broken and barely put back together pieces. The woman who has a dog trained to protect her and nine hidden guns in her house with an alarm system that I thought would protect me as much physically as emotionally. I've spent years building a carefully crafted wall, and with one random kiss from your brother in a coffee shop, it crumbled and let you all in."

I stand and bring her with me. Cradling her in my arms, I rest her head on my chest so she can hear my heartbeat. There's no way this is the Spencer I've known all these years. How could she think so little of herself?

"You're wrong."

"What?"

I stroke her head and repeat myself. "You're wrong. We do worship and adore you. You deserve it and so much more. But Tucker's kiss didn't crumble your wall; you let it down. Piece by piece, you've brought down that wall and let us in. I know because you've fortified it so well we could have huffed and puffed, and it would have still stood. Look how long Miller and Axel tried. You built your wall out of bricks, Dream Girl. The kiss with Tucker might have rattled your mortar, but *you* took it down."

"I took it down?"

"You did."

Spencer's breathing increases as she considers my words. I begin to sway and hum—a small dance to redirect her focus. She can still think, but my words aren't as deep as she's making them out to be. I speak the truth and nothing else.

In the pale green gazebo, surrounded by the thick green

trees, we dance. I hold her and forget about what lives outside these branches. Her feet shuffle with mine, and our back-and-forth sway now has a purpose. We slowly spin in a circle as I continue to hum. There's no song in my head, just the notes flowing.

"Are you alright, Dream Girl?" I kiss the top of her head, and her body relaxes even more in mine.

"Yes. Are you?"

"How could I not be with you here in my arms?" Her moan of contentment lets me know she likes my answer.

"Lincoln?" I hmm, my response. "Make love to me."

My breath hitches at her request. I'm the only one who hasn't had her yet, and she's asking me, no, she told me, to make love to her in the middle of these woods.

"Here?"

She pulls away and removes her white t-shirt. "Yes, here."

She's wearing the same shorts and sports bra she had on earlier, but paired with her words, they seem sexier.

"When I came out here looking for you, Nicole told me she was taking the kids inside and let me know that this gazebo was very private back here." She turns behind her and flips a switch I hadn't seen. Twinkling lights illuminate the underside of the roof and let off a soft glow. The sun has just started going down, so they aren't very bright at the moment, but they soon will be.

"She told you that?"

"She did."

Spencer crosses her arms over her chest and lifts off her sports bra. Her shorts come next, and this woman, whom I don't deserve, stands gloriously naked in front of me. Her creamy white skin, lightly painted with freckles, starkly contrasts the greens around her. I'm struggling to breathe, looking at her. I feel frozen in place. This must be a dream, and I don't want to move and wake up. Spencer, my Dream Girl, is standing before me, offering herself to me. I've been here before, in deep slumber, waking up fisting myself.

Spencer takes a step forward, and I wait for her to dematerialize as my alarm goes off. I'm afraid if I blink, she'll disappear. But when petite fingers brush along the hem of my shirt and nails lightly scrape my sides as she lifts my shirt over my head, the soft breeze that sweeps around us when my shirt hits the floor is undeniable. She's here, and she's real.

I pull her into me, the feel of her pebbled nipples against my chest like razors to my skin. Her blue eyes blink up at me through her thick lashes. Her freckles seem to glow under the soft light. Everything about this woman enchants me, and here she is, offering herself to me.

"Are you sure?"

"Make love to me, Lincoln." She steps away again and opens one of the benches. Inside, she pulls out a few outdoor pillows and a lush-looking quilt.

"I have so many questions for Nicole and Justin." I take the blanket from her and lay it on the floor. I kick off my shoes and pants as Spencer lays back on the pillows, waiting.

"I don't deserve you, Dream Girl."

"Come show me how much you *do*."

Lowering my body to hers, I want to begin everywhere. I want to taste and suck every part of her flesh, but right now isn't about exploration; it's about connection. I can worship her when we have more time, in a bed. It can be alone or with the guys; it doesn't matter to me. Right now, all that matters is I convey to her how much she means to me. How much this relationship means to me, and most of all, how much her trust means everything.

Slowly, I lower my lips to hers and taste the world around us. The earthy smells permeate my senses. I dip my head to her neck and kiss my way down her body.

"Lincoln," she whines as I dip my tongue into her belly button.

"Shhh, I have to get you ready."

"I'm ready. I'm wet. Please, Lincoln. I need you." I slide my hand between us, and she gasps as I run my fingers through her soaked lips.

"Is all this for me?" I circle her clit, and her yes is more of a moan than a word.

Grabbing the base of my cock, I line up. I've never had sex with a woman, without a condom. In my profession, all of our professions, you learn the hard way to just be safe and wrap it up. This gift she gives me of her body is more precious than she can understand.

"Are you sure?" That question asks so much in three simple words. Are you sure you want to do this without a condom? Are you sure you want to let me in your body? Are you ready to take our relationship to the next level? Are you ready to let me into your heart?

She may not understand the magnitude of that last one but, by the time we're done, she will. Giving myself to her as much as she is giving herself to me. I'm all in.

"I have no doubts." With her confirmation, I line myself up and slowly rotate my hips, pushing inside inch by painful inch. The pain isn't physical. It isn't even mental. The pain is my soul being split apart and remolded just for her.

When I'm fully inside, I stop and wait. The blood rushes through my ears, my arms want to give out, my heart runs a marathon, but all I feel is peace. Spencer stares up at me with eyes full of awe and contentment. She has the final piece of a puzzle in her hands. With our eyes locked, I slowly pull out, and as I push back in, the puzzle piece snaps into place.

"Lincoln…" she trails off, unable to put into words what I already know she's feeling. The air around us heats as our bodies move together. I kiss her lips, her neck, the tops of her breasts, as we keep our rhythm steady.

My fingers continue to rub her clit, not because I'm trying to make her orgasm, because I need to keep hearing the moans and mewls of pleasure she's making. But when I feel her legs quiver and her inner walls flutter, I'm excited that she might share that gift with me.

I kiss her neck and whisper all the words my heart wants to tell her.

"For years, I waited with anticipation every shift to hear your voice."

"Your confidence and willingness to help people fills my heart."

"Thank you for giving me the treasured gift of your body."

When I feel like I've spilled out all of my truths and there's only one left to say, her nails dig into my shoulders, her breath quickens, and her orgasm spasms around me. It's not as intense as the ones I've seen her have, but her moans are longer and deeper as if this orgasm is more consuming than the others. And when I follow behind her a few minutes later, I feel it, too. It's a release of energy and love.

I fucking love this woman. She should know. It's unfair to hold it back.

"Dream Girl, I—" she covers my mouth with her hand.

"Not yet. Not like this. Not after a disagreement when you're still buried inside me. Another time. Another day, when the sun is shining, and there are no monumental decisions or apologies. When I haven't doubted my worth or spent twenty minutes digging gum out of Axel's hair."

"Okay. But know it's true. Without words, please know. I'll show you everyday with my actions. I don't want there ever to be a minute that goes by where you doubt my feelings for you. You're my Dream Girl." I kiss her long and tenderly before pulling out. I use the t-shirt she was wearing to clean us and we slowly get dressed.

By the time we make our way up the path to the house, the sun is fully down, but strings of lights illuminate the trail. I wonder if this was here before or after Nicole.

When we walk in the door hand in hand, the crowd of assholes cheer for us. Even the kids join in because the adults are doing it. I take a deep bow, and Spencer freezes.

With a stiffened body, she turns to Justin. "Tell me there aren't any cameras out there." A smile slowly creeps up his face. Spencer's grip on my hand tightens before Nicole smacks Justin across the chest.

"There is, but I turned them off when we came in. Whatever you did out there is safe." Justin kisses Nicole, mumbling how not fun she is.

"Eww. Gross."

Axel puts a hand on Katy's shoulder, looking concerned. "What's wrong?

"They almost made a sex tape out there."

The adults scramble to cover tiny listening ears, but it's too late. Hannah looks up at Justin with an inquisitive face.

"Daddy, what a ses tape?"

"Escape. Aunt Spencer and Uncle Lincoln almost made an ESCAPE."

"Oh, a sescape." Hannah seems satisfied with Justin's answer while Katy and Axel try to contain their laughter.

"Anyway…" Justin looks relieved. "Katy, what do you want to do for your birthday next week?"

"Birthday? Spencer, did you know it was her birthday next week?"

Katy looks around the room and shrugs. "Surprise?"

44

Miller

M oving day. I hate fucking moving. Even if we're only swapping houses, it still requires boxes, and bubble wrap, and more boxes. Luckily, with so many men around, there's enough muscle that it's easier. How does that saying go? Many hands make light work? Or some shit like that.

Justin and Cole are here helping. Dempsey is with the girls having a girls' day with Katy for her birthday tomorrow, and all the kids are at a mother's morning out program except Miles, who's being doted on by Spencer's father.

We refused to let Eddie help, but he insisted he wasn't going to sit around and do nothing, so the girls gave him the most important job. Baby duty.

"Are you ready for baby number three, Cole?" Blake is two days overdue, and you'd never know it. She was so excited to get a pedicure because that's how Annie went into labor.

"More than ready. I can't wait to find out if it's a girl or a boy. I'm thinking boy." After much convincing, Annie persuaded them not to find out the gender of the baby. They already have everything they need since they had boy/girl twins the first time. Cole whined the most when the decision was made, but after a while, he understood the excitement. He enjoys the reactions of others when he tells them they aren't finding out.

"Has everyone picked rooms yet?" Eddie sits on Spencer's couch in the pool house, cuddling Miles while he watches us load everything onto a trailer to tow it down the driveway. Most of the furniture is being swapped since Eddie said it isn't his style.

"Only Katy. The rest of us don't care." I lick my lips and turn away from Lincoln's shirtless form. We've been so busy packing and working that there hasn't been much time for the fun stuff.

"Tuck, is everything all set for tonight?" I pass him a box labeled GUEST BATH with red tape across it.

Being in a relationship with the owner of a nightclub has its perks. Tucker has closed the restaurant portion for the night, and we're having a party for Katy. She confided in us that she's never had a birthday party before and we want to make the first one with her in our family special.

"Of course. My manager has been texting me all day with the details. We've posted to our social medias that the restaurant is closed for a private party. The cake has already arrived, and the decorations are looking perfectly girly." He pulls out his phone and turns the screen toward us.

"Oh my god." Axel bursts out laughing. "Does the bull have a unicorn horn?"

"Of course it does. It's a unicorn party. I don't do things small, especially for the ones I care about."

We had Hannah ask Katy what her favorite animal was,

and she told her unicorns. It feels fitting despite her turning seventeen. She's never had a party before, and what little girl didn't imagine, once in their lifetime, having a unicorn-themed celebration?

"Alright, Eddie. We need the couch. It's the last thing to go on the trailer before we head back up the driveway. Cole, grab an end." Eddie stands with the baby, and Cole and I load the couch. Justin drives it up to the house, and the rest of us walk.

"This was really nice of you, Mr.—" Eddie arches a brow at Cole before he finishes his sentence. "Eddie, the extra space will be so nice for them."

"Not nice, just practical. Have you seen all of these men crammed into this small pool house? It's like a can of Vienna sausages. Besides, now I can hire a housekeeper to come once a week. It'll be a quarter of the price, and I won't have to clean. I may be old, but I'm no fool, son."

I slow my pace and grab the belt loop on the back of Lincoln's pants so he'll walk with me. "I really need you to put a fucking shirt on before I start licking the sweat off your chest. I'm so goddamn horny, and you're not helping walking around looking like fucking sex on a stick." He spins and stops short in front of me. Our chests crash together, and it does nothing to tamp down my arousal.

"Are you struggling, Fireball? Are you needy?" His hand slides up my chest, grazing my nipple. My cock jumps, and I groan.

"You aren't fucking helping." Before we moved in with Spencer, we were splitting time between our two apartments and talking about downsizing to one. Our playtime was anytime, anywhere, but since moving into the pool house and

341

having Katy so close, we've been limited to shower quickies, and they just aren't as satisfying.

I'm excited to move into the new house. Katy is taking the downstairs master with the attached bathroom, so she has everything she needs for her and the baby. She hasn't officially told us yet that she's keeping it, but we all know without needing her words. But even if she decides not to continue with the pregnancy, she still has her privacy.

The other bedrooms and the bonus room are upstairs. We decided the bonus room would be the community bedroom, but anyone who wanted privacy could use the extra rooms. Somehow, I don't think any of the other rooms will get used.

Cole informed us that Annie was gifting us a special bed, called a Family Bed, that will fit us all. I won't argue with her if she wants to purchase a seven thousand dollar bed. Oh, and several sets of the special sheets needed. In a few days, we'll be sleeping in luxury.

"Let's go, boys," Tucker yells down the driveway. "Spencer just texted, and they're done at the salon. We need to get this trailer unloaded so we can get ready."

"Coming."

"Not yet, you aren't." Lincoln runs his hand over my semi-hard cock through my pants, and I want to strip for him right here and now. "Katy is spending the night at Justin's since the house isn't set up yet. If you can be a good boy for the rest of the night, I'll take care of this and more." He punctuates his words with a squeeze to my head, and I bite my lip to stop the carnal growl that desperately wants to come out.

"I make no promises."

"I do." He jerks my cock twice and walks away. I have to lean over and brace my hands on my knees. Two tugs. Two fucking tugs is all it takes for me to almost lose control. I inhale several deep breaths to calm myself from not blowing my load in my pants like a fucking teenager.

Lincoln's retreating ass is just as enticing as his shirtless front, and I force myself to stare down at my feet as I walk the rest of the way to the house.

We quickly unload the furniture and boxes and put them in their proper rooms. Spencer is meticulous with her packing. Every box is sealed with a different-colored tape, and each corresponding room has a piece of the same tape color, indicating to anyone with eyes which boxes and furniture go where. It's genius and foolproof.

"The girls just got to my house, so we have about an hour to get ready." Cole waves his cell, indicating he got a notice from Annie and Blake about their location. Since we were already here and they were all going out together, we decided to meet at the club to save time. Nicole is a hairdresser and will help everyone get ready at Annie's house, which is also where the highly vetted babysitters will be staying. Babysitters, plural, because we learned the hard way when you get the kids all together, it requires lots of adults.

"There's two showers in the pool house and three here, so we can all get the washing-up part done quickly." Tucker lifts off his hat and swipes his forehead with the back of his hand. Even that is fucking hot.

Shit. I need a cold shower.

"You're drooling, Fireball." Lincoln's whisper in my ear makes me shiver. His deep voice vibrates under my skin.

"I'm fucking horny, Babe. Shower with me so I can take the edge off."

Lincoln's hand rises, and he toys with the collar of my t-

343

shirt. "I could, but wouldn't it be so much sweeter to wait for later?"

"No, no, it fucking wouldn't." Grabbing his hand, I brush it over my erection. "I wonder if Tucker would help me out?" I tip my head to the window where Tucker stands just outside. I see it in his eyes; the reaction I'm looking for.

"Why don't you ask him and see how red I make your ass tonight." He squeezes my cock again, but this time, I'm in control of the game, and the pleasure courses through me.

"Maybe I will." I step back, adjusting myself before walking out of the house and straight to Tucker. I lean into his ear with a quick smile over my shoulder to Lincoln, who's followed me out.

"Lincoln threatened me with a spanking if I came over here and asked you if you'd like to shower with me. It sounds like a really fucking good time to me, but he's trying to kill me with delayed gratification. Will you walk with me to the pool house so I can pretend to earn my punishment?"

Tucker's lips lift into a devilish grin, and he grabs a fistful of my shirt.

"Bruiser, did you really just come over to me, with all this bravado, and tell me you want me to *pretend* to tease your boyfriend because you want a spanking?"

Oh fuck. Why did I think this was a good idea?

"Let's go." He tugs on my shirt in the direction of the pool house.

"What...where are we going?"

He gives me a stern look. "To take a shower together. I don't fucking pretend to do anything, and I'm sure as hell going to be there to watch him tan your ass later. Now, let's get going before we're late meeting the girls."

I stumble behind Tucker, stunned that my teasing has become torture.

"Tucker?"

"Bruiser?"

"You're just fucking with Lincoln, right? Or me?" He peers back at me, and the tilt of his lip tells me I'm in for it. "Shit."

"Like I said, I'm a grown adult, and I don't play pretend." He pauses and huffs. "Well, that's not the truth. I'll certainly be *pretending* that you're going to come while we take our shower. I'm with my little brother; delayed gratification is fun.

"Fuck."

Tucker was telling the truth. He drags my ass into the shower and washes my hair, lulling me into a false sense of security. When his soapy hand slips around my hip and pumps my cock I almost burst on the spot.

Tucker's hands are larger and more calloused than Lincoln's. His grip is firmer as he strokes me.

"Don't you fucking come, Bruiser. You already have one punishment coming to you, and I promise you don't want to add another one."

"Are you sure?" I rotate my hips and rub my ass across Tucker's hard cock, poking me from behind. The air at my back quickly turns cold as Tucker steps away from me, and a loud crack echoes through the room.

"Holy shit balls." The heat from his slap radiates across my ass cheek as his hand rubs over the sting.

"Do you want nine more of those for being a brat?"

Before I can answer with a resounding no, Tucker moves his hand back to stroking my cock, and my body falls against his.

"I'll be good."

"That's right, you will. You'll be a good boy for me and my brother."

I fucking hate that I love being called that so much. It's emasculating and arousing at the same time, but I wouldn't change it for anything. I'll be their good boy. Their good fucking boy.

45

Katy

I've never had a birthday party. My mother never cared to celebrate my birth. I'm not sure I would even know when my birthday was if it wasn't for my teachers in school celebrating it for me.

The scene around me is a flurry of organized chaos. Annie lives in a house that looks like an ordinary, everyday residence from the outside, but the inside tells a different story. Everything is top-of-the-line, including her fancy Doberman, Candy, who keeps licking my ankles. Blake told me it's because I used cherry-scented lotion, and Candy loves...well, candy.

Blake also told me a hilarious story of the time Candy stole one of their dildos, and Cole had to chase her around the house trying to get it back. I love Blake. She's fantastic and doesn't treat me like a child. The only hesitation when she told me that story was making sure no one else heard and tried to stop her from sharing. I'm going to be a mother. A dildo story is probably the least of my worries at this point.

Mother. I've officially decided to keep the baby and plan

to tell them tonight. Despite the circumstances that he or she came from, seeing the loving families and relationships around me solidified what I already knew I wanted. How could I not want to bring another life into this incredible group of people? I know it won't be easy, but Annie, Blake, and Nicole are such amazing role models. I feel confident in my decision and can't wait to tell them.

"Dempsey, eyes," Nicole calls from across the room. Mr. Viking bodyguard has followed us around all night. He's under strict instructions not to let us out of his sight, and he's taking it very seriously, including being inside Annie and Blake's massive bedroom with us. Someone must be changing because that's the code for him to turn and face the wall.

I like when he's facing away. I can linger a little longer on his large muscular body. At Nicole's request, he took his hair down. The hairdresser in her wouldn't allow her to not check out his dirty blond locks, and then she stole his hair tie.

I was envious of her hands and wished I could run my fingers through them.

Down girl.

Man, these pregnancy hormones are no joke.

"I agree." I jump at Blake's whisper in my ear.

"You what?" She moves from behind me to stand and gawks at Dempsey's backside.

"He's yummy looking."

"No, I wasn't…I mean, I was…well…" I drop my head and huff, and hear her snicker.

"It's written all over your face, Katy. Your cheeks are flushed, and I swear I can see your heart beating through your shirt." I raise a hand to my cheek and feel the heat. "He's a very handsome young man."

"He's not that young. And even if he was, I'm only barely seventeen and pregnant. They make TV shows about girls in my situation, Blake."

"Hmm." She taps her lip, and I don't like the look on her face. I can tell she's about to embarrass me. "Hey, Vik the Viking."

"Blake," I hiss her name through gritted teeth and grab her arm, trying to pull her anywhere else in the room to avoid this conversation.

"Ma'am?"

"Relax, Katy. He knows how good-looking he is—most men who look like him do. So Vik, how old are you?"

I see the lip twitch he tries so hard to hide when he finds something funny. "I'm twenty-two, ma'am."

"Excellent. And do you like kids? Ever thought about having a family of your own?"

I could die right now. I want the ground to open up and swallow me whole. He knows she's asking these questions for me. I'm standing right next to Blake, and I'm probably as red as a tomato.

"I like kids just fine. A family is always the dream, but dreams can be futile."

"Huh. Interesting. Thank you for your answers." I don't know if I like his last answer. There was a hint of sadness that I'm not sure Blake picked up on. I can't help but hang on to his every last word and notice the slight change in his pitch.

"All clear, Dempsey," Nicole says nonchalantly from across the room. She has no idea of our conversation as she was in the bathroom. No clue when Viktor turns, and his eyes immediately meet mine, searching. What are you searching for, Viktor?

Instinctively, I cup my non-existent stomach, and his eyes fall to my hand. Of course, he knows about my pregnancy. When his eyes roam back up to meet mine, there's a new look on his face before he turns his gaze back to the middle of the room.

Was that guilt? He has nothing to be or feel guilty about.

"Katy. Get your young ass in this closet, and let's find you something to wear." Blake swats at my butt, and I give Viktor one last glance before disappearing into a room that might as well be a department store.

On a normal day, I wouldn't be allowed into Midnight Moonshine, and I guess, technically, I'm not going *in*. The restaurant is open to anyone, but the dance floor is eighteen and over, except on Sunday afternoons when family dancing is allowed.

As we walk into a foyer that looks like a movie theater entrance, I notice a sign that reads, "Restaurant Closed for a Private Party." I hope that's not for me. I can't imagine Tucker would close his entire restaurant on a busy Friday night...for me.

"I've been told you need to close your eyes, but if you're not comfortable with it, you can just walk in." I know Spencer's offer comes from a place of her own comfort level.

"I'm comfortable. And I know I've told you already, but

you look beautiful, Spencer. I feel bad for the guys." Spencer is wearing a form-fitting, devil-red dress with a halter top and a hemline that's borderline sinful. Red is usually a color that someone with Spencer's complexion can't pull off, but somehow, it highlights her dark strawberry-blonde hair, that is down and perfectly styled thanks to Nicole, and looks absolutely gorgeous. I'm glad I'm spending the night at Justin's house because I don't want to be anywhere near her and a bedroom.

"As do you, Katy." Blake was all too happy to play dress up with me. She was nostalgic looking at some of the clothes in her closet and wondering if she'll ever get to wear them again. She picked a dark pink strapless dress for me with a sweetheart neckline. The bottom of the dress flows down to just above my knees, and Blake made sure to point out that it has pockets. She practically squealed while showing me.

While my eyes wandered their amazing closet of shoes, I fell in love with a pair of sparkly black four inch heels; I didn't want to look like a baby doe all night wearing shoes I had no right trying to pretend I could walk in. I opted for a two-inch strappy sandal instead, and I'm glad I did. This place is huge and I'll most likely end up doing a lot of walking.

Tucker walks out from a pair of tinted glass doors and looks handsome. His usual attire of dark jeans and a button-up shirt has been replaced with dark gray slacks. He has one of those string tie things that cowboys wear in the movies over his maroon button-up shirt.

He walks up to Spencer and me and removes his hat to bow at us.

"Well, look at my two favorite girls. Absolutely stunning. Let me look at you. Spin for me." Spencer's smile is bright as she spins, and Tucker's eyes beam with pride. When I turn, Tucker whistles, and I swat his chest at his ridiculousness.

"Please tell me that's not for me?" I gesture toward the closed restaurant sign, and he looks at me like I'm crazy.

"Of course it is."

"Tucker, that's too much. You can't close your entire restaurant for me to eat dinner here." He rolls his eyes and steps behind me. Placing his hands over my eyes, he slowly walks me forward. I hear the door open, and the air shifts. Soft music plays around me, and it smells heavenly.

"Of course I can. It's the perk of being the owner. And it's not just dinner, Katy." He removes his hands and steps back. "Open your eyes, birthday girl."

I open them, blinking a few times because I don't believe what I'm seeing. The entire restaurant is draped in pink and gold. There are unicorn balloons, centerpieces, and even a cake. The delicious smell is various mac n cheeses based on the signs in front of the serving platters.

"It wouldn't be a Katy party if there wasn't mac n cheese." I spin and throw myself into Justin's arms. Tears prickle my eyes as he wraps his arms around me. "Happy Birthday, Katy."

"Justin. How? Why?"

He laughs, and I feel the vibrations on my cheek. "The *how* would be this cowboy standing next to us. The *why* is because you deserve it."

"You're special, Katy, and deserve to be celebrated." I release Justin and throw my arms around Tucker. I shake my head into his chest.

"I don't deserve all of this." Tucker grabs my shoulders and pulls me away at arm's length.

"You deserve this and so much more. I heard about your history with Justin, and I know what happened before you came to live with Spencer. You're a strong, resilient woman, and we are honored to have you in our lives. We're going to celebrate your life, and you're going to eat your mac n cheese and unicorn cake with a smile."

"Can it be a teary smile?"

I'm pulled away from Tucker into Axel's broad chest. "It can even be a snotty smile, Katy girl. We'll still love you." *Love me?*

"Nope. We aren't doing that. I just felt you get stiff. We love you and all of your stubborn brattiness. Don't ever doubt that." I know Axel means every word he says; it's just sometimes hard to believe. After so many years of feeling unloved, these random adults took me in on the worst day of my life, and they haven't looked back once. I'm the same person in Spencer's house as I was in the apartment I grew up in, but I never felt loved there. I barely felt cared for.

Once again, I'm pulled from one embrace into another. Well, two others. Miller and Lincoln sandwich me between them, Miller to my front and Lincoln to my back.

"Katy doesn't think we love her," Axel tattles.

"I never said that."

"You didn't, but your body language did." I can't argue with him there.

"Okay, okay. You all love me." I shift away from Lincoln and Miller and wave my hands in the air. "I'm a lovable, adorable, angsty teenager. A pregnant one that really wants to eat her weight in mac n cheese until she's about to pop and then top it off with unicorn cake that better be strawberry flavored because that's the only acceptable way."

"Told ya," Axel boasts.

"What? Told who, what?" There are grumbles and sour faces all around me.

"Axel here," Tucker throws a thumb his way, "said you'd want strawberry. We all disagreed."

"All?"

"Yes. We thought you'd want chocolate." Lincoln plays with the cuffs on his silver dress shirt paired handsomely with black slacks.

"So there's no strawberry cake?" I try to keep the disappointment out of my tone but I fail.

Miller huffs. "No, there's a strawberry cake *and* a chocolate cake. Axel was persistent."

I step over to Axel, who's wearing a purple dress shirt with cuffed sleeves and navy dress pants. It suits him and his personality perfectly.

Lifting on my toes, I kiss his cheek and whisper shout so everyone can hear me. "That's why you're my favorite." His face beams as I skip off toward the food table and hear the gasps and commotion behind me. They're fun to rile up and so easy.

Dinner is amazing. I stuff myself with the most delicious mac n cheese I've ever eaten, but no matter how good it is, nothing will ever compare to the blue and orange box that Justin made me the first day I wandered into his apartment.

When it's time for dessert, as promised, there are two identical unicorn cakes. As I blow out the candles on both, because they insisted on lighting both, I decide it's time to tell them.

"Before we eat these, I'd like to make an announcement." Everyone in the room turns their attention to me. This is my family—the one the universe made me wait almost seventeen years for. Not a single one of them is my blood, but it doesn't matter to any of them, and it definitely doesn't matter to me.

"I want to thank everyone from the bottom of my heart. I've shared the worst day of my life with some of you…and now I share the best day with all of you. And because of you and the support you've provided me, I've decided to keep the baby."

They all stare at me with smiles of admiration. I don't deserve any of them.

46

Axel

Tonight has been incredible—good food with great friends, surrounded by people we love. As we stand around, all saying our goodbyes, I watch everyone interact with each other.

Blake is the bubbly sunshine of the group, a perfect match for Annie's stoic nature and Cole's relaxed attitude. Justin hides his inner demons, but Nicole nurtures him and gives him peace. Katy fits seamlessly into our ever-expanding group, soaking up life like a sponge.

Miller and Lincoln might as well be an old married couple, knowing each other so well, inside and out. Miller has stopped hiding his relationship and is open with Lincoln out in public. Tucker and Spencer have this undeniable bond that defies every standard of relationships. He *knows* her. He sees her even when she's hiding behind her mask.

Where do I fit in?

My chemistry with Spencer is evident in every kiss and caress. I'm the jokester in our five-some, but I sometimes can't help feeling like a fifth wheel. I'm no one's calm; my

ADHD wouldn't ever allow that. I'm the chaos—the one who blurts out my thoughts without thinking. My humor is a shield that keeps me from thinking too deeply.

"What do you need, Darlin'?" Tucker's breath on my ear snaps me out of my pity party.

"Just observing."

He steps around me, blocking my view of the room. "There's more going on in that head of yours. You look far too contemplative just to be observing."

Does he see everyone?

"You and Spencer have something special." That's part of what I was thinking, hopefully enough that he doesn't push for more.

No such luck.

"We do. But what else were you thinking about?" He lifts his hand to my forehead and smooths the creases with his thumb. His touch is gentle and comforting. "You're worried about something. Is it Katy?" He shakes his head before I can answer, seeing something in my face. "Not Katy. Hmm. Something at work? Not that, either. Something at home? Ah. Talk to me." His hand trails down my temple, my cheek until he's holding my chin in his hands. His blue eyes pierce me.

"I'm fine."

"You're not." His objection is as quick as mine. "You're not okay, and you can tell me willingly, or I can persuade you to tell me." Tucker's thumb runs along my bottom lip, and he grabs my belt and pulls me into his hips. I look around the room to see who's still here to witness us, and he pulls my chin back to him. "This is my club, and I don't care who sees. Eyes on me, Darlin'."

"I'm fine, Tucker," I insist again trying to get my point across, but he ignores me.

"Hard way it is." He releases my chin but not my belt and drags me behind him toward the doors leading to the club. He takes a left into an office and locks the door behind us. I'm slammed up against the wall and Tucker puts one hand on my neck and the other at my waist. He stops his lips just before we connect, his hand stopping me from closing the space. An involuntary whine escapes me, and I realize how much I've missed this connection.

"Please." I want his touch—his soft lips and rough beard against my skin. "Tucker, please kiss me."

"Tell me what's wrong." Closing my eyes, I dip my head as much as his hand allows. I don't want to feel broken and vulnerable right now. I want to feel wanted.

"Nothing. I'm f—"

"I promise if you finish that sentence, you'll regret it." He nips my jaw, and I want to melt into a fucking puddle.

I'm hard. I'm so fucking hard and turned on, and he hasn't even touched me.

"Talk to me, Darlin'. I don't want to ask again. You've been reserved lately, and I don't like it."

It's hard to think or form words when his mouth is hot and wet on my skin. He traces the angle of my jaw with licks and kisses. The shell of my ear, the hollow of my neck. His simple touches are so erotic. My brain is misfiring more than usual with the need and want coursing through my body. I drum my fingers on my thigh with the need to tell him and the crushing anxiety not to.

"Axel." My growled name reverberates through my brain like a ping-pong ball. Squeezing my eyes closed, I take a deep breath and whisper my doubts.

"I don't...fit."

He pulls away, and I can tell he's misunderstood what I said.

"Not like that." I puff out a heavy sigh. "Miller has Lincoln, and you have Spencer and..."

Tucker must see the pain in my eyes that I'm trying so desperately to hide. I shouldn't complain about the pieces of each of them that they offer me. I'm so grateful for what I get. I have more than I ever wanted, and it feels selfish to want them to give more of themselves to me.

"Fuck." He rests his forehead on mine. "Axel, no. You're as much a part of this relationship as any of us. Are you feeling left out?"

Is that what I'm feeling? No. That's not it. I can join in with any of them whenever I want. We're all open with our affection.

"Not left out. Just...extra."

Tucker finally closes the distance between our lips, but it's not fast or dominating. It's soft and tender, and the rawness I was already feeling from this conversation seeps out. Tucker removes his hand from my neck and wipes away a stray tear.

"I'm so fucking sorry that you're feeling that way. It's the farthest thing from the truth, Darlin'. Everyone has their part."

"Yeah, I'm the stupid, funny one." Wow. That wasn't self-deprecating or anything, but I'd be lying to myself if, some days, I didn't feel exactly like that.

A growl that tells me exactly how much he disapproves of my thoughts echoes around the room. "Stop that right fucking now. You're more valuable than that. Please tell me that's not actually how you feel you fit in here?" He listens to my silence and knows it's my answer. "I'm so fucking sorry, Darlin'. I'm so sorry."

His low, muffled apologies continue as he kisses down my neck. Tucker reaches for my shirt, and his lips trail after his hands as he slowly undoes the buttons. I grab his hat before it falls off his head and run my fingers through his dark auburn hair. He hums his approval, and the sound vibrates through my chest.

"You're just as much wanted as everyone else in our family."

With all the buttons undone, he stands and slides my shirt off my shoulders.

"I've never felt unwanted. Sex is never the problem."

"Then what?"

I don't know how to put into words exactly how it makes me feel. It's just an extraness.

"If I'm not just the funny one, then what am I?" I realize these are lifelong insecurities I'm burdening my relationship with. It's a general feeling of my entire life, not necessarily only in my relationship with them.

"Hmm. Answering my question with a question. Okay. You need to know your worth in our relationship?"

"I-I do." His hands roam my bare chest, and I'm struggling to do anything but feel.

Tucker steps back and pulls out his phone. He types a few lines and then grabs my hand, taking me to a dark green velour couch in the corner of the office. When he sits, he pulls me down to straddle his legs. It's a very different position than I'm used to, as I'm usually the one being sat on.

"What are we doing?"

Tucker looks into my eyes, and he rubs the tops of my

thighs. The warmth from his hands burning a line on my skin.

"We're waiting."

"Waiting? For?" Tucker's phone buzzes between us, startling me. It buzzes again and again. I stare at the phone, wondering when he's going to pick it up. When he finally does, the smile that crosses his lips melts my inner soul. It's beautiful.

"Look."

He hands me the phone, and I see he's received a handful of texts.

Miller: Axel is the best friend I could ever ask for. He's loyal to a fault and always makes me smile. He has the biggest heart, and I'm happy to call him mine.

I lift my gaze to look curiously at Tucker. "What is this?"

"Keep reading." His hands glide back up my thighs as I read the next text.

Blake: Axel is like the big cuddly brother I always wanted. A smile from him could brighten my day.

Lincoln: Axel inspires me to always look on the bright side. Even on my darkest days, he brings me light and joy. I love the big guy.

Justin: I love the shit out of that man. He doesn't put up with my bullshit, and in a world of people-pleasers, I need someone like Axel to keep me grounded.

Cole: Axel is the only person I know whose humor can rival mine. I love the conversations we've had that are deep but laced with enough comedy that we always come out better on the other side!

Nicole: No one will ever commiserate curly hair with me as well as Axel. We hold each other's secrets close to our hearts.

Katy: Axel is MY big teddy bear. Nothing more needs to be said.

Annie: I have great respect for someone who can do the job Axel does and still finds humor in everyday life.

Spencer: Every one of my men holds a special piece of me. Axel holds my laughs and my smiles that I didn't know I still had after such a long time of being locked away.

Tucker swipes his thumbs across my cheeks, collecting my tears. The last few texts were blurry to read through my emotions.

"And me. Do you know what you mean to me? You're a breath of fresh air after a day in the dirt. A cold glass of water after baking in the sun. You're my sunshine. You're all of our sunshine. You're not the stupid, funny one like you said. You bring us all so much joy in this terrible fucking world. I'm sorry we haven't been doing a better job showing you how much you mean to us. Sometimes, we forget that just because you smile all the time, it doesn't mean there aren't deeper emotions hiding behind it. But you need to let us in and talk to us. For you to think so little of yourself, you must see your humor as a burden, and we can't have that. Your humor is a beautiful thing, but we can walk alongside you through sadness, fear, and love, too."

I hunch over and bury my face in my hands. I feel so raw right now. The words everyone said about me were incredible, but more than that, Tucker's words spoke the truth. I hide behind my humor because, like Spencer, it's my mask. No one ever bothers the funny guy. The one who always wears a smile but never gets upset. But the flip side to that is if I'm always smiling, no one takes me seriously. It's a heavy burden to wear on either side of the coin. But if Spencer can learn to drop her mask and let us in, then I can do the same with my humor.

Gentle hands encircle my wrists and pull to uncover my face. I probably look like absolute shit right now, and I keep my head hung low.

"Don't hide from me, Darlin'. What do you need? What can I give you right now?"

"You've just given me so much." My cup is full with all the love everyone just poured into it.

Tucker kisses my knuckles and the heat flares in my body. His beard scratches my fingers, and my cock twitches. "If I've satisfied your mind, is there something your body needs?"

47

Tucker

My heart is in pieces because of what Axel just told me. I'm usually so observant, but I've been distracted lately and clearly haven't been at my best.

I took a chance when I texted everyone, but I knew they'd come through.

Group Chat:

Tucker: Axel is struggling with his position in our family. He feels like he's an extra person. Can each of you reply to this text with your favorite thing about him? I want to show him how needed and loved he is.

Watching the tears fall down the cheeks of the brightest sunshine I know almost gutted me, but I knew he was reading things that he needed. They were tears of happiness for the love that our family and friends were pouring into him.

"If I've satisfied your mind, is there something your body needs?" He may believe everyone's words, but his body has been carrying this stress for a while. He got mental relief from crying, but his tense body shows me he could still use a physical one.

Releasing his hands, I slide mine up the soft fabric of his slacks.

"Did anyone tell you how incredible you look tonight? Purple is your color." He looks over his shoulder at his shirt haphazardly laid on the floor near the door. When he turns back, he looks between our bodies and laughs.

"This isn't a position I'm used to. I'm usually the one being sat on."

I run my hands from his stomach to his chest and back. His muscles contract under my touch, making him look even more delicious.

"I happen to like you right here, but if you'd rather change positions, I have some other ideas." I flip him to the right and lay his back on the couch, hovering my body over him. "Is this more familiar to you?"

"Even less." I sometimes forget that this is all new to him. He's so easygoing for a former straight man.

Shit.

"Darlin', are you okay with this? Would you like me to call one of the others to come in and join us?" I don't think he's been one-on-one with any of the other guys, and he might not be into this.

Nails dig into my shoulder blades, and Axel's hips arch to bump with mine. "Don't call anyone else. I'm one hundred percent okay with this." I take that as permission to explore his chest with my mouth.

"And what exactly are you okay with?" I'm willing to take this little romp wherever he needs and wants it to go.

"I need—" His words stop when I suck on the sensitive spot just below his ear.

"What do you need?"

Axel's hips buck up when I nip the spot I just sucked. "Yes. That. More. You."

"I'm going to need all of your big boy words, Darlin'."

"C-can you fuck me, Daddy Tucker?" *Brat.*

"You're going to sass me while asking me to fuck you? Sassy brats get punished."

"Fuck, yes," he moans.

God, I want to punish him so badly.

"If my brother didn't already have plans to punish Miller tonight, I'd tan your ass right now. But I now want to include you in it. How does that sound? You and your best friend are both getting punished for being brats. It sounds like heaven to me."

"Fuck me now, punish me later?" Axel phrased it as a question, but I hear the hint of demand in his voice.

"Flip over. Hands and knees." I sit up and almost fall off the couch with how quickly he moves under me. His hands fumble with his belt and pants as he sheds his clothing before he gets into position.

"Are we eager, Darlin'?" He drops his chest to the couch, making his ass stick out even farther. I happily massage his ass cheeks, pulling them apart to see his glorious hole he's allowing me to own.

"I'll warn you, not only am I bigger than Miller, this angle will be deeper. Do you think you can handle me?"

"I want you, Tucker. I can handle it."

I smooth a hand up his back. "I know you can. Don't move." I grab a bottle of lube out of my desk drawer and take my time undressing while I stare at the man offering himself to me. I'll do better for him. We will all do better. We've been focused on Katy and Spencer, but there are five people in our relationship, and each of us deserves to feel wanted and loved.

When I reposition myself behind him, he's shaking. He jumps when the lube bottle clicks, and I chuckle.

"Nerves or anticipation?"

"Anticipation. Adrenaline." I feel the same. Watching Miller take him for the first time, hearing him being talked through everything, and the noises he made were as exciting for me as being inside Spencer for the first time.

"Darlin', we're going to need to be quick about this. Every-one is waiting for us. I promise we can take our time later." I lube my finger and rim his hole. He tenses, then exhales and relaxes. He wants this just as much as I do.

"Just need you, Tuck."

"I know. I'm going to take care of you. Relax and let me in. Deep breaths." He's so compliant, and it isn't long before I slip in one, then two fingers. He's eagerly bucking under me when I slip in a third, and whining for me to take him. His body jolts when I remove my fingers completely and add lube to my throbbing cock.

"Tucker," he pants, and it's music to my ears to hear my name said so breathy and needy.

"This is the hard part, then the pleasure." I spread his cheeks apart and watch him contract at the loss and need of me. "Deep breath in, then breathe out." I take the opportunity the moment he relaxes and push in. He gasps.

"Oh fuck."

"Shhh, you're doing so well. Give me another deep breath.

Good boy." He relaxes even more on the exhale, and with quick shallow pumps, I go deeper. His sounds of pleasure mixed with pain and need spur me until he's taken everything I have to offer.

"Need. You."

Axel's voice is strained as he waits for me to fuck him. The anticipation that's rising as I kneel, unmoving with my cock buried deep in his ass, is just as torturous for me as it is for him.

His pleading whine cracks any semblance of restraint I have left.

"Hold on, Darlin', I'm going to give us what we both need." I pull my hips back and thrust in hard. The grunting moan that erupts from Axel can surely be heard outside my office door, but I don't give a fuck. There are perks to being the owner.

I set a brutal pace that has us both panting and grunting. He's tight and keeps flexing his muscles, constricting me even farther.

"Axel, your ass is too sweet, and you're pulling me over the edge too quickly. Jerk your cock, I want you to come before I do."

"Your couch?"

"Fuck the couch. I'll buy a new one. I want your pleasure. I didn't make a request. I gave you an order." He growls his approval and shifts to reach under him. He moans a sigh of relief when he wraps his hands around his swollen cock.

I can feel my balls drawing in and my spine starting to tingle.

"Need you to come, Darlin'." I adjust my hips and angle myself to go deeper with each thrust. I can tell by the change in his moaning, I've found his sweet spot.

"There it is. Give it to me." I pump my hips harder, faster. Axel's mouth opens on a silent scream before he turns his head into the cushion, and a guttural sound pours out of him. I pull out just as my orgasm overtakes me and spill onto his back and ass. Hot ropes of come burst from my cock that are so powerful I have to brace myself on the back of the couch so I don't crush Axel.

I sit back on my heels when I'm done and run a finger over his ass, smearing my come along his cheeks.

"I can't wait to do that again later with my hand prints proudly displayed on this ass." He mumbles unintelligible words, still muffled by the cushion, and I laugh lightheartedly. It seems I was feeling as much stress as he was, and this was the relief I needed, too. "Don't move. Let me get you cleaned up. I place a kiss in the middle of his back and get wet paper towels to clean us.

As we're getting dressed, Axel looks at the darker spot on the couch and frowns. I grab his chin as his mouth is opening and smash my lips to his with a searing kiss.

"If you were about to apologize for my couch, don't. It's an improvement, and I'm looking forward to fondly remembering how it got there." He drops his forehead to mine and sighs.

"Okay. Yeah, okay." He kisses my nose, and I laugh at his playfulness.

"Better?"

"Better. Thank you."

I pull him into my chest and wrap my arms around him—a simple hug. Axel melts into my embrace, and I hug him a little harder.

"Don't keep your feelings from us. We can take it. We're a team, a family. We're stronger together. Okay?" He answers me with a kiss. My phone buzzes in my pocket, and I groan at the interruption.

Lincoln: Out front. Now.

48

Lincoln

Tonight has been perfect for Katy. Everyone celebrated our favorite teenager, and we got to enjoy spending time together as ourselves without judgment.

I watched Tucker pull Axel away as everyone said their goodbyes, and I silently thanked him. He's been in a funk lately, and I couldn't figure out why. Hopefully, my arrogant, stubborn brother can get to the bottom of it.

When the text came through to a group chat from Tucker, my heart fell to my feet. Have we been that neglectful of his feelings? Miller and I had a routine before we moved into Spencer's house, and we can all see the connection Tucker and Spencer have that's different from the rest of us.

"I feel like shit. How could we be so terrible to the guy?"

Miller tucks me into his arms and kisses my temple.

"No one has been terrible to him. We just need to make more effort. It's an adjustment for all of us. We'll get settled into the big house and make new routines. We've been crammed into the small space, making due, living our separate lives together. We need to be a family. Annie is making it possible for us to all be together in one room, and I, for one, can't wait."

I cuddle further into his chest and relax. He's right. We need everyone to make the effort, and we will.

Miller, Spencer, and I are chatting in a booth, waiting for Tucker and Axel to finish, when Dempsey strides back into the restaurant with a grave face.

"Dempsey, what's wrong? Is everyone okay?" Everyone left about twenty minutes ago. Blake, Annie, and Cole left in Cole's car, and Nicole, Justin, and Katy left with Dempsey to pick up the kids from Annie's house.

"Miss Katy forgot her purse." He steps over to a booth and picks up a small black bag. "But we have a problem. Lincoln, could you come with me."

"Oh, hell no." Miller stands from the booth. "If there's a problem that involves my family, we're dealing with it together." Dempsey looks around the room, looking for the other two missing people. "They're busy. What's wrong?"

Dempsey sighs, and his shoulders fall. "There's something on your truck, Lincoln. I didn't move it, but you should probably come and see."

"Not here." Spencer sounds mad, which isn't an emotion she shows often.

"You're fucking kidding me." How is this asshole still following us? "Let's go."

I see it as soon as we get close. There's a large, thick envelope under my windshield wiper.

"He can't reach us at home anymore, so he's resorting to this." I reach for the envelope, and Dempsey grabs my wrist.

"You don't want to call the cops?"

"First, don't ever grab me again." I shake my arm away and glare at him. I know I shouldn't direct my anger toward him, but I'm pissed. I grab the envelope, and it's lighter than I expect.

"Sorry, Sir."

"Second, I *am* the cops. And so is this asshole, that's the problem. He's on his home turf, and we need to be careful how we deal with it. We thought he'd just been sending pictures until we realized he'd tampered with Spencer's security system. He's slowly escalating."

Everyone gathers around as I open the envelope. Spencer gasps when I pull the pink lacy panties out.

"Please tell me these aren't yours, Dream Girl."

She shakes her head. "They aren't."

Thank fuck. I would have lost my mind if they were.

"What else is in there, Linc?" Miller reaches his hand in and pulls out a picture. Spencer and Katy stand next to each other, laughing. It's a Polaroid from tonight. Was he *in* the club? Miller flips the image over, and written in the all-too-familiar handwriting is the worst note yet. PINK IS MY FAVORITE COLOR ON HER

"Fuck."

Whatever Tucker is doing, I hope he's done.

Lincoln: Out front. Now.

Tucker: Coming now.

A few minutes later, Tucker comes charging out the front door with Axel on his heels.

"What's going on, brother?"

The two of them were definitely up to something. Axel's

373

shirt is untucked, and Tucker's is only buttoned halfway, having lost his string tie. If this were any other situation, I'd be happy for them and want all the details, but not right now.

Miller hands Tucker the envelope contents, and while they look everything over, I pull Axel aside.

"Everything good?" I put my arm around his shoulder and pull him into my side.

A smile that spreads ear-to-ear flashes on his face. "Yeah. I'm good. Thank you guys. I just had a moment."

"Tucker helped you through it?" His eyes lift to Tucker, and I swear, in the dim parking lot lights, I see him blush. "I'll take that as a yes. I'm happy for you man."

"Me too. Now, what's going on?"

I explain to him about the picture and the underwear, and he visibly becomes as pissed off as the rest of us.

"What the fuck do we do now?"

I wish I could answer Axel's question, but even though we're on the right side of the law, they won't be of any help.

"Dempsey, get back to Katy. She's your main priority. I know Annie and Justin have top-of-the-line security, but you're her security everywhere outside their houses. I'll watch her at school. Spencer, don't protest. You go nowhere without at least one of us."

"I'm protesting." I smiled because I knew she would. "I've been dealing with this for over a decade. I'm not running scared of him. I'll never run scared of him again. I'm not that woman anymore. Now, I will happily allow any of you to escort me, but please don't think it's for my protection. It's because I understand there is safety in numbers."

"And apparently guns," Axel murmurs, but Spencer hears him and gives him a deadpan look that he hunches away from, mouthing "Sorry."

I fucking love this woman. She's fiercely independent, but she's letting us in. Stepping up to Spencer, I pull her into my chest and kiss her forehead, whispering thank you.

"There's no use standing around in the dark. Let me go close up inside, and the four of y'all head home." Tucker tips his hat to Dempsey, steals Spencer away from me for a kiss that has my heart racing, then leaves us.

The ride home feels tense. I want to go straight to the carwash and rinse this fucker right off my truck, but getting Spencer safe and secure in our new-to-us home is my focus.

"I'm beat." Miller drops his head to the back of the headrest and closes his eyes. I reach into the back seat and squeeze his thigh.

"Rest while you can. You still have a punishment coming to you, and I'm not letting it slide." He puffs out a breath, but there's a smile on his lips.

"Fuck. Me." Axel's semi-panicked voice catches everyone's attention.

"What's wrong?" Spencer looks around at the windows, trying to see any signs of Axel's distress.

"Tucker owes me a punishment too and said he would enjoy punishing me while Lincoln punished Miller."

An evil laugh starts in the back of my throat. I try to contain it, but it escapes, and I let it. Soon, everyone is laughing through our stress, and it feels cathartic.

"What did you do, Axel?" I've got to know.

"I asked him to fuck me and called him Daddy Tucker."

"Holy shit." I choke on the air around me.

Miller lifts his arm, eyes still closed, and high-fives Axel. "You're a crazy shit. He's gonna get your ass good tonight."

Axel wiggles in his seat. "He already did."

"Axel. Shut the fuck up before I crash my truck, or I'll tell Tucker to punish you harder. Well damn." I've just come to a realization. "My brother is an instigator. He got both of you in trouble today."

"What the hell *did* you do, Miller?" I've been waiting for Axel to ask. This is going to be good.

Miller huffs and crosses his arms like a child throwing a tantrum.

"I'm horny. So fucking horny, and my lovely boyfriend here has been denying me all day."

"Watch it, Fireball." He heeds my warning.

"So I asked Linc to shower with me, and when he told me no, I acted like a brat and teased that I bet Tucker would do it. When I asked Tucker to *jokingly* walk with me to the pool house to *pretend* we were going to take a shower, he told me he doesn't play pretend. The evil man made me shower with him to earn my punishment and still denied me any release."

Spencer giggles, and every one of us stops to listen.

"What's so funny, Dream Girl?" I run a single finger up her inner thigh, and her gasp stops her laughing.

"You all joke and call him Daddy Tucker, but it really is like he's the father to a bunch of children."

Spencer's relatable comment kills any tension left in the truck, and the conversation is light-hearted the rest of the way.

When we get home, everyone showers and gets comfortable, waiting for Tucker to return. Miller and I are relaxing on the couch when Axel approaches. He huffs with his hands on his hips and quickly starts pacing in front of us.

"Problem Axel?" He stops and gives me a deer-in-headlights look, then drops to his knees in front of Miller.

"How much trouble am I in? Tucker can be scary as fuck when he turns all Daddy Dom. I never even knew I was a brat until he called me out on it. My ass is already sore from the pounding he gave me earlier." He drops his head in Miller's lap and groans, "I'm scared."

"Axel." My sharp tone snaps his head up to meet my eyes. "What's the safeword?" He looks at me, puzzled. "Safeword. Tell me the safeword."

"Code Blue."

"Good boy," I croon. "What does the safeword mean?"

"I want to stop."

"Very good."

"But what if I'm not sure about it? I've never been spanked before."

I reach over and run a hand through his damp curls. He closes his eyes and hums.

"Would you like to add a yellow safeword?"

"Yellow?"

"Yes. Yellow, like a pause. Or a slowdown. When Miller and I first started dating, we used stoplight safewords. Red, yellow, and green. He was new not that long ago."

He rolls the word yellow around on his tongue, trying it out.

"Y-yeah. I'd like that. I like that a lot, actually. Thanks." Axel stands and flops on the couch next to Miller, laying his head on his lap and hanging his feet off the arm of the couch.

"You're welcome to play with my hair some more." He looks at me upside down and smiles. It's sweet and innocent, and one of my favorite things about him.

377

49

Spencer

"Little Miss. Time to wake up." Blinking my eyes open, I see a smiling Tucker.

"Hi."

"Shhhh. Don't wake them yet."

After my shower, I came out to the couch, and Lincoln, Miller, Axel, and I watched a few TV shows and must have all fallen asleep.

Tucker offers me his hand, and we walk to the kitchen. I'm not used to this house yet. The pool house has an open floor plan, but my father's house is a little more traditional, with separate rooms.

"Did you get stuck at work? It's late." Tucker's hands find their favorite spot in my hair, and he lowers his lips to mine. There's no urgency to our kiss; it's relaxed and enjoyable.

"I stayed behind to see if I could catch anything on the cameras, but it was just someone dressed head to toe in black. I'm sorry I couldn't see more." A hand leaves my hair to hold the small of my back, and his warmth melts into my skin.

"You have nothing to apologize for. I'm glad you're back.

Let's go to bed."

I know the smile creeping up his cheeks. He's up to something.

"I had an idea while I was watching y'all sleep, but I wanted to pass it by you first."

"That sounds ominous." Tucker runs a soothing hand over my back.

"Did Miller and Axel tell you about their punishments?"

It's my turn to smile. "They did...*Daddy Tucker*." He growls and nips at my neck. I hold in my yelp of shock.

"Be careful, Little Miss. Punishments are fair game for all. Now, I was thinking, since those two boys are such sound sleepers, I'd use my cuffs and handcuff them before we wake them up. But I don't know if they have become triggers since you first used them. The choice is yours."

How do I feel about the cuffs? Reaching behind me, I grab the arm, rubbing my back. I examine the cuff, rubbing my fingers over the smooth leather. I love the way they look on him as they wrap around his muscular forearm. Without having to bring the cuff any closer to my nose, I can already smell the leather scent that I associate uniquely with him.

"Will you...will you try one on me again? I don't think it's a trigger, but I'd rather know now than while they're being used."

"Of course." Tucker turns his wrist so I can unsnap the black buttons. The leather strands separate easily as I unravel them from his wrist. Once they're a long strand, he takes it from me.

"No need for a safeword here, Little Miss. If you want me to stop or remove it, just use your words."

"Okay." That's one less thing to worry about, and I love

that he took it into consideration for me. Tucker expertly twines the strands around one wrist, then the other. Before he closes the snaps, he looks at me silently, asking if I'm okay. I nod, and he snaps the buttons.

"How does it feel?"

I wiggle my fingers and turn my wrists as best as I can. Nothing pinches or pokes. There's a light pressure, but nothing uncomfortable. I don't realize I'm squeezing my thighs together until Tucker's fingers brush my leg.

"Shall I take this as a sign you're still okay with these?"

My breath shudders as I inhale. "I am."

"Shall we go wake up Lincoln and get our evening started?"

"Too bad there's only two of these." Tucker pulls me into his chest, crushing my hands between us and knocking the breath out of me.

"I'll have another pair tomorrow, and we can keep them in the bedside drawer next to your Glock."

"That sounds like a fun piece of furniture."

Tucker eases back and reaches for my hands to undo the cuff. When it's removed, he kisses my wrists, takes my hand again, and walks me back into the living room.

The guys haven't moved much since we fell asleep. Lincoln's head is on Miller's shoulder, and Axel is still draped over Miller's lap.

Tucker leans over and softly licks Lincoln's lips. I'm not sure I've seen them kiss, but it sparks something inside me. Lincoln grabs the back of Tucker's neck, startling us both, and kisses him fully.

"Brother," Lincoln growls when he pulls away. There's fire in his eyes as he stares at Tucker. I reach down and grab Lincoln's hand, and he glances next to him at the now empty spot where I was sitting. A light tug at his hand makes him understand that I want him to get up. Lincoln releases Tucker, and both men stand.

Tucker removes the cuff he's still wearing, and using his fingers he explains to Lincoln the plan. He puts up two fingers and points to the cuffs, then Axel and Miller. Then he puts his palms together and puts them next to his cheek, simulating someone sleeping on a pillow.

Lincoln's eyes light up when he understands the plan. He turns and lightly moves Axel's arms until his wrists are close together. He steps back to let Tucker do his work.

Miller is a little more difficult. His one arm is draped on the back of the couch, and his head uses his bicep as a pillow. Lincoln moves to the back of the couch so he can lift Miller's head while I help pull his arm down, careful not to hit Axel in the head.

Somehow, the three of us manage to cuff both men, and we admire our handiwork before waking them.

"How should we do it?" Lincoln and Tucker have pure mischief on their faces.

"We could be mean and make a loud noise," Lincoln suggests.

"Or we could be evil and rub their cocks awake before them."

"I love the way you're thinking, brother." Tucker elbows Lincoln playfully. "Do you have a cock preference?"

"You can take mine, and I'll take yours." Lincoln winks and crouches next to the couch in front of Axel. Tucker does the same in front of Miller, and they smile at each other before carrying out their devilish plan.

Both sleeping men wear sweatpants, so finding their

targets is easy. Gently, they glide their hands over Miller and Axel's pants. I love being a spectator to their antics. Whether funny or sexual, I get humor and pleasure from how they love each other.

Does that make me a voyeur?

As much as I get enjoyment out of each man, if they focused on each other, I would be just as content.

Axel is the first to show any signs of waking. His hips shift, and a soft moan slips through his lips. The sound makes me rub my thighs together again, and Tucker notices. He always notices.

"Like what you're seeing, Little Miss." I nod, not wanting to give away just how affected I am by these two men taking what they want from the sleeping men in front of us.

"Mooooore," Axel moans.

Tucker leans over, running a hand through Axel's hair. "You awake, Darlin'?" The only response is more moaning but nothing coherent enough to be an answer.

Miller still hasn't stirred, and I can tell Tucker is about to up the ante. He tips his head at Lincoln, whose smile widens, and they lower the sleeping men's pants. Semi-erect cocks lay thick over their thighs, and both men lower their heads to take them into their mouths.

My heart races at the sight of them and the erotic nature of what I'm doing. Watching these men take the pleasure they want from their sleeping partners. I think…I think I need to tell them I want to wake up with one of them between my legs.

I moan as the memory of Lincoln coaxing an orgasm from me in my sleep comes to the forefront of my mind. When I look up, Miller's eyes are wide and darting between me and Tucker. He sinks lower into the couch when he realizes what's happening, just in time for Tucker to pop off and give him a saccharine smile. When Miller reaches to bring him back, he finally notices the cuffs.

"What the—" Tucker puts his hand over Miller's mouth to stop his protest.

"One down, one to go," Tucker whispers. "Do you need lessons, little brother?"

Lincoln increases his activity, and Axel bucks his hips as "fuck" pours from his lips. He tries to put his elbows on the couch to sit up and see what's going on when the cuffs stop his mobility.

"Oh fuck." Axel tilts his head to see Miller is in the same situation as he is. "We're fucked aren't we?"

Lincoln releases Axel's cock and sits back. "Not yet, but you will be." He sits back on his feet and pats Axel's thigh. "Tucker, we made an adjustment to the safeword after Axel expressed some unease earlier."

Tucker looks down at Axel with concern and runs a finger over his cheek. "What's wrong, Darlin'?"

Axel closes his eyes and takes a deep breath. "I-I was nervous about the spanking. Lincoln suggested we use yellow as a second safeword." He opens his eyes, clearly concerned about Tucker's reaction.

"Ah. As in red, yellow, green? But only the yellow part of that?" Tucker continues to stroke Axel's cheek, comforting him.

"Yeah. Like that. Is that okay?"

Tucker leans down and kisses Axel's cheek. "Of course, it's okay. Your comfort and security are always the top priority. That goes for everyone. Yellow and Code Blue are the safewords. Agreed?" We all agree, and Tucker smiles. "Well, then, I guess we have punishments to dole out. Let's go, brother."

50

Miller

Waking up to Tucker swallowing my cock was not something I ever thought I'd experience, but it quickly tops the charts as one of my favorites. Seeing I was handcuffed and realizing what was about to occur, not so much.

Lincoln tucks Axel back into his sweatpants and helps him stand, then Tucker does the same for me and passes me to Lincoln.

"Hey, Fireball. How was your wake-up call?"

"Something you should try doing sometime soon and often."

"Me too, please." I spin to see Spencer looking sheepish. Her vulnerable side is so fucking sexy, made even more attractive by the fact she's comfortable enough to put her walls completely down and tell us what she wants.

I lift my arms to wrap around her and remember they're currently cuffed together. Raising my arms over her head, I rest my elbows on her shoulders and pull her in for a kiss.

"Any fucking time. But Smithy, with four men in your

bed, you might not want to say that too loud, or you could be waking up every day with a different man between your legs."

She leans forward and kisses me. "I'm failing to see a problem with that."

God, I love this woman.

What?

"That sounds like fucking permission, men." Axel's exuberance excites us all.

As I'm being led upstairs to the bedroom, I seriously contemplate my last thought. It was so natural when I said it to Lincoln. Can I love more than one person? Logically, I understand I can, but I never have before. If I tell Spencer I love her, am I betraying a part of Lincoln? We're all in this relationship together, and obviously, feelings will develop within our family. I need to discuss this with Lincoln. I need to tell him first how I feel.

"I have a plan, brother." Tucker having a plan sounds more dangerous than the spanking I'm about to receive.

"Please share." Lincoln sounds way too eager.

Several minutes later, I find myself bent over the side of our bed with Axel in the same position on the opposite side. We face each other in this vulnerable position that's equally as hot as it is terrifying. Lincoln has taken me over his knee before, but Axel and I have no choice but to look at each other as we take our punishments.

"How many, Fireball?" Lincoln rubs circles around my bare ass. "You showered with my brother after I told you not to. How many does that deserve?"

"But he made me."

Lincoln bends over me to get close to my ear. "Did you use

your safeword?"

Fuck.

"No."

"Then you did it willingly. How many?"

"Four?" He'll never go for such a small number, but I had to start low.

He hums in thought. "How many does Axel get, Tucker? His infraction was far less than Miller's."

"Little Miss, how many should they get for their punishment?"

Spencer could be the right or wrong person to ask. She'll be fair and logical but could also give a high number.

Be nice, Smithy, please.

"Four for Axel and eight for Miller. While they both made infractions, there is a drastic difference in being sassy and disobedient."

She went with fair instead of nice.

Without looking back at Lincoln, I can see Tucker's smug face and imagine Linc's looks much the same.

"Excellent choice, Dream Girl, now lay down."

"What?" She looks at Lincoln like he has four or eight heads. "Why am I lying down?"

"Because, while they are getting their punishment, you won't be left out. Their hands are perfectly capable to make you feel good. Lay on your back between them and help them remove their cuffs so they can explore and pleasure your body."

Oh, I fucking love this idea, and Axel's wicked smile tells me he does too. At least the thought of touching Spencer has erased the unease on his face.

She crawls onto the bed and gently removes the cuffs,

kissing each of our wrists when she's done. There isn't much room between us, but Spencer manages to lie down like a buffet of sex.

"Where do you want me?" Axel and I adjust Spencer's body until we can easily reach her in every place we want.

"Alright, boys, are y'all ready?"

It's hard to focus on one thing with so much nakedness around me. Spencer is on full display; Lincoln keeps rubbing his cock over my ass, and I have a straight line of sight down Axel's muscular back, which leads to a thick, bobbing cock that Tucker keeps slapping onto Axel's ass.

My yes is muffled as I take in a mouthful of Spencer's incredible breast.

"Just a reminder, Code Blue and yellow are the safewords. Everyone good with those?" Tucker waits for everyone's response.

When I'm too busy listening to the sweet moans of my incredible woman to answer, Lincoln gives me a warning swat. "Words, Fireball."

The sting radiates to my stomach, and I pop off Spencer's nipple with a gasp.

I manage to pant out an "I understand" before returning to Spencer's body.

The first true smack comes without warning. I have a split second to react when I see the flash in Axel's eyes, but it's not enough. Heat instantly courses through my body, immediately soothed by Lincoln's consoling hand.

"So gorgeous. Fuck I love seeing my mark on you." I hear movement, and then Lincoln's lips caress his stinging handprint.

Another smack cracks the air, and Axel's eyes squeeze tight.

He's holding his breath.

"Darlin', are you good?" Tucker's hands move over Axel's ass, and everyone in the room waits for his reaction. When his eyes finally pop open, there's a fire in them I've never seen before.

Yeah, he's fucking good. He loved it.

"More," he pants out. Axel's voice is thick with lust.

"Fuck." Lincoln gives me a matching set of handprints.

"Don't neglect our woman, Fireball. You should be touching, kissing, fondling, and licking her at all times.

My eyes roam Spencer's body, and the blush that's crept down her chest. She's as turned on as we are.

"What do you need, Smithy?"

"Touch me. Anywhere. Everywhere."

"Your wish is my command." I capture her nipple in my mouth again and let my hand roam down her body. She parts her legs for me when I tickle her landing strip of hair. She's hot and wet already, and as I hum my approval, Axel grunts from his next punishing smack.

"You're doing so well," Tucker praises in his ear. You're halfway done.

"No."

"No? Do you need to use a safeword, Darlin'?"

"Eight. I want the same eight as Miller."

"Are you—" Axel's growl stops Tucker's words. "Alright. You'll get your eight, but I'm not going any softer because you doubled your own punishment.

"Good." The man in front of me looks feral. He wants every ounce of pleasurable pain he's getting.

Spencer's moan pulls me back to her as my fingers make lazy circles over her clit. I love the little sounds of pleasure she makes.

Smack.

This one stings more than the first, as my skin is now raw. Here's where I have to remind myself it's about the after, not during. It's about the sensation of Lincoln's hand smoothing his mark, the praises he whispers in my ear, and his tongue licking a line of fire down my spine.

Smack.

Axel's response is different from mine. The fire in his eyes ignites with every new mark on his body. I don't know Tucker's level of punishment, but I trust him when he said he wasn't going softer on Axel. His smacks echo in the room as loud as mine.

Spencer gasps when I feel Axel's hand brush mine, and he enters a finger inside her.

"Fuck, Tails. I'll never get used to your heat. You're a fucking furnace."

Smack. Smack.

Axel's moan mixes with my groan as Lincoln and Tucker dole out joint punishments. Our mouths roam over Spencer's body while our fingers pleasure her pussy. Tucker and Lincoln begin to grunt with their efforts, and Axel is...gone.

Tucker's arm rears back for number seven, and I'm concerned.

"Yellow."

The room goes silent, and all eyes are on me except Axel's, who are off in the distance. He isn't looking at anything in particular; he's looking through it all. His fingers have stopped moving on Spencer, and he's simply lying on the bed.

Lincoln's worried breath whispers in my ear, "Talk to me, Fireball."

I turn my head to Axel but look up at Tucker. "Where is he?"

Tucker arches a brow, not understanding my question. He runs a hand up Axel's spine and turns and presses his body to him.

"You okay, Darlin'?" When Axel doesn't answer, Tucker moves to the side to look at his face. A smug smile tugs at his lips and he runs a finger across Axel's cheek. "This is beautiful."

"What's going on?" Spencer questions him with concern.

"He's…in subspace." Tucker caresses Axel's back, his body erupts in goosebumps, and a delicious moan purrs from his lips.

"In what?" I've never heard of subspace.

"He's blissed out, Fireball. It's a state a submissive can enter that's like an altered headspace. The pain is so pleasurable his mind has taken him away."

"Is he okay?"

"Oh, Bruiser, he's in ecstasy. Let's finish the scene, and I can give him some aftercare while you two take care of our girl.

I was so concerned with Axel, I didn't realize Spencer had turned onto her stomach.

"Are you sure he's okay to finish?"

"He's perfect, Fireball. Are you? You called yellow."

"I'm good. Green."

Smack. Smack.

Axel moans again, and all my anxiety fades when I see his smile. One more, and our punishment is over.

"Dream Girl, do you want to do the last one?" *Oh shit. Yes, please.*

"I like your thinking, brother. Do you want them, Little Miss?

"I…" Spencer's cheeks flush, but her nipples are hard, and her breathing is labored. She's not nervous or embarrassed; she's turned on by the thought.

"Do it, Smithy. Don't hold back."

Lincoln steps aside, and Spencer crawls off the bed to stand behind me. My body shutters when her cool hand touches my heated skin.

"It looks so…does it hurt?" Her fingers trace lines across my raw ass.

"Hmm, not when you touch me like that. You could never hurt me. It's your choice."

Spencer's hand falls away from me, and I hear a low moan. Looking over my shoulder, I see Lincoln's head buried in her neck and his hands coming from behind, rolling her nipples between his fingers.

"Brother, why don't you go take care of Axel? The three of us will finish up here."

I feel the whoosh of air as Tucker gives Axel the last of his punishment. A guttural moan, long and low, rushes from him.

"Linc, watch him while I go start a bath."

Lincoln nods at Tucker then steps away from Spencer. "Dream Girl, take care of Miller, and I'll take care of Axel." Lincoln rounds the bed and stands behind Axel. He gently massages him from upper thighs to lower back, and it sounds like he's purring.

"Miller, can I…"

"Do it, Smithy. I want it from you. Add your mark on my ass." And she does. Spencer steps back, and when her hand hits my ass, the sting is unlike the first seven. Her hand is smaller, and the power behind her swing is different. The sting is sharper, and she rubs her hand over her punishing mark as Lincoln did, but she's softer and gentler, and fuck do I need to come.

My impatience has gotten the better of me, and I'm done playing around. I flip over on the mattress and grab Spencer around the waist, rolling her with me until I'm hovering over her.

"I need you, Smithy. So fucking bad."

51

Tucker

I've had some outrageous ideas in the past, but duel punishments might top the cake. After tonight's events and reviewing the tapes to find nothing helpful, I needed to relieve some stress.

Seeing my four sleeping partners together, I almost woke them solely to sleep, but sleep wouldn't help me. I needed release. My idea required Spencer's approval, and seeing my cuffs around her wrist only stirred my need for more relief.

I'm in my glory, watching and doling out punishment, when I hear one of the two words I never want to hear. "Yellow."

What proceeds the safeword is a glorious sight. I knew Axel would make a good sub. His bratty ways are all for show and enjoyment, but I've seen the flashes in his eyes when one of us asserts dominance over him.

Subspace is something people hope to achieve. The fact he achieved this during his first true scene is incredible. My concern now is subdrop. Axel's body needs to reconnect with his mind, and the process is different for everyone. It could be minutes, hours, or even days.

I draw him a hot bath and hope he's one of the lucky ones that bounces back easily with no lingering effects.

When I reenter the bedroom, Lincoln is massaging Axel, and Spencer and Miller are preparing to have their own fun. "Lincoln, will you help me get him into the bath?" We each put an arm under his shoulders, and although his feet move, he's still not coherent.

"How are we going to get him in the tub? I assume you're joining him?" I look back and forth between the tub and an incapacitated Axel and realize I need reinforcements.

"Bruiser, I hate to interrupt you, but we need another hand in here." I hear a groan, and Spencer tells him to "Go help."

Miller enters the room and looks at our situation. "What's the plan?"

"If you take over for me, I'll get in the tub, and we can all get him in together."

After rearranging and lifting Axel, we finally settle him between my legs, and the guys eagerly leave the room to rejoin Spencer. I run my hands over his body above and below the water, trying to bring him back to me. After several minutes, his head rolls around on my chest, and his calm sleep-like breathing increases.

"Relax, Darlin'. I'm here, and you're safe." At the sound of my voice, his breathing slows. He's not entirely back yet, but it's a start, and I have high hopes that he'll come out of it sooner rather than later.

I'm enviously listening to the moans coming from the next room when Axel finally stirs. Like someone waking from sleep in a place different from where they fell asleep, he's disoriented.

"T-Tucker."

"I'm right here." He jumps when I glide my hands down his arms and realizes we're in water.

"What-How did I get here?"

I chuckle, thinking of the struggle it was to get a limp, full-grown man into this tub. "It wasn't easy."

He sits up and frantically starts patting his body down. "Did something happen? Am I hurt? Is Spencer okay?"

Wrapping my arms around his chest, I pull him back to me and hold him. His body instantly reacts and melts into mine.

"Everyone is fine. You, Spencer, everyone. Have you heard of subspace before?"

"Subspace? Yeah, I've heard of it, but..." He turns in my arms, and I loosen my hold to make it easier. "Is that what happened to me? I remember the fifth smack, and then everything kind of...blended together."

"How do you feel?"

"A little like I have a good buzz going, I got a massage, and I've just saved someone's life all at once."

"Interesting." The water splashes as he turns around to face me on his knees.

"What's interesting? Is that bad?"

"Not at all." I run soothing hands from his shoulders to his elbows. "Everyone's experience is different. It should be pleasurable during and after, but some experience negative after effects."

"Do I need to plan for that? Where are the others?"

"I can't tell you what to plan for because I assume this is your first time?" Axel nods. "Close your eyes and listen?"

If he wants to know where the others are, he can find out for himself. He gives me a puzzled look, and I run a hand over his face, closing his eyes.

"Listen, Darlin'." There are a few quiet heartbeats before a growl echoes in the room, followed by Spencer's moans.

Axel's eyes pop open, and he tries to stand, but I hold his shoulders down. "Fuck, I want in on that. I need her. I need you." He grabs my cheeks and smashes his lips with mine. My cock instantly hardens at his advances, and I push back for dominance.

"Easy. You've just come out, and we don't know what will happen."

"Please, Baby. Please. I need them. I need you." Axel peppers kisses down my neck and across my chest.

"Baby?"

"Fuck, I'll call you whatever you want. Baby, sweetie, Daddy Tucker, anything. Just...I just...fuck."

His hips grind on my stomach, and I can feel the need coursing through him like adrenaline.

"Let me help you get out of the tub and dry off. I want to make sure you're alright. Subdrop can be traumatic."

He agrees, and I step out and get both of us towels. Once we're dried and Axel is enthusiastically bouncing on the balls of his feet, I acquiesce and tell him we can join the others. I grab his hand before he runs away so we can enter together.

"Holy fuck." Axel stops in his tracks at the sight. Spencer is on her back with Miller on all fours, eating her pussy. Lincoln is on his back with his head between Miller's legs giving him a blowjob. "Please?"

Axel looks at me with pleading eyes, and I let go of his hand. He stops at the end of the bed and crawls between Lincoln's legs, taking his cock almost fully into his mouth in one move.

"Jesus fucking, fuuuuuck. Axel? Are you good man? Oh fuck. Yeah, I think you're good." Lincoln goes back to Miller, and I'm looking at an erotic chain of sexuality.

Let's complete the set.

Axel kneels in a squatters position at the end of the bed and I step up behind him and rub his firm ass cheeks. There's still visible marks of my fingers and slight bruising around some edges. I pull his cheeks apart, and instantly, he clenches. I put my thumb in my mouth and swirl it around to coat it with my saliva, then use it to rim his hole. Axel's gasp of surprise turns into a moan, and when I replace my thumb with my tongue, I think his next gasp of shock accidentally makes him deepthroat Lincoln. The moans in the room are loud and mingle together. Miller's hips jerk as his orgasm takes control of his body. Lincoln doesn't give up until Miller removes himself completely.

Miller lays next to Spencer at the head of the bed and rolls her on top of him.

"Sit on my face, Smithy. Don't say no. Just do it."

Spencer opens her mouth to protest but thinks better of it and gets into position. He pulls her down onto his face and smothers himself in her pussy.

"I need someone inside me." Axel sounds as desperate as his words.

"Get the lube, and you can sit on my cock." Linc looks down his body at Axel and smiles.

"Are you stealing my fun brother?"

"Never. Let's play with him together."

Axel jumps up and grabs the lube from the nightstand, and Lincoln prepares Axel while I prepare him.

With Lincoln lying on his back, I tuck a couple of pillows

under his hips, and Axel slowly sits on him. It's so fucking sexy to watch Axel's ass stretch around Lincoln's cock. They're down toward the bottom of the bed, with Lincoln's feet braced on the edge. Standing in front of him, I lube up my cock and prepare to enter Lincoln.

"Why do you look nervous, Brother."

"Because you're fucking huge, Tuck."

"Aww." I run my hands up his inner thighs until I reach where he's connected with Axel, and I massage the area. They both moan, and I bask in the power of my simple touch. "Don't worry. It will fit." I give him a devilish smile over Axel's shoulder as I line up and tell him to breathe.

He's tight, or I'm big, or both. I know he's the top for Miller, so he's probably not used to being fucked, but I couldn't pass up the opportunity when he offered. I pull Lincoln's legs around my hips so they're in a more natural position, and together, the three of us find a rhythm. It's sloppy and uncoordinated but feels so fucking good.

"Mind if we join you?" Miller scoots closer to the bottom of the bed and lays next to Lincoln.

"Do what Axel's doing, Smithy." Spencer mounts Miller, and it's the perfect position. If she leans back, I can kiss her, Axel is directly next to her, and I already see Lincoln's hands slinking toward them to play with her clit.

"Okay, but what do I do up here?" Spencer's question is so innocent.

"Anything you want to, Little Miss. Trust me, our boy there is already in heaven with you just sitting on his cock. Any movement will bring him pleasure."

She tests the water by jerking her hips front and back, and he grabs her hips and moans.

"Yep, just like that Dream Girl. Rock his world."

Spencer reaches over and grabs Axel's cock, and he practically roars. The five of us, connected by various body parts, tease and pleasure each other through our orgasms. Lincoln goes first deep inside Axel and I pick up my pace. Moments later, Axel spills all over Lincoln's stomach from Spencer's hand.

Spencer is panting, and I can tell she's getting close but needs that last push to get out of her head. I help Axel crawl off of Lincoln and get lost at the sight of the come dripping out of his ass and coating Lincoln's softening cock.

"Talk to her, Axel. Praise her and give her amazing tits attention. Make her explode on Miller's cock. It's fucking fantastic." He's like an eager puppy when he kneels behind her and does exactly as he's told. It seems his punishment may have taught him a lesson.

With my girl being pleasured by two of her men, I turn my attention back to the one I'm currently wrecking.

"Are you ready? I'm done being easy."

"Give me everything you've got, Tuck." I push Lincoln's knees up to his chest and lean on them for leverage as I push in deeper and angled exactly where I need to be to make him come again.

"Fuck, fuck. Goddammit. I just fucking came. You're... you're gonna make me—shiiiiit."

"Gonna make you come again? Yes, brother, that's the point." One, two more thrusts against his prostate is all it takes for him to coat his stomach with his come. I fall right behind him just as I hear Spencer's moans of ecstasy next to me. Her arms are wrapped around the back of Axel's neck, putting her entire body on display as she gyrates on top of

Miller, who's enjoying his own release. All eyes are on her because who could resist the sight of our stunning woman coming apart at our hands.

When her moans subside, she breaks into a fit of laughter. Loud, tear-inducing laughter that we all join in on as we collapse onto the bed in a tangle of sweat, come and love.

52

Katy

I thought getting my license would give me freedom. Unfortunately, when a psycho ex-lover is stalking your family, you get a gorgeous Viking bodyguard taking and following you everywhere. Even though we haven't gotten anything from the stalker in over three months, everyone is still on high alert.

"Can't I just drive to the ice cream place, and you can drive back?" I realize I'm being a whiny teenager, and I should be lucky I've convinced Dempsey to let me sit in the front, but I'm still blah about the entire situation.

"Sorry Miss Katy. You know the rules."

"But who will know except us?" He gives me a side-eyed glance. "Yeah, yeah. The dash cams. I know." I sink lower into my seat and huff. At least I get my ice cream.

"How is school going? Are you liking it?"

A few weeks ago, I asked if I could be home schooled. I'm beginning to show, and while I'm confident in my decision to bring this baby into the world, I'm not comfortable with all the questions that will come along with being a pregnant seventeen year old. Mostly, "Who's the baby daddy?"

"It's a lot easier than sitting in a classroom. How are you enjoying being my chauffeur?" Justin put Dempsey on guard duty full-time when I officially left school. Even though I'm never alone, whatever adult is home with me during the day is usually sleeping. It makes it quiet to get my schoolwork done quickly, but it also gets lonely. Viking Viktor keeps me company, though.

"You're always a delight, Miss Katy."

"Ugh. I wish you'd quit the 'Miss' thing. There's no reason to be so formal."

"Just part of being a gentleman, Miss Katy."

I flip back on the seat, grunting my frustration.

"I wish you'd be less of a gentleman sometimes." *Crap.*

"Miss Katy?"

"Um. I didn't mean it like...THAT. Not like less of a *gentleman,* gentleman. Like, just less gentlemanly. Less formal. More fun. Not that you aren't fun. Well, I actually wouldn't know because...oh my god. Kill me now." Leaning forward, I bury my face in my hands and hear Viktor laughing.

Of course, he's laughing at me. I just made a fool of myself. I can feel the heat on the tips of my ears. I can't imagine how red my face must be.

"Katy, look at me." *No Miss.*

I spread my fingers apart over my eyes and turn my head, peeking at him.

"If it will make you more comfortable, I will do my best to drop the Miss." He smiles at me, and my ears heat all over again. He rarely smiles. Not because he's grumpy but because he takes his job extremely seriously.

"Okay." My response is muffled, but I'm sure he understands.

Warm, thick fingers wrap around my wrist, pulling my hands away from my face. When I don't look up, he tilts my chin with his finger to face him.

"Katy." Why does my name sound so different without the Miss in front of it?

"Yes?"

"We're here." Here? "Did you decide what flavor ice cream you want?" Ice cream. We're at the ice cream shop. Duh. His hand falls away, and I blink several times.

Get yourself together.

Man, these pregnancy hormones are no joke. Viktor chuckles at my apparent lack of brain function and grabs his door handle.

"Don't move. I'll get your door." Chivalry. No. No, you idiot. He's your bodyguard. He's probably checking the perimeter or something. Stupid, pregnant, hormonal seventeen year old. Don't forget that.

Viktor opens my car door and then the door to the ice cream shop for me. I wonder what we look like to the people around us. There isn't too large of an age gap between us, but I'm obviously young, and he's, well, a 10. A total 10.

As we stand in line waiting for our ice cream, I get a text from Spencer.

Spencer: I have a surprise for you. I sent Dempsey an address.

They've rotated back to nights again, so everyone's been sleeping during the day, and I've been trying to do my schoolwork at the library or a coffee shop. Justin decided to go per diem, so he only works when needed. Miller has become Spencer's official partner in the ambulance and fills in at the firehouse occasionally.

Katy: Grabbing some ice cream. I like surprises.

"Hey, Dempsey, Spencer just told me she has a surprise for me. Any idea what it is?" A small smile spreads on his cheeks, and it's obvious he isn't going to share whatever it is he knows. He checked his phone a few minutes before I got my text, so I assume Spencer was giving him instructions.

"Sure do." This man is like a bank vault, and there's no use in trying to get any information out of him.

"Hi, what can I get for you?" Finally, at the front of the line, the perky brunette smiles and asks for our orders.

"I'll take two scoops of Butter Pecan, and she'll have a vanilla soft-serve cone with extra rainbow sprinkles. Thank you, ma'am."

My mouth drops. "How did you know that's what I wanted?"

"Because it's what you always get. Unless you look in the coolers, then you want birthday cake ice cream in a cup, also with extra rainbow sprinkles." He knows what kind of ice cream I eat? It's probably part of his job to notice everything. But wait...

"Butter Pecan. Really, Dempsey? Who says Pee-can? It's Pecan." I reach into my purse to grab my wallet, but he beats me to it. "You don't have to pay for me."

"It's my pleasure, Katy." A genuine smile lights up his face, and I think my heart stops beating. His cheeks are round and full under his beard, and even his eyes beam with the expression.

"Th-thanks."

"You're welcome. Pee-can is an acceptable way to pro-
nounce the nut. I know it's an old man's flavor, but that's
why I order it. It reminds me of my father, who passed away
five years ago."

"Oh." That's all I can manage to say. I'm parentless, but it's
bettered my life. I can tell by the sadness that just eclipsed
Viktor's eyes that he had a good relationship with his father.

"Hey Katy?"

"Hmm."

"You don't need to call me Dempsey. My friends call me
Vik."

Is he considering me a friend? He's offering me an olive
branch to a friendship. But everyone else calls him Dempsey.
Would it be weird if I started calling him Vik? I much prefer
to call him Viktor.

"What if I wanted to call you Viktor?" He pauses, mouth
open, hand mid-air with a spoonful of ice cream, and his
eyes meet mine.

"I think I'd like that."

After our ice cream, Viktor takes me to a building downtown.

"What are we doing here?" I look out the window at the
tall buildings around us.

"Taking you to the address Spencer gave me." It's after six
in the evening, and the Chicago business crowd has changed
to a tourist crowd, with people milling in and out of shops
and taking lots of pictures.

Viktor pulls into a parking deck and finds a space close to an elevator. It's a generic office building connected to the garage with no clues to what we're doing here.

"Where are we?" Viktor puts his hand on the small of my back and directs me to the elevator. Inside, he pushes the button for the eighteenth floor, and the elevator ascends. When the doors open, he turns left down the hallway before I get a chance to look at the bulletin board directory.

"You're no fun. I can't even look for clues."

"Thirty seconds, and you'll thank me for not ruining the surprise."

He stops at a door with a sign that says "RainbowDreams" and pushes it open for me. Inside is a waiting room filled with all of my people.

"What's going on? Where are we?" The room is decorated with posters of adorable babies and rows of chairs.

"Is this the mama we've been waiting for?" A blonde woman in pink scrubs stands behind a window in the waiting room with a smile on her face. "Katy?"

"Um. Yeah. I'm Katy."

"Wonderful. I can take…" She looks around the room at Spencer and the five men surrounding us. "Okay, if you can squeeze in and don't tell, you can all come into the room. You're the last appointment of the day."

Smiles radiate around the room, and I'm still clueless as to what's going on.

"I can wait out here. The family should all go in. It will make more room." Viktor takes a step back, and I grab his forearm and shake my head at him. He's become a good friend over the past several weeks with all the time we've spent together since I've been out of school.

"Whatever is about to happen, you can be a part of it." He looks down at my hand, then into my eyes. I see the look. The one he thinks no one sees when he looks at Hannah or Miles. His face softens, and his silver-blue eyes glow.

"If you wish, Katy."

We follow the pink scrub lady to a room with a bed, a large-screen TV, and a...

"An ultrasound? Don't I have one scheduled in a few weeks with the OB?"

"You do." Tucker takes my hand. "But we know how excited you are to find out the sex of the baby and thought this would be a nice surprise."

I'm in shock. I've been excited to find out. I know you can do an early blood test, but I declined because I wanted to find out by seeing my baby, not a word on a piece of paper.

"This is...oh my god." A squeal comes out of me as I hop up on the table.

"Let's find out if we're decorating with pink or blue, Katy girl." Axel looks more excited than I do, bouncing on the balls of his feet.

"Axel, did you forget to feed your squirrels today?" I gently grab his arm. "You're bouncing like a kangaroo."

He scoffs at me. "Squirrels have been fed. This is pure excitement."

I smile and lay back on the bed and get set up. When the technician starts moving the wand around my belly, all eyes are on the large TV screen.

We listen to the heartbeat first, and the thumping fills the room. We see the tiny hands and feet, and my excitement grows.

"Let's see if we can get this little one to show us the goods.

A boy will look pretty obvious, and a girl will look like a hamburger."

"Really?" Miller questions. "A burger?"

Axel smacks him across the chest. "Shut up and watch."

Spencer reaches down and grabs my hand. I wonder if this is hard for her.

"It's riiiiiiight...here." The tech freezes the screen, and we all stare. It's obvious what the baby is but no one makes a sound until the tech types and the letters appear across the TV. B-O-Y.

"Congratulations, Mom. You're cooking a baby boy."

My eyes shift to Spencer, who's staring at the screen.

"Spencer?" She doesn't respond to me.

"Little Miss. Let's take a walk." Tucker's hand on her arm pulls her out of the trance.

"It's a boy, Katy." She sighs and I wonder how this affects her when she squeezes my hand. "Don't you think we have enough penises in the house already?"

Lincoln laughs first, and I'm grateful because I'm in shock. I knew this would be hard for her, but she's joking around, so maybe it's not as hard as I expected.

She smiles down at me, and I know she's okay. The machine whirs to life, and a long string of picture prints emerges from it.

"Here you go. Some trophies to take home. Congratulations again, Mom."

"We have just enough time for dinner before some of us have to get to work." Miller claps a hand on Viktor's shoulder as we all file out of the ultrasound room. "Dempsey, you're welcome to join us. I know you're off the clock now that we're all here, but a man needs to eat, right?"

Viktor's eyes quickly flash to me. If I hadn't already been looking at him, I wouldn't have noticed.

"Sounds wonderful. Thank you. You're welcome to call me Vik. You all are."

53

Dempsey

D inner last night was wonderful. It's been a while since I've been out with people I can enjoy myself with. While I never let my guard fully down, I was much more relaxed knowing Spencer and Katy were surrounded by men who could take care of them.

The rain outside this morning is torrential. I wasn't surprised when Tucker called to ask if I could come in early. Typically, I've been coming over around ten so he could go to the club and work. Lincoln would be long gone to the high school, and Spencer, Miller, and Axel would be home sleeping.

Because of the terrible weather, they're all stuck at work, and Tucker has to leave earlier than usual to meet a supplier.

When I arrive, I walk in using my door code, and Tucker anxiously waits to leave.

"Thank you so much, Dem—Vik. I'm so sorry to bother you, but I can't miss this delivery. They've been stiffing my manager, and I need to be there."

I shake his hand and clap his back. "No problem. Be careful

out there. The roads are slick." He nods and passes me out the door, pulling up the collar of his jacket and hunching his shoulders under his cowboy hat.

Katy is sitting at the kitchen counter eating breakfast when I walk in. They've slowly been updating the outdated house. The kitchen cabinets have been painted navy blue on the bottom and white on the top to open the space. Katy sits on a fancy metal chair at the new gray counter top.

"Are you planning to share?" I give her a half smile and try not to notice how she lights up when I do.

"Your plate is in the microwave. Just hit the start button to warn it up."

"I was joking."

"I'm not. Tucker makes the best pancakes, and this is maple-flavored bacon." She picks up a piece and bites off a chunk. "I think food is Tucker's love language. Before you protest, that plate is specifically for you. There are already leftovers for the others in the refrigerator."

I don't have any more reason to argue, so I hit the start button as instructed. The timer on the microwave starts at thirty seconds and counts down. My back is to her, but I can feel the holes she's boring into me with her eyes.

I'm not blind to the way she looks at me. Most women do, and in any other situation, I'd welcome it. Katy is young. Too young. I may only be five years older than her, but she's still a baby at seventeen, and I need to make sure I thwart any possible advances.

"I know we had plans to go shopping today after I finished my school work, but we can take a raincheck..." She snorts, and I turn to see her laughing silently. When I arch a brow, she puts up a finger to compose herself. "Sorry. It's raining,

412

and I said raincheck. Totally ridiculous, I know. Ignore me. Anyway, if you wanted to go shopping another day, I'd understand."

Spencer asked if I'd take her window shopping for nursery ideas. Nights are rough on their bodies, and Katy is a touch-and-feel kind of person. If possible, she'd rather see what her options are than scroll online.

"Why don't you finish your work? Then we can see how the weather looks. There's supposed to be a lull in the rain."

"Deal."

I sit at the counter but leave an open stool between us. Tucker does, in fact, make delicious pancakes, and the bacon is cooked to perfection.

After we've eaten, Katy brings her schoolwork to the living room since no one is home. The weather was bad enough that everyone stayed at work for extra hands. I like that they feel confident enough in my protection of Katy that they don't rush back.

I hand wash our dishes while she works on her homework because I need something to do and don't want to feel like a creeper. Once everything is clean and put away, I pull the gun cleaning box out of the front closet and sit at the kitchen table to do more busy work while Katy finishes. My gun could use a good cleaning so it's not wasted energy.

It's around lunchtime when she's done with her work, and the rain has slowed.

"How about that shopping trip, Katy?"

She stretches on the couch, and I turn to see her shirt lift over her belly. "Sure. Let me just change." As she walks past me, she gives me a friendly smile.

Seventeen. Pregnant. Don't be a pervert. Seventeen. Seven-

413

teen.

I take a deep breath to ground myself and grab Katy's jacket and umbrella from the front closet.

When she returns, she's wearing black rain boots with colorful polka dots, black pants, and a light pink hooded top. There's no baby bump showing, and I'm sure she did that on purpose.

"You shouldn't be ashamed."

"What?"

I step closer and hold the jacket up to her. She turns and finds the arm holes, putting it on.

"You shouldn't be ashamed of your pregnancy. You made an informed decision. You're making good of a bad situation. I'm proud of you, and everyone in this house is too."

She startles me when she quickly turns and wraps her arms around my back. I hesitate a moment before I return the embrace because it's something she needs. She sniffles and pulls back, wiping her face.

"Sorry about that. I'm ready."

"Stop apologizing, or I'll forget to drop the Miss, Katy."

"Oh, that's just cruel. You wouldn't?"

"Try me?" She stares me down with fake bravado before relenting with a huff. "Exactly. Now get your butt out of this house."

As we step outside, she pulls the hood of her rain jacket over her head and refuses the umbrella I offer. I open her door and get her tucked inside before running to the driver's seat.

"I'm not made of sugar, Viktor. I won't melt."

"No, more like cayenne pepper. Good in small doses, but too much will have you choking." *Fuck.* That was not meant

414

to be dirty. How did talking about spices become dirty?

"Vik-tor." Katy giggles my name, and I instantly laugh with her at the absurdity of the situation.

"Let's just not talk about this, please. If the guys heard what I said, they'd probably fire me. I meant no disrespect, Miss Katy."

She stops laughing and shifts in her seat to face me. "Don't do that. Don't *Miss* me because you're embarrassed or feel guilty or whatever negative emotion is going through your head. It was an innocent joke that…Well, maybe I'm not the only child here."

How she took a potentially bad situation and turned it around is incredible.

"I appreciate you, Katy."

"Good." She turns back in her seat to stare out the windshield. "You should. I'm a big deal around here." She adds a little twang to her words, and I'm laughing again.

"Working on your Tucker impression?" She shrugs and sucks in her bottom lip. "What's wrong?" Her brows crunch, and she looks at her lap.

"Justin said his lawyers are almost done with the paper-work for the adoption. I'm super excited that it's Spencer who's adopting me but…but no one has asked me about my last name. I don't want to give my little boy the same last name as the woman I want nothing to do with ever again. She threw me away for some money. She doesn't deserve for her name to be shared. She doesn't even know I'm pregnant."

I'm stunned to hear they haven't discussed this with her. As a group, I'm generally impressed with their communication skills.

"There's been nothing said at all?" I catch the slightest

shake of her head out of the corner of my eye. "Talk to them then. Maybe it slipped their minds." Katy shrugs, and I can tell by her body language she's done talking.

Her attitude perks up when we get to the baby store Annie recommended. I've never seen so many tiny things in one store. I pick up a bodysuit and compare it to the size of my hand. They match. Katy starts hysterically laughing next to me.

"What's so funny?"

"I can't decide if that's tiny or your hand is giant."

"Both." She takes the pink scrap of fabric from me and puts it back on the rack, picking up a blue one instead. Lifting her hoodie, she reveals a tight, white shirt underneath with a small round belly. She usually wears loose-fitting clothes, so I didn't realize she had much of a baby belly.

Katy lays the blue outfit over her belly and proudly smiles.

"You picked the wrong one. He can choose to wear pink when he can see in color."

"That's very progressive thinking, Katy."

"Viktor, I live in a house where I basically have four dads and their best friends are a throuple. If I thought any other way, I'd be homeless." Just then, her stomach growls, and we both look at her belly and laugh.

"Either he doesn't like the blue, or he's trying to tell you he's hungry."

"I can always eat." She rubs her belly and puts the outfit back on the rack. "I have a good idea of what I like. I can look online now. Let's go get something greasy from the food court. Please." She bats her eyelashes at me like a doll, as if I would say no.

"Keep your flirting to yourself little girl. Let's feed that baby." I instantly realize I've said the wrong thing. Calling her a little girl and, even worse, calling her out on her flirting clearly pisses her off.

In all fairness, she probably wasn't flirting. She was just Katy being Katy and having fun. But I'm a giant asshole who keeps needing to remind myself that not only is she only seventeen, but she's also my job. A job, who right now is storming away from me because I made an asshole comment.

"Katy." I should apologize, but that could also give her the wrong impression. I need to keep a clear boundary in my head regarding her. "Katy, please wait, the food court is in the other direction."

"I'm not hungry. Let's go home." She picks up her pace, and for a small person, she walks really fast when she's angry. When I catch up to her, I reach out and touch her shoulder, and she spins around, glaring at me.

"Look, I get it okay. I'm sorry. You're just so easy to be around. Sometimes I forget you're just my babysitter." She walks past me back in the direction we came. "Let's just get some food and then we can go home." She sounds defeated, and I hate that I made her feel that way.

The food court is surprisingly crowded for the middle of a workday, but Katy decides she wants pizza, and while she waits, I need to use the bathroom.

"I'll be right back. Wait here for the pizza. Don't move."

"I have enough male figures in my life telling me what to do. I don't need another one. Go take your potty break. I'll wait for the pizza."

She's angry with me, and I understand it, but that doesn't mean I have to like it. I also wish I hadn't drank that extra coffee, needing me to leave her alone, even if it is only for two minutes.

I'm in and out of the bathroom in record time, thankful the restrooms are next to the food court. When I come out, I hear the employee calling my name, searching for someone to pick up the food. When I don't immediately spot Katy, I panic. I told her not to move. The kid behind the counter recognizes me and tries to get my attention, but I ignore him to look for her.

I'm trained to be good under pressure, and I don't like the feeling I have right now. I'm sure Katy's here and is just mad at me and walked off out of spite, but until I have eyes on her, that knowledge is not enough.

My thoughts are confirmed when I see her standing in the line for the cinnamon sugar pretzels. She's just pulling out her wallet, having placed her order, when I approach her with more anger than I know is needed.

She doesn't understand what's been going on because they haven't told her. We can't figure out why Shane's pictures and notes have become more focused on her. They didn't start that way. We noticed the pictures started coming with more of Spencer and Katy together, but slowly, Spencer began disappearing, and it was just Katy.

"I told you not to move."

She whips her head around and glares at me with all the hatred she can muster. "And I told you I didn't need another *Daddy.*"

The cashier awkwardly passes Katy her pretzels, and she stalks past me again.

"Where are you going now?" Without turning, she throws her angry response over her shoulder.

"Apparently, to get the pizza you couldn't even get despite

them calling *your* name."

How could so much aggression and frustration be wrapped up into one little package?

"I've got it, Katy," I try demanding, but she continues to ignore me.

She stops at the pizza counter, and the teenage boy smiles when she approaches. She glances at me with a glower, but her face transforms when she turns her head. Her eyes soften, and a smile brightens her face.

"Hi, I'm picking up a pizza for,"—she side-eyes me and leans over the counter—"my dad and me. The name is Dempsey." Her voice is high-pitched and over-the-top flirty.

The growl escapes me without my permission, and when the pimply-faced idiot hears it, he practically falls backward, fumbling to grab our pizza.

"Thank you," I say through gritted teeth as I grab the box from him before he can hand it to Katy.

"Thank you so much...Joseph." She leans in even farther to read his name tag, making him blush when she says his name. She gives him a saccharine smile that he returns, and I have to fist my free hand to stop myself from throttling this poor, unsuspecting teenage boy.

Closing my eyes, I count backward from ten, despite knowing I could start at one hundred, and it wouldn't be enough to combat the brattiness she's exuding.

"Let's. Go. Katy." It takes every ounce of willpower I have left to get those three words out. She's intentionally taunting me all because I called her a little girl. It was an honest mistake, and I should have known better. There's nothing about Katy that's a little girl.

"Sure thing, Daddy. I'll drive since I know your eyes aren't the greatest."

I'm at my breaking point, and if she doesn't stop, I might just snap. I lean close enough to her ear so only she can hear me. "I'm only five years older than you, and the only people that call me *Daddy* are thanking me the next morning for rocking their fucking world. I suggest you put your big girl panties on and put away the sass so we can go home and eat our pizza."

As crude as my statement is, it does what I intended it to do. After a moment of staring at me with her mouth open, she turns on her heels, and I follow behind her with a smug smile.

When we reach the exit doors it's pouring again. If we hadn't just gone through what we did, I'd let Katy wait in the vestibule while I get the car, but she lost the privilege of being dry.

"Could you—"

"Not a chance, sweetheart. You made your bed, and now you have to lie in it. Pull your hood on and avoid the big puddles."

54

Dempsey

She's ignoring me. It might be from the argument in the food court or the laugh that escaped when Katy stepped into the giant puddle in her stubbornness. Or it could be from the standoff we had in the rain when I opened the passenger door for her, and she didn't want to accept my gesture.

Now she sits cold and wet, and every time I try to turn the heat on for her, she glares at me for attempting to be nice. I was able to sneak the seat warmer on, so I feel a fraction better about her wet state.

I need to fix this. I've crossed the line. She's a job, and I've been treating her as a friend, which has been sending mixed signals.

"Katy, I—"

"Whatever you have to say, I don't think I want to hear it."

"Katy…"

"Just stop, Dempsey. You made your point." I really fucked up. She went back to my last name.

"And what point is it that you think I was trying to make?"

She turns in her seat, and I can feel her defenses come up. "That I'm just a kid, and I'm a pain in your ass you have to basically babysit. I'll stop. I know you're not my friend. Justin or Spencer or whoever, pays you to watch my every move, and that's the extent of our non-existent relationship."

"Katy," I growl, looking over at her.

"Keep your eyes on the road. It's pouring."

"Katy." This woman is going to let me talk if it's my last fucking breath.

"What!" she snaps back at me. I open my mouth to finally speak my peace when my phone rings through the Bluetooth speaker in the car.

"Fuck." I punch the button on the steering wheel harder than necessary. Tucker's name flashes on the screen for a split second before his panicked voice fills the car.

"Where are you?"

"On the way home from the mall. What's wrong?" Tucker is the calm, level-headed one of the group. If he's bothered by something, then there's cause for concern.

A loud crack of thunder drowns out Tucker's response, and I have to ask him to repeat himself.

"We got pictures...from an unknown number."

"Another one? Wait, unknown number? He sent you a text?" This fucking asshole is pushing his luck.

"He sent them to all of us in a group text, but you're driving right now, right?" Lightning and thunder light up the sky, and I let my foot off the gas to slow down. The storm is right above us.

"Tucker, what's going on?" I hear him sigh and can just imagine him running his hands through his beard.

"The first picture was Katy with a blue baby outfit over her

422

belly. There's one of you both getting pizza. Dempsey, one of them has Katy alone in the food court. Please tell me you were just out of the frame."

"Fuck. I had to hit the head. I'm so sorry, Mr. Bennett. I was only gone a few minutes."

"That's all it takes, Dempsey."

"Tucker, we're fine. Shit!" *Boom.*

Katy screams, and Tucker panics. "Katy, what's wrong?"

"Oh my god. I'm sorry. That thunder was so loud. This storm is crazy." Katy's chest heaves as she holds her hand over her heart.

"Dammit, Dempsey. Get her home safely but as soon as possible. She's precious cargo."

"Absolutely, Mr. Bennett. We are about ten minutes out." The line disconnects without another word. I guess he's not in a goodbye mood.

Out of the corner of my eye, Katy pulls at her seatbelt, making sure it's secure.

"Katy, are you alright?"

She glances at me, and I can see the fight from earlier is gone.

"Please watch the road. It's really coming down out there and…" She rubs her hands up and down her thighs, trying to calm herself down. "I'm sorry. Why was he there watching me? Spencer wasn't with us. Why would he send pictures to them of *me*? I walked away from you. You told me to stay near the pizza place, and I was so mad. I'm sor—"

"Stop." I cover her hand with mine, trying to calm her rambling. She stares at it before turning her hand over and lacing our fingers together with a sigh. She's trembling. "It's all going to be okay. We're almost—FUCK!"

"What was that? What happened?"

I'm wondering the same thing. I'm trying to watch the road while glancing in the rearview. Someone hit us from behind. Did they hydroplane?

"Sit back, Katy," I bark. She's trying to twist to look out the back window, and I need her to stay in her seat.

"I'm going to pull over up here to assess the damage. They probably just lost control in this rain." This doesn't help her already frazzled nerves. "Are you alright?"

She's nodding before she finally says, "Yeah."

I pull into a mostly deserted parking lot, and the car's headlights follow me through the rain. I park and turn to Katy, taking both hands.

"I'll be right back, okay? Hopefully, there isn't too much damage, and we can just exchange numbers and deal with it on a dry day. I'll leave the car on if you want to call someone so you aren't alone.

She pulls up the call list on the screen before I'm out of the car. Opening my umbrella, the owner of the other vehicle is already heading toward me. They're dressed in a black hoodie pulled over their head and they're hunched over trying to keep the rain out of they're face. Relatable.

"Hey, what happened back there? This rain is something else?" Based on stature, the man continues to come toward me with no apparent plan to stop. "Man, is everything alright?" I'm getting a bad feeling and back up toward the car door. Katy is talking to Spencer over the Bluetooth, and when my hand reaches the handle, the hooded man yells over the rain.

"I wouldn't, Dempsey."

"Who the fuck are you? What the hell do you want?" He

looks up just enough for me to see his eyes and the gun he pulls from his hoodie pocket.

"I want you to step away from that door."

"The fuck I will, and if you know my name, you know I won't walk away." Lightning lights up the dark afternoon sky, and I get a better look at his face. I memorize every feature I can. Dark hair and eyes; they could be black or brown. A crooked nose, and the evil smile he's giving me has a slight chip to one of the front teeth. There's no hesitation in his grip on the gun he's holding, which means he's most likely trained or at least comfortable with firearms.

"I had a feeling you'd say that. Do you really want to do this the hard way? You could step aside, and I can drive off with Katy, and no one gets hurt." My Glock is under my jacket. He'll hit me before I can grab it. I'm a fucking idiot for putting my defenses down. *Fuck!* There's a backup piece in the glove compartment. Maybe I can warn Katy.

I quickly shift my eyes to see inside the car, but the windows are fogged and full of rain. The hooded man cocks his head to the side, listening. I can hear Spencer, but I'm at the driver's door. He's near the rear wheel. Can he hear her?

"Is that...my beautiful bride, I hear?"

What the fuck? Beautiful—No fucking way.

"Shane."

His smile turns into something straight out of a horror movie.

"You know my name. Does that mean she still talks about me? I bet she does. Maybe I can say hi." He takes a step forward, and so do I.

"Don't you fucking come any closer."

"Or what, Dempsey? I'm holding a gun on you, and yours

is buried under all your clothes. Pretty clever of me to catch you off guard, huh? I thought about hitting you harder or trying to push you off the road, but you have my precious cargo in there, don't you? A sweet little girl carrying an even sweeter little boy, right? That blue outfit you were looking at was pretty cute."

How the fuck does he know so much. Why does he want Katy?

"Oh, that's right, you're new. You weren't around for my handy work."

What the fuck is this guy talking about?

"I'm done talking. Just move aside." We both freeze when the window motor whirls down an inch and Katy innocently checks on me.

"Can we go yet, Viktor?"

"Close the fucking window, Katy," I try to warn her, but it's too late. Shane uses my distraction to lunge toward me. I pull open the door, realizing I'd have a better chance of trying to get the Glock out of the glove compartment than fighting with the wet clothes I'm wearing.

Katy's eyes widen with shock and fear as the sound of the gun going off pierces the air. It's louder than any of the thunder we've been hearing, and Katy screams as the burning radiates through my abdomen. I use my frame to cover the open door in an attempt to keep Shane from getting to Katy. Spencer is yelling over the Bluetooth, but I can't make out a word she's saying over the screaming and the sound of the blood rushing through my ears.

Every second feels like an eternity as I wait for Shane's next move. I feel the warmth of the blood spreading through my shirt. Katy lunges toward me as her car door swings open, and the rush of air blows her beautiful chocolate-colored hair across her face.

I slump forward in exhaustion, knowing he's not behind me anymore, and watch helplessly as Shane wraps his arms around Katy's chest.

"Someone fucking talk to me!" Spencer is panicking and cursing. It's going to take her a lot to get her through this emotional trauma.

"Spencer," Shane hisses, and all the air goes still in the car. Katy's struggling in his hold, and I'm using all my energy to stop the blackness trying to consume my vision. "Spencer, I've come to collect our girl. I'm going to be taking her with me. I'm sad to say I don't think Dempsey is going to make it." He looks at me and sucks in air through his teeth as he watches the blood now dripping freely onto the seat below me. "He's losing blood fast."

With my breathing labored and the feeling of pain dulling instead of increasing like it should be, I know he's probably right. I've fucking failed her.

Using my last bit of strength and Shane's distraction with Spencer, I mouth "glove compartment" to Katy. She shakes her head, not understanding, or maybe she can't see me through her tears. She's pleading my name as the rain pours into the car from both open doors.

A loud clap of thunder roars over our heads, and I take a chance to speak up.

"Glove compartment." She glances to her right, and I know she's heard me this time. The question is, can she trust me enough to understand those two words and put the pieces of the puzzle together?

"Spencer, my love. Do you really not know? I thought I

427

was making it so obvious."

Shane's words sound like they're echoing through a tunnel. The blackness is taking over, and I don't have any fight left. I have to hope Katy understands me.

The last moments flash as I try to open my eyes every time they close from the weight of my exhaustion.

"The baby is mine. I took her in that alley."

Katy dips her head forward.

"I'm finally getting my boy, Spencer."

Crack.

"You fucking bitch."

Blood.

Shane holds his nose.

OPEN YOUR FUCKING EYES VIKTOR!

Click.

Blackness.

Screaming.

DON'T LEAVE HER ALONE. EYES OPEN ASSHOLE!

Bang.

Warmth all around me. I feel so light.

One. Last. Look.

Blood everywhere.

Katy...

I'm. Sorrrrr

The End for now...

55

Author Notes

S o, I wrote a cliffhanger. Please don't hate me. Spencer's book was never meant to be anything more than a story about a neurodivergent woman finding love with four incredible men through her diversity and her traumatic past...enter Katy.

I had an idea, and my Alpha said, DO IT. I know I've put Katy through the wringer, and the more I wrote Spencer's book, the more I realized there was an entire story still left to be told...enter Viktor Dempsey.

Could I have written a 200K book and gotten the entire story under one roof? Sure. But where's the fun in that?

While Katy's story will primarily shift to her and life after the incident, there will still be lots of Spencer and her merry band of men.

Please still love me, and know that I won't keep you hanging for long. Katy's release date, Never Fear Again, is set for July 10, 2024. One year to the day that I published my first paperback novel.

If you haven't read Hazel's Harem, now's your chance! Or pick up either of my novellas in my Single Parent Series: Caffeinated Passion and The Wrong Hookup.

Much love and thanks to you, me readers.

~Casiddie

About the Author

Casiddie is a single mom to five wonderfully crazy kids. When she's not carting them to activities, she's getting lost in her head with her friends as she brings them all to life.

You can connect with me on:

🅕 https://www.facebook.com/casiddiewilliams

🔗 https://www.tiktok.com/@casiddiewilliams_author

Also by Casiddie Williams

Hazel's Harem

A new job opportunity brings curvaceous, single mom Hazel Gibson, back to her hometown where she finds her hands full with a little more than just her 12 year old daughter.

When two gorgeous men offer her a six week proposition to be with both of them together, no strings attached, Hazel decides you only live once, and why choose if you don't have to?

But life has a habit of throwing Hazel curve balls, and she finds herself having to make some major life decisions to protect her family. Curve ball #1: When you're already juggling two men, what's one more?

Caffeinated Passion

Stella has been the focus of Penny's desire for almost a year. She watches her work while silently longing for her, wishing she could make Stella hers.

Though Stella is a down-on-her-luck waitress, she makes the best out of life with her son Cooper. She's desperately trying to get out of her terrible situation with her drunk boyfriend, one shift at a time.

When Stella finds herself in need of an extra hand, Penny takes the opportunity to swoop in and help her, offering a job to nanny her daughter, a safe place to live, and a relationship if she's interested.